Married Lovers

Jackie Collins

Married Lovers

SIMON &
SCHUSTER

London · New York · Sydney · Toronto

A CBS COMPANY

First published in Great Britain by Simon & Schuster UK Ltd, 2008
A CBS COMPANY

1 3 5 7 9 10 8 6 4 2

Simon & Schuster UK Ltd
Africa House
64–78 Kingsway
London WC2B 6AH

www.simor vs.co.uk

Simon & Schuster Australia
Sydney

A CIP catalogue record for this book
is available from the British Library

Hardback ISBN: 978-1-84737-258-1
Trade Paperback ISBN: 978-1-84737-259-8

Typeset by M Rules
Printed and bound in the UK by CPI Mackays, Chatham ME5 8TD

For my three daughters –
Tracy, Tiffany and Rory.
My greatest achievements.

ANYA

*A*nya Anastaskia was an exquisite child. From the moment she was born in a small village outside the city of Grozny, in the Republic of Chechnya, people commented on her fair looks. Her mother – a former Russian ballerina – was not surprised, for she had fallen in love and left Moscow to spend her life with Vlad Anastaskia – a farmer – and the most handsome man she had ever laid eyes on. Anya was born on 1 August 1985, a home birth with no complications. Not only was she beautiful, she was also a sunny-dispositioned and extraordinarily sweet child. The Anastaskia family lived a peaceful life, that is until the Chechen-Russian war, which started in 1994 when Anya was just nine years old. At first it seemed as if the fierce fighting between the Chechens and the Russians would not affect the Anastaskia family. But that was not to be; Anya's father was called to the city to fight and never returned.

Anya's mother was heartbroken. She seemed to lose all will to live, and before the war ended in 1996 she went to sleep one night and never woke up. Anya was eleven, alone and petrified. A neigh-boring family took her in, but they were not kindly people and treated her harshly. It did not help that Anya's ethereal and some-what delicate beauty – inherited from her mother – upset Svetlana, the daughter of the family – a stocky, darkly vicious girl with a

1

cruel tongue. Although Svetlana was only a few years older than Anya, she treated the younger girl as if she were her personal slave. Svetlana's parents were not much better; they gave Anya all the hard jobs, such as cleaning out the pig pens, scrubbing the cold stone floors and other menial tasks. They might have taken her in, but they used her for their own purposes, and made her sleep on an old blanket in a corner of the kitchen. At night, when the lights were turned off, cockroaches and mice roamed the kitchen floor – sometimes a rat or two. Anya huddled beneath her blanket too scared to move.

Eventually the inevitable happened; the mother of the household became pregnant, and the father took the opportunity to force himself on Anya, appearing night after night with an erection, ready for her to service him any way he wanted. At first she resisted, but what was the point? She had no money, nowhere to run, this was her home now, so she gritted her teeth and endured the sexual abuse. It began when she was twelve and ended two years later when the war started up again with air strikes and ground troops.

One night seven soldiers invaded the house. Seven drunk, out of control rebel soldiers with nothing but destruction on their minds. They beat up the father, raped the mother, and then set upon Anya and Svetlana. Anya was the lucky one, they merely raped her – taking their turns one by one. But with Svetlana they played vile sexual games until they finally ended up slitting the young girl's throat. Then, laughing drunkenly, they shot the parents in the head and set the house on fire, leaving everyone for dead.

Huddled in a corner, frozen to the spot, Anya waited until she was sure the soldiers were gone, then somehow or other she willed herself to move and was able to escape the burning house.

She had no idea why she'd been spared death, but the fact that she was still alive forced her to try and forget about her ordeal and concentrate on survival. She joined a procession of Chechen refugees who were fleeing across the border to the neighboring province of

Ingushetia. Befriending a young mother with three children, she tried to pretend she was part of a family again. But she knew that this wasn't so. She was half-starving, all alone in the world, and she had no idea what would happen to her next.

Chapter One

Present day, Los Angeles

Cameron Paradise hit *Bounce*, the private Members Only fitness club, running – literally.

"'Morning," she said breathlessly, waving at Lynda, the pretty Latina girl perched behind the white wicker reception desk. "Am I late? Is my eight o'clock here yet?"

"Of *course* he is," Lynda said, rolling her expressive brown eyes in an exaggerated fashion. "Mister Old Fart himself is ready and waiting with the same filthy mouth as usual. Nothing changes."

"Great," Cameron sighed, brushing back a lock of natural blonde hair from her eyes. "Can someone please tell me why he always manages to get here early?"

"'Cause it gives him more time to sharpen his twisted old tongue," Lynda answered knowingly. "Besides, you know he *loooves* you."

"Thanks a lot," Cameron murmured, making a face.

"That man talks nothing but sex, sex, sex," Lynda complained. "I dunno how you take it."

"I take it," Cameron replied patiently, "'cause he pays over the top, and very soon I'll have enough money stashed away to open my own place, and when I do, *you'll* come work for me, and any client who talks dirty to either of us is history. How's that?"

"You'd better make it soon, before I slap his disgusting mouth shut once an' for all," Lynda said, reaching for her nail file.

"Now, now," Cameron chided. "We all know that violence is not an option."

"Hmm . . ." Lynda mused, playing with one of her gold hoop earrings. "If my boyfriend, Carlos, ever heard the things that perv says to me, he'd break both his spindly little legs."

"Tune him out, that's what I do," Cameron said, stretching her arms above her head.

"I try," Lynda wailed, "but c'mon, sister, y'know it's impossible!"

"Nothing's impossible," Cameron shot back, heading for the staff changing room.

"Maybe for you," Lynda yelled after her.

Cameron was a stunningly beautiful woman in a sporty casual way. Five feet eight inches tall with a well-toned body, flawless skin, high cheekbones and dirty blonde hair worn short and spiky with long bangs that drifted sexily above her pale green eyes.

She'd worked at *Bounce* for almost three years, ever since fleeing Hawaii and an abusive relationship with her Australian husband, Gregg. *Bounce* was the perfect place for her; she paid the owner rent to use the facilities, plus a commission on each of the clients she brought in. Everything else went straight into her pocket, which meant that she could charge what she liked, and she did.

She was twenty-one when she'd first landed in L.A., and because of her exceptional looks she could've easily followed the actress or modeling route. But that kind of career was not for her, she was after something more substantial, so what better plan than working toward eventually opening her own fitness studio? And since everyone in L.A. seemed to be obsessed with the way they looked, it was a business she could definitely tap into. She knew plenty about health and how to be in optimum shape – at least Gregg had taught her *something*. And best of all she was smart enough to realize that she could achieve her goal if she worked hard and didn't allow herself to get caught up in the whole L.A. scene of recreational drugs, too many late-night clubs and endless parties.

"Hey, beauty," Dorian, a buff trainer with a Fabio-style mane of flaxen hair and several flamboyant tattoos, called out as she pulled on a fresh tank top. "That old dude of yours is gettin' impatient. He's mutterin' obscenities under his breath."

"Oh God!" Cameron exclaimed. "That man is such a wanker."

"Somebody needs to put him *down*," Dorian warned. "And I do *not* mean in a good way."

"I'd love to," Cameron quipped, hurrying toward the main work-out area. "Only I suspect he'd get off on it."

"She's *so* right," Dorian agreed, tossing back his precious mane.

Her un-favorite client, Mr Lord, was indeed waiting. A bizarre figure in red and black bicycle shorts stuffed with what could only be described as a fake penis; a Rat Pack T-shirt circa tour 1965; and a crooked slime-brown toupée perched jauntily on top of his head. He was the author of crap biographies, stuffed with information gleaned from newspaper files, all out-of-date and totally inaccurate. The celebrities he'd written about regarded him as a pathetic joke who couldn't write his way out of a corner, but he kept on trying.

He threw her a disapproving look while tapping the dial of his fake gold Rolex. "You're late," he grumbled. "If I wasn't so hot t' fuck you, I'd find myself another trainer."

What an asshole, she thought, smiling brightly. She had a mind to dump him as a client, but right now she needed all the money she could get, so she charged him double her hourly rate, and gritted her teeth while trying not to listen to his obscene ramblings.

7

"My bad, Mr L.," she said, attempting to avert her eyes from the fake bulge in his bicycle shorts. "Let's get you started. As you're always telling me – no time to waste, right?"

"You need a boyfriend," Mr Lord said, leering at her breasts. "And I'm talkin' about a man, not some boy. A *real* man who knows how to lick your pussy, an' finger your—"

Cameron tuned him out as he began pontificating about the joys of oral sex – at which he was – according to him – the absolute master. The very idea of Mr Lord giving head to anyone was repugnant.

Her thoughts drifted to Gregg as they often did, and the memories that came up were still painful and difficult to think about.

* * *

She and Gregg had met in his native Australia when she was nineteen and backpacking across the country. She'd left her Chicago home at eighteen shortly after burying her mother who'd died of cancer. Her dad was long gone, and since she couldn't stand her stepfather, she'd decided to take off. For the year before hooking up with Gregg she'd indulged her wanderlust, exploring Asia with Katie, a friend from school. They'd stayed in youth hostels and beach communes, working as part-time waitresses and babysitters, until they'd decided to be even more adventurous and head for Australia. Pooling their money, they'd purchased a couple of cheap plane tickets to Sydney, and from there they'd made their way to the Great Barrier Reef.

Within days she'd run into Gregg at a beach party. It was lust at first sight. He was six feet three, a muscled twenty-five year old, and quite a big deal in the surfer world.

She was just nineteen and surprisingly still a virgin.

Gregg went after her with a vengeance, soon dropping the several girlfriends he was seeing at the time. It wasn't long before he'd invited her to move into his ramshackle house on the beach. She'd agreed, providing that Katie could move in with her, and that moving in certainly didn't mean she was going to sleep with him.

Hmm . . . wishful thinking. Gregg was not a man to take no for an answer.

The first time they made love was not so brilliant, she was shy and intimidated and trying too hard to please him. But the second time it was explosions all round.

After a few months Gregg received an offer of a highly paid job at one of the big luxury hotels in Maui, and since the money was too tempting to turn down they'd taken off for Hawaii, full of plans for their future. Six weeks later they were married on the beach at Sunset, and Cameron had felt truly happy for the first time in her life.

Everyone regarded them as the golden couple, both so bronzed and tall and blond and beautiful, both so crazy about each other.

For two years it was all more or less perfect, until one day – after a surfing accident which put Gregg out of commission for several months – he began to change, turning from a sunny-dispositioned champion surfer into a mean and miserable shut-in who seemed to get his kicks from barraging her with endless tirades of verbal abuse.

At first she was too shocked to do anything. But after a series of vicious screaming and yelling attacks, she'd decided to fight back.

Gregg hadn't liked that, and soon he'd turned violent, which was enough to make her know for sure that things were veering totally out of control. Her mom had been trapped in an abusive relationship with Cameron's stepdad, and over the years she'd watched her mom change from a vibrant outgoing woman into a cowering frightened wreck. She'd vowed she would never allow it to happen to her, so even though she still had feelings for Gregg, it was time to get out.

In her mind she'd worked out an escape plan, but before she could put it into action she discovered she was pregnant. It was a surprise, and after the initial shock she'd thought that maybe she could turn it into a blessing. Naively she'd convinced herself that having a baby would change everything, so feeling pretty sure about things she'd decided to give Gregg one more chance.

It was a fatal mistake, for seven weeks later, in the middle of another of his rants, he'd shoved her to the floor, kicked her viciously in the stomach, and several agonizing hours later she'd lost their baby.

After that there was no more doubt. She knew that she had to escape.

A few days later, still battered and bruised, she'd attempted to flee in the middle of the night while he was sleeping, taking only one small bag, her passport and the money she'd saved teaching kids to surf.

Unfortunately Gregg awoke and went berserk with fury when he'd realized she was trying to leave. With a massive show of brute strength he'd knocked her down and pinned her to the floor screaming expletives in her face, blaming her for the loss of their baby, and everything else he considered wrong in his life. Then he'd beaten her so badly that both her eyes were blackened, her arm broken, and blood flowed from a deep cut on her forehead. It was almost as if he was trying to kill her.

Somehow or other she'd managed to grab a table lamp and smash it over his head knocking him unconscious. Then she'd fled from the house and never looked back.

At the airport she'd booked herself on the first plane to San Francisco, where her backpacking friend Katie was now living with Jinx, a struggling rock musician. Once she arrived in San Francisco, Katie and Jinx had taken her in, made sure she got medical attention and generally looked after her.

She'd stayed with them for several weeks while recovering from her ordeal, but as soon as the cast came off her arm, she'd decided to take the train to L.A. where she was determined to make a better life for herself and forget about the past.

It was possible. Anything was possible. Although she realized that one of these days she had to do something about Gregg, there was no way she could stay married to him. And yet she wasn't ready to return to Hawaii and divorce him, not until she was established and felt confident that she could face him and tell him exactly what a piece of cowardly shit he was.

*　*　*

Mr Lord didn't like it when he felt he wasn't receiving her full attention. "What're you thinking about?" he demanded, sweating his way through a series of arm reps.

"Nothing that would interest you," she answered, keeping it vague.

"Ah, but everything about you interests me," Mr Lord said with a toothy leer. "Your magnificent tits, your hot little ass, your—"

"Let's not get carried away," she said, interrupting him before he could say any more. "Quite frankly, I'm not in the mood to listen to your chauvinistic crap today, so can it."

"Me? A chauvinist?" Mr Lord objected, adjusting his padded crotch. "I love women. I honor them. I love their wet—"

Once more Cameron tuned him out. He talked a good game, but deep down she was sure he was just another dirty old man who couldn't get it up. And how sad was that?

Chapter Two

"I'm bored," Mandy Richards announced, sitting cross-legged on the oversized couch in her enormous living room overlooking a shimmering blue swimming pool. "Nothing's exciting anymore. I'm totally bored."

Ryan Richards regarded his thirty-two-year-old Hollywood Princess wife with her compact body and glossy auburn hair pulled back into a girlish ponytail. Sometimes she managed to sound like a whiney teenager. Today was one of those days and he wasn't in the mood to indulge one of her childish fits.

She was obviously expecting him to say something. He didn't. He kept his silence, it was safer that way.

"I said I'm bored," Mandy repeated, twisting several expensive diamond tennis bracelets on her delicate wrist while throwing him an accusing look. "Didn't you hear me?"

"Well," he said at last. "If you're so bored, why don't you do something about it?"

His reply did not please her. "*You're* my husband," she said, throwing him a baleful stare. "Why don't *you* do something about it?"

Ryan was not slow. Once again Mandy was on the warpath looking for a fight, and once again he was target number one. It didn't take a genius to figure *that* out. "Sorry," he said, edging toward a fast exit. "I got a shitload of stuff to take care of today."

Actually he didn't have a shitload of anything, but getting out of the house seemed like a wise idea.

"What stuff?" Mandy demanded, her back stiffening. "It's Saturday, aren't we supposed to be spending the day together?"

"No," Ryan said, a tad abruptly. "I thought I mentioned that I'm having brunch with that Argentinian director I've been waiting to meet – he's flown in specially to see me. Then later I promised my sis I'd drop by to see the kids."

"Which sis is that?" Mandy sneered as if "sis" was a dirty word she could barely get out. "The one with the jailbird husband?"

"Don't go there, Mandy," he warned, temper rising. Christ! It drove him nuts when she went after his family, and she knew it. "Marty got arrested for a DUI – it could've happened to anyone."

"His *third* DUI," Mandy said pointedly. "Even Daddy couldn't help with that one."

Yeah. Daddy. Mandy's father. Hamilton J. Heckerling. Movie Mogul Supreme. Überproducer. Starmaker. Egocentric pain in the ass. Not a conversation took place without her bringing Hamilton up one way or the other.

"Where *is* Big Daddy?" he asked, not really caring, but determined to steer the conversation away from his sister, Evie, whom he loved dearly, and whom Mandy couldn't stand. He knew she was jealous because he and Evie were so close.

"Hamilton is in New York," Mandy said, uncrossing her yoga-pant-clad legs. "I suspect he has a new girlfriend."

"*Another* one?"

"He's divorced," Mandy said, immediately jumping to her father's defense. "He can have as many girlfriends as he wants."

"He sure can," Ryan answered – adding a dry – "*How* many times has he been married?"

13

"You know how many times," Mandy sniffed.

"I'm no expert."

"Oh, for God's sake!"

"What?"

"Perhaps that's where *I* should be," she said, hurriedly changing the subject because she did not appreciate discussing her father's love life – especially with Ryan.

"Where?" he asked, purposely needling her.

"In New York *with* him," she snapped.

"Well, if you—"

"No!" Mandy said, throwing her husband a sharp look. "You'd like that, wouldn't you? You'd enjoy having me out the way so you could hook up with some little tootsie whore and play around."

Jesus Christ! Why did she say such things? Why did she go out of her way to piss him off?

Seven years they'd been married. Seven long years, and not once had he cheated on her, although the opportunities that came his way were abundant. He was thirty-nine and not bad-looking, above average in fact. He was over six feet tall, quite fit – thanks to daily jogging. He had longish sandy-brown hair, extremely intense blue eyes – his best feature – and a slightly crooked nose busted in a football game when he was twelve. The vibe he had going for him was a kind of younger Kevin Costner thing – it was a vibe women found most attractive. He got hit on all the time by actresses, models, young executives, other men's wives, but he always turned them down. Ryan Richards was one of that rare breed – a man who believed in the institution of marriage. He'd married Mandy for better or worse – and just because it had turned out to be a nightmare did not mean that he should cut and run – although sometimes he yearned to. Neither did it mean that he should cheat the way most of his married friends did. He had principles, and staying faithful was one of them.

It had all started out so well. Mandy – pretty and sweet and caring – she'd presented herself as perfect wife material.

He'd met her at the première of the second movie he'd produced. A gritty drama about a woman on Death Row. And even though he was in his early thirties at the time, he was more than ready to hook up with the right girl. He'd had it up to here with the wanna-be model/actress types. He found them to be vacuous, boring, ambitious and too pretty for their own good. Mandy appeared to be the right girl at the right time. She made interesting and insightful comments about his movie, and not in a fan-like way. Her words were smart and to the point, and he was delighted to discover that she could actually hold an intelligent conversation about film-making. Another major plus was that even though she was very pretty in a petite way, she had no desire to be an actress. "One of these days I plan on raising a family and being there for my children," she'd informed him. Ryan was immediately impressed.

At the time he had not realized that Mandy was Hamilton J. Heckerling's daughter. Of *course* she knew exactly what to say to up-and-coming producers; she'd been raised by one of the biggest showmen of all time – Hamilton J. Heckerling – a legend in his own lifetime – a throwback to the moguls of yesteryear.

By the time Ryan discovered who her famous father was, they'd been on three under-the-radar dates, and had extremely satisfying sex several times. Young Mandy was certainly no slouch in the bed department; she'd given him a series of blow-jobs the like of which he'd never experienced before, and he'd been around – nobody could say that he hadn't enjoyed his single days.

After he found out who her father was, he'd decided that it didn't matter – in fact, it was kind of a kick. And even though all his friends warned him about marrying into the Heckerling family – he'd done it anyway.

Foolish.

Stupid.

Dumb.

But he was in love at the time, or at least he'd thought he was.

Several of his friends got together and insisted on throwing him a bachelor party. They'd told him they were taking him to Vegas. Instead they'd commandeered a private plane and flown him off to Amsterdam for a long weekend of lust, adventure and debauchery. His final fling.

It had turned out to be one long memorable weekend, four days he would never forget.

When Mandy learned that he'd flown to Europe without her, she'd been furious. If she'd found out what had really gone on during the trip, she would've been more than furious. But she'd married him anyway. Mandy was a girl who always got what she wanted, and the man she wanted was Ryan.

Their marriage had taken place on a private beach adjacent to Mandy's father's twenty-five-million-dollar estate in Puerto Vallarta. Ryan had opted for a close family affair, but Mandy had begged him to acquiesce to her wishes. "Daddy doesn't ask for much," she'd said, all sweetness and light. "I'm his only daughter and you can't blame him for wanting my wedding to be a memorable event. It's the least we can do for him."

So he'd given in.

Their wedding was attended by six hundred guests – eighty were his friends and family – the rest of the people he didn't know, although Mandy assured him they were all important players in the film industry.

So be it, he'd thought. *We only have to do this once.*

Except it turned out to be once a week, for Hamilton hosted weekly soirées at his magnificent hill-top home in Bel Air, and he expected them to attend every time.

"This is bullshit," Ryan had complained after the fourth weekend in a row.

"No, it's not," Mandy objected.

"I can't take all this socializing," he'd said. "It's not my scene."

"Daddy calls it networking," she'd answered. "You should thank him. You're meeting all the most important people in town."

"Why would I want to do that?" he'd demanded.

"For your career," she'd countered. "You never know when you'll need a favor."

"My career is progressing very nicely," he'd said irritably. "In case you've forgotten, I have two movies in development, and one about ready to shoot."

"Daddy thinks you should make bigger movies," Mandy had informed him. "He thinks you should come work for him."

"Are you kidding me?" he'd said, outraged. "I certainly wouldn't want to work for your father. I make small independent movies, that's my style."

"Sometimes style is not enough."

"What does *that* mean?"

"It means that if you *did* work for Daddy, you could do anything you wanted."

"I was under the impression I was doing quite well on my own," he'd said dryly.

"It's just a thought," Mandy had said, deftly reaching for his fly, because she knew exactly when to stop pushing and concentrate on other things. After all, they were newly married, so it might take some time to turn Ryan around.

But Ryan was no pushover. He might have married a famous man's daughter, but when it came to the movie business he walked his own path – he needed neither help, advice nor interference from Hamilton J. Heckerling.

A year into their marriage Mandy reluctantly admitted defeat when it came to Ryan's career. He was indeed his own man, and she could do nothing to change that. At least she'd persuaded him to accept her father's wedding gift – a house in the flats of

Beverly Hills with six bedrooms, lush gardens, a pool and a tennis court.

At first he'd objected. "It's way too big," he'd said.

"Not when we have children," she'd replied, cannily playing the family card. "Besides, Daddy will be heartbroken if we turn him down."

After arguing about it for a couple of weeks he'd finally given in, and they'd moved into the house on Foothill. He'd had to admit that the idea of a large family appealed to him. He'd been raised with three sisters and loving parents, so family was extremely important, he couldn't wait to start one of his own.

Unfortunately it was not to be. Over the course of their seven-year marriage, Mandy had become pregnant three times. She'd lost the first two babies to miscarriages, and their third baby was stillborn.

It was heart-breaking for both of them. It was also the main reason he stayed, for how could he desert her after all she'd been through? It wouldn't be right, and throughout his life Ryan had always tried to do the right thing.

* * *

"Okay, Mandy," Ryan said impatiently. "I have to get going."

"If you must," she said in an uptight voice. "What time will you be home?"

He hated being questioned, but Mandy could never resist going there.

"Around five," he answered vaguely.

"Don't forget we're having dinner with Phil and Lucy at the beach," she reminded him. "*Geoffrey's.* It's our check. We should leave before six. One never knows what the traffic will be like on P.C.H. and you know how I hate being late."

Funny, coming from a woman who always kept him waiting.

"Got it," he said, finally making it to the door.

Geoffrey's restaurant with Phil and Lucy Standard wasn't such a bad thing. Phil was a close friend, and Lucy could be entertaining when she wasn't zoned out on her favorite Vicodin/Xanax combination.

Yes, an evening with the Standards sure beat out an evening at home with Mandy.

Chapter Three

Six clients later, Cameron finished her day at *Bounce*, although she was by no means done; she still had several house calls to make, which would take her way past eight p.m. When she was finally through, she'd collect her two dogs from Mr Wasabi, her friendly Asian neighbor, fix herself something to eat, and fall into bed ready for tomorrow's early start.

She knew she was a workaholic, but nobody was about to do it for her – and she was determined to put away enough money to enable her to open her own studio soon.

Fortunately she was well on her way to achieving her goal, proof that all her hard work was worth it.

"Where you off to now?" Lynda inquired as she made her way past the front desk.

"Charlene Lewis," she replied, pausing for a moment. "Isn't she your unfavorite Hollywood Wife?"

"Oh, *her*," Lynda said, tapping her overly long manicured nails on the counter-top. "That woman is a true *puta*. A typical double-trophy wife with an alcoholic old dude husband."

"You think?" Cameron said, tongue-in-cheek.

"Oh, *c'mon*," Lynda insisted. "Everyone *knows* she's waiting for him to drop so she can inherit his millions an' start bumpin' an' grindin' with cabana boys."

Cameron raised an amused eyebrow. "Cabana boys?"

"You get what I mean," Lynda said with a dirty giggle.

"Do you hate *all* my clients?"

"Only the bad-ass ones," Lynda retorted. "You got a few hot actors I wouldn't say no to hopping in the shower with. An' I *looove* Joanna P. – she knows how to have fun."

"How bad can my bad-ass clients be when I get them to pay double my usual rate?" Cameron said. "They're helping us, you know."

"No," Lynda argued. "*You're* helping them get their saggy asses into shape."

"Whatever."

"You work too hard," Lynda said, wrinkling her pert nose. "Thing is, sister – you got no personal life, an' that ain't healthy."

"I have a perfectly fine personal life, thank you," Cameron replied tartly.

"Y'know," Lynda began with a sly smirk, "Carlos has a friend—"

"No!"

"*What?*" Lynda said innocently. "I can't even remember the last time you went on a date."

"*I* do, and it was a total disaster," Cameron said, recalling a short, hairy agent with a handle-bar moustache, who'd kept on insisting he could get her into movies – a place she had no desire to go. She shuddered at the memory.

"All work an' no sex—" Lynda sing-songed.

"Makes me stronger," Cameron said, cutting Lynda off.

"Yeah, yeah, you're Superpussy!" Lynda teased.

Dorian appeared in the doorway flexing his considerable muscles. "You called?" he said archly.

"You wish!" Cameron said, grinning.

"Bitch!"

"Slut!"

"Ah, she knows me so well," Dorian said with a proud smile.

"Me and half of West Hollywood," Cameron drawled. Dorian *was* a major slut, but she loved him all the same; he had a big heart, and could always be relied on in a crisis.

Smiling to herself, she made her way out to the lot at the back where her 1969 fastback silver Mustang was parked. It was a fantastic car that got her where she needed to go and was major fun to drive. She especially enjoyed firing up her iPod, and on one of her rare days off, driving to the beach with the dogs in the back, and L.L. Cool J and The Black-Eyed Peas serenading her. That was her relaxation, simply doing nothing much, certainly not going on useless blind dates with one of Carlos's "hot to get laid" friends. Besides, unbeknownst to Lynda or anyone else – she had sex whenever she wanted it with Marlon – a nineteen-year-old college student she'd met running the UCLA track. They'd struck up a "friends with benefits" relationship. Nothing serious, simply uncomplicated sex whenever either of them felt like it. It suited both of them just fine. Although sometimes she did feel a bit guilty because technically Marlon was still a teenager, although his twentieth birthday was just around the corner, so it wasn't as if she was sleeping with a *boy*. Besides, she was only five years older than him.

Nobody knew about Marlon, and that's the way she intended to keep it. Lynda would criticize, and Dorian would be after Marlon for himself.

Cameron's three best friends were Lynda, Dorian, and Cole de Barge, another gay trainer who was black and totally hot. Three close friends, but she kept her secrets to herself.

She made it in record time to the gated community where Charlene lived with her rich husband. Their luxurious mansion was perched atop a hill with a magnificent view from every room. To reach the house, visitors had to drive through security gates and inform the guards – who kept a detailed log of everyone who entered – exactly which house they were visiting.

As she drove down the neatly kept streets past a series of

enormous gated mansions, she decided the set-up was like some kind of surreal billionaires' ghetto. The thought made her smile.

Charlene Lewis had been around Hollywood for twenty years. First married to a Vegas singing star, then a famous composer, she was now on her third husband, Aarron Otterly, an eccentric billionaire who was twice widowed and fast approaching eighty. Charlene knew a thing or two about promising prospects, so the moment she'd realized Aarron was available, she'd moved in on him like a hooker intent on getting paid for sucking cock. Her sell-by date was fast approaching, and she was well aware that most billionaires liked their women to be twenty-something, or if any older, at least Asian.

She'd hooked Aarron by allowing him to try on all her clothes and parade around in full drag – it turned out that he was especially fond of her vintage Valentinos and Dolce & Gabanna ultra-sexy evening gowns.

The good news was she didn't have to indulge in sex with him, he preferred to pleasure himself while admiring his dolled-up image in a full-length mirror. As long as she was there to watch along with him, he was happy.

The bad news was he had grown offspring who couldn't stand the sight of her; they were convinced she was after his money.

Cameron realized that Lynda was probably right, Charlene *was* merely biding time until her dear hubby dropped so she could get on with her life and not be bothered by pesky financial problems. She'd never worked and she never intended to.

A Filipino butler greeted Cameron at the door and informed her that the lady of the house was waiting for her. She made her way through luxury until she reached the gym out by the pool.

"You're late," Charlene admonished, sitting astride a stationary bike clad in a shocking-pink leotard that clung like a second skin.

Charlene was an ode to Botox, Juvena, silicone, collagen, and any other facial fillers on the market. Lipo-suction was her best friend. She didn't believe in the plastic surgeon's knife unless it was for her overly large breasts, but she did believe in everything else. At forty-six she was immaculately preserved with disturbingly enhanced lips, and not a line on her smooth face.

"I'd hardly call five minutes late," Cameron retaliated.

"You know I'm a stickler for punctuality," Charlene said petulantly. "Every five minutes count. I could've been doing something else."

Like what? Cameron wanted to ask. *Lending your husband your mascara? Shopping for more designer outfits? Screwing the pool boy?*

"Take your ring off," Cameron said cheerfully, indicating the twelve-carat diamond monstrosity Charlene wore on her middle finger. "It's time to get limber."

Reluctantly Charlene removed her enormous ring. It was her security blanket and never left her sight. Cameron mused that if Charlene sold the ring, the money could feed a family of five for at least ten years.

"C'mon, let's hit it," Cameron said, beginning a series of deep stretches. "Gotta suffer for that amazing bod."

"Why?" Charlene snapped.

"'Cause if you want to keep on looking great, that's what you have to do."

"One of these days," Charlene muttered, "I'm gonna sit on the couch an' do nothing but scarf down Krispy Kremes."

"No, you're not," Cameron said briskly, switching on the sound system. "You'll be buff forever. It's your destiny."

"Really?" Charlene said, preening.

"Absolutely," Cameron responded.

Positive energy always got her through the day. And motivating her clients was one of the keys to her success.

It was past nine by the time she made it home to her modest one-bedroom house situated in a quiet street behind Von's supermarket on Santa Monica. She rented the house from a flamboyant

24

interior designer who was one of her favorite clients. The house was tiny, but it did have a small garden in back where Yoko and Lennon – her two golden Labradors – loved to stretch out and bake in the sun. Yoko and Lennon were great company; with them around she never felt lonely.

After fixing herself a cup of Miso soup, she listened to her answering machine. It was mostly calls from clients booking or changing appointments. The final message was from Jill Khoner, a TV producer client, who wanted to know if she was available to pay a house call to Don Verona – the talk-show host. She was aware of his name, but she'd never got around to watching his show. However, new clients were always welcome, so after finishing her soup, she called Jill back and took down Don Verona's details. Then she led Yoko and Lennon outside, ran them around the block, and finally made it to bed.

It had been a very long day.

Chapter Four

Once he was sitting in his car, Ryan called his best buddy, Don Verona, who immediately told him to come on over. Their friendship went way back to their college days when they'd shared a tiny apartment near USC and harbored big ambitions and a never-ending stream of nubile girlfriends. They'd both made it in their chosen careers, and they'd always remained close in spite of numerous girlfriends and wives who'd tried to split them up. Some women were extremely threatened by their man's long-time buddies, but Ryan and Don weathered all attempts to break up their friendship.

Don lived in an ultra-modern house he'd personally designed and had built after the demise of his second marriage to a French movie star. Perched at the top of Sunset Plaza Drive, his house was a true bachelor's paradise with all the accoutrements. A professional-size pool table; three flat-screen high-def TVs with full sports packages on every one of them; a fully equipped gym; a state-of-the-art sound system; and a virtual reality games room – which included an immaculate poker table. Outdoors there was a scaled-down golf course, a full stainless-steel barbecue pit, and a six-car garage to house his impressive collection of automobiles.

"Hey," Ryan said, walking into the living room and flopping straight onto the couch.

"What's up?" Don asked. He was movie-star handsome, with jet-black hair, dark eyes, rugged features, and a trademark two-day stubble. He was also an extremely successful and popular late-night talk-show host. Don Verona was Letterman without the Mid-Western hang-ups; Leno without the insults; Craig Ferguson without the Scottish accent; and Conan without the red hair. Don had his own particular style and it worked.

Don's big problem was women. They loved him, and he loved them back. But with two divorces behind him he was having difficulty getting it up for the parade of gorgeous women who threw themselves at him. Since his last divorce from the French movie star, the only time he felt he could really relax in bed was with a paid professional. His shrink informed him it had something to do with alimony anxiety. Yeah, he was paying out plenty to both ex-wives, so he could understand that.

"Dunno," Ryan said, shrugging. "Had to get out of the house. Mandy's driving me nuts."

"Yeah," Don answered knowingly. "I remember the feeling well. Women can do that to you; they've got this misguided idea that it's their right."

Picking up a copy of *Sports Illustrated*, Ryan began studying the bikini-clad supermodel on the cover.

"Mandy's in one of her clinging moods," he remarked.

"Big surprise."

"Huh?" Ryan said, throwing the magazine back on the coffee table.

"C'mon," Don said, trying to talk some sense into his friend. "You know your wife's a world-class manipulator; she gets off on fucking with you, that's her deal."

"Maybe . . ." Ryan said, trying to convince himself Don was wrong, but knowing that he was right. Mandy *did* get off on fucking with him, sad but true. And he let her get away with it because . . . well, because it was easier that way.

"I speak the truth, bro'," Don continued. "The way I see it, you haven't been happy in a long time."

"Not true," Ryan said, still hovering in a state of denial.

"You've got to start thinking of an exit strategy," Don said, opening up the enormous glass doors that led out to an infinity lap pool.

"Hey," Ryan objected, getting up and joining Don by the open doors. "Just because *you* had two failed marriages doesn't mean that I should give up. Mandy has her good points."

"Like *what*?" Don said, as Butch, his black Labrador, wandered into the house from outside and rushed over to nuzzle Ryan. "Every time I see the two of you, she's on a major nagging binge."

"Mandy's been through a lot," Ryan said, absentmindedly bending down to stroke the dog.

"And how long are *you* supposed to pay for it?" Don asked bluntly. "Shit happens. You need to move on. Either that or get something going on the side."

"That's not my thing."

"Maybe it should be, 'cause I'd bet money you're not getting laid."

"What makes you think that?"

"You're so fucking tense lately it's ridiculous."

"I'm not like you," Ryan said defensively. "I don't believe in giving up easily. And I certainly don't believe in cheating."

"Who's cheating?" Don said, raising an eyebrow. "I'm single, remember? It's *you* we're talking about."

"Do me a favor and get off the subject of my marriage," Ryan said. "I came up here to relax."

"Relax away," Don said, stifling a yawn. "I got a new trainer coming over. One of my producers recommended her, she's supposed to work it like a drill sergeant. I need some discipline." He patted his flat stomach. "Getting flabby."

"Yeah, sure," Ryan said disbelievingly.

"You should work out with us," Don suggested. "It'll shake you out of the dumps. Then we can take in some college football. I'm in an insane betting mood."

"'Fraid I gotta pass," Ryan said. "I'm going over to my sister's, then stopping by the editing rooms."

"I thought you were done with your latest masterpiece," Don said, strolling into his hi-tech steel and concrete kitchen, Butch at his heels.

Ryan followed. "A movie is never done until it hits the theaters, and even then . . ." he trailed off.

"Yeah, yeah, I know," Don said, tossing Butch a dog biscuit. "When it comes to work, you're a perfectionist."

"And you're not exactly a slacker," Ryan responded. "Five shows a week, and every one a ratings winner."

Don shook his head as he filled a ceramic mug with coffee. "The difference is that you're doing what you always wanted, while I'm swimming in crap."

"Crap? Are you kidding me? Having one of the three top-rated talk shows in the country is hardly crap. And let's not forget that you make a helluva lot more money than me."

"Ah yes," Don said immediately. "But we both know it's not about the money, it's about the passion. And when it comes to work – you got it. I don't."

"That's not true."

"Yeah," Don said ruefully. "Unfortunately it is."

"Anyway," Ryan said, "I should go. Whyn't you join us for dinner tonight?"

"Where?"

"*Geoffrey's*. Seven-thirty. It's my check, and Phil and Lucy are coming. Bring a date, and not someone you're paying – Mandy'll suss that out in two seconds flat."

Don laughed. "Sounds like a plan. I'll see you at seven-thirty."

*   *   *

The moment Ryan was out of the house, Mandy called her father in New York. To her fury his pissy housekeeper refused to put him on the phone, claiming he was otherwise engaged. Mandy clicked off her phone and threw it on the couch. She hated her father's "protectors" as she called them. He employed a whole coterie of housekeepers, assistants, drivers and bodyguards who made sure nobody could get to him unless he wanted them to.

"*I* should be the exception," she was constantly reminding him.

"Why's that?" he would reply.

"Because *I'm* your daughter, and that should give me privileges nobody else has."

Hamilton usually chuckled when she tried to elicit privileges.

That was another thing she hated about her father – his chuckle. It had no warmth, it was a mean-spirited sound. She preferred him in serious mode. Unfortunately he spent most of their time together giving her "the chuckle."

"I want to marry Ryan Richards," she'd informed him seven years ago.

Chuckle. Chuckle.

"I'd like to produce one of your movies with you."

Chuckle. Chuckle.

"Can I get my Trust Fund early?"

Chuckle. Chuckle.

He never took her seriously.

The rumor on the street was that Daddy Dearest had a new girlfriend. Mandy wasn't too pleased about *that*. He'd gone through five wives, wasn't that enough for any man?

She'd heard about the latest girlfriend from her secret confidante, Lolly Summer, who worked for one of the major gossip sites on the Internet. In exchange for juicy tidbits about the stars, Lolly made sure to tell Mandy absolutely *everything*.

After not getting through to her father, Mandy called Lolly. "Any more news?" she asked.

"He's throwing a dinner party tonight," Lolly responded. "A big deal dinner party – everyone from Rudy to Trump. It promises to be quite an affair."

"And the purpose of this dinner party is . . .?"

"I'll let you know. I have two contacts on the guest list."

"If you find out anything at all, text me. I'll be out tonight, but I need to know what's going on."

"Of course," Lolly said. "Now, about that Owen Wilson item you promised me . . ."

* * *

Ryan's sister, Evie, lived in a small house in Silverlake. She had three children, all boys, and all under the age of eight. Marty, her husband, worked as a stuntman. He was also a raging alcoholic.

Alcohol and stunts. A dangerous combination. Ryan had used him on one of his movies, and that was enough for him. His brother-in-law was an unpleasant bully with few friends; Ryan couldn't wait for the day when Evie finally decided she'd had enough.

At the present time Marty was languishing in jail on account of a third D.U.I. arrest.

Financially, Ryan knew things were tight for his sister – because any film company with any sense refused to hire Marty – but Evie flatly refused any help.

Evie greeted her brother with a warm hug. Seven years younger than Ryan, she was pretty in an exhausted kind of way. Her three boys were transfixed, sitting on a worn couch watching cartoons on TV.

"Thank God for Saturday mornings," she sighed. "It's the only time they're quiet, bless their murderous little hearts."

"Hey guys," Ryan said, bending down to greet his nephews. "What's goin' on? Anything I should know about?"

The boys didn't budge.

"They want a dog," Evie said, tucking a strand of curly brown hair behind her ear. "It'll mean more work for me, but they *really* want one. And with Marty away so much . . ." she trailed off, as if the very mention of her jailed husband was too painful.

"Maybe I can get them a dog," Ryan suggested.

"Well," Evie said, hesitating for a moment. "Only if you *promise* no fancy breeds. They've made me swear I'll get them a rescue dog from the Pound."

"Proper little citizens and so young," Ryan said, ruffling the youngest's hair.

"I know," Evie said ruefully. "Petey refuses to eat chicken anymore, which makes planning family meals so much fun."

"I could take them for burgers at *In 'n' Out*," Ryan said, aware that Evie looked like she could use a break. "Then I'll run 'em through the park and we'll kick a ball around. What do you think?"

"I think I love you," she said gratefully.

"That's nice to know," he said. Of course the perfect day would've been taking them to his house and letting them splash in the swimming pool, but Mandy would throw a fit. Since they couldn't have children of their own, she didn't want someone else's around, especially Evie's three rambunctious little boys. They argued about it often.

"Gotta use the john," he said.

On the way to the bathroom he stopped off in Evie's bedroom where he took a stack of tens and twenties from his jacket pocket and artfully distributed them around the room. That way it didn't look like a hand-out; hopefully Evie would think she'd left the money lying around.

It was ridiculous that she wouldn't allow him to help her out. There he was living in a ten-thousand-square-foot mansion in Beverly Hills, making an excellent living, while she was stuck with her dead-beat husband in Silverlake barely able to pay the bills.

The three boys were happy to devour their *In 'n' Out* burgers along with cartons of unhealthy French fries and scads of tomato ketchup. After watching them stuff themselves, Ryan took them to the park where they ran riot, and on the way back to the house he stopped at Best Buy and bought them each Sony PSPs. They were beyond excited.

By the time he delivered them back to Evie he felt as if he'd taken a five-mile hike.

"Your kids have worn me out," he complained. "Dunno how you do it."

"You're not as young as you used to be," she remarked with sisterly candor. "Face it, big brother, you're getting up there."

"I'm thirty-nine," he objected.

"Soon to be forty," she pointed out.

Jesus! Was it true? Was he about to score the big four O? Crap! No longer the hot shot young producer in town, he, Ryan Richards, was hitting middle age. He could hardly believe it.

He started thinking about his earlier conversation with Don. Deep down he knew Don was right, he wasn't as happy as he should be with Mandy. She was always on a rant about something or other, always complaining and nagging. And for the last year their sex life had been practically non-existent – ever since the stillbirth of their son. Whenever he made a move, Mandy shied away from him, coming up with yet another lame excuse. This from a woman who'd once prided herself on giving the superlative blowjob.

Perhaps they'd both be better off if they weren't together.

Suddenly the word "divorce" slipped into his head.

No. Impossible. His mom would be so disappointed if he couldn't make it work. Before his dad had passed, his parents had been married for forty-five blissful years. Divorce was not a situation his mom would take lightly. And as for Hamilton J. Heckerling – Jesus! The old man would probably put a hit out on him.

Ryan smiled grimly as he imagined himself running around L.A. scrutinizing every other person as a potential assassin, while checking under his car to see if there was a bomb planted there.

Your imagination is out of control, he told himself as he kissed his sister goodbye.

"Take care," Evie said, squeezing his arm.

"No, *you* take care," he responded. "When's Marty getting out?"

"This week."

"Is he going to A.A.?"

"He says he doesn't need to."

"Evie—"

"I know, I know," she said, refusing to look him in the eye. "Please don't lecture me. It'll be fine."

But they both knew it wouldn't be.

She touched his arm again. "Is everything okay with you and Mandy?" she asked as they walked toward the front door.

His sister had excellent instincts when it came to him, but he didn't care to get into it.

"Yeah, sure, everything's great," he said breezily. "Why?"

"I don't know, you look tired."

Hmm . . . reminding him of his upcoming birthday wasn't enough, now he looked tired. Great!

Today was not turning out to be the best of days.

ANYA

*L*ife in the city of Magas was harsh. With so many refugees pouring in – over two hundred and fifty thousand – food and housing was short. Anya soon found herself separated from the mother and children she'd traveled with. Before long she ended up alone with only the clothes she was wearing and a chunk of stale bread a kindly old woman had given her. No money. No identity. But still, nobody could take away her delicate beauty.

The refugee camps were filled to bursting, nowhere to go, nowhere to settle. Anya hovered on the perimeter, shivering, half-starved, her thin body trembling, unable to speak as she remembered the horrors she'd witnessed.

This was how Sergei found her. A resident of Magas, he'd been given a job to do by his boss, fat old Greedy Boris Pinski, a man of many trades. Greedy Boris dealt in arms and black-market goods. He also dealt in women, and his young henchman, Sergei, was dis-patched to the refugee camps to see if he could come up with any strays Greedy Boris might put to good use in the underground brothel he ran in the middle of the city.

Serge drove a dusty American station-wagon his boss had won in a card game. By the time he came across Anya the wagon was already filled with two sisters, a scrawny girl with lank red hair, and a short fat woman who Sergei knew Greedy Boris would reject – but what could he do? The pickings were not exactly abundant.

He almost didn't stop for Anya. Such a skinny little thing and much too young. Then he caught a glimpse of her face, and for a moment he was lost in her pale blue eyes – so filled with pain, so expressive. He pulled the wagon to a sharp stop. "Get in," he ordered, jerking his thumb.

She did as she was told and climbed into the back of the station-wagon. The other women ignored her; they had their own problems.

Sergei drove his carload of women to the center of the city and delivered them to Greedy Boris, all of them except Anya, whom he hid in the trunk. "Stay quiet," he warned her. "If you behave and give me no trouble, you'll get food and a place to sleep."

She stayed quiet. She was fourteen. She didn't know what else to do.

At first Sergei decided he would keep Anya for a few days, have his way with her, then hand her over to Greedy Boris. But this was not to be, for twenty-year-old Sergei, who'd lived most of his life on the streets using his wits to survive, fell in love with the child.

He took her to the room he rented in a run-down house, made her strong tea and pieces of burnt toast with thick black pudding spread on top, then after washing her in a communal bathroom, he allowed her to sleep in his bed, while he settled on his one ratty chair with loose springs and a torn cover.

He considered himself mad to do this, but there was something about Anya, he didn't quite know what it was. She refused to speak, not one word; all she did was look at him with those big sad blue eyes and that was enough.

He realized she must have been raped, for when he'd washed her he'd discovered dried blood stuck to her thighs. It was obvious that the girl had suffered a terrible ordeal.

Yes, he could have left her with Greedy Boris, but why would he do that? She looked at him with such longing, a yearning in her eyes that begged to belong, to be close to someone.

Sexually he forced himself not to touch her. He wanted to, but

36

somehow he felt it wouldn't be right. In a way he was afraid. This was strange, as Sergei had never been afraid of anything.

Every day he tried to persuade her to speak. She steadfastly refused.

When he had to go out to work, leaving her alone in the room, he sternly instructed her that under no circumstances was she to answer the door.

She nodded her head.

"One of these days you will say something to me, yes?" he asked her in the Russian language they shared.

She nodded again.

"I can be patient," he said.

He thought about all the whores he'd screwed, all the women who'd passed through his life. He thought about his stepmother, who'd forced him to have sex with her when he was twelve. His stepmother's best friend had also used him for her own pleasure. And then a procession of women all shapes, sizes and ages. Those women he'd used for his own benefit.

Sergei had developed a tough exterior. He'd had to.

After two nights of sleeping on the chair, he decided it was okay to move into the bed next to her.

She immediately shied away from him, those sad eyes of hers filled with fear.

"I will not touch you," he promised. "You don't have to be afraid."

He turned his back to her and slept fitfully.

Early in the morning she leaned over and whispered in his ear. "My name is Anya."

"Oh," he said, startled. "You can talk."

"Thank you," she murmured. "Thank you for your kindness."

The girl was thanking him. Nobody had ever thanked him before. He was filled with a strange feeling.

Now he could never hand her over to Greedy Boris. It wouldn't be the right thing to do.

Meanwhile, Greedy Boris was on his case. "Is this all you bring me?" Greedy Boris screamed, eyes bulging with fury, fat arms waving in the air. "Two sisters who aren't worth shit, and a ratty girl with bad teeth. Go back to the refugee camp and get me more girls. There must be plenty of pussy. Get it for me and bring it here."

Greedy Boris's clientele was not of the highest caliber. Mostly they were married workmen who came by at all times of the day, stayed five or ten minutes and went on their way. Greedy Boris worked his girls hard; sometimes they were forced to service fifteen or sixteen clients a day.

Sergei did not want this fate for Anya. His Anya. His little bird. For in his heart he knew they were destined to be together.

One day he decided they had to make an escape from the ravaged war-torn city. They had to get away from Greedy Boris and everything he represented.

It was time for them to run.

Chapter Five

"Hi," Cameron said, when Don Verona flung open his front door. "I'm Cameron Paradise, Jill Khoner set this up. You must be Don Verona."

"Whew!" he exclaimed, slowly checking her out. He saw a tall natural blonde in a white tracksuit with long legs and intoxicating green eyes. "Jill told me you were a beauty, but I wasn't expecting perfection."

"Not only is he famous," Cameron murmured, tongue-in-cheek, "but he has the corny lines to go with it."

Don threw her a quizzical look as Butch came bounding over, making a fast run for her crotch. The dog excitedly stuck his nose between her legs and began sniffing.

"Easy, boy," Don said, pulling back on Butch's collar. "Sorry about that."

"Don't worry," Cameron said, bending to scratch Butch's neck. "I have Labs of my own. They're overly friendly, but that's cool."

"You have a Labrador?"

"Two," she said, as Butch started licking her hand. "They're incredibly loyal dogs."

"They sure are," he said, taking a step back. "So – Miz Paradise – you'd better come in."

She entered his immaculate house.

"Paradise is quite a name," he remarked. "Where did you make that one up?"

"Actually, it's my mother's maiden name," she said, glancing around. "Jill told me you have your own personal gym. Where is it?"

"Straight to business, huh?"

"That's why I'm here," she said, unimpressed with his handsomeness. Good-looking famous men were a staple in Hollywood, especially when you worked at a high-end sports club. She'd had many a Hollywood hot shot make a play for her, it was not unusual.

"You come highly recommended," he said, heading for the circular all-glass staircase custom designed by himself. "Jill says you're the best."

"I work hard for my reputation," she answered coolly. "I expect all my clients to do the same for their body."

Don was not used to people – especially women – who didn't fawn all over him. After all, as Ryan had pointed out earlier, he had his own extraordinarily successful talk show and made megabucks. However, in spite of her acerbic attitude he found himself liking Cameron immediately, for not only was she knock-out gorgeous, she had a grittiness about her that appealed to him.

"Here's the deal," he informed her over his shoulder as she followed him upstairs to his gym. "I'm used to working out with male trainers. Fewer distractions, y'know what I mean?"

"Should I leave now?" she shot back, thinking that he was pretty full of himself.

He stopped on the stairs and she nearly ran into his back. "Only if you want to," he said.

"You're the client," she responded. "If you care to work with a male trainer I can easily fix you up."

"You can, huh?"

"Most definitely. I have two male colleagues, both gay." She paused for a moment. "Would that be a problem?" she said, challenging him.

"Not for me," he answered smoothly. "But y'know," he added, shooting her a half-smile, "right now I think I'll stick with you."

"We'll see," she answered.

He raised an eyebrow. "We'll *see*?"

"This is a test run," she said. "I only work with clients I feel I can help."

"Well," he said lightly, "let me know when you make your decision."

"Oh, I will," she assured him.

* * *

By noon Cameron was back at *Bounce*.

"You worked out *who*?" Lynda asked, after Cameron had filled her in.

"I told you, this guy – Don Verona," she said, repeating herself.

"Man!" Lynda exclaimed, rolling her eyes. "You couldn't tell me earlier so I could've come with you."

"To do *what*?"

"Enjoy the view!" Lynda said with a lustful sigh. "Watch an' *wish*. That man is hot hot hot!!!"

"Who's hot?" Dorian inquired, appearing right on cue as usual.

"Missy here went over to Don Verona's crib an' worked his gorgeous ass out. That dude is sooo sexy. I'm in *love* with that man!"

"Me too!" Dorian agreed. "I sleep with him every night! His monologue rocks."

"C'mon, sister," Lynda pleaded, leaning across the reception desk. "What's he *really* like? I wanna know *everything*, no details spared."

"Yes," Dorian agreed. "We want all the dirty bits. Is he hung? Did you notice? A lefty or a righty?"

"Will you two quit it," Cameron scolded, shaking her head in exasperation. "He seemed like a nice enough guy. A lech, but aren't they all?"

"Oh yes," both Lynda and Dorian chorused.

"I've never watched his show," Cameron said. "Is it really that good?"

"Never watched his show?" Lynda repeated, brown eyes widening in disbelief. "You're certainly not *screwing* anyone, so what *are* you doing at eleven p.m.?"

"Sleeping," Cameron replied, thinking they'd both freak if they found out about Marlon.

"Sleeping!" both Lynda and Dorian cried out in shocked unison.

"Yes, sleeping, so I have the strength to do this every day and make enough money for us to move on," Cameron said, thinking that the two of them should form a group they were so in tune.

"You're major *disciplined*," Dorian said, as if it was a bad thing. "I myself like to party."

"No, *really*?" Cameron said, feigning surprise. "Who would've guessed?"

"Don Verona," Lynda sighed dreamily. "Any chance of persuading him to come work out here?"

"Now *why* would I do that?" Cameron said. "He has his own perfectly set-up gym, and besides, I don't want anyone here getting their hands on him. I'm building up our private client list so that when we leave we're not accused of stealing any *Bounce* clients."

"When?" Dorian wanted to know.

"Soon," Cameron assured them. "We're well on our way. I'm checking out a few locations next week."

Dorian's next client entered the premises. He was a buff-looking soap actor who was firmly in the closet. Flashing a set of newly crowned teeth he winked at Lynda.

"Hi Roger," Dorian said, greeting his client with a macho punch on the arm. "Are we ready to stretch those lovely muscles?"

Roger threw another wink – this time at Cameron. "Let's go, Dorian," he drawled. "I couldn't be more ready." He and Dorian walked off.

"Why does he *do* that?" Lynda complained.

"Do what?"

"Act all sexy and straight. We all know he's even gayer than Dorian."

"He's an actor," Cameron said sagely. "It's all about the image."

"I suppose," Lynda said, adjusting a display of lotions and oils sitting on her desk. "What you doin' tonight?"

"Nothing much," Cameron replied, deciding not to mention that Don Verona had invited her to dinner, an offer she'd declined. Lynda would throw a fit if she knew.

"Here's the thing," Lynda said casually. "Carlos has a cousin from Mexico City in town. Apparently this dude is *mucho* hunky. I haven't met him, but if my Carlos says he's hot, then—"

"No!" Cameron said, vigorously shaking her head. "How many times do I have to tell you?"

"Tell me *what?*" Lynda asked innocently.

"No! No! No!" Cameron insisted.

"It's not a set-up," Lynda wailed. "Just a friendly feast at *Houston's*. You know how you love the spare-ribs there, an' you'd be doing Carlos a big favor."

"She's not doing anyone a favor," Dorian interjected, returning to collect an armful of clean white towels. "Don't you get it – our Cameron is all work and no play."

"Please don't speak about me as if I'm not here," Cameron said. "As a matter of fact, Katie's in town. We're going to her boyfriend's gig at *The Roxy*. I'm taking Cole."

"Cole!" Dorian said, pausing on his way back to his client. "How come you didn't invite *me*?"

"Because I invited Cole," Cameron answered briskly. "Next time I'll invite you."

"Thanks a lot," Dorian huffed. "Just because he's the most handsome black man on earth."

"No. Blair Underwood is," Lynda insisted. "An' then Boris Kodjoe an' oh yeah – Taye Diggs – only Taye is kinda short, an' I like my men tall."

"Carlos is five feet ten inches," Dorian sniped. "Hardly a giant."

"Yeah, well let me tell you this – he's a giant in the place where it *really* matters," Lynda shot back, brown eyes flashing.

"Okay, okay, you two," Cameron said. "Quit with the bickering. And Dorian, I had no idea you were into rock concerts. They're all rough and noisy and filled with sweaty rock fans."

"Sounds *très* sexy," Dorian purred. "Take me! Take me!"

"Anything sounds sexy to you," Lynda snapped.

Cameron had three afternoon clients left, then she was through for the day. She thought about how much she was looking forward to meeting up with Katie, whom she hadn't seen in two years. Katie and Jinx were the only people who knew about Gregg and what had taken place between them. None of her other friends had any idea that she was actually married.

Oh God! She was *still* married. How depressing. Had to do something about *that*. And she would. Soon. Eventually she'd hire a lawyer and discuss her options.

As she worked with her final client – an overweight woman who was getting married in four weeks' time and needed to lose twenty pounds – her mind wandered back to that morning and Don Verona. She had to admit that he was very attractive. He was also major charming and a smooth flirt, although when he'd invited her out it had come as a surprise.

"Hey," he'd said, concentrating on perfecting his already

impressive abs, "I'm having dinner with some interesting people tonight. Care to join me?"

She'd shaken her head and said a very firm no.

Two minutes after she'd declined, he'd reached for his iPhone and called someone else, a female who'd apparently said yes.

"You don't wait around, do you?" she'd remarked.

"Why waste time," he'd replied with a jaunty wink.

"By the way," she'd added, thinking that it was to her advantage to put him straight upfront, "it's nothing personal, but I think I should warn you – I never mix business and pleasure. So, if we *are* going to work together . . ."

"I'll bear that in mind," he'd said, giving her the famous Don Verona self-deprecating grin.

Better be careful of this one, she'd thought. *He could be trouble, and the last thing I need is distractions.*

* * *

There was something about Cole de Barge that Cameron had always found very appealing. Not only was he undeniably handsome with his milk-chocolate skin and well-defined features, plus a body straight off the cover of *Men's Health*, he was also a truly decent person with no agenda, and he was smart – so smart that she was considering offering him a business partnership, although that might not sit too well with Lynda and Dorian, who would be most put out that she hadn't chosen them. The truth was that Lynda wasn't business-partner material, she was too intent on getting Carlos to marry her so she could settle down and raise a slew of kids. Lynda's maternal instincts were way out of control. And as for Dorian . . . well, Dorian was Dorian. An excellent trainer, a big flirt, and not to be taken that seriously.

Cole, on the other hand, had a serious side. It was no wonder every gay mogul in town fell in lust with him. First lust and then love.

Cole had experienced several high-powered relationships with major Hollywood players, but he always got restless when they started parading him around like a piece of meat. He deserved respect, and that never happened when you were some rich big-shot's boyfriend. Like Cameron, he was determined to achieve something on his own.

They'd met when she'd first arrived in L.A. and been searching for a job. She was sitting at a table in *Starbucks* on the corner of Robertson and Beverly, thumbing through a *Fitness* magazine, when Cole had wandered over. "Can I take a look at that when you're done?" he'd asked. "There's an interview inside I've been meaning to get to."

She'd given him an appraising once-over. "Only if you tell me where the best sports club in town is," she'd replied.

"You looking for a personal trainer?" he'd asked.

"No. I'm looking for a job."

That's how they'd met, and that's how she'd gotten to work at *Bounce*, where Cole was already one of the most popular trainers.

At first she'd been wary of working there, especially when Cole told her the deal. "You mean *I* have to pay them rent and commission?" she'd said. "I can't afford to do that. I need a job that pays *me*."

"I got your back, girl," he'd assured her. "You'll make a lot more money controlling your own clients. I'll even set you up with a couple of mine to start you off."

Cole had been right, he'd kept his promise and given her three of his own clients with whom she was still working. He'd turned out to be a true and valuable friend.

"What's this Katie babe like?" he asked as they left *Bounce* and strolled out to the parking lot.

"She's a great girl," Cameron said. "Very pretty in a rock chick kind of way."

"And you're old friends?"

"Uh huh. We've been through a lot of stuff together,"

Cameron said, opening her car door. "But I guarantee you'll prefer her boyfriend – he's a skinny Brit, full of sexy rock 'n' roll moves."

"Who cares?" Cole said, heading for his motorcycle. "After my last crash 'n' burn I've decided to go the celibate route."

"That's good to know," Cameron said, grinning, "'cause he's not gay."

"Honey, they *all* are, given the right circumstances," Cole replied with a knowing wink. "You can bet on it."

"So cynical," Cameron sighed, getting in her car.

"So right," Cole responded, jumping astride his motorcycle.

They met up with Katie at a coffee shop on Sunset. Katie was petite, with a halo of curly red hair and an abundance of freckles. Cameron was pleased to note that she and Cole hit it off immediately. Katie was special, and as for Cole – he was a prince.

They sat around talking for a while before heading off to Katie's boyfriend's gig at a club down the street.

"Tonight is like kind of a showcase," Katie confided excitedly as they settled into a booth. "There's reps from two big record companies coming. Jinx is way out psyched, this could lead to something major big like a record deal."

"Sweet," Cole said, ordering a beer.

"I hope it works out," Cameron said, opting for a Red Bull.

"So do I," Katie sighed wistfully. "'Cause we got a really tight thing going, and if Jinx scores a deal, then who knows . . ." she trailed off.

"What?" Cameron asked curiously.

"We might even get married," Katie giggled.

"Is that what you want?" Cameron asked, amazed that anyone would even think of committing to a lifetime relationship.

"We've been talking about it," Katie said.

On stage Jinx came across like a young Mick Jagger, with all the hip-snaking moves and a skinny body in perpetual motion. His group – *Satisfy* – were loud and energetic.

Cameron was impressed, and even though it wasn't her kind

47

of music – too rock 'n' roll – the teenage girls in the audience freaked. She could tell that Jinx possessed a kind of quirky star quality.

Cole thought Jinx was hot. And corruptible.

"I'm telling you – he's not," Cameron whispered.

"There's no way he'd turn down a blow-job on a cold night," Cole responded with a knowing smirk.

"From a *girl*," Cameron insisted.

"You're such an innocent," Cole teased.

"Isn't he fantastic?" Katie enthused, leaning over.

"Right on," Cameron agreed.

Later, after a backstage drink with Jinx and the band, Cole took off and Cameron and Katie got a chance to sit back and talk.

"You look amazing," Katie said, peering at her. "How's everything going?"

"I'm working toward what I want to do," Cameron said. "It's all good, I'm getting there."

"And Hawaii is—"

"Nothing but a faded memory," Cameron interjected. "I never even think about Gregg anymore. He's past history."

"No more bad memories?" Katie asked sympathetically.

"I'm telling you, it's all forgotten."

"Who'd have thought Gregg would turn out to be such a bastard," Katie said. "I hate that—"

"Can we not go there?" Cameron interrupted, willing Katie to drop the subject. "I want to hear more about you and Jinx and those marriage plans of yours."

Katie couldn't wait to tell her everything.

Later, when Cameron left the club, she stood outside, called Marlon on her cell, and asked if he was up for a visit.

"All clear," Marlon said, referring to the fact that his current girlfriend wasn't around. "Come on over."

So she did, and as usual he was delighted to see her. Marlon was always delighted to see her. A college student and aspiring screenwriter, she knew nothing about him except that he was originally from Tennessee, tall and lanky with bleached-by-the-sun hair, deep hazel eyes, a smoking body, and always available.

The moment she walked into his shack at the beach, she began unbuttoning her Cargo pants. Neither of them talked much, they both knew the deal.

Marlon was in his Calvin jeans with nothing underneath. "Hey," he said, hurriedly dropping his Calvins.

"Hey," she said, peeling off her T-shirt.

He grabbed her in an embrace and they began kissing, long, hot kisses, his tongue darting in and out of her mouth. One thing about Marlon, he was a great kisser, full of enthusiasm. Unfortunately his foreplay skills needed honing, but she wasn't there to teach him, she was there for the sex, the feel of him inside her, filling her up with his strong, overpowering manhood.

Sex was comforting. Sex was real. She didn't need the hassle of a relationship, this thing she had with Marlon would do just fine.

They fucked for a long time, until they both came. Then within minutes of their grand climax, she was out of there, in her car and on the way home.

It wasn't perfect, but it was a lot better than getting stuck with one of Carlos's horny friends.

Chapter Six

Most people would pass out mixing Vicodin and Xanax, but Lucy Standard – formerly Lucy Lyons – movie star – thrived on the combination, although sometimes she almost nodded off at the dinner table – prompting her husband, Phil, to joke about his wife the drug addict.

Their friends did not consider it too amusing, but Phil assured everyone that Lucy knew exactly what she was doing.

"It's her back," he explained. "She suffers from excruciating pain from a stunt she insisted on doing herself when she starred in that action movie with our current Governor – the so-called actor. He shoulda stopped her, but he was too busy worrying about his close-ups."

Lucy and Phil lived in a sprawling ranch house in Brentwood, with their two children and a menagerie of animals – including three dogs, a black pig and a parrot who screamed *Fuck you!* at anyone who came within two feet of his perch.

Phil – a big bear of a man with several Oscars on his mantel – was affable, slightly overweight and bearded, with reddish hair and an extremely hearty laugh. He was also a notorious philanderer. "Pussy is my hobby," he was known to boast to his male cohorts. "Pussy and tits – that's what makes the world go round."

Lucy chose to ignore the fact that her husband slept with anything that had a pulse, although she had to be aware of it. Everyone knew that Phil suffered from a major zipper problem.

Lucy was forty, a tough age to be for an actress in Hollywood. A once super-successful star, she hadn't worked in several years, and since Phil was a much-in-demand screenwriter she pretended that it didn't bother her, but of course it did. However, she had no desire to play anyone's mother on screen, so she'd bided her time waiting for the right opportunity to make a startling come-back. Lucy was still extremely beautiful with a sweep of waist-length black hair and a ferocious body. She was also quite a competent actress.

Phil scored big bucks and was extremely generous, so shop-ping, expensive lunches and cutting-edge beauty regimes kept Lucy busy enough. Maintenance was a bitch, and even though she wasn't currently a working actress, she was still chased by the paparazzi everywhere she went. They were all after that one shot of her looking like crap, and she refused to give them the pleasure.

Lucy had a plan. And that plan was to make a major come-back in a major movie and all the people who'd written her movie-star days off could go eat shit. Ryan Richards was part of her plan, although he didn't know it yet. Ryan Richards was going to produce the movie that would make her a star again. And her husband, Phil, was going to write her the role of a life-time – although he also didn't know it yet.

Lucy, when she wasn't zonked out of her mind – knew exactly how she would maneuver the two men into position. And Mandy would help her, because Mandy was her friend.

Of course Mandy didn't know it yet, either, but Lucy was going to let her in on the plan very very soon.

*　*　*

"Who decided on *Geoffrey's* for dinner?" Ryan asked as he and Mandy sat in his Lexus trapped in a major traffic jam on the Pacific Coast Highway.

"Lucy's choice," Mandy replied, pulling down the visor and peering at her reflection. "Our check."

"If it's our check, then why was it *her* choice?" Ryan persisted.

"You know Lucy," Mandy answered vaguely.

"By the way," Ryan said as casually as possible. "I invited Don and a date to join us."

"What?" Mandy said, sitting up ramrod straight, a sure sign she was annoyed.

"Didn't you say it's our dinner, so no problem, right?" he said calmly.

"You should've told me," Mandy snapped.

"I forgot. Big fucking deal."

"You know I do not appreciate surprises."

"I invited him 'cause he had nothing to do. I thought you'd be pleased. You like Don, don't you?"

"Sometimes," Mandy answered guardedly. Yes, she did like Don. And she'd like him even more if he paid attention to her. He was always so dismissive, and it pissed her off. She was Hamilton J. Heckerling's daughter, for crissakes. Most people jumped. Don never had. "Who's he bringing?" she asked.

"I'm sure he'll bring someone nice."

"Nice!" Mandy scoffed. "Don wouldn't know nice if it slapped him in the face! He's into hookers, everyone knows that."

"Not true."

"You were the one that told me," she said accusingly.

Shit! He'd mentioned it once. He wished he hadn't.

"Did you at least change our reservation?" she asked.

"All done."

"I really wish you'd told me earlier."

"I wasn't aware I had to check in with you."

Mandy pursed her lips and gazed out the window. He'd

known she wouldn't take it well. Mandy was a control freak exactly like her father; she wanted *everything* run by her before it happened. The only time he got away from her controlling ways was when he was in production on a movie, although during the first few months of their marriage she'd attempted to interfere in that too. Not for long though, because he'd stopped her at the pass. Making movies was *his* thing, and she'd soon learned – albeit reluctantly – to stay out of his business.

Stuck in traffic, his mind started drifting back to the early days before they were married. The sex had been great, *really* great. One night they'd been driving home from dinner, and the moment they'd hit the flats of Beverly Hills she'd leaned across, unzipped his pants, and given him a fantastic blow-job while he was driving. It was one of his most memorable experiences.

They'd had some laughs then.

Now, seven years later there were no more laughs, and his life was moving forward at a frightening speed. Forty was looming and if he was truthful to himself, he'd admit that he was stuck in a marriage with a woman he didn't like anymore. It was time to do something – anything.

"I've been thinking," he said, drumming his fingers on the steering wheel as they continued to crawl along P.C.H.

"Good for you," she responded, in full pissy mood.

"Seriously, Mandy," he said, persevering, "I've been thinking that maybe it might help us out if we went to couples counseling."

"What?" she exclaimed, quite horrified. "Couples counseling! I can't be seen doing something like that. How would it look?"

"Couples counseling is about two people seeing a counselor privately," Ryan explained. "And, I might add – paying big bucks to do so."

"Why would you even *think* about us doing something like that?" Mandy demanded, staring at him accusingly.

"'Cause surely you must realize that we're drifting more apart every day." There, he'd said it. He'd opened the gates and he was glad.

"No, we're not," she said stubbornly. "Why would you say that?"

"Because it's true," he said, wishing the traffic would move faster. He paused for a moment before plunging ahead. "When was the last time we had sex?" he asked, thinking that he may as well go for it, this was as good a time as any.

"Ha!" Mandy snorted. "So *that's* what this is about. Sex. I should've guessed."

"You can't fight the truth, Mandy. We haven't had sex in months."

"Is that *all* you can think about?"

"Jesus Christ! Face it. When a married couple stops having sex—"

"Y'know," Mandy said, interrupting him, because he was saying things she did not wish to hear, "I should listen to my father more often. He taught me that most men think of nothing else."

"Your father taught you a lot of things," Ryan muttered. "None of them good."

"Are you criticizing Daddy?" she shrieked, outraged.

"Would I do that?" he replied.

"Yes, you would," she answered feverishly. "You hate Daddy, you always have."

"I do not hate him."

"Then why won't you work for him?" she demanded.

This conversation was a constant in their marriage; so much for talking about what was really on his mind.

"How many times do I have to tell you?" he said evenly, attempting to remain calm. "I make independent movies, not box-office pieces of money-grabbing crap!"

"I can't believe you said that!" Mandy exclaimed, her face reddening. "How dare you!"

"For crissakes, cut it out, Mandy," he said, finally losing patience.

"Don't you tell *me* what to do."

By the time they reached the restaurant they were not speaking.

* * *

"Why the fuck do we have to drive all the way out to *Geoffrey's*?" Phil demanded as he and Lucy sat in his Range Rover stuck in the major traffic jam on P.C.H.

"It was Mandy's suggestion," Lucy said.

"Of course it was," Phil grumbled. "Mandy suggests and we all go along like little sheep. That woman is something else."

"It's their dinner," Lucy said. "So they get to choose."

"Mandy's problem is she thinks she's her father," Phil snorted. "Doesn't she get it that *Hamilton* is the one with the balls and the power. Mandy better wake up and smell the fact that she's simply the daughter of."

"Oh, c'mon, Phil," Lucy chided. "Just 'cause you never got to fuck her."

"What *are* you talking about?" he said, outraged. "There's no way I'd screw Mandy. For a start she's too fuckin' short. I like my women tall."

"You like your women any height, shape *or* size," Lucy said dryly. "They can be a midget for all you care."

"Why do you come out with crap like that?" Phil said, refusing to acknowledge the truth.

"Like what, Phil? Surely you're aware that your reputation stretches way before you."

"Shit!" he roared, honking his horn at the car in front. "What the fuck are these morons waiting for?"

"For the traffic to move," Lucy said patiently. Pulling down the visor, she peered in the lighted mirror inspecting her flawless complexion. Botox was the greatest invention ever, not a line on her porcelain skin. And she was younger than most of the comeback kids out there. Demi Moore was over forty when she played her return role in *Charlie's Angels*. Michelle Pfeiffer was fifty-something and she'd starred in several major movies recently. And Sharon Stone was almost fifty when she made *Basic Instinct 2*. Not to mention Madonna and a host of other older actresses still going strong.

Lucy decided she was a mere youngster compared to all those other women.

Yes, she thought to herself, *tonight I'm going to start things in motion. Tonight I'm resurrecting my career.*

Dinner with Ryan and Mandy was the perfect opportunity.

*   *   *

Don drove like a maniac, one hand on the steering wheel of his black Ferrari – chosen for the night from his six cars – the other groping for a cigarette or a mint or his iPhone. Don was always in motion.

His date, a famous "girl next door" TV star, gripped the side of her seat in a panic. This was their first date and she didn't want to spoil it by asking him to slow down.

Ignoring the backed-up traffic on P.C.H., he zipped down the middle lane – totally illegal.

"Who are we having dinner with?" Famous "girl next door" TV star asked, desperate to take her mind off his insane driving. Her name was Mary Ellen Evans, and she'd recently suffered through a very public and humiliating divorce when her movie-star husband had taken off with his gorgeous co-star. The public were firmly on Mary Ellen's side; they would be very happy to see her out on a date with Don Verona – who, since his last divorce, was considered as eligible as George Clooney, and equally as attractive.

"Friends of mine," Don said casually. "You'll like 'em."

He'd met Mary Ellen when she'd appeared on his show the previous week. Having a late-night talk show was a fertile ground for meeting women; many beautiful actresses passed through his studio enabling him to pick and choose. Although some of them were unavailable, most of them were only too delighted when he asked them out.

"Will I know your friends?" Mary Ellen inquired, asserting herself. She was so sick of the tabloid headlines about how lost and lonely she was. It was about time she got out and about.

"Maybe," Don said. "But I thought I'd surprise you."

"Okay," Mary Ellen said, wondering if perhaps they were meeting up with Tom and Katie, or could it be the famous Beckhams? Don Verona knew everyone.

Don threw her a quizzical look, taking his eyes off the road for a moment which terrified her even more. "You're into surprises, aren't you?" he inquired.

"Absolutely," she said, tossing back her sleek bobbed golden hair, and contemplating whether they would sleep together later. She was ready. A revenge fuck was exactly what she needed after the way her husband had publicly humiliated her. Don Verona was the perfect choice.

"Actually," Don said, "it's Phil and Lucy Standard, and Mandy and Ryan Richards."

"Oh," Mary Ellen said. "I was in one of Ryan's movies."

"Yeah? Was it a good experience?"

"I think he's great," Mary Ellen gushed, remembering the major crush she'd harbored. "It was my very first job, a tiny role, and Ryan was so caring and helpful. Everyone on the set adored him. I haven't seen him since – this is exciting."

"Hey – should be a fun evening."

"I'm also a big fan of Phil Standard's work," she added, quite pleased with the way things were turning out. "He's surely one of the most talented screenwriters around."

"Phil's a character," Don said. "He'll probably try to feel you up under the table, so you'd better be prepared."

"Really?" Mary Ellen said, eyes widening.

"Just keep your knees firmly together and you'll be okay."

Mary Ellen threw him a look. "Thanks for the advice."

"Any time," he said, reaching for a cigarette.

Oh damn, he smokes, Mary Ellen thought. *Who smokes in L.A.? It's so unhealthy, and if I sleep with him my hair will smell and so will my clothes. Damn! Damn! Damn!*

"The smoke doesn't bother you, does it?" Don asked.

"Not at all," Mary Ellen replied.

Don Verona was a hot date. She had no intention of ruining it.

Chapter Seven

Hamilton J. Heckerling was big and brash. Loud-mouthed and overbearing. Married five times. A patron of the arts and from all reports a total sonofabitch. Whenever Hamilton entered a room, everyone knew it, especially Ryan, who always tried to avoid him if possible. It wasn't that he was intimidated by his father-in-law, he just didn't like him very much. A lot of people felt the same way. Not that it bothered Hamilton. He was a man who walked his own path full of confidence, and anyone who disliked him – well, his philosophy was fuck 'em. He simply didn't care.

Hamilton inspected the six round dining tables set up in his New York apartment – a penthouse located in Donald Trump's most prestigious building. Hamilton was finicky about entertaining, everything had to be exactly right. He'd learned the art of giving perfect dinner parties from his second wife, Marlee, Mandy's mother, a socialite who now lived outside Cape Town with a black game ranger she'd met on safari in South Africa. Mandy was two at the time, so Hamilton had informed the child that her mother was dead, and he'd paid Marlee a fortune never to return to America. It made things simpler that way.

Marlee was his dirty little secret. And that's the way she would remain.

"Florence!" Hamilton yelled for his housekeeper, and the woman came running. Sternly he informed her that one of the wine glasses had a smudge on the rim.

Florence couldn't see it, but she attended to the offending glass anyway. Whatever Hamilton J. Heckerling wanted, he got.

Hamilton waited until she placed the glass back on the table, then he was satisfied.

Tonight was a special night. Tonight he was announcing his engagement to the sixth and next Mrs Heckerling.

He marched around the room one last time before retiring to his bedroom to prepare for the occasion. Hamilton was fastidious about personal grooming, and his valet awaited his presence, along with all the accoutrements of the well-groomed man.

Hamilton was well aware that when news of his engagement broke tomorrow, Mandy would be upset that she wasn't present. She'd try to berate him over the phone – calls he wouldn't take; she'd attempt to bombard him with e-mails that he wouldn't read.

Ah . . . Mandy . . . sometimes she acted more like a nagging wife than his only child. She was spoiled and capricious, but in his own way he loved her all the same. If only she could learn to stay out of his personal life things would be so much easier between them. Who he dated or slept with or indeed married, was his business and his alone. When Mandy learned that, they'd experience a vastly improved relationship.

He wondered how Mandy would react to Pola – his new wife-to-be. At twenty-something Pola was a whole lot younger than his daughter, and when Mandy found out, he knew that the information would not go down well.

But who was she to criticize? She'd had her pick of all the men in Hollywood, and what man had she chosen? Some loser independent film-maker who wasn't interested in going mainstream, didn't want to come work for him, and insisted on making meaningful movies instead of a shitload of money.

Ryan Richards. He couldn't even knock Mandy up so that it stuck. The man had weak sperm, that was the problem. No grandchildren for Hamilton J. Heckerling.

Hamilton fervently wished that Mandy would do herself a favor and divorce the loser.

At least he'd made sure there was a pre-nuptial in place – drawn up by the most litigious lawyer in town. Pre-nuptials were God's gift to rich people. Only fools would consider marrying without one.

In Hamilton's experience women always signed the agreement – even though they demurred at first. Show them enough cash benefits, allow them to keep any gifts he might buy them – and they signed their money-grabbing little hearts away. Men too, although when Ryan had signed he'd asked for nothing, hadn't even checked it out with his own lawyer, which proved he was stupid.

Hamilton thought about his five ex-wives for a moment. Five beauties who'd ended up boring the shit out of him.

Perhaps Pola would be different.

Perhaps she'd be the one who lasted.

A man could hope, couldn't he?

*   *   *

Mandy was on her second martini when she received the text from Lolly. She jumped up from the table. "I'm visiting the little girls' room," she said, hoping that the other two women would not come with her. She wasn't in the mood to listen to Lucy, who seemed in a particularly aggressive state, and as for Mary Ellen, she was an actress, and Mandy couldn't stand actresses, they were all so dull. The poor dears harbored nothing but thoughts about themselves – their acting classes, their Pilates lessons, their diets, their yoga, their strength training, their psychics, their perfect little bodies, their designer gowns chosen for special events, and their borrowed jewelry. Borrowed jewelry indeed!! How crass was that! Besides, Mary Ellen was pathetic, a girl whose husband had dumped her. Since when was Don into another man's cast-off?

Fortunately neither Lucy nor Mary Ellen seemed inclined to go with her, so Mandy trotted off on her own.

She immediately locked herself in a stall and read the text.

DINNER STILL IN PROGRESS. YOUR FATHER ANNOUNCED YET ANOTHER ENGAGEMENT! POOR YOU. APPARENTLY THIS ONE'S A BABY.

Mandy had to read it twice before she could absorb the full impact of the information. *Crap!* she thought. *The old fool has gone and gotten himself engaged to some woman he's only been seeing for a month or so. It's totally ridiculous. There is no controlling this man.*

Once more she attempted to call him on her cell. Once more his voicemail picked up.

Was he avoiding her?

Probably. That would be just like him, afraid of hearing the truth. And she was the only person who could get away with telling him the truth; everyone else around him was too scared.

It was imperative that she got hold of him. God, she'd be lucky if there was any money left at all by the time he got through marrying all these women. This one would be bride number six!

Of course, she had her Trust Fund to keep her warm, the bulk of which she inherited when she was thirty-five. She'd already inherited a chunk, and spent it happily on herself. Why not? She was entitled.

For a moment she thought about Ryan and their conversation in the car. What *was* he going on about? It occurred to her that maybe she should spend some money on him, buy him something extravagant. His birthday was coming up soon, and perhaps it might be a good idea to plan a party to celebrate.

Yes, that was it, she'd put together a surprise party, and he could stop all this nonsense about couples counseling because no way was she getting into that. As far as she was concerned their marriage was perfectly fine, and if Ryan thought otherwise, that was *his* problem.

But he had sounded restless in the car, especially when he'd started on about their sex life or lack thereof. She decided that if he was very lucky she'd give him a blow-job on the way home, oral sex always shut him up. But then she started thinking about how it would look if they were stopped by the police. She could just imagine the headline in *Variety*.

HAMILTON J. HECKERLING'S DAUGHTER CAUGHT GIVING ORAL SEX TO INDIE PRODUCER IN CAR.

Ha! Not so clever.

She re-read Lolly's text before returning to their table, where Don was at the end of a long involved story about the time Drew Barrymore guested on his show the week after she flashed David Letterman, and then proceeded to do the same to him.

"I never was a guy for sloppy seconds," he mused, finishing the story.

Ha! Mandy thought. *Then what are you doing with Mary Ellen Evans?*

Everyone laughed. Mary Ellen quite politely, although she didn't think it was a particularly funny story. She wondered if he'd talked about her after *she'd* guested on his show. She always attempted to do the best she could on talk shows. She was flirtatious and amusing and tried to wear something sexy – or at least "girl next door" sexy. She hated that label almost as much as she hated doing TV interviews, but at least it had gotten her access to Don, and he was quite a score. Unattached and not gay. Drop dead handsome with a stellar career. What better way to get back at her ex?

"I have an announcement," Lucy said, commanding everyone's attention.

"Something *I* don't know about?" Phil asked, nursing his third Scotch.

"You don't know *everything* about me, dear," Lucy said with a wink. "Even though you *think* you do."

"Christ almighty!" Phil groaned. "Wives!"

"Anybody interested in hearing my announcement?" Lucy said, slurring her words ever so slightly.

"I am," Mary Ellen piped up. She was quite in awe of the beautiful Lucy, whom she'd grown up admiring in many movies, although she would never say that to Lucy, because actresses did not like to be reminded of their age.

"In that case, I'll go ahead," Lucy said, then, pausing for effect she added a breathless – "Guess what, everyone?"

"I thought you had an announcement," Phil grumbled. "Spit it out, this is not a fucking guessing game."

"I've decided to make a comeback," Lucy said grandly, ignoring him.

"From *what?*" Phil snorted.

"A career comeback," Lucy said, shooting him a daggered look.

"Oh," Mandy said, surprised that Lucy hadn't confided in her. "That's interesting, isn't it, Ryan?"

Ryan muttered something under his breath. He'd barely spoken all evening, even though he knew this was making Mandy mad, and somehow he didn't care.

"Do you have a project in mind?" Mandy asked.

"Yes," Lucy said enthusiastically. "I have an original idea for a movie, and I've put together an outline." She paused for a moment before turning to Ryan. "I know it's something *you'll* be interested in," she said. "And Phil," she added, including her husband, "you'll love it."

Phil made a face like he couldn't believe his wife was coming out with such crap.

"So," Lucy continued, "I suggest the three of us get together for a business meeting as soon as everyone's schedule permits."

"Are you *shitting* me?" Phil said, bushy eyebrows shooting up.

Lucy narrowed her eyes and gave him a cold look. "I'm sign-ing with a new agent," she said. "He'll be representing me. I'm giving you first shot at this exciting project."

"Y'know," Phil mused, glancing around the table, "sometimes I think I married a girl from the backwoods who knows nothing about how things work in this town – not a former movie star."

"There's no such thing as a *former* movie star," Lucy said pointedly. "You're either a star or you're not. It doesn't matter whether I'm working, I *still* get all the attention I can handle. And the fans still love me."

"Jesus Christ!" Phil muttered. "I don't believe this shit. Why is she embarrassing me like this?"

"I think it would be a treat to see you back on the screen," Mary Ellen said, taking up the slack before a nasty fight erupted.

"Thank you, dear," Lucy said, wishing the TV star would butt out. Mary Ellen was too young and too pretty, and surely she knew that Don preferred hookers?

"My father just got engaged again," Mandy said, immediately taking the focus off Lucy, who was not pleased to relinquish the spotlight.

"Who to this time?" Don asked.

Mandy shrugged as if she couldn't care less, although inside she was seething. "Some woman he's been seeing for all of five minutes."

"No shit?" Don said, his interest perking. "How many does this make?"

"Too many," Mandy said ominously.

"Never too many for me," Phil chuckled.

Lucy threw him another cold look. How dare he move on without addressing her comeback news. It was important to her, and he was treating her news as if it was a joke. This was unac-ceptable.

The rest of the dinner passed quickly, each person having their own reasons for getting out of there.

After coffee and dessert, the three women went off to the Ladies Room, and Ryan finally felt able to relax.

"Can you believe my wife?" Phil exclaimed. "She's fucking nuts."

"Why didn't she tell you first?" Don asked.

"I thought she'd gotten over all that acting crap," Phil growled.

"Apparently not," Ryan said. "But if it's something she wants to do—"

"It doesn't make any sense," Phil complained. "I give her everything she wants, an' now this outta left field. She's lost it if she thinks *I'm* getting involved."

Ryan shrugged. "They're all difficult," he said. "On the way here I was trying to talk to Mandy about going to couples counseling."

"Couples counseling!" Phil roared, tugging on his beard. "You, her and Hamilton, 'cause she ain't gonna do shit without Daddy."

"She won't do it period," Ryan said glumly.

"I met someone," Don interjected, his mind still on Cameron.

"We can see," Phil said. "The kid's pretty in a kind of unsexy way. Nice tits. You fucked her yet?"

"I'm not talking about Mary Ellen," Don said irritably. "Someone else."

"And who would the lucky lady be?" Phil asked, downing the last of his drink. "Not one of your midnight call girls, I hope."

"Why do I have this reputation?" Don said, exasperated. "Three times I've had a girl come over. Three fucking times. Big fucking deal."

"Who's criticizing?" Phil said. "If I was single I'd be doing the same."

"No you wouldn't, you're too cheap," Ryan joked.

"Let's get back to me," Don said. "This girl I've met is a personal trainer and gorgeous."

"*Hot* gorgeous?" Phil interjected. "'Cause lately your taste seems to be veering offtrack."

"*Classy* gorgeous," Don said. "I asked her to dinner tonight, she turned me down."

"Now that *is* classy," Ryan dead-panned.

"What's wrong with you guys?" Don said, shaking his head. "You never take anything seriously."

"I'll tell you what I'm taking seriously," Ryan lamented. "My birthday coming at me like a goddamn express train. I'm about to hit forty. I feel a mid-life crisis slamming me squarely in the balls."

"He's not getting laid," Don offered. "Mandy's closed shop."

"Not getting laid!" Phil bellowed. "That's tragic."

"Scream a little louder," Ryan said. "The table in the far corner didn't quite hear."

"Ryan Richards is not getting laid," Phil yelled.

"Oh, Jesus!" Ryan said, quickly signaling for the check. "It's time we got the hell out of here."

ANYA

*S*ergei stole a gold watch, money and a selection of drugs from *Greedy Boris's safe. Before the old man found out, he and Anya were on their way out of the city. By this time they were lovers, the fourteen-year-old girl and the twenty-year-old petty criminal. Anya had come to realize that the only thing she had left was her sexual power, and she used it on Sergei so that he would protect and look after her.*

He was very different from the men who'd raped and abused her. Living in his room, she'd grown used to sharing his meals and his bed, so when he'd first had sex with her, she'd gritted her teeth and decided that it was a lot better than being out on the violent and dangerous streets all alone in the world. Sergei wasn't so bad. Wiry and skinny as a stick, with pointed features, two missing front teeth and a facial tic, at least he was young – like her – and after a while they began exchanging their personal horror stories and a closeness and intimacy grew between them.

Sergei realized he had scored a prize, for Anya was indeed a beauty with her porcelain skin, fair hair, and exceptionally pale blue eyes. She was becoming more of a woman as each day passed.

Their escape from Ingushetia was arduous and treacherous, involving a dangerous trek around the mountains, countless rides on dusty trucks, two days on a delapidated train, and many nights sleeping outside in the open with only one tattered blanket between them.

Sergei's goal was to reach Poland, but getting across the border presented a challenge even he found difficult to solve. However, he was street smart and determined, plus he had drugs to sell – and he used them as currency. Eventually he bribed a farmer to hide the two of them in the back of his truck with the livestock, and that's how they crossed the border into Poland, where Sergei had a cousin.

Sergei's cousin, Igor, was not exactly thrilled to see them, but he took them in all the same. Family was family, and Anya was such a tasty little morsel.

Sergei soon noticed the lecherous way his cousin looked at Anya, and it worried him, so he lied and informed Igor that Anya was his wife. "Your wife?" Igor sneered. "Why would any man be foolish enough to marry?"

Like Sergei, Igor was a minor pimp. And just like Sergei he had a boss, although his boss was a lot more sophisticated than Greedy Boris. Since Sergei was in need of a job, Igor took him to meet her.

Olga Gutowska was a stony-faced, stout Polish woman known as The Empress. She lived in a house with seven bedrooms, and ruled her stable of girls with an iron fist. Nobody ever questioned Olga Gutowska. She had connections in all the right places. Instinctively Sergei knew that if she ever saw Anya, she'd immediately want her. So after Olga agreed to hire him on a trial basis, he made sure that he kept Anya well out of sight.

Igor thought he was crazy and urged him to put Anya to work. "She make you plenty money," he said slyly, reminding Sergei of Greedy Boris. "She make us both money if we work her on the side and no tell Olga. She be our whore."

Sergei said an emphatic no. In his mind Anya was his wife, she did his washing and ironing, she cooked for him, and she was always available for him sexually. She didn't speak much, but that was understandable.

Then one day while Sergei was out, Igor began pawing Anya. She backed away from him, terrified. But her fear only seemed to excite him more, and when she resisted, he brutally raped her, then later he forcibly dragged her out of the house.

Sergei returned home at dusk to find both Anya and Igor were gone. So were all of Igor's possessions.

Suspecting what had taken place, Sergei flew into a crazed fury and raced over to Olga's house, where he was denied entry. "You no longer work here," the bodyguard at the door informed him. "Go away. Don't come back."

They'd stolen his Anya, and Sergei was beside himself with grief and anger. But he wasn't about to accept what they'd done to him. Oh no. Sergei was not going quietly.

He purchased a gun on the black market, and later that night he returned to Olga's house. When the guard at the door attempted to prevent him from entering, he shot the man in the shoulder, and forced his way inside. Sergei had one goal and one goal only, and that was to get Anya back.

When Olga heard the gunshot, she picked up the shotgun she kept handy at all times and marched into the front hall where she confronted a wild-eyed Sergei.

"Where's my Anya?" he screamed. "Give her back to me, or so help me I will kill all of you."

"You're too late, she's gone," Olga said flatly.

"Don't lie to me!" Sergei yelled, waving his gun at her. "I will not be lied to."

Olga lifted her shotgun and pointed it straight at him. "Go," she commanded. "Before I shoot your sorry ass. It's not worth dying for a dirty little whore."

With an agonized cry of frustration, Sergei lunged at her. True to her word Olga shot him in the stomach, blowing him almost in two.

Leaning over the banisters with the other girls, Anya gasped in horror.

Once more she realized she was all alone.

Chapter Eight

Cameron's realtor acquaintance, Iris Smith, had two properties to show her. The first one was useless. Depressed, Cameron called Cole and asked him to meet her at the next one. She valued his opinion and she also thought it might be the perfect opportunity to talk to him about partnering up.

Cole arrived on time.

"What do you think?" she asked, standing back and surveying the rather cramped dark basement space on Melrose.

"Way too gloomy," he responded, wandering around the empty space. "And too damn small. No windows, no sunlight. Doesn't do it for me."

"You could lighten it up with the right decoration," Iris offered, trying to be helpful. "A coat of white paint, perhaps some flowers."

"Are you kiddin' me?" Cole said, kicking at a loose floorboard. "No amount of paint's gonna liven this place up."

Cameron agreed. Cole had excellent instincts and he was right.

"Well," Iris said hesitantly, "there is one more situation I could show you. But I should warn you that the rent is higher."

"How much higher?" Cameron asked, thinking that there was no way she could pull off a higher rent.

"A substantial jump."

"Okay . . ." Cameron said unsurely. "I suppose it wouldn't hurt to see it."

The location Iris had mentioned was on Wilshire, and it turned out to be perfect. It was an enormous open space penthouse, with high ceilings and a large surrounding outdoor terrace.

"This is totally it!" Cameron exclaimed.

"It sure is," Cole agreed.

"Give me the bad news," she said to Iris. "How much more is it?"

"I hate to tell you, but it's a lot more than the other two locations," Iris said apologetically.

After hearing all the figures, Cameron turned to Cole. "It's way out of my range," she said ruefully.

"I might have an idea," he said. "We gotta talk."

"What's to talk about?" she said, shrugging. "I can't venture out on my own only to immediately go broke 'cause I fail to make the rent each month. Plus they require two months' security deposit, and then there's all the other expenses – phones, electricity, a ton of stuff."

"You gotta factor in that wherever you go, right?" he pointed out.

"I guess so," she said hesitantly. "It's just such a downer. What I need is a Sugar-Daddy, some old dude with big bucks to throw around."

"Maybe I should go get *me* a Sugar-Mama," Cole suggested, laughing. "Between us we'll make it work."

"You'd do that for me?" she said wistfully. "You'd really change tracks?"

"For you," he said gallantly. "Anything."

"Y'know, Cole, you're such a good friend," she said warmly, grabbing his arm and squeezing.

"I try."

"And you succeed."

It was true. He did succeed. Along with Katie in San Francisco, Cole was the best friend she had. But even though they were close, she'd never told him about Gregg. Somehow she couldn't bring herself to do so. In a way she was ashamed that she'd allowed the situation with Gregg to happen to her. When things started to escalate, why hadn't she walked out on him? Was she an accomplice in the abuse she'd endured? Or even worse – was she an enabler?

"Let's go get coffee," Cole said, glancing at his watch. "My first client's not until twelve."

"Exactly what I need, a heavy jolt of caffeine." Iris was hovering. "We'll have to let you know," Cameron said. "Can you hold it for us?"

"Only for a few hours, so you'll have to let me know soon," Iris replied, gathering up her papers. "This is a prime location – I can assure you it'll move fast."

Cameron nodded. "I understand."

She and Cole made their way outside, strolled down the street, and settled in a nearby *Coffee Bean*.

"Here's what I've been meaning to talk to you about," she said earnestly, brushing a lock of blonde hair out of her eyes.

"Go ahead."

"The thing is, I was kind of wondering if you might be interested in coming in as a partner?"

"I got a few bucks stashed away," he said thoughtfully. "But here's what *I* was thinkin'. Maybe I'll speak to my sister. Natalie's always carryin' on about investing her money – she could be interested."

"Really?"

"Why not? Big sis is scorin' plenty of bucks on her TV show, this could be her thing. I'm gonna set somethin' up."

"Wow!" Cameron exclaimed excitedly. "Make it fast, you heard what Iris said – that space won't stay available for long, and it's just *so* right."

"Believe me – I'm onto it."

"Once we get off the ground I *know* we'll be successful," Cameron said, nodding her head as if to reassure herself. "We both have great client lists."

"We sure do."

"And I was thinking that we should make it membership only. Very exclusive."

"Yeah, but how about the whole stealing clients deal?" Cole ventured. "You thought about that?"

"I never signed anything with *Bounce*, did you?"

"Not a thing."

"Anyway, why *would* we need to steal? If our clients want to follow us, they're free to do so. I dunno know about you – but I have more recommendations than I can handle."

"Lynda's coming, right?"

"She can't wait."

"An' Dorian won't wanna be left behind."

"Does this mean you're my partner?" she asked hopefully.

"You got it, babe," he said, breaking out a big grin.

"This could be so amazing!" she exclaimed. "I love you!"

"Yeah, but right now I'm outta here," he said, jumping up. "Client waitin'. I'll speak to Natalie right away."

Cameron watched him leave. Tall handsome Cole was absolutely her best friend. How stupid was she? She'd been so busy saving money when she should've been making him part of her plan way earlier. Now she had someone to help make it happen, and whether Natalie invested or not, it was a major plus.

Later, on her way back to *Bounce* her cell buzzed. "Yes?" she said, hoping it might be Cole with some news.

"Remember me?" said a smooth voice. "Don Verona, your client from Saturday, the one you turned down for a date."

"It wasn't a date," she said, wondering what he wanted.

"It could've been," he answered, sounding slightly amused.

"I invited you to dinner, and you informed me that you never mix business with pleasure."

"I did say that, didn't I?" she said, surprisingly pleased to hear from him.

"Look – here's what I've decided," he said. "I want to hire you on a regular basis."

"You do?"

"Yes, so can you fit me into what I'm sure is your busy schedule?"

"Well . . ." she said, hesitating for only a moment. "I suppose if we can work out a time that suits us both."

"You know what I like about you?" he said, sounding even more amused.

"Do tell."

"Your manic enthusiasm."

"I save my enthusiasm for my work," she responded, suppressing a smile.

"Glad to hear it."

"I'm sure you work hard too."

"That I do." A beat. "I was thinking, mornings are good for me, and since I'm an early riser, how about seven a.m. five days a week?"

"You're willing to work out five consecutive days?" she said, surprised, because big stars usually weren't so into it, not unless they were preparing for a movie role, and then it was all systems go.

"I'm hosting an awards show and it's coming up fast. I plan on getting into really good shape."

"You *are* in good shape," she said, flashing on the memory of his well-defined abs.

"Thanks," he said modestly. "Didn't think you noticed."

"Seven is okay, although I'll have to charge you a higher rate because of the time."

"You trying to gauge me?" he teased.

"No, I'm merely telling you the way it is," she said, all busi-ness. "When would you like to start?"

"Tomorrow. Does that suit you?"

"Seven a.m. at your house. I'll be there."

"I'll be waiting."

She clicked off her phone, excited in spite of herself.

No involvements, her inner voice warned.

Why not? she reasoned. *He's a very attractive guy.*

Yes, with charm to spare and an enormous ego. Besides, an involvement will get you offtrack. Right now all your energy has to go toward creating your future.

Yes. Her future. Building the dream.

And if Cole's sister came through, things were looking prom-ising.

Putting it all together was going to be a big challenge, but she could do it, especially with Cole's help.

Instinctively she knew that her inner voice was right. No involvements. No distractions. No more time-consuming rela-tionships period.

Gregg was enough bad memories to last a lifetime.

Chapter Nine

Lunching at *The Grill* was a weekly ritual. Ryan and Don were there, but Phil couldn't make it, he was too busy with his own problems trying to talk his movie-star wife out of resuming her "dead-on-arrival" career.

"How'd it go on your way home last night?" Don asked, ordering a bottle of flat water. "Things didn't seem so smooth at dinner."

"We resolved a few issues," Ryan answered carefully, not about to reveal what had happened in the car on their drive home. Mandy had suddenly reverted to her old ways and attempted to give him head on P.C.H. Once he would've got off on it, but this time he'd shoved her away with a vengeance. It wasn't the time, nor the place. Besides, a blow-job from Mandy didn't seem right; he'd had a horrible suspicion she'd stop mid-blow and complain about something or other. Mandy had turned into a world-class nag.

The bottom line was that sex with his wife was no longer sexy. She didn't turn him on in any way, shape or form.

"You know how I feel about your situation," Don remarked, consulting the menu.

"Everything's fine," Ryan lied, spinning his answer to suit himself. "Mandy was upset about Hamilton getting married again, that's all."

"Surely she's used to his crap by now?"

"Seems not."

"By the way," Don added, "his latest is on the front page of the *New York Post*. She looks about twelve!"

"That's when you know you're getting old," Ryan said glumly.

"How's that?"

"When you think everyone looks twelve!"

"You're the one heading for a mid-life crisis, not me," Don said, picking up a breadstick. "I have another six months before I hit the big four O. And y'know what – I don't give a shit."

"Why would you?" Ryan said restlessly. "You've got it made. You built your own home, you have plenty of money, a great career, your health, your freedom, *and* you're fucking famous, not to mention good-looking. Shit! Who wouldn't be happy being you?"

Don signaled for their waiter. "Y'know," he confided, "I called that girl I told you about, the personal trainer. I'm working out with her every day at seven, starting tomorrow."

"Working out?"

"My body, jerk," Don said, flashing a grin. "Gotta keep the machine in action."

"I thought you liked her."

"I do. So this way I get to know her on neutral ground. No dating hassles."

"You're paying her, right?"

"Of course I am."

"Then isn't it kind of like having a hooker come over without the sex?"

"You're sick," Don said, shaking his head, but laughing all the same.

"Think about it," Ryan insisted. "You're *paying* the girl to spend time with you. No commitments."

"Do me a fucking favor, straighten out your own crap before you start criticizing mine."

"I'm trying to be helpful, Don."

"You're about as helpful as a sack of shit."

"Thanks!"

"What's bothering you anyway?" Don asked. "I thought you said everything was okay between you and Mandy."

"Hey – nothing's perfect," Ryan said gloomily.

"Then do something about it," Don suggested, determined to jog Ryan into taking some kind of action. "Divorce is not such a disgrace, it's more a rite of passage, especially in this town. Man, I did it twice. It cost me, but damn it was worth it!"

"In my family divorce is admitting total failure," Ryan said, thinking of his mother's disappointment if he even so much as mentioned the word divorce. "My parents were married forever."

"C'mon, Ryan, it's not as if you have kids. You're feeling it's over, so you owe it to yourself to make a move."

"I don't know," Ryan said unsurely.

"It's about time you hauled your sorry ass in to see my shrink," Don said. "She'll set you straight. I'll find out if she does couples therapy."

"Mandy won't go for it."

"Too bad she has your balls in a vise," Don said dryly. "I can remember when—"

"Can we drop it?" Ryan interrupted. "It's not that easy."

"Okay, okay, I get it," Don said as their waiter approached. "I'm ordering a big juicy steak and a shitload of French fries. Gotta get my strength up for my new girlfriend."

"Girlfriend?" Ryan questioned.

"She could be."

"You really like this one, huh?"

"I'm giving her a test run. We'll see."

* * *

"You're jealous, that's what your reluctance to help me is all about," Lucy yelled. "But trust me, Phil, I'm going to make a big comeback with or without your help."

"What is it that you want that I don't give you?" Phil yelled back. "You've got everything you could ever want. I fucking don't get it."

"You wouldn't. You're too busy screwing any piece of ass who looks at you sideways."

"Oh for Christ sakes, that again."

"How would you like it if I did the same?" she retaliated, determined to get her point across.

"I'd break your fucking neck."

"Fuck you, Phil."

"Fuck you, Phil," screamed their parrot, hopping around his cage.

"I'm going to kill that goddamn bird," Phil roared.

"Make sure you don't fuck it first," Lucy responded, before stalking out of the kitchen.

She was making a comeback, and no one was stopping her.

* * *

Mandy spent the morning attempting to reach her father while avidly studying the coverage about his engagement in the newspapers and on the Internet. She was particularly incensed with the story in the *New York Post*. Not only did they have his new girlfriend's picture on the front of the paper, but there was a bitchy piece on page six about the age difference between Hamilton and his intended, also the number of wives he'd had. Fortunately it didn't mention her, although it should have, since she was far more important than any of his damn wives, considering *she* was the heir apparent to the Heckerling fortune. Mandy Heckerling. They should kiss her Hollywood Princess ass. Everyone should.

She was also furious that Ryan had flatly refused her offer of sex last night. It was hard to understand why. Yes, she had to admit that their sexual activities had kind of dwindled in the last couple of years. But when she'd offered him head in the car he'd turned her down when he should've been wild with enthusiasm. What was *that* all about?

The thought occurred to her that maybe he had a girlfriend on the side.

Then she decided – no – absolutely no way. One thing about Ryan – he was not a cheater.

Or was he?

Doubts began creeping into her mind.

According to her father, all men cheated. That was the way of the world according to Hamilton J. Heckerling.

Men are cheaters.

Women are not to be trusted.

And most people are dumb.

When she called Lolly again to find out if there was any further news, Lolly's voicemail picked up. Frustrated, Mandy set off to get a manicure, a pedicure and a facial.

At least a few hours of maintenance would take her mind off things. Temporarily.

Chapter Ten

The meeting between Cameron, Cole and his sister, Natalie, took place at the bar in the Beverly Wilshire Hotel. When Natalie de Barge walked in, heads turned. Clad in a black cashmere sweater and white pants, a grey fedora perched on her head, conversations stopped as people observed this vibrant black woman with stunning good looks. Natalie was also a successful TV entertainment reporter, co-host of a popular nightly TV show that rivaled *E.T.* and *Extra*.

After fifteen minutes of small talk, Cameron began carefully laying out her business plans. Natalie slowly sipped a Cosmopolitan and listened intently, asking pertinent questions here and there.

When Cameron was finished she finally spoke. "Okay, this is what I want," she said, tapping her glossy nails on the table. "If I'm about to invest my hard-earned money in this venture, then my baby bro' gotta be a full partner. I'll put up fifty per cent of the upfront money. But that's the deal. Cole, full partner – fifty fifty. No negotiation."

"Wow!" Cameron said, trying to remain cool, although she was thrilled that her dream might just be coming true. "That's no problem, Natalie. Cole and I get along great, and believe me – it'll be a relief to go into business with a partner, someone I can absolutely depend on and trust."

"Yeah," Cole agreed, laughing. "Someone you don't havta sleep with."

"You mean you haven't converted him?" Natalie asked, straight-faced. "A gorgeous girl like you?"

"Not yet," Cameron replied, playing along with the joke. "But I swear I'll keep trying. I can be very persuasive."

"In that case, I'm definitely in," Natalie said, with a big smile.

"For real?" Cameron said, her green eyes gleaming with excitement.

"Yup," Natalie said, still smiling. "You can go over all the details with my business manager, Laura Lizer. She's one tough cookie, so don't even think about screwing me."

"*Puleeze!*" Cole interjected. "As if."

"Okay, kids, then that's it," Natalie said.

"Fantastic!" Cameron exclaimed, turning to Cole. "It means we can go for the location we saw, and start renting equipment immediately."

"Thanks, sis, you won't regret it," Cole said, standing up.

"I'd better not," Natalie said, also getting to her feet and exchanging a warm hug with her brother. "Oh, and I expect free use of the facilities for me and my friends whenever we feel the urge to get fit."

"For you – it's free," Cole said, all business. "Your friends – they gotta pay."

"Hard ass," Natalie said, mock-pouting.

"I learned from the best – *you!*"

"Such a sweet talker." Natalie sighed, picking up her Fendi purse. "Have fun, kids. We'll talk some more tomorrow. Right now I got a hot date with Brad and Angelina."

"I can't believe it!" Cameron said, as Natalie strolled off. "We're actually on our way! Shall we tell Lynda?"

"Tell whoever the hell you want," Cole replied. "I knew Natalie wouldn't let us down."

"Hmm . . ." she mused. "Maybe we should wait until every-thing's settled, then we can go out and celebrate."

"You got it," Cole said, psyched that his sister had come through; it proved that she really believed in him, and that was something he hadn't expected.

He and Cameron exchanged hugs.

"To partners!" Cole said. "We're gonna kick it, girl. We're gonna open the best fuckin' sports club in the city!"

"You bet we are," she agreed. "And right now I'd better call Iris and secure that space."

"Go ahead. Do it."

Cameron fished out her cell and punched in the realtor's number.

Iris picked up the second ring. "Oh dear," she said, all embar-rassed. "I think it might be gone."

"We asked you to put it on hold," Cameron said sharply. "We saw it first and now we want it."

"Yes, dear, I know," Iris said, quite flustered. "But you prom-ised to get back to me."

"We *are* getting back to you," Cameron said, pulling a face at Cole and deciding she'd go freaking nuts if they lost the space. "C'mon, Iris, it hasn't even been twenty-four hours."

"I'll see what I can do," Iris said.

"Not good enough. Write up an offer, that space is *ours*!" she said, clicking off her phone.

"Aint nobody gonna mess with you," Cole joked. "You're one hard-assed woman."

"She'll come through," Cameron said. "She'd better."

After they left the hotel, Cameron was too wired to go home, and not in the mood for a return visit to Marlon. Cole had a hot date, so on impulse she stopped by Mr Wasabi's, picked up her dogs, bundled them in the back of her Mustang, and set off for the beach.

She drove fast all the way down Sunset, making it to Paradise

Cove in under an hour. After parking the Mustang she let Yoko and Lennon run wild on the beach. It was a beautiful night with a strong breeze and a high surf. Watching her dogs romp along the sand, she felt as if she could fly. What a day! It all seemed such a long way from two years ago when she'd fled Hawaii battered and bruised with nothing but bad memories and a broken arm.

Sometimes she wondered why Gregg had never come looking for her, then she realized he was probably too ashamed to face her. Ashamed and sorry – at least, she *hoped* he was sorry.

She didn't care. He'd turned out to be a monster, and she prayed that she'd never have to set eyes on him again.

Yoko and Lennon were racing all over the place, splashing in the surf, barking, rolling in the sand, reveling in their freedom.

After a while she realized it was time to rein them in and start doing some serious planning. Iris had better come through with the location, it was so damn perfect. And now she had a partner. One of her best friends. What could be better?

By the time she got back to her house it was almost midnight. She'd forgotten she had Don Verona at seven in the morning. Damn! Too early!

Setting her alarm for six she slept fitfully. She needn't have bothered, because she was up at five anyway, too charged up to sleep.

After walking her dogs, and eating a healthy breakfast of wheat toast and scrambled egg whites, she pulled on a tracksuit and her favorite Pumas, then set off for Don's house.

When she got there she had to ring the doorbell several times before a bleary-eyed Don opened the front door himself. It was apparent that he'd rolled out of bed to do so, because he was barefoot, his dark hair ruffled, wearing nothing but baggy blue pajama bottoms and a winning smile.

"You're not ready," she said, meaningfully tapping her watch. "It's seven a.m."

"Ah, jeez," he said, attempting to stifle a yawn. "I got caught up in something – ended up having a late night."

"When you're set to work out at seven a.m. you're not supposed to have late nights," she said briskly, entering his house.

"Can we leave it today?" he said, yawning again.

"Fine with me, but you should know that I'm charging you anyway."

"Send me a bill," he said, scratching his head. "I'm good for it."

She almost turned to leave, then thought better of it. "Can I ask you something?" she said, giving him a direct look.

"Ask away," he said, enjoying her refreshing beauty. She was so damn . . . glowing.

"Maybe I got the wrong impression," she scolded, "but I thought you *wanted* to do this." She paused, allowing her words to sink in. "Weren't you the one all gung-ho about getting into shape?"

"Didn't you tell me I was already *in* shape?" he responded, hardly able to take his eyes off her lips which were begging to be kissed.

"Kind of. But that doesn't mean you couldn't use some extra toning."

"You think so?" he asked, imagining those lips on his, imagining her naked and in his bed next to him.

"Yes," she said, her eyes checking out his physique – which she had to admit was quite impressive. Hard abs, firm arms, a muscular chest. She wondered what had happened to his previous trainer, because it was quite obvious he was into working out.

"Look," he said, wishing she'd shut the fuck up and come into his bedroom with him, "whyn't you do us both a favor, go in the kitchen and make a pot of coffee while I throw something on."

"Are you kidding?" she said incredulously.

"*What?*" he said, squinting. "Did I say something wrong?"

"You want coffee, then I suggest you make it yourself."

"Huh?" he mumbled, not getting it.

"Surely you have a housekeeper?" she said, incensed that he was treating her as if she was merely there to do his bidding.

"It's not my deal to have anybody around on a permanent basis."

"Then I suppose a wife is out the question?" she drawled sarcastically.

"Why?" he said with a sly grin. "You applying for the job?"

"Some job," she murmured scornfully.

"Jeez, you're difficult," he grumbled.

"No," she said, answering quickly. "I'm merely professional, and you should be too."

"Okay, okay," he said, holding up his hand. "Stop lecturing me. *I'll* put on the coffee, then I'll get into my work-out clothes and we'll do fifteen minutes."

"Fifteen minutes?" she said, shaking her head in disbelief. "You're paying me for an hour."

"You've got money on the mind, lady. I *said* I'll pay you. Do I look like a welsher?"

"I hate wasting *my* time and *your* money."

"And she's thoughtful too," he teased.

"I try to be."

They exchanged a long look.

"How about dinner tonight?" he said, tired of wasting time.

"Excuse me?"

"Dinner. Tonight," he said patiently. "Two people sitting at a table eating food. It's a local custom. Very popular."

"No."

"No what?"

"No thank you."

He threw her a quizzical look. "Are you gay?"

"What?" she said, outraged.

"Into women?"

"Oh, I see," she said. "I don't want to go out with you, so automatically you assume I'm gay."

"Not that there's anything wrong with it – I mean if you *were* gay," he said, studying her beautiful face. "Although, I have to say, it'd be a terrible waste. However—"

"I am not gay," she said firmly. "Not that it's any of your business."

"Married? Engaged?" he pushed.

"What is this – an inquisition?"

"Kinda. I'd like to take you to dinner and you keep on saying no. There has to be a reason."

"How about you're not my type."

"Now *you're* kidding, right?"

"I don't date actors."

"I'm not an actor."

"You're on TV. Same thing."

"I host my own talk show. Totally different."

"I don't date celebrities."

"Who *do* you date?"

"You know what – *I'll* make the coffee," she said, deciding to put an end to a conversation that was becoming far too personal and going nowhere. "Go put on your work-out clothes and we'll get in half an hour of weight training."

"And so she changes the subject," he drawled.

"Go!" she ordered.

"Yes, *ma'am*," he said, mock-saluting.

He couldn't help smiling as he made his way into his dressing room and grabbed trackpants and a T-shirt. This one was so different from the women he was used to. She was beautiful – but they all were. She had a great body – but they all did. Cameron had something else going for her; she struck him as not only stunningly beautiful, but honest, self-confident and unimpressed with his fame. Very refreshing. And best of all she was not prepared to succumb to his considerable charms, and that *was* most unusual.

But she didn't want to go out with him, and he had to find out why. It was in his nature to get to the bottom of things. It wasn't as if he was some crazy pervert she'd met on the Internet or picked up in a club. He was Don Verona, and most women creamed at the thought of any interaction with him.

So what was wrong with her?

By the time he got back to the kitchen the coffee was bubbling in the pot and she was busy chopping fruit.

"What are you doing?" he asked.

"You can't work out on an empty stomach," she said crisply. "It's not the right way to start the day."

"I never eat in the mornings."

"You do now," she said, pushing back a lock of blonde hair that kept on drifting into her very appealing green eyes. "It'll give you more energy."

"Are you always this bossy?" he asked, picking up a slice of mango with his fingers.

"Only when I need to be."

"And that would be now?"

"Seems to be the case," she said, handing him a slice of banana.

"Who *are* you?" he said, wondering for a moment if one of his friends had sent her to mess with his head. That would be their idea of a joke. Not too funny.

"Your new trainer," she answered briskly. "I don't know what kind of excuses the last one let you get away with, but things they are a-changing!"

"They are?"

"Oh, yes."

And once more their eyes met, and once more Cameron silently warned herself to be careful. This guy was a player, and she wasn't about to fall for his game. No. She had far more important things on her mind, and Don Verona could turn out to be an unwelcome distraction.

Keep on remembering that, she warned herself. *No involvements. Work first.*

And yet . . . Gregg was almost a distant memory, and she'd had no one to share things with. No man to hold her at night. Marlon didn't count. And . . .

No! No! No! a stern voice screamed in her head. *It ain't gonna happen. No way. No how.*

End of story.

ANYA

*A*nya *soon realized that with Sergei gone, she had nobody to depend on but herself. Sergei had treated her with kindness, but it seemed kindness didn't pay, because Sergei was dead, and with Olga's connections, the woman was never accused of the crime.*

The morning after the shooting, Olga had Igor bring her upstairs to the bedroom she occupied on the top floor of the house. Anya had spent the night huddled in a locked closet where Igor had deposited her after Sergei was shot. She'd hardly slept at all and when Igor came to fetch her, she was painfully aware that she smelled, her hair was matted and her clothes grimy.

"What's your name?" Olga barked.

"Anya," she replied, quite startled by the luxury of Olga's bedroom. There was an enormous bed, long satin drapes hanging from the windows, and a big white furry rug on the floor. Anya had never seen such luxury.

"How old are you?" Olga asked, rubbing her hands together in anticipation of the money this morsel of a girl would bring in.

"Fifteen," Anya whispered.

"Fifteen an' not a virgin," Olga muttered. "But you can pretend, can't you?"

Anya nodded, although she really didn't understand what the woman was getting at.

"Take your clothes off," Olga ordered.

Anya stiffened.

"Don't be shy," Olga said. "I've seen it all before."

Timidly Anya slipped off her dress. Sergei had never thought to buy her underwear, so she stood in front of the intimidating woman and Igor – who skulked by the door.

Standing there, naked and shivering, a feeling of hopelessness overcame her.

"Not bad," Olga said, reaching for a porcelain mug filled with sweet black tea. "Nothing that a bath and a delousing can't take care of."

At that precise moment Anya made a promise to herself that one day she would be treated as a human being and not a piece of meat. One day she would take her revenge on all these people.

In her heart she knew that day would come.

Chapter Eleven

"I've decided to throw a surprise birthday party for Ryan," Mandy informed Lucy as they sat at an outside table at *The Ivy*.

"And *I'm* thinking of divorcing Phil," Lucy responded, adjusting her Dolce & Gabanna sunglasses, wondering if she was being observed by sneaky paparazzi hiding in the black SUV parked across the street.

"Oh my God! What's he done now?" Mandy exclaimed, thinking that she should actually be saying – *who's he doing now?* Because Phil Standard's sexual activities were general knowledge. He was a bad bad boy, but lovable all the same.

"He's refusing to cooperate on my career comeback," Lucy said petulantly. "Phil can be a jealous prick when it suits him. He doesn't relish the idea of me attracting any more attention than I already have."

"Phil, jealous?" Mandy said, not quite believing it, for Phil always seemed so easygoing.

"Oh yes," Lucy said, filled with the unfairness of it all. "If Phil had his way I'd be permanently knocked up and stuck in the kitchen cooking him three meals a day. He doesn't get that I'm a movie star, for God's sake."

"I'm sure he is very proud of you," Mandy murmured.

But Lucy wasn't listening, she was on a roll. "I took time off to have his kids, and now that I plan on resuming my career, the selfish jerk is being about as helpful as a boil on the tip of his dick! Asshole!"

"How *are* the children?"

"Fine. They're with their nanny. I don't know what I'd do without her, she's a gem."

Mandy wasn't that interested, she had her own problems, but she made a few more sympathetic noises anyway.

After Lucy had finished complaining Mandy repeated her desire to throw Ryan a surprise party. "Upstairs at *Mr Chow*," she said. "Only twenty people. And do *not* tell Phil, because he'll blab to Ryan, and that'll spoil the surprise."

"How am I supposed to get him there if I can't tell him?" Lucy asked, biting into a crab cake.

"Say it's dinner with Don, that'll do it," Mandy said, nodding to herself. "I'll call Don and warn him; he's a lot more capable of keeping a secret."

"He's screwing his assistant, you know," Lucy revealed.

"Who, Don?" Mandy asked, quite surprised.

"No, Phil," Lucy said scornfully. "Fucking around is in his genes, or so he tells me – like *that* makes it okay." She paused for a moment and narrowed her eyes. "Now, if *I* did it, he'd go berserk. *That's* why he doesn't want me going back to work; he thinks I'll be exposed to all kinds of temptation."

"How ridiculous," Mandy said, pushing her grilled vegetable salad around the plate.

"I know," Lucy agreed. "It's not as if I'm about to walk on the set and fuck George Clooney." She took a long beat, grinned and added – "Although . . ."

They both giggled at the thought.

"Have you ever cheated on Phil?" Mandy asked curiously.

Lucy paused for a moment before answering. Mandy was a notorious gossip and anything she told her would be repeated all over town, so although she was mad at Phil, she wasn't about to castrate him by blabbing to Mandy about the tennis pro and the masseur she'd had brief but satisfying flings with. She'd managed to keep her extra-curricular activities firmly under wraps, and that's the way it would stay.

"No," she said at last. "Have *you* ever cheated on Ryan?"

"Of course not!" Mandy responded, blushing slightly. "I would *never* do that to him."

"Do you think he cheats on you?"

"Who, Ryan?" Mandy pealed with laughter. "He wouldn't dare. I'd cut off his balls and use them for earrings!"

"Ryan's a very attractive man," Lucy mused. "And you know what the women are like in this town . . . especially when they're on the loose. Predatory bitches."

"Oh, I know," Mandy said, nodding her head in agreement. "But Ryan's not a cheater."

"You'd be shocked if I told you the names of some of the women who've set their sights on Phil," Lucy continued. "Fortunately he just fucks them and moves on. Bastard!"

"Tell me names," Mandy said, eyes gleaming with anticipation. "They're safe with me."

"Can't do that," Lucy said, pursing her lips.

"I don't know how you've taken it all these years," Mandy said, slightly aggrieved that Lucy wouldn't reveal anyone's identity. "Don't you sometimes have to conquer the urge to kill him?"

"Ten years of marriage, and probably five hundred women," Lucy sighed, tossing back her sweep of long dark hair. "I suppose I must love the cheating sonofabitch, so what can I do?"

"You can divorce him, just like you said."

"I *said* I was thinking of it," Lucy frowned. Telling anything at all to Mandy Heckerling was a big mistake. Mandy lived for juicy information so she could pass it on to her coterie of so-called girlfriends.

Sometimes Lucy wondered why she was friendly with her. But

if one lived in Los Angeles Mandy was a social necessity; the woman had a hand in everything, therefore it wasn't wise to get on her bad side.

Funny how everyone referred to her as Mandy Heckerling and not Mandy Richards. She never wanted anyone to forget that she was Hamilton J. Heckerling's daughter. And nobody ever did.

Ryan deserved better, he was such a sweetheart. Of all the men in the business, Ryan was certainly the nicest, and not in a boring way. Ryan was undeniably attractive, smart, fun and very sexy – although he didn't seem to know it like Don Verona. He was also an extremely accomplished film-maker. Lucy would give anything to work with him, and she'd hoped that he would feel the same way. But no, judging from his non-reaction to her news of a comeback, it was not to be. However, she was not prepared to give up. She was determined to get Ryan to take a look at her story outline. Maybe he'd love it so much he'd want to produce it.

"Well," Mandy said wisely, "thinking about it is the first step. If you did decide to go ahead, what lawyer would you use?"

"I wasn't serious," Lucy said, managing to steer Mandy off the subject and back to Ryan's surprise party.

Truth was that she had no intention of divorcing her cheating bastard of a husband. She'd put in ten years' hard time, and one of these days she planned on reaping all the benefits.

* * *

Every morning Don sat down in his office at the studio and met with his production team and his chief writers. First they dissected the previous night's show, then they went over the upcoming show. Don had a big input on which guests were booked. He kept a list of favorite guests – celebrities who could appear on his show any time they wanted. His list included everyone from Tina

Fey to Don Rickles, Jimmy Woods and Dennis Miller. All brilliant guests who knew exactly what they were supposed to do. He also favored edgy political commentators, writers, and sharp comedians. However, his segment producers and bookers were always pushing major movie stars and gorgeous minor actresses or models.

Usually they compromised, and the show ended up being an interesting mix, although as a host Don got bored easily and sometimes his behavior pissed publicists off when they believed one of their more important clients had been insulted.

Don didn't care, he did his thing and the eager public couldn't get enough of his wry sense of humor. Young actors and actresses with an overblown sense of their own importance were his biggest annoyance. Especially when the female celebrity on his show considered herself God's Gift and went into what he referred to as a "flirting frenzy." Some of the women put on an exhibition not to be believed. Skimpy backless dresses, minuscule skirts, no panties, see-through tops, erect nipples. He was so used to it that they simply had no effect on him. Mary Ellen was the first one he'd dated in a long time.

One date was all it had taken for him to realize that Mary Ellen was too needy for him. After their dinner at *Geoffrey's* he'd driven her home. She'd asked him in for a drink, but he'd declined and not called her again. She'd waited a week before texting him with an invitation to the opening of a low-budget movie she was in. Feeling sorry for her, he'd said yes. Now it was tonight and he was kicking himself. Why had he agreed to go, that was the question.

If it was Cameron . . . well, that would be a date to look forward to.

But no, the lovely and reclusive Cameron was playing hardball, turning up at his house every day at seven a.m. looking incredible, forcing him to sweat his way through a vigorous workout, then turning him down every time he asked her out.

Don was not used to turn-downs. Cameron Paradise was a first, and he didn't like it.

Although . . . she was a challenge. And if there was one thing Don excelled at, it was meeting challenges.

Cameron Paradise would come around. They always did.

* * *

Catching Don on his cell, Mandy filled him in about the surprise party she was planning.

Don didn't know what to say. He was sure that the last thing Ryan needed was a surprise party, but it wasn't up to him, so he assured Mandy he'd be there.

"Who are you bringing?" she wanted to know.

"It depends."

"On what?"

"On how I feel that night, Mandy," he said, irritated. She was such a pushy woman.

"You could come alone," she suggested. "It isn't necessary for you to always be seen with one of your transient dates."

What a bitch! "My assistant will let you know," he said, abruptly clicking off his cell.

Who the fuck did she think she was, talking to him like that? Transient dates indeed!

The sooner Ryan dumped her, the better.

* * *

Mary Ellen wore a low-cut pink dress and extremely high stilettos. She had great legs and an admirable body, but Don did not find her at all sexy.

He picked her up at her Brentwood house in his silver Lamborghini, and drove her to the Academy Theater on Wilshire, where the screening of her movie was taking place. It was her first starring role in a theatrical movie and she was excited. On TV she was a big star, movies were a whole other thing and she was desperate to make the jump from TV to the big screen.

The legitimate photographers and hovering paparazzi went wild when the two of them entered the theater. They were a dream duo. Flashbulb frenzy took place, while Don gritted his teeth and wished he were somewhere else. The whole red-carpet scene had never appealed to him. It brought back bad memories of his second wife, Sacha, a luscious French movie star who'd reveled in the spotlight. After the divorce she'd moved back to Paris and now lived with a starving artist. No alimony relief there.

"I'm heading inside, I'll wait for you in the lobby," he whispered to Mary Ellen.

"Please don't," she whispered back, clutching onto his arm, slightly panic-stricken. "I can't do this alone."

So he was stuck as the flashbulbs continued to flash, microphones were thrust in his face, and questions were yelled at them.

Are you two an item?
How long have you been seeing each other?
When's the engagement?
When's the wedding?
Is Mary Ellen pregnant?
When's the divorce?

Nobody actually said *When's the divorce?* But Don knew that they wanted to.

Shit! What had he gotten himself into?

Suddenly a hand clamped down on his shoulder, and there was Ryan, grinning at his discomfort.

"Come on, you two," Ryan said, rescuing them both. "Let's go take our seats or we'll miss the beginning of the movie."

"Thank God!" Don said as they headed upstairs. "I forgot what a nightmare these things can be. What are you doing here anyway?"

"The director's a friend," Ryan replied. "And by the way, Mary

Ellen, he raves about your performance. Says you have a very special quality."

"Thank you," she said modestly, quite aglow from all the attention.

"Where's Mandy?" Don asked as they took their seats.

"Attending one of her charity gigs. We're meeting at *Spago* later, care to join us?"

"Love to," Don said, relieved. He'd had enough alone time with Mary Ellen – she simply wasn't his type.

Not that he had a type, but whatever it was, she wasn't it.

* * *

The next morning the newspapers, TV gossip journalists and Internet blogs heralded the big new romance. Don Verona and Mary Ellen Evans. The famously attractive talk-show host and the famously jilted-by-her-movie-star-husband girl next door.

The ladies of *The View* decided the two of them were a perfect combination. Jillian, Steve and Dorothy dished about them on *Good Day L.A.* Even Regis and Kelly gave the supposed new couple a few minutes.

Don wasn't pleased, but he had no one to blame but himself. He should have known better than going to a movie première with a well-known and much-loved TV star.

Mandy was on the phone first thing. "I assume you'll be bringing Mary Ellen to the party," she said. "I'm ordering extremely expensive place cards with gold calligraphy, so I'm double checking."

"I told you yesterday, Mandy," he answered patiently. "I have no idea who I'm bringing."

"But I thought—"

"Do me a favor, don't jump to any conclusions."

"But last night—"

How did Ryan live with this woman? Even her voice got on his nerves. And the thought of fucking her . . .

She was droning on about how much fun *Spago* was the night before, and how great he and Mary Ellen had looked together. "You make a beautiful couple," she concluded.

"Yeah, well, we're not," he said flatly, and hung up.

If Mandy wasn't married to his best friend there was no way he'd waste his time talking to her.

But she was Ryan's wife, so he had to put up with her – that was just the way it worked.

Chapter Twelve

Cameron and Cole met with Laura Lizer, Natalie's business manager, and put their signatures on the relevant papers. Then Iris came through, and they were able to sign the lease for the space they'd seen on Wilshire. It seemed that things were moving right along.

As soon as everything was done, Cole arranged a celebratory dinner at *Obar* – a fun restaurant/bar on Santa Monica.

He and Cameron arrived together; Lynda brought her boyfriend, the very macho Carlos; Dorian walked in with a young male assistant who looked after a major singing star; and Natalie was accompanied by her latest live-in, a successful real-estate developer, and one of her best friends, Ty Morris, a talented black photographer who specialized in artistic nudes.

Ty took one look at Cole and Cameron, and to Natalie's annoyance spent the majority of the evening begging them to pose for him. Meanwhile the young personal assistant fell in lust with Cole, causing Dorian to go off in a snit, while Carlos strutted around acting as if he was doing everyone a favor by being there.

"This is a nightmare," Cameron whispered to Cole halfway through the evening. "We should never have allowed significant others to come. It was a mistake."

"So right," Cole agreed, although he was quite enjoying all the attention coming his way.

"Can't wait to get outta here," Cameron muttered, informing Ty for the fourth time that no – she was not planning on posing nude anytime soon.

Meanwhile they needed a name for the new place, and everyone had a suggestion. Dorian thought *Flow* sounded right; Natalie liked *Energy*, Ty opted for *Strip*; then Cole came up with the winner. "We're calling it *Paradise*," he said. "It's got exactly the right vibe."

And so *Paradise* was the chosen name.

* * *

Apart from arranging to rent the equipment, and then having it all installed, Cameron soon realized there was plenty of hard work to be done, and that either she or Cole needed to be at the new premises making sure everything went smoothly. This meant that both of them had to give up some of their clients, then Cameron had to inform the man who ran *Bounce* that she would no longer be working there, which turned out to be more of a drama than she'd anticipated.

The owner of *Bounce* was an Iranian in his fifties, commonly known behind his back as Mister Fake Tan. He paraded around the premises once or twice a week, usually with an interchangeable blonde in tow, favoring girls with enhanced boobs, referring to them as his new assistants.

Since Cameron rented her space and paid Mister Fake Tan commission on every one of her clients who used the facilities, she'd felt no obligation to give him much notice. But when she informed him that she was leaving, he threw a fit. "How can you do this to me?" he screamed. "After I give you job, look after you. How can you be so ungrateful?"

Ungrateful? He'd made a ton of commission over the two

years she'd been at *Bounce*. What did *he* have to complain about?

"Where you going?" Mister Fake Tan screamed. "Nobody treat you as good as I do."

His reaction had scared the hell out of Lynda, who was a salaried employee.

Cole had taken it in stride. "Do *not* tell him we're openin' our own place," he warned. "'Cause that'll really get his balls in a sweat."

So Cameron lied and informed him she was only planning to work with private clients in their own homes. That shut him up.

"He'll find out, you know," Lynda ventured.

"And there's nothin' he can do," Cole assured her. "You'd better give your notice asap."

"What do I tell him?" Lynda wailed.

"Tell him you're gettin' married."

"I wish!"

Meanwhile Cameron was wondering if she'd taken on too much responsibility. It was one thing dreaming of opening her own place, it was quite another actually doing it. And money was draining away at an alarming rate. *Her* money. Cole's money. Natalie's investment. Money was hemorrhaging out of the place. It was a big worry, but she and Cole were convinced they could make it happen. They had no choice.

*　*　*

Every morning Cameron worked out Don Verona at seven a.m. Following him she had two more clients, and by ten-thirty she was at the new premises organizing painters and installers and plumbers and electricians. Cole took over at four, enabling her to spend the rest of the day working with her other clients.

It was a grueling schedule, but as the place started to take shape, it was worth it.

Don was still on her case about going out to dinner with him. She'd steadfastly turned down every invite, but he didn't seem inclined to quit. She refused to flatter herself, she knew it was only because he was unused to hearing "no."

"You look kind of tired," he said to her one morning as he ran on the treadmill and she stood beside the machine, stopwatch in hand.

"Hey – I'm averaging five hours' sleep a night," she said ruefully. "I guess it's catching up with me."

"I know you hate me asking questions –" he said tentatively. "But what the hell *are* you doing all night?"

She hadn't mentioned her new venture to him. She'd thought of doing so when they were ready to open, which didn't appear to be any time soon as none of the workmen they'd hired seemed to be capable of completing on time. And their so-called contractor was useless. The bathrooms weren't finished, the phone lines weren't in, the lighting needed attention, and only half the exercise equipment had arrived. It was totally frustrating, not to mention expensive. She was getting more worried each day that they'd run out of money before they even got started.

"I'm opening my own place," she said, glancing at her watch. "Five more minutes, then we're moving on to weights."

"What kind of place?" he asked, continuing to run.

"A fitness studio."

"*You're* opening it?"

"Don't sound so surprised."

"I'm surprised you haven't mentioned it before," he said, wondering why she was always so damn secretive.

"I hardly plan on being a personal trainer all my life," she said. "This is my dream."

"Good for you," he said, slightly out of breath. "How's it progressing?"

"Slowly," she sighed. "It's an ongoing saga of no job gets

finished on time, which means I'm kind of stuck there permanently, overseeing everything. If I'm not around, my partner is."

"You have a partner?" he said, on immediate alert. Was this
why he was getting nowhere with her? She had a goddamn partner! Did she live with him? Were they fucking? Shit!

"Yes, I have a partner," she answered coolly. "Cole de Barge.
He's a personal trainer too."

"You didn't tell me that you're involved," Don said, frowning.

"Involved?"

"A partner."

"Oh!" She started to laugh. "Cole is my *business* partner. I'm
hardly his type."

"You're everyone's type."

"Cole is gay."

Now why did he feel so relieved? "No shit?" he said, keeping
it casual.

"He's a great guy, and his sister, Natalie, is our investor."

"You have investors?" he said, slowing down the treadmill.

"Only one. Natalie de Barge."

"I think I know Natalie," he said, stepping off the treadmill.
"She's on that early evening entertainment show, right?"

"That's her," Cameron said, handing him a towel.

"Yeah, she's one of the good ones," he said, throwing the
towel around his neck.

"I hope so, 'cause we're running out of money fast."

Damn! Now why had she said that? Too much information.

"You are?" Don said, sensing an opening.

"I might be forced to increase your rate," she said quickly,
lightening things up. "Think you can afford me?"

"Maybe you should bring in more investors," he suggested.
"I mean I could—"

"No thanks."

God! She certainly didn't want Don Verona thinking that she

needed his money, because she didn't. They'd manage. They had to.

"When's the opening?" he asked.

"Two or three weeks is our goal," she said, as they moved over to the free weights. "Perhaps you'd like to come."

"Ah . . ." he said wisely. "She needs me for publicity."

It hadn't occurred to her before, but having celebrities at their opening couldn't hurt.

"Can I count on you to be there?"

"Tell you what," he said, sitting down on the bench and picking up a pair of hand weights. "I'll make a bargain with you."

"Uh-oh," she said warily. "This doesn't sound great."

"I'll come to your opening, if you'll come with me to a friend's birthday party Sunday night."

"You know I don't—"

"Yeah – I know, I know – you don't mix business with pleasure. But think of the coverage you'll get if I'm at your place when you open your doors to the hungry public. They love me, you know," he added dryly. "I have many loyal fans."

"That's blackmail," she said sternly.

"Never said it wasn't."

She couldn't help smiling. "You're something else, Mr Verona."

"And you're not?" he responded, shooting her a quizzical look.

"Okay, it's a deal," she said, thinking how thrilled Lynda would be to finally meet him.

"You're sure? You're not going to back out on me at the last minute?"

"As if I would! And if you like," she added, "bring some of your famous friends." They may as well make the opening as starstudded as possible; after all, this was L.A., and getting the word out with some positive P.R. was a smart move.

"Got no famous friends," he said, going through a series of upper-arm reps. "Merely acquaintances."

"Then bring your girlfriend."

"I don't have a girlfriend."

"According to the press you do."

"Yeah? And who would that be?"

"Mary Ellen Evans."

"Aw, jeez," he groaned, putting down the weights. "Do not believe everything you read."

"It's all over the Internet."

"It is?"

"Not that I'm glued to the Internet, but it's there."

"Jealous?" he said, teasing her.

"Oh sure," she drawled. "Losing sleep and everything."

"Ah, so *that's* why you're only sleeping five hours a night," he said, grinning. "You're sad and disappointed that you didn't get me first."

"I hardly think so," she demurred.

"You don't, huh?" he said, still teasing.

"Nope."

"Then what *can* I do to make you lose sleep?"

"Absolutely nothing."

"You're sure?"

"Quite sure, thank you."

"We'll see."

"Oh my! You have a very big ego!"

"And that's not all!"

"Okay, okay," she said quickly. "I don't need to hear any more."

Don flashed another of his famous grins. She was coming around. His charm had not deserted him.

Soon he and the delectable Cameron Paradise would be a couple.

Chapter Thirteen

As she walked into the dinner party upstairs at *Mr Chow*, Cameron realized two things. One, she was the youngest woman there. And two, the other women did not take kindly to a stranger in their midst – especially a stranger who did not resemble a wanna-be actress/model with the requisite fake tits, plumped up lips and Botoxed forehead. And especially as she was with Don Verona.

It soon became patently obvious that even though they were married, every woman in the place felt that she had a strong claim on Don. He was their favorite famous, straight single man, and given half a chance they'd all be willing to hop into bed with him were he to ask.

The party was full of couples, and the women descended on Don as if he were a rare steak at a barbecue. Mandy was at the forefront, sparkling in a silver sequined Valentino cocktail dress, diamonds dripping, her hair swept up in a chic chignon, which didn't really work because she was too short to carry it off.

"Hello, dear," Mandy gushed, her eyes inspecting Cameron from head to toe. "And your name is—?" she trailed off, not really interested. She'd hoped that Don would bring that TV girl, Mary Ellen, the one whose husband had dumped her, making her Queen of the tabloids, poor thing. At least she was famous in her own way.

"My assistant *told* you her name," Don said good-naturedly, plucking a spring roll from the tray of a passing waiter. "It's Cameron Paradise. Surely even you can't forget a name like that, Mandy."

"Hi," Cameron said, feeling awkward and out of place in her simple white pantsuit, with no diamonds in sight.

"Welcome, dear," Mandy said, distracted as more people entered.

"Mandy is the birthday boy's wife," Don revealed. "Get her to your gym and every Hollywood Wife in town will follow. Mandy gets off on discovering new places."

"I'm not sure Hollywood Wives are the clients I'm looking for," Cameron said coolly.

"You want to make money, don't you?" Don questioned, going for another spring roll. "Believe me, getting Mandy on your side is step number one." He paused for a moment and raised an eyebrow. "You do know who she is, don't you?"

"Yes. You just told me, she's Birthday Boy's wife."

"*And* the daughter of Hamilton J. Heckerling, the mega-producer with power up the kazoo."

"The what?" Cameron asked, suppressing a giggle, because she sensed Don was a little bit nervous bringing her here, therefore he wasn't his usual smooth in-control self, which she was rather enjoying.

"Let's go find Ryan," he said.

"That would be Birthday Boy?"

"It sure would. He's probably having a major melt-down somewhere quiet."

"Why's that?"

"'Cause it's his fortieth, and he's freaking out like it's the beginning of the end."

"What does he do?" she asked, attempting to sound interested.

"Indie producer. We went to college together. Ryan's probably my closest friend."

Three over-dressed women descended on Don, enveloping him in clouds of *Angel, Sapphire* and *Something Very Exclusive.* They all started talking at once, and even though he attempted to introduce Cameron, their interest level was nil.

"I'll be right back," she whispered, discreetly slipping out the door.

She'd thought about taking a break in the Ladies Room, but it was filled with chattering women, so feeling claustrophobic, she made her way downstairs and out to the front of the restaurant, where a gathering of paparazzi jumped to attention for a moment, then realizing that she was nobody, they chose to ignore her.

She walked a few steps away from the front of the restaurant and took a deep breath. Ah . . . fresh air, although smoke was in the air from a few resolute smokers who lingered outside indulging their vice.

It had been a mistake to come with Don tonight. This wasn't her world, filled with powerful men and rich women, some of them famous. Her idea of a fun night out was a movie and dinner at a small neighborhood restaurant. Don couldn't do that, he was a star; his freedom to do whatever he wanted was non-existent.

No more nights out with Don Verona. He was off her radar.

A man was pacing agitatedly up and down in front of her muttering to himself. He did not look like the kind of man who spent his time spilling expletives under his breath. He had on a well-cut suit with a blue shirt and a darker blue silk tie. And when the street light caught his face, she noticed the bluest eyes she'd ever seen. Blue and intense, in a craggy face with generous lips and a slightly crooked nose. For a moment she couldn't help staring. He was not perfectly handsome like Don, but he was extraordinarily attractive.

As he passed her for the third time she couldn't help herself. She took a tentative step forward. "Uh, are you okay?" she asked.

He stopped abruptly; now it was his turn to stare at her. "Yes," he said, after a moment of silence. "I'm letting off steam before I explode."

"Exploding is not a good plan," she said lightly, wondering why her heart was starting to beat at an accelerated rate.

"Tell me about it."

Oh, I'd like to, she thought. *I'd like to take you to my bed and tell you all about it.*

What the hell was happening here? She was getting turned on by a total stranger. A man who muttered under his breath and had blue eyes that mesmerized her. She hadn't felt like this since the first day she'd met Gregg. It was instant attraction.

How to get his attention, that was the problem, although he didn't seem to be going anywhere.

"Uh, are you eating at *Mr Chow*?" she asked, knowing that she probably sounded utterly foolish.

"Kind of," he said.

And suddenly their eyes locked into an intense sexually charged exchange that neither of them seemed inclined to break.

"Hey, *there* you are," Don said, appearing out of nowhere as the paparazzi zoomed into action, flashbulbs popping non-stop.

Cameron dragged her eyes away from the blue-eyed stranger and attempted to regain her composure.

"And you," Don said to the stranger, ignoring the cameras that were flashing in his face, "you'd better get your sorry ass inside before your wife blows a fuse. Believe me – she's getting close." Don then gave them both a pleased smile. "I see you two have met. Didn't I tell you she was a winner, Ryan? Was I right or was I right?"

Shell-shocked, Ryan nodded. This woman, this exquisite creature, was his best friend's new passion. And what was he supposed to do about *that*?

Nothing. Because he was a married man, so even if he wanted to do something, there was no way, no way at all.

"You must be Birthday Boy," Cameron murmured.

"That's me," Ryan responded.

And once again their eyes locked.

* * *

Cameron got through the rest of the evening in a semi-daze. Don introduced her to plenty of other guests, but she couldn't have cared less. She found herself unable to stop watching Ryan Richards, who did not seem to be having a great time. Later she found out from Don that Ryan was furious at his wife, because although Mandy had thrown him a surprise party, she'd failed to invite any of his family, to whom he was extremely close.

A man who loved his family on top of everything else. How refreshing was that?

Casually she asked Don if the Richards had children, and Don relayed the story of the miscarriages and the stillborn baby.

Cameron felt a lump in her throat imagining the disappointment and heartache he must have gone through.

In the car on the way home she asked if Mandy and Ryan were happy.

"You seem awfully interested in the Richards," Don remarked, driving with one hand on the steering wheel, another draped around her shoulder.

"It was their party. I should be."

"Did you enjoy yourself?" he said, ignoring her question.

"Well . . ." she replied, hesitating for a moment. "The food was amazing."

"You're not answering me."

"Those people," she mused. "They're not really my scene."

"And what's your scene?" he asked, his hand beginning to massage her shoulder as he turned on Sunset.

Oh no! she thought. *He's expecting me to come home with him. And that's just what I don't need.*

"Something more . . . casual," she murmured. "And I think I should point out that you're heading in the wrong direction."

"I am?"

"You are."

"I thought that since we're working out at seven, and it's late, it would be more convenient for both of us if you stayed over."

"Convenient?" she said, raising an eyebrow. "That's a new one."

"I do have a guest room," he assured her. "No pressure."

"And I do have two dogs who'll rip up my house if I fail to return home. So . . ."

"I suppose that means I'm turning the car around and taking you home," he said wryly.

"That would be the plan."

"You're a hard woman."

"No. I'm a hard-*working* woman," she said, correcting him.

He dropped her off without an argument. At least he knew how to behave.

"See you bright and early," he said, waving as he drove off.

She collected Yoko and Lennon from her neighbor and hurried into her house.

Birthday Boy.

Ryan Richards.

Her mind was spinning.

She hadn't felt this way in a long, long time.

ANYA

"How can I please you?"

These were the words Anya used every day. Her mantra. She'd learned to say the same thing in several languages. She'd also learned that if she was to survive she could not be shy and retiring, she had to be aggressive and not lie back and accept everything that happened to her. Velma, a twenty-year-old Polish girl – the most popular whore at Olga's – had taught her that.

Anya had spent the first two months cowering away from the men she was supposed to service. They came to the room she was allotted – all shapes, sizes and ages. They unzipped their pants and used her in any way they saw fit.

She was horrified and ashamed. There was no one to protect her, she was a prisoner with no choice except to lie there while a parade of transient men used her body for their own sexual gratification.

Twice a day she was allowed to go downstairs to the kitchen where she was given a lackluster meal – mostly soup and bread. It was there that she first saw Velma – a big girl with huge breasts, beehived dyed black hair, lots of dark eye make-up and jammy red lips.

At first Velma chose to ignore the slip of a girl with the terrified expression. But then she decided that this new girl might have a pretty face, but she was certainly no competition, so after a while she relented and began speaking to Anya. Mostly she relayed what she considered to be great words of wisdom.

"You'll never get a man to request your services again if you lie there like a dead cat."

"Don't you have makeup? You're paler than a glass of milk."

"Offer to suck his cock first. That way you can get off easy."

Sometimes Velma came into the room where Anya slept at night and got into her bed. And sometimes Velma touched her with a far gentler touch than the men she was forced to service – including Igor, who felt that because he had brought her in, it was his right to use her whenever he wished.

"Tell the bastard no more free trips," Velma advised. "And if he doesn't listen, complain to Olga, she'll soon stop him. Olga makes sure everyone pays to use her girls."

"How long have you been here?" Anya ventured.

"Too long," Velma responded, lighting up a cigarette. "But now Olga give me money, and when I put away enough, I leave."

"Where will you go?"

Velma shrugged. "Who knows? Perhaps Holland. I hear a girl can make lots of money in Amsterdam."

"Can I come with you?" Anya asked, her eyes alive with the thought of getting away from the life she'd been forced into.

"Maybe," Velma replied. "I also hear two girls together can be very popular."

And from that day on the seed was planted and Velma began planning their escape.

Chapter Fourteen

Driving his car with total disregard for anyone's safety, Ryan was furious, plus he'd had too much to drink, but he was not about to spare his wife's feelings. "You're a fucking mean-spirited *bitch* an' I want a divorce," he snarled, barely acknowledging a Stop sign.

His harsh words shocked Mandy into a stunned silence. A divorce! Was he insane? An outburst like this was so unlike her husband, but she was forced to realize that she'd finally pushed him too far by not inviting his stupid family to the party. She should've understood that not including his family was red flag time. *Dumb! Dumb! Dumb!*

"You don't understand—" she began, ready with a dozen excuses.

"Oh, I understand only too well," he responded. "You hate my family, you always have. They're not grand enough for you, are they, Mandy? They're not fucking *rich* enough for you. They don't own big important companies and film studios, they're not movie stars or celebrities, so why the hell would *you* bother with them?"

"That's not fair," she objected.

"I'll tell you what's not fair," he raged. "You throwing me a surprise fortieth and not even inviting my mother, let alone my sisters."

"That's because there's so many of them," she said, stumbling over her words. "I thought we'd have a private celebration later this week, a *family* evening at the house. After all, it's not as if they know any of our friends. They wouldn't have enjoyed themselves tonight, they'd have felt out of place."

"Screw you, Mandy, you're full of shit," he said, turning the car onto their street.

"Look," she said, exasperated, "if I'd invited your mother *and* your sisters *and* their husbands, that would've been seven extra people. Now where exactly would I have put them?"

"For crissakes save me your dumb excuses," he muttered as they pulled up to their house.

"I'm not making excuses," she said stubbornly.

"Get out the car," he ordered.

"Excuse me?"

"Get out the fucking car. I'm not coming in."

"Where are you going?"

"None of your fucking business."

She had never seen him so angry, nor heard him swear so much. He'd be sorry in the morning when he sobered up. But in the meantime, how was she supposed to deal with him?

"Out!" he repeated impatiently. "Now!"

Reluctantly she got out the car, and before she could say a word, he roared off.

Mandy stamped her way into the house. This was not the way she'd planned on ending the evening. Ryan's behavior was inexcusable. How dare he talk to her in such a disrespectful way! If her father knew about this, he'd be livid.

But her father wasn't around, was he? He was on a luxury yacht cruising around France and Italy with a woman she hadn't even met. No doubt another gold-digging bitch with her hands deep in Daddy's pocket.

Damn Ryan Richards. He did not appreciate anything she did for him. She'd gone to great lengths to throw him a fabulous party, and this is the way he repaid her.

She hoped he got himself arrested for a DUI just like his dumb brother-in-law. It would serve him right.

And with that thought in mind she marched upstairs, stepped out of her designer gown, gulped down two sleeping pills and went to bed.

*   *   *

Ryan was sober enough to realize that he probably wasn't thinking straight, and he certainly shouldn't be driving. Christ! The lectures he'd given Evie about her alcoholic husband getting behind the wheel. And now here he was, doing exactly the same thing.

He was filled with mixed emotions. Anger – because of Mandy dissing his family. Guilt – because he'd just met his best friend's latest crush and he had experienced an overwhelming attraction. And sadness – because there was absolutely nothing he could do about it.

Reasons?

One – he was married.

Two – she was with his best friend.

Or was she? Because according to Don nothing was going on between them. She wouldn't go out with him, let alone sleep with him.

And yet . . . there she was earlier, very *much* with Don, and maybe even now as he drove aimlessly around, they were sealing the deal.

Swerving the car over to the side of the street, he flipped open his cell and made a call. If Don didn't answer his phone then it was a sure thing that he and Cameron were an item.

And if he did . . .

"Hey." Don's voice.

He'd answered, which meant that she wasn't there.

Ryan experienced a strong sense of relief.

119

"What's up?" Don asked, suppressing a yawn. "Why are you call-ing? How come you're not curled up in bed next to your darling wife?"

"My wife's a mean cunt," Ryan muttered.

"And so the truth finally dawns."

"I'm coming over an' sleeping on your couch."

"Hey – you're sure as hell not sharing my bed," Don quipped.

"I'm on my way over now."

"Can't wait!" Don drawled sarcastically.

"Where's your girlfriend?"

"Unfortunately she chose to go to her own home," Don said dryly. "Who'd've thunk?"

"She's too good for you," Ryan said, slurring his words.

"And you would know that after five minutes in her company?"

"Too fuckin' good."

"Jesus! You're out of it, pal. I suggest you get your ass over here, and make sure you drive slowly. I'll put on the coffee."

He made it over to Don's, staggered inside, shrugged off his jacket and immediately collapsed on the couch. By the time Don came at him with a cup of strong black coffee, he was snoring.

Don shook his head, threw a blanket over him and left him alone.

*   *   *

In the morning Ryan awoke with the light streaming through the huge glass doors leading out to the pool, and Don's dog, Butch, sniffing around his crotch.

"Shit!" he muttered, abruptly sitting up. The events of the previous evening began spinning around in his head. And his head hurt, oh how it hurt. A jackhammer seemed to be pounding away near his right temple, and his mouth felt like a rat might've crawled in and died there.

Rolling off the couch he made his way into the guest bathroom.

After peeing, he stared at his reflection in the mirror and realized how crappy he looked. Not only crappy, but there was an unsatisfied look about him. Truth was, he looked fucking miserable. And then it dawned on him – he *was* miserable. Life with Mandy was finally unbearable. He'd said it in anger last night, but the sad reality was that he was seriously thinking of asking her for a divorce. He couldn't go on living a lie with a woman he did not love anymore. Besides, in the long run it would be better for both of them.

Don was still asleep, his bedroom door firmly shut. Ryan wandered into the kitchen and put on the coffee, then he let Butch out, and contemplated going home and facing the wrath of Mandy. She had an uncanny habit of turning everything around and making *him* feel like he was the one who'd screwed up.

But not this time, oh no, not this time. She'd gone too far leaving out his family on his birthday. It was a big mistake.

He'd spoken to his mom yesterday morning and she'd wanted him to come by their house and celebrate. Not that turning forty was any kind of celebration. Forty was middle-aged, the very thought sent him spinning into a deep depression. He'd told his mother he couldn't make it because Mandy had planned a quiet dinner for two.

And so the quiet dinner for two had turned into him and her and twenty-six of her fucking friends.

He was *still* angry. What a *cunt*!

After downing a mug of coffee, he decided there was no point in waiting around for Don to surface. Don would only lecture him once more about what a fool he was to stick with Mandy, and he didn't need confirmation. He finally got it.

Picking up his jacket, he left the house, and who should be walking toward the front door – Cameron Paradise.

They were both startled.

"Oh!" she said, standing quite still. "It's you. Birthday Boy."

"Do me a favor and stop calling me that," he said, unable to take his eyes off her beautiful face. She looked even better in the light of day with her lightly tanned skin, clear green eyes and natural blonde hair.

"I guess your big day is over," she murmured, thinking that he looked like he'd slept in his suit. It didn't matter – he still gave her chills. And those eyes, so blue and intense. She felt short of breath and yet desperately excited for absolutely no reason at all.

"Uh . . . Don's not up," he said, clearing his throat. "Still sleeping."

"I'm early," she responded, glancing quickly at her watch. "Couldn't get to sleep last night."

Why not? he wanted to ask. *Why couldn't you sleep? Were you thinking of me?*

How ridiculous would *that* sound? Of course she wasn't thinking of him, she barely knew him. In fact he was surprised that she even remembered him.

"You could ring the doorbell," he suggested, sounding like Idiot of the Year. "Or . . ." he took a long beat and then surprised himself with the next words that came out of his mouth. "You could come and have breakfast with me."

Silence hung between them. A heavy silence fraught with unsaid words.

He finally broke it. "I think I'm in desperate need of nourishment," he said.

"Breakfast sounds like a plan," she replied, experiencing tiny shivers of delight. So what if she missed out on Don's appointment; she could always call him with an excuse.

"I know a little place on Sunset where they serve great bacon and eggs," he ventured. "You interested?"

Yes, I'm interested. I'm very interested.

And then came that annoying voice in her head. Some called it the voice of reason. She called it bullshit.

He's married.

I don't think happily.

That's not your concern.

There's no harm in breakfast.

Who are you kidding?

"Okay," she said breathlessly. "Breakfast it is."

"My car or yours?" he said, his hangover improving by the minute.

"Uh, you take your car, and I'll follow," she said, already deciding that if she was to blow off her standing appointment with Don, it wouldn't be smart to leave her car sitting in his driveway.

"I'll drive slowly," he promised, ridiculously elated.

"You don't have to, I can keep up."

Their eyes met, and electricity was in the air.

Cameron jumped into her Mustang and waited until the Lexus moved, then she trailed his car, and while they were on the way to wherever he was leading her, she left a message for Don, informing him that something had come up and she couldn't make it, but that she'd see him tomorrow.

This is an adventure, she thought.

Yes. An adventure you should not be embarking upon.

Why not?

You know why not.

Dammit! Nothing was stopping her now. There was an irresistible force at work, and she was powerless to resist.

Chapter Fifteen

When Mandy awoke and discovered that Ryan had not come home all night, she was at first surprised, followed by aggravated and finally very very angry. Concern did not enter her head.

Immediately she called Ryan on his cell. Her call went straight to voicemail.

She slammed the phone down in a fury. How dare he do this to her! And where exactly had he spent the night?

Don, of course. Don Verona – his bad influence single buddy who did not like her that much. Oh, he tried, putting on a good face for Ryan no doubt, but she could sense that he didn't warm to her as much as she felt he should.

She would like nothing better than to see Don safely married again. There was something vaguely threatening about single male friends, especially friends who had liaisons with hookers.

Oh yes, *everyone* knew that Don Verona used the services of hookers. He was probably with one of them last night – the tall blonde with the body and the attitude. It was infuriating that he would bring such a girl to her exclusive dinner party. Sometimes Don exhibited no class at all, and it was a shame, because he had everything going for him except picking the right woman. Why hadn't he brought Mary Ellen? She might be a dull little actress, but at least she was famous, that had to count for something.

Mandy's fingers itched to punch out Don's cell number and ask if her husband was there. But no, she was not about to do that. She refused to play the needy little wife chasing after her man.

What if in his drunken state Ryan had gone after another woman, had *sex* with another woman?

The very thought sickened Mandy. Her father was a known philanderer. What if her husband turned out to be one too?

No. Not Ryan. Not true blue Ryan – the man with a steadfast moral compass that never wavered.

She knew that other women found him attractive, and that made *her* feel good because it was a testament to her excellent taste. But Lucy was right, the single women in L.A. were predatory and beautiful and unscrupulous when it came to getting their hands on a man – whether he be available or not.

Impulsively she picked up her phone and called Don. "Can I have a word with Ryan?" she said sweetly, as if she did not have a care in the world.

"Huh?" Don mumbled, being his usual unhelpful self.

"Are you asleep?" she asked, noting that it was only seven fifteen, probably too early to call anyone unless you were sure they were an early riser.

"Yes, Mandy, I'm asleep," he answered, determining that it was definitely time to change his number and make sure that Mandy did not get hold of his new digits.

"Sorry, Don, but I need to speak to Ryan," she said, not sorry at all.

"What makes you think he's here?" Don said, messing with her.

"Because you're the first person he'd run to," Mandy said, her voice rising.

"Run to?"

Why did he have to be so goddamn *difficult*?

"We got into a minor tiff and he'd had too many Mohitos, so naturally he took refuge with you," Mandy said, keeping her voice even and pleasant. "Right?"

"You'll have to call back at a decent hour," Don said, yawning. "Like I said, I'm asleep."

And once more Don Verona hung up on her.

Mandy was speechless, she was not used to such rudeness. She resolved to somehow or other get him out of their lives on a permanent basis. And if Ryan didn't like it – too bad.

*   *   *

Jesus! The woman's a clinger, Don thought, groping for his watch and noting the time. Normally he was up much earlier, but he'd slept past seven, and where was Cameron with her boot-camp moves? She was usually right on time.

He rolled out of bed and into the bathroom where he peed, brushed his teeth, then went looking for Ryan who, he discovered, was no longer on his couch. The poor bastard had probably gone home, sober and defeated.

The coffee pot was hot, so he poured himself a cup, and finally checked his messages. There were several, most of them from the night before. His agent, his clothes stylist from the show, Mary Ellen inviting him to her birthday party, and then the first message of the morning – which was Cameron informing him that something had come up and she couldn't make it today.

He was strangely disappointed. He'd gotten quite used to starting the day with her, and now she wasn't coming.

Was it something he'd said?

Something he'd done?

No. The previous night – their first date – he'd behaved himself. No smash and grab moves. No going for a good night kiss, although he'd wanted to – oh, how he'd wanted to.

Cameron was on his mind big time. He was beginning to feel like a teenage boy who couldn't make it to first base with the prettiest cheerleader in school. What was going on here? He was Don Verona. He could take his pick of any woman he wanted, so what was so special about Cameron Paradise?

Her lips, her eyes, her cheekbones, her body, her hair, her smell . . .

Man, he had a major schoolboy crush. How *about* that?

It was kind of exciting really, because recently he'd become somewhat jaded – hence the whole call-girl scene. They came, they did whatever you wanted, they got paid, and that was that. A nice clean transaction.

But he'd known it was just a fad – a phase he was going through – nothing permanent. And then Cameron had landed at his front door, and he was hooked, couldn't stop thinking about her, couldn't wipe the smile off his face.

He had a strong feeling that if he played it the right way, there were nothing but good times ahead.

* * *

By ten a.m. Mandy had called the editing rooms, Ryan's office, and finally – out of options – she reluctantly called his mother.

Noreen Richards was gracious and charming as usual. "Mandy, dear, how lovely to hear from you. Ryan told me you were taking him out for a cozy dinner for two last night to celebrate his birthday. Romantic gestures are so important for a relationship. Did you have a wonderful time?"

Mandy immediately realized two things. One – Noreen had no idea about the dinner party at *Mr Chow*. And two – Ryan had obviously not spent the night at his mother's house in Calabasas.

"Hi, Noreen," she said, thinking quickly. "I . . . uh . . . thought it might be a nice surprise for Ryan if you – and of course your daughters and their husbands – came for dinner tonight at our house. Kind of the day after the big day celebration."

"That sounds delightful," Noreen responded. "Have you phoned Ryan's sisters?"

"No. Actually I thought you might do it, then you can call me later and let me know who's coming. Is that okay?"

"Of course it is, dear. I'll get right on to them."

"Oh, and Noreen," Mandy added quickly, "if you speak to Ryan, not a word. I want it to be a surprise."

"Certainly, dear."

"Seven o'clock, our house. See you then."

She clicked off her phone, triumphant. This would show Ryan how much she cared.

On the other hand, now she had to get hold of a caterer and spend an entire evening with Ryan's family. How tedious was *that*? What was the old saying – *No good deed goes unpunished*.

However, if this was the only way to appease Ryan, so be it. She could suck it up and be the perfect little wife for once. No problem.

Chapter Sixteen

Ryan had no idea where to take Cameron. It crossed his mind that *Hugo's* on Sunset might be the right place, then he decided it wasn't, so he ended up driving to the Four Seasons Hotel.

Dumb move. What if one of Mandy's friends spotted him at a hotel with another woman?

The way he was feeling right now – he didn't care. It was a perfectly innocent breakfast with a potential new trainer. Yes, that was it, he'd hire Cameron to work him out, exactly like Don had done.

He drove up to the hotel where the parking valet greeted him by name. After surrendering his Lexus, he informed the out-of-work actor type that the lady in the Mustang was with him, and he'd take care of both tickets.

Cameron pulled up and he hurried over. "Nice wheels," he remarked. "What year?"

"Sixty-nine," she replied, alighting from the car. "Fourteen years before I was born and it's still going strong. How about that?"

He managed a quick calculation in his head and worked out that she was twenty-five. A mature twenty-five, not a ditz like so many of the girls out there.

Still . . . twenty-five was young compared to his advanced years. He was forty, for crissakes. Fucking forty!! How did *that* happen?

"This is a hotel," Cameron said, stating the obvious.

"Best breakfast in town," he said.

"I'm not really dressed—" she began.

"You look beautiful," he interrupted.

There. He'd said it. Did that make him a dirty old man coming onto her with such an obvious line? Although it wasn't a line, he really meant it. She was the girl of his dreams.

Correction. She was the girl of *Don's* dreams.

Shit! Shit! Shit! This wasn't happening. It was all too surreal. And above all else he was married. Fucking *married*, for crissakes.

But they could be friends, couldn't they?

Yeah, Don would love that, he could just imagine Don's words. "What the fuck are you taking my girl out to breakfast for?" Don would say. "Back off, you forty-year-old horny married *prick*. She's mine!"

"I *am* hungry," Cameron admitted, which wasn't exactly true. She had a feeling in the pit of her stomach, but it wasn't hunger, it was more a feeling of excited anticipation.

"Me too," Ryan said, taking her arm as they walked into the lobby of the hotel, steering her toward the dining room, where the maitre d' made a big fuss of him, seating them at a prime window table.

A waiter immediately came over with menus. Cameron studied the many choices, hiding her face behind the menu as she tried to get a handle on exactly what she was doing.

She'd blown off Don for breakfast to be with a total stranger who had the bluest eyes she'd ever seen, a slightly crooked smile, and what looked like an in-shape body beneath the slept–in suit. Oh yes, and he had great hands with long artistic fingers, and— *dammit*! One of the fingers wore a wedding band, and what the *hell* was she thinking?

130

"Anything in particular you fancy?" Ryan asked. "Eggs or the Continental breakfast?"

I fancy you, she thought, putting down her menu. Their eyes met across the table. For a moment time stood still for both of them.

She finally broke the look and heard herself mumbling something about Eggs Benedict might be nice. Ryan agreed, so a double order of Eggs Benedict it was, and suddenly they started talking, about movies, books, TV, politics, art.

He knew plenty about everything, and she was able to keep up. Every morning she always made time to scan the *New York Times* and *USA Today* so that she'd have plenty to converse with her clients about. She was also a bit of a CNN junkie, and she was definitely addicted to the Discovery channel. It turned out that he was too.

Breakfast came and went. They both ate plenty and never shut up. Cameron took time out to run to the Ladies Room and cancel her two appointments after Don. She didn't care. She was having fun for once. And the more they spoke, the more she realized that she really liked Ryan as a person, not just as an incredibly attractive man.

He was nice. He was decent.

And he's married, so stop with the fantasies.

They were on their third cup of coffee when his cell vibrated for perhaps the fifth time. He picked it up off the table and glanced to see who the caller was.

"It's my sister," he said. "I'd better take it."

Oh God! Great family values. All the other calls he'd ignored, but for his sister he made an exception. *This man is perfect*, she thought, as he walked away from the table speaking on his cell.

Yes, and so was Gregg once upon a time, that is until he'd changed into a wife-beating, baby-killing monster.

She'd lost her baby because of Gregg, and the unbearable hurt of what he'd done to her always lingered. Forgetting was too

131

hard, too painful. It was also the reason she had not forged any meaningful relationships since fleeing Hawaii; she was much too wary of getting hurt again.

Her eyes filled with tears and she groped in her purse for her sunglasses to cover her vulnerability as Ryan came back to the table, his face grim.

"Is everything all right?" she asked.

"My sister needs me," he said abruptly. "It's an emergency."

"Oh, well, don't let me hold you up."

"I have to go over to her house," he said, signaling for the check. "Her scumbag of a husband got out of jail yesterday, and he's threatening her."

"Threatening her, how?" she questioned, experiencing a sudden chill. It all sounded horribly familiar.

"Long story," Ryan said. "Her husband's got a drinking problem, always needs money, and it's not as if they're exactly flush."

"Can I come with you?" she asked, surprising herself, forgetting that she should be getting over to *Paradise* where they were supposedly putting in the phone lines.

"Why would you want to do that?" he asked.

"Maybe I can help. If it's you and him it could get difficult. But if I'm there . . . it might diffuse the situation."

Not only was she beautiful, she was caring too. Mandy would never consider putting herself out for his family, she'd rather die than travel to Silverlake.

The check came. He threw down a handful of bills and got up.

"Let's go," he said. "Leave your car here, we'll pick it up later."

* * *

"Natalie," Don said over the phone. "This is Don Verona."

Natalie de Barge cradled her cell phone under her chin, and

mouthed *Don Verona* to the makeup girl who was painstakingly applying individual lashes to Natalie's lids.

The makeup girl looked duly impressed.

"Uh, hi Don," Natalie said, attempting to maintain her cool – although she was quite excited that Don Verona was actually calling her. "What can I do for you?"

"I heard you're investing in a fitness studio," he said, getting right to the point.

"Wow!" she exclaimed. "News travels fast. Where did you hear that?"

"It doesn't matter where I heard it," he said briskly. "I'd like in."

"In what?" Natalie asked, confused.

"I want to be part of it. Put in money. Make it the hottest place in town."

"Well, Don," Natalie said slowly, "that sounds great. But obviously I'll have to speak to my brother, he's in charge."

"Cole?"

"You know him?"

"I don't, but I do know Cameron. They're partners, right?"

"You seem up on everything."

"Here's what I want, Natalie," he said, not about to waste any more time. "Total anonymity. I'm prepared to be a silent investor – putting up as much extra money as they need. Only they can't know it's me. Can you arrange that?"

"Don, I don't even know if they *need* another investor."

"Every business does. We want to make this thing fly. So my business manager will call your business manager and you'll tell your brother you've got a friend who wants in – but you will not tell him or Cameron who it is. Do I have your word?"

"I suppose *why* you want to get involved is a question you're not prepared to answer?" Natalie asked, wondering what kind of agenda he had in mind.

He laughed. "S'right."

"And what do I get in return?"

"What do you *want* in return?"

Taking a deep breath, she plunged right in. "An exclusive three-part interview at your house to run during sweeps."

"Natalie, Natalie," he sighed. "You know I don't do sit-downs. And I *never* do my house."

"Yes or no?" she said boldly.

"You're tough."

"Never pretended I wasn't, Don."

"Okay."

"Okay what?"

"A one-off – no more than ten minutes. And at the studio, not my house."

"We're in business," Natalie said, clicking off her phone somewhat dazed. She didn't have a date with Don Verona – but what she did have was far more important. An exclusive interview with a man who was notorious for never doing interviews!

This was a coup. Natalie de Barge was one happy camper.

ANYA

*E*scaping from Olga's was not easy. But Velma was a smart one, smarter than both Sergei and Igor put together. She began working on a few of her regulars, feeding them sob stories in between sucking their cocks. Telling them she had a sick mother to care for, and a baby who was virtually starving. And because Velma was so convincing, and her cocksucking skills so fine, the men believed her and began slipping her cash on the side. A little bit here, a little bit there, it soon mounted up.

"You can do the same," Velma informed Anya. "Men are easy and dumb. You've got to make them feel they excite you like no other man – that way you can get anything from them."

Anya nodded, not quite sure what she was supposed to do other than lie there like meat on a slab while they had their way with her.

Velma began teaching her certain tricks such as how to behave in bed, the things she should say to the men to feed their hungry egos.

At first Anya found it repellent and sickening to even speak to these men who were so rough and out for a quick stab of pleasure at her expense, but once she started doing and saying the things Velma taught her, the men's attitude toward her began to change. They treated her better, they requested her when they came to the house, they even touched her in places she didn't want to be touched – except by

Velma – but it was more bearable than being used as nothing but a vessel for them to invade.

After a while she began dropping hints about a sister who couldn't walk, and a mother who'd been blinded in a terrible accident. Once she started, the lies came easily, and soon – like Velma – she was pocketing money on the side and hiding it from Olga.

For the first time since the invasion of her home and the murder of her surrogate family, she felt that she had some kind of control. Velma was right, once you learned how to lie to them, most men were easy.

Gradually she embraced the feeling of sexual power that overcame her, finally understanding how important it was to her survival.

It took almost two years of plotting and planning and squirreling money away, until one day Velma decided it was time for them to go. Anya was excited, but also terrified. What if Olga came after them? What if the unknown was even more scary than servicing a series of men she'd grown used to? And worst of all – what if Velma deserted her?

However, she was prepared to take a chance, because Velma was her everything and she couldn't risk losing her.

They set off at three in the morning while everyone in the house was sleeping. Velma had a regular customer with an old car whom she'd persuaded to help start their journey. Another customer had gotten them fake passports. Velma's sexual skills were extraordinarily persuasive.

Their journey out of Poland was harrowing, especially when they reached the border. Anya was petrified their fake passports would be discovered and they'd be sent back. But Velma worked her magic on the border guards, flirting and exchanging vulgar jokes. Anya knew that Velma would've gotten out of the car and blown every one of them if she'd deemed it necessary. It wasn't. However, once they'd crossed the border, the driver of the car wanted sexual gratification from both of them before dropping them off at a railroad station.

After he'd left, Velma cussed him out as a dirty Polish pig. She was not at all grateful for the help he'd given them.

The next few days they spent on trains making their way toward Amsterdam, where Velma swore she had a connection. Sometimes the trains were okay, but most times they were dirty and crowded, and Anya found herself wondering if she'd made the right decision.

Velma was not slow at plying her trade. Whenever she spotted a likely prospect, she took him off into the lavatory and gave him what he required.

"Easy money," she informed Anya. "You must do the same."

Anya shook her head. "I don't want to."

Velma gave her a hard look. "You'll do what it takes," she said. "Otherwise you'll see the back of me."

So Anya did as the older woman told her, and found herself once again servicing a series of men as the various trains rattled and bumped their way across Europe. By the time they reached Amsterdam she was exhausted. Not Velma.

"We're spoiling ourselves and staying in a hotel for the night," she informed Anya. "Tomorrow we start afresh. Tomorrow we start making real money."

Anya was excited. She'd never stayed in a hotel, and the thought of a proper bed and a shower was quite energizing.

Velma hailed a cab at the train station, and after she'd chatted up the driver, he'd recommended a modest motel. After checking in, Velma threw herself on the bed and declared that Amsterdam was the most beautiful place on earth.

Anya was inclined to agree.

"This," Velma announced, "is where we belong."

Chapter Seventeen

Sitting in the passenger seat next to Ryan on their way to see his sister in Silverlake, Cameron felt completely comfortable. It was almost as if they were old friends, not two people who'd only met the night before.

She could tell he was preoccupied – thinking of his sister, no doubt – and she did not wish to pry, but suddenly he started opening up about the situation.

"I've got three sisters," he began. "Evie's the youngest. She ran off with this moron when she was eighteen. Now three kids later, she's stuck with him."

"What does he do?" Cameron asked quietly.

"Drinks and spends any money he can get hold of."

"I mean, what does he do professionally?"

"The jerk's a stuntman, and not at all skillful. I'm amazed he hasn't killed himself by now, 'cause believe me – stunts an' booze do not mix."

"Has he threatened your sister before?"

"Not that she's told me. But I wouldn't be surprised."

"I'm sorry," Cameron said softly.

"Yeah," Ryan said, his face grim. "So am I."

They drove the rest of the way in silence, a companionable silence. Neither of them felt the need to talk, there would be plenty of time later. And in spite of everything, Cameron was sure there would definitely be a later.

*   *   *

Lucy Lyons Standard had a plan. Since her recent announcement of a career comeback had apparently left her husband cold, she'd decided to develop the project herself. After all, it was she who'd come up with the story idea, so why wouldn't she get a script written? That way she'd have something to show Ryan, because she was convinced that once he read it, he would be very interested in developing the project further.

Phil steadfastly refused to discuss it with her. Every time she tried to bring the subject up, he walked out of the room.

She retaliated by refusing to cook his meals or share his bed. Not that either of her punishments were a big deal, since their housekeeper was a better cook than she was, and she imagined that he was getting plenty of sex from his twenty-three-year-old Asian assistant who had small pointy tits and a laugh like a hyena.

The problem with Phil was that he had no taste; he'd fuck a plant if it looked at him sideways, he'd fuck the plainest woman in the world, and make her feel like a goddess. He might not be the best-looking man in the room, but women were drawn to him like bees to honey. It was as if they sensed that Phil was a master in the bedroom; it was as if they knew he possessed a golden tongue and was expert at using it. Over the years he'd perfected the art of pleasing a woman orally, zeroing in on the precise pleasure points that could bring her to the dizzying height of ecstasy. Damn him!

Lucy drove toward the beach in her white convertible Mercedes, the latest model. Phil was generous when it came to material things, not so generous at sharing his powerful talent. How easy it would've been for him to offer to write a script for her, help her get her career back on track.

But no. He continued to refuse to discuss it.

So now she was forced to hire an unknown writer, because as Phil Standard's wife she could hardly go to an established screenwriter – it would make both of them look ridiculous.

A few weeks ago a lawyer friend – more of an acquaintance really – had sent over a couple of spec scripts written by his college kid son for Phil to take a look at as a favor. Phil hadn't bothered to read them. Lucy had.

The scripts were surprisingly fresh and sharp. Lucy was impressed, so much so that she was on her way to meet the kid – a student at UCLA – and discuss her story idea to see if he might be the writer for her.

She was determined – one way or the other – to show Phil that she could make a comeback – with or without his help.

*　*　*

Evie met them at the door to her house with a burgeoning black eye. She was shivering uncontrollably.

Suddenly Cameron experienced a hollow feeling in the pit of her stomach, the feeling she'd always gotten after Gregg had finished beating her up – it was a mixture of fear, hate, and helplessness.

Evie had the same emotional look in her eyes as she flew into her brother's arms, sobbing.

"Sonofabitch!" Ryan muttered furiously. "Sonofafucking*bitch*! *Where is he?*"

"He left," Evie said, her voice no more than a whisper. "He grabbed my purse and ran out of here."

"And the boys? Where are they?"

"In school, thank God."

Cameron took a tentative step forward. "Uh . . . hi," she said.

"This is Cameron," Ryan said quickly. "She's a friend of mine."

"Maybe we should get you inside and put some ice on that eye," Cameron suggested in her best sympathetic tone.

Evie looked questioningly at Ryan.

He nodded. "She's right, let's do that."

The three of them went inside the house which looked like a hurricane had hit it: furniture was overturned, a glass vase was shattered in the center of the room, and books and CDs were scattered all over the floor.

"What exactly happened?" Ryan asked, keeping his voice even, but both women knew that inside he was seething with rage.

"Marty got out of jail yesterday," Evie said in a low voice. "When he came home he was angry, accused me of not pulling any strings to keep him out of jail in the first place. We fought about that, then he took my ATM card and went out. He came back this morning still drunk from the night before, smelling of whiskey and . . ." she hesitated for a second, glanced at Cameron and stopped talking.

"Go ahead," Ryan encouraged. "I told you – Cameron's a friend."

"Well . . ." Evie managed. "I could smell another woman all over him." Her eyes filled with tears. "I . . . I accused him and that's when he went berserk, screaming like a crazy man. He wrecked the room, hit me, demanded more money, and walked out."

"Has he ever hit you before?" Ryan asked, barely able to control his anger.

"No," Evie said, not meeting her brother's stern gaze.

Yes, Cameron said silently. *He's hit her before. It's etched on her face. Believe me, I've been there. I know the look.*

"I can assure you that he's never doing it again. Never," Ryan said, his bluer than blue eyes blazing with rage.

"He didn't mean to do it," Evie blurted helplessly. "He was frustrated."

Sure, Cameron thought. *And why not take it out on you?*

You're an easy target. A woman. And women find it hard to fight back. In fact, we're programmed not to.

"Jesus, Evie, I don't care what he was," Ryan said, pulling a chair back to its rightful position and sitting his sister down. "Hitting a woman is an inexcusable act of cowardice."

"Where's the kitchen?" Cameron asked. "I'll get some ice for that eye."

Ryan pointed her in the right direction.

"She's nice," Evie said softly, asking no questions.

"She's . . . uh . . . my trainer," Ryan managed.

"Yes," Evie murmured. "I can see you're all dressed for a work-out."

Ryan felt a flash of guilt. What did Evie think was going on?

His cell phone vibrated, and he pulled it from his pocket to check on the caller. It was Mandy. Call three. She was anxious and he didn't give a shit.

"You can't stay here," he said to Evie. "We're collecting the kids from school, then I'm driving you over to Mom's. After everyone's safe I'll come back here and deal with Marty."

"I'm not going to Mom's," Evie said, panicking. "She'll think I'm such a failure."

"No, she won't. Mom'll understand."

"Says you," Evie said, shaking her head.

Cameron came back into the room with a dustpan and brush. She was also holding a packet of frozen peas which she instructed Evie to put on her eye. Diligently she began sweeping up the broken glass from the shattered lamp.

Watching her, Ryan was bemused. This girl was so utterly unlike Mandy. The thought of Mandy dealing with this situation in such a concerned and efficient way was laughable. Cameron seemed to know exactly what to do.

"I'm over my hysteria," Evie said, holding the frozen peas to her damaged eye. "I can deal with him. I know my husband, he'll be full of apologies."

Of course he will, Cameron thought. *He'll tell you how sorry he is, and how much he loves and adores you, and as soon as he's in another nasty mood, he'll beat the crap out of you again.*

"I'm not leaving you here," Ryan said. "No way."

"Please, Ryan," Evie begged. "You have to. I can handle him."

They argued back and forth some more while Cameron cleaned up the room, until finally Evie convinced him that everything would be okay.

"If you're *sure* . . ." he began, reluctant to leave.

"I'm sure," she said, quite recovered. "So go have your . . . work-out, and I promise I'll check in with you later." She reached out and touched Cameron's arm. "I'm sorry you had to see me like this. Thanks for being so sweet."

"Hey –" Cameron said, wishing there was more she could do. "I understand."

Oh yes, I really do. I've been there, and the only answer is to get out while you still can. Do not procrastinate, because once it happens, it's a sure thing that it will happen again.

After hugging his sister, and making her promise to call him at any time of the day or night, Ryan took Cameron's arm and led her outside to his car.

"This doesn't feel right," he said, shaking his head. "Don't you think I should stay and give the sonofabitch a taste of what he gave her?"

"She doesn't *want* you to stay," Cameron pointed out. "She has to work out what she needs to do on her own."

"You think?"

Cameron nodded. "That's usually the way it goes."

He studied her face for a moment. "How come you know that?" he asked at last.

"I had a . . . uh . . . friend who suffered through the same thing," she said, taken off-guard. "Eventually she . . . uh . . . wised up and got out."

His blue eyes were intense as he continued staring right at her. "It was you, wasn't it?"

"Excuse me?"

"You wised up and got out."

Inexplicably her eyes filled with tears. How did he know? Just thinking about what had happened to her was too upsetting to go there. Gregg was her past. She was strong now, invincible, and she would *never* allow anyone to get close enough to hurt her again.

That was the plan, and she was sticking with it.

Chapter Eighteen

Everything was organized. Mandy had hired a chef, three waiters and a barman, which was excessive for nine people, but what the hell – she wasn't about to help out, and her housekeeper was unable to come back that evening on such short notice. Mandy had a mind to fire the woman, but then she'd have to train someone new, and she had no intention of suffering through *that* nightmare again.

It was all Ryan's fault. When they were first married she'd insisted that they hire a live-in couple, but he'd said absolutely no way – he enjoyed the freedom of *not* having help living on their property. It was a battle he'd won. Usually when it came to domestic matters she got her own way, but sometimes Ryan was adamant, and that had been one of those times. No live-in help.

She was embarrassed to tell any of her friends. Lucy and Phil employed a couple from Guatemala, two daily housekeepers, a laundress, an English nanny for their two children, and three assistants who worked from their house. According to Lucy, she needed all the help she could get, what with Phil – the messiest man on the planet – the kids and their menagerie of assorted animals.

Impulsively Mandy reached for her phone and called Lucy, who answered immediately.

"I'm in the car," Lucy announced, driving with one hand on the steering wheel. "On my way to interview a writer for my idea."

"Does Phil know?" Mandy asked.

"Fuck Phil," Lucy snapped. "He's a dictatorial asshole."

"Are you two still not speaking?"

"Oh, we're speaking all right," Lucy said ominously. "I just won't let him anywhere near me in the bedroom, and as much as he gets on the side, Phil hates it when I don't allow him his nightly fix."

"Nightly?" Mandy was impressed. It must be true about Phil and his insatiable sexual appetite, not to mention his enormous penis. Not that size was that important, and besides, Ryan was hardly lacking in that department.

Once, at their annual Christmas party, Phil had come onto her in the bathroom. He'd locked the door, muttered that she was a hot little piece of ass, shoved her back against the vanity and attempted to stick his thick tongue down her throat.

She'd pushed him away and informed him she was not the kind of woman who cheated on her husband, especially when her husband was supposedly one of his closest friends.

Phil had laughed himself red in the face (he was totally drunk), unlocked the door, and promptly informed anyone who'd listen that she was a frigid bitch.

Ha! she'd thought at the time. *He should only know the things Ryan and I get up to in our bedroom. Frigid, my ass.*

Of course that was then – early days – before two miscarriages and a stillborn baby, before marriage took over and she and Ryan grew so used to each other that sex didn't seem that exciting anymore.

However, if Ryan was dissatisfied with their sex life, she'd better do something to liven it up. He'd uttered the dreaded word "divorce" and that was quite unthinkable. She realized he was drunk and angry at the time, so of course he hadn't meant it. But still . . .

Mandy couldn't stand her father's shrieks of triumph if she and Ryan ever got a divorce.

"I warned you he was a goddamn loser," Hamilton would yell. "A loser with weak sperm!"

Yes, Hamilton never tired of informing her that the miscarriages and the stillborn baby were all the result of Ryan's weak sperm. Even Mandy was shocked that he would say such vile words.

She sighed, and considered how best to make the peace with Ryan. The first step was the family dinner, and having arranged it, she saw no reason why she had to suffer through it alone.

"Are you guys busy tonight?" she asked Lucy.

"Why?" Lucy responded. She'd learned never to say yes until she found out the reason the question was being asked, especially when the question was coming from Mandy.

"I'm putting together a small, more intimate dinner for Ryan," Mandy said, trying to make it sound enticing. "It's at the house. I'd love it if you and Phil could come."

Lucy took a moment before answering. An intimate dinner at the Richards' house sounded like the perfect opportunity for her to corner Ryan and talk to him about her story idea. "I'll have to check with Phil, but that sounds nice," she said, slowing down as she approached her destination. "I'll call you back."

"Do that," Mandy said, thinking that at least she wouldn't have to entertain Ryan's family by herself, which was a big relief. Plus the Standards were always good value – a once-big movie star and an Oscar-winning screenwriter. The Richards family should be so lucky.

* * *

Sitting in his office with panoramic views of Burbank, Don was irritable, and he was taking it out on everyone around him. He complained that his coffee was lukewarm, his morning Danish was stale, the air-conditioning in his office was too cold, and the line-up for that evening's show was weak.

"What didja do, *fall* outta bed this morning?" his producer, Jerry Mann, inquired. Jerry – who was in his late fifties with a bald head, deep suntan and easygoing manner, had been around the block and then some. In his time he'd worked with Carson, Griffin and Letterman. He was knowledgeable and smarter than most people, old-school seasoned, and there was nothing about the talk-show business he didn't know, plus nothing threw him, which is why Don enjoyed working with him. They were partners in a show Don had never wanted to do, but within months of being talked into it by the head of the network, his ratings had started to rise and now, eight years later, he was at the top of his game. His original ambition had been to become a news journalist for a network like CNN, covering war zones and places of interest. But no, fate had taken him in a different direction.

"Never got to do my work-out this morning," he grumbled. "My trainer didn't show."

"You sound like a fuckin' poodle," Jerry quipped. "Get on one of those fuckin' machines you got stashed at your house, an' do it yourself."

"He needs Cameron," Jill Khoner, the segment producer who'd recommended Cameron in the first place, said. "She's the best trainer in town, really motivates you to do more and more. Am I right, Don? Are you grateful? Even if I say so myself, I did you the biggest favor."

"Yeah," Don said, careful not to sound too enthusiastic. "Cameron is pretty motivating."

"We all think she's gay," Jill confided with a secretive little laugh, as if she knew more than she was saying. "Never dates. Never talks about men. What do *you* think?"

I think I want to slap that snide smile off your face. My dream girl is not gay.

Or is she?

Was it possible *that* was the reason he was getting the big turn down? Could it be that Cameron Paradise was a muff diver, a carpet muncher, a dyke?

No!

Maybe.

Oh shit! Wouldn't *that* be something. And yet . . . when he'd asked her . . . what *had* she said?

He tried to remember. Something like – *because I won't go out with you, does that make me gay?*

"Don?" Jill persisted. "What *do* you think?"

Jill wasn't leaving it alone. She was probably waiting for his expert opinion, because everyone knew that when it came to women – Don Verona *was* an expert. Or so they imagined.

"Never gave it any thought," he said, as casually as he could manage. He didn't want anyone getting a sniff of the fact that he really liked Cameron. A lot. "She's an excellent trainer, that's all that matters to me."

"Yes, and she's opening her own fitness studio," Jill said enthusiastically. "I can't wait!"

"Are we discussing tonight's show or what?" Don said, rapidly changing the subject.

The truth was he was pissed that Cameron had cancelled on him, and he didn't want to listen to one more word about her.

"Birdy Marvel," Jerry said, clearing his throat. "She's performing a song from her upcoming CD. It drops next week. Then maybe a short interview with you?"

"No!" Don said adamantly. "There's no way I'm talking to that no-brains pop star who *you* insisted on booking. One song and she's gone. No plopping her panty-less ass down on my couch. Has everybody got it?"

"Yes, Don," Jill replied, thinking how sexy her boss looked when he was in a foul mood. She wondered who he was fucking.

Rumor had it that recently he'd been into hookers. She couldn't blame him. The press were relentless when it came to famous people and dissecting their relationships.

"Whatever you want," Jerry said, shrugging. "But you gotta know, her fan base is huge."

"And I don't give a shit," Don said. "So, are we clear? One song and goodbye."

* * *

"Faster!" Phil groaned.

A muffled sound came from the young Asian woman crouched between his legs.

"I said faster, woman!" Phil urged as her mouth clamped even more tightly onto his dick, attempting to pick up the pace.

It wasn't happening for him, she simply didn't get it. No technique, and if a woman didn't have technique he couldn't come.

He felt himself softening and pushed her away.

She laughed nervously. Lucy had accused her of having a hyena laugh, and Lucy was right, as usual.

Lucy gave great blow-jobs. Movie star blow-jobs. Although she wasn't a movie star anymore. And that's precisely why they were fighting, because he wouldn't help her become one again.

Phil Standard was no dummy. He had an incredibly beautiful, sexy and talented wife whom he did not wish to share with a voracious public. When he and Lucy had first met ten years ago she'd been surrounded by agents, publicists, directors, handsome co-stars, producers, stylists, makeup artists and a whole coterie of hangers-on. He'd managed to lure her away from the entourage, made her fall in love with him, knocked her up, married her, and somehow or other he'd weaned her off all the movie-business crap and got her living a normal life – well, about as normal as it gets when you work in movies. As a hugely successful screenwriter he'd never felt the urge to surround himself with an entourage, so gradually he'd gotten rid of hers.

They lived a pretty good life. Great house, interesting friends, two pre-teen kids who so far had not given them too much trouble, their beloved animals. Plus he gave Lucy anything she wanted. A new car. A beach house, a vacation in Bali, designer clothes and handbags and shoes galore. She could buy anything she desired.

And now this bombshell. She wanted her career back.

No! He wasn't having it.

A career would expose her to all kinds of temptations, and even though – in his mind – it was perfectly okay for him to screw around because it meant absolutely nothing – it was certainly *not* okay for her. When it came to his wife, Phil Standard had a ferocious jealous streak.

"That's enough, Suki," he growled, as the Asian girl started up with a little hand action. "I'm not in the mood."

Suki crawled out from beneath his desk. "Something I did wrong, Phil?" she asked, looking hurt.

"It's not you, it's me," he said, using the most famous line known to man.

"I could . . ."

"No, Suki," he said, zipping up his pants. "Not today."

* * *

"Hi," Lucy said, staring at the young man who opened the door to his run-down beach shack in Venice. He was wearing a ripped UCLA T-shirt, faded jeans and no shoes. His bleached blond hair was mussed and slightly damp, as if he'd just stepped out of the shower.

She had not expected studly. She'd expected studious.

"I'm Lucy Standard," she began.

"Pleasure to like . . . uh . . . meet you, ma'am," he said, offering her a handshake.

Ma'am? Was he kidding?

"C'mon in," he said in his vaguely Southern drawl. "'Fraid it's a bit of a dump, but like my dad taught me – ya gotta do it for yourself. No hand-outs."

"Ah yes," she said, stepping inside. "Your dad is a very fine lawyer."

"He sure is. My mom always told me that, even though they got divorced when I was seven."

"That's a shame."

"Yeah. He moved to L.A. We stayed in Tennessee. But now that I'm in L.A. too, my dad and I are getting close again."

"That's nice," Lucy said, stepping inside and surveying the bright one-room apartment overlooking the Venice boardwalk. There was a futon in the middle of the floor, clothes tossed in heaps, stacks of newspapers and magazines, and an old pine desk piled high with books, plus a computer and various pieces of electronic equipment.

"I suppose I should tell you what I have in mind," she said, observing a thick layer of dust everywhere except the desk.

"Shoot," he said. "I'm hot to get on it right away."

"I bet you are," she murmured, while wondering if it was a bad thing to entertain impure thoughts about a strapping teenage boy. "By the way," she said, keeping it casual. "How old are you?"

He threw her a look. "Does age make a difference, Mrs Standard?"

"Call me Lucy," she said quickly. "And . . . uh . . . no difference at all. It's just that—"

"Yeah, I know," he drawled, favoring her with a boyish grin. "My mom always says I look younger than I am. But you liked my scripts, didn't you?"

"That's why I'm here."

"Then age isn't a problem, is it?" he said confidently. "Don't wanna blast my own achievements, but I got a lot more going for me than some clapped-out thirty-five-year-old fart."

He thought thirty-five was old-fart time! Which meant that he probably viewed her as ancient. Charming!

"I'm nineteen," he added with another disarming grin. "An' I am so freakin' ready to conquer Hollywood. So . . . uh . . . Mrs Standard – Lucy – let's get right to it."

Chapter Nineteen

"W here've you been?" Cole demanded stony-faced. "I had to cancel two clients an' hustle my ass over here quick time."

"I'm so sorry," Cameron said, overcome with a sudden rush of guilt. "A friend had . . . uh . . . an emergency. I went to help out."

"What friend?" Cole asked suspiciously, peering at her. There were no secrets between him and Cameron – or so he thought.

"It was . . . uh . . . Katie and Jinx, they got involved in some kind of crazy fight," she lied. "I ran over to their place to prevent them from killing each other."

Now why wasn't she telling Cole the truth? That she'd met someone with whom she'd fallen madly in lust, he was married and totally unavailable, which meant there was nothing she could do about it.

"And your cell quit?" Cole said, still uptight. "You couldn't let me know you wouldn't be here? The phone guy called *me* to say he didn't know what lines were supposed to go where. You were the one that was dealing with him. I had to leave in the middle of a work-out with the head of a network. Man, he was *way* pissed."

"Oh dear," Cameron said sheepishly. "Guess my phone must be off."

"I left you three messages," Cole said accusingly, his handsome face quite sulky.

"Yes, I can see," Cameron said, checking out her voicemail. Three from Cole. Two from Don.

"I gotta get back to work, that's if you're *sure* you got no more emergencies to deal with," he said sarcastically.

"I'm sure," she replied, wondering if he noticed that for some unknown reason she couldn't stop smiling. Not that anything had happened between her and Ryan, it was simply an amazing connection, a meeting of the minds, a feeling she could spend twenty-four hours a day with him and never get bored.

After leaving Silverlake they'd talked some more. She hadn't revealed much. Didn't care to.

He hadn't pushed. Ryan Richards was special, she'd sensed it the first time she saw him.

When they'd arrived back at the hotel to pick up her car he'd asked her if she could fit him into her schedule for some personal training.

"Of course I can," she'd said, thinking, *Thank you, God! Married or not, at least I get to see him again.*

They'd settled on six p.m. five days a week, which meant that she'd have to cancel a client she already had booked at that time, but the way she felt, she would've cancelled Brad Pitt.

Then he'd suggested that their breakfast and the trip to Silverlake might be better if it was kept between the two of them.

She'd agreed.

One day and they already had shared secrets. Why did that make her heart beat even faster?

You're getting off track.

No, I'm not.

Excuse me? You're opening up your own studio with weeks to go and a thousand things to do. Yet you spent the morning hanging out with a virtual stranger.

155

He's not a stranger. He's a new client. I need every new client I can get.

Who the hell do you think you're fooling?

Her conversation with herself was halted by the entrance of Lynda, accompanied by Carlos. Lynda was all smiles, and Carlos was in full macho strut.

"Oh my! This place is amazing," Lynda exclaimed, looking feisty in a clinging red tank top and tight jeans which emphasized her Jennifer Lopez-style butt. "Do we get the tour?"

"Sure," Cameron said. "As long as you don't trip over any loose wires."

"Yesterday was my last day at *Bounce*," Lynda announced, fluffing out her clouds of brown curly hair. "I think Mister Fake Tan's got a suspicion about what's going on."

"Well, if he does, there's nothing he can do. None of us signed any contracts."

"He says that doesn't matter," Lynda worried. "He says he's gonna sue you an' Cole for loss of business."

"Let him try," Cameron said calmly. "I'm not bothered, are you?"

"Not me," Lynda said boldly. "I'm coming to work here, an' sister, this girl can't wait!"

Carlos gave her an obvious nudge.

"Oh yes," Lynda continued. "Carlos met this contractor guy, some dude who owns his business, makes mucho bucks. An' we were thinking—"

"No!" Cameron interrupted. "Absolutely no more fix-ups!"

"It's not a fix-up," Lynda objected, managing to look pained. "This dude is a *building* contractor. Carlos thought he might be able to help you out here."

"Yeah," Carlos said, joining in. "He's into cash deals only – but everything for the right price and fast. You should meet him."

"Whaddya think?" Lynda asked.

"I think I'll take his number."

"It doesn't hurt that he's not bad-lookin'," Lynda giggled. "Kinda hot in a Tony Soprano way."

"Oh for God's sake," Cameron sighed.

"Gotcha!" Lynda squealed, clutching onto Carlos's arm. "This one's married, which means that even if you fell madly in love, the man is taken!"

Yes, Cameron thought, *and so is Ryan. He's married and off-limits so why even go there?*

Because I can't help myself, that's why.

*   *   *

Ryan rented offices in a small building on Ventura Boulevard. This suited him fine, because when he was in production there was plenty of extra space to rent, and when he was between projects he made sure his expenses were at a minimum, keeping just two offices and one assistant. He'd never believed in wasting money, it all went into the movie he was currently working on. This infuriated Mandy, who thought that like her father he should have grandiose offices to impress potential investors, and when he was making a movie, she thought he should allot himself a much bigger piece of the pie.

Ryan refused to work that way. If his movies made money, so did he. If they didn't . . . well, he wasn't about to steal from anyone. And why should Mandy worry? She had plenty of money of her own.

His assistant, Kara, a competent black woman who'd been with him for over ten years – handed him his message sheet. He shut himself in his office and checked through the list. There were the usual business calls, plus Don, Phil, and two from Mandy. She'd already left three messages on his cell; obviously she was anxious, and probably deeply pissed. Well, too bad, because so was he.

He thought about his breakfast with Cameron for a moment. They'd had a real connection, and he was sure she'd felt it too. But there was nothing he could do about Cameron until he'd told Mandy he wanted out.

God! If he was truthful with himself he knew he'd been postponing the inevitable. Their marriage was over, surely Mandy knew it too? The thing about not inviting his family to his fortieth birthday was the signal he'd been waiting for. It was time to end it.

He reached for the phone and called his wife.

He was expecting screaming, but what he got was the nice Mandy, the sweet Mandy, the Mandy who rarely put in an appearance anymore.

"Are you all right?" she asked, all solicitous and low-key.

"I'm fine," he answered guardedly.

"When you didn't come home last night I was worried about you," she said softly.

"Listen, Mandy," he said, clearing his throat. "We need to talk."

Ah . . . Mandy thought. *We need to talk*. The words no woman ever wants to hear.

"And we will," she said quickly. "But first you should know that your entire family is coming to our house for dinner tonight."

"Huh?" he blurted, taken by surprise.

"I tried to tell you last night," she continued, squeezing a note of hurt into her voice. "But you weren't in the mood to listen."

Oh *shit!* Was she kidding? His family. At their house. Could he have misjudged Mandy?

"All of them?" he said at last.

"Yes, all of them," she replied. "I spoke to your mom five minutes ago, and she assured me that everyone is coming. I wanted it to be a surprise, but you were so mad last night that

158

I thought I'd better tell you. I've had it planned for weeks." A long silent beat. "Are you pleased, sweetie?"

She didn't usually call him "sweetie", but the occasion merited it. She wanted him to feel as bad as possible about the way he'd treated her. Ryan Richards needed a healthy shot of guilt.

"Uh . . . yes," he said. Christ! He'd been screaming at her about not including his family, and she'd had this planned all along. Why hadn't Evie said anything?

Probably because her mind was elsewhere.

"I don't know what to say," he muttered.

"That's all right," Mandy said, all magnanimous and forgiving. "You were upset. You thought I'd left your family out. You should know that I would never do that."

Damn! He felt like the world's biggest shit. He'd had all these negative thoughts about her – including asking for a divorce – and now this.

"What time will you be home?" she asked.

"Later," he said.

"Not too much later," she said. "You'll want to shower and get ready, they'll be here at seven."

He wished she would turn into her usual nagging self, but it was not to be.

She left him with a trapped feeling in the pit of his stomach.

Trapped in a marriage with a woman he did not love, and there seemed to be nothing he could do about it.

* * *

Driving home from Venice Beach, Lucy felt quite invigorated. Telling Marlon – yes, that was the kid's name – apparently his mom had been a big Marlon Brando fan – about her story idea was so exciting, because he got it, he actually got it, and not only that, he immediately began coming up with his own ideas to add to the story, and they were fresh and edgy. There was a lot to be said about dealing with someone so young. Marlon wasn't jaded, he had an enthusiastic attitude she admired.

It occurred to her that if he wrote a hot script she wouldn't need Phil or Ryan, she'd have her agent shop it with her name attached to star, and they'd go for the best deal.

Although she had to admit that she liked the idea of working with Ryan, he was sensitive when it came to his actresses, and she needed – in fact craved – Ryan's particular brand of sensitivity.

Hmm . . . she thought. *How about if Phil agrees to be script consultant as a gesture of good will toward me?*

Reaching for her cell, she called her cheating husband.

"Where have you been?" he asked, sounding put out that she wasn't at home tending to his every need.

It was too soon to tell him what she was up to. "Shopping," she answered vaguely.

"Shopping? Again? Don't you have everything you need?"

"Not quite," she answered. "Oh, by the way, Mandy and Ryan invited us to come by their house for dinner tonight, a small group. Okay with you?"

"Whatever you want."

I want my career back.

"Good. Have your assistant call Mandy and accept."

"Are you on your way home?"

Are you still fucking anything that moves?

"I'll be there soon."

*　*　*

"You ruined my day," Don said, waving everyone out of his office as he spoke to Cameron on the phone.

"Why's that?" she asked.

"Last night at Ryan's party I was kind of under the impression we had a connection," he said, drumming his fingers on his desk. "Then come this morning an' you bale on me. That's not nice."

160

"Sorry," she murmured. It seemed as if she was having to apologize to everyone today.

"Sorry doesn't cut it," he replied, mock-stern. "What was so important that you couldn't make it?"

Revealing that she'd skipped out on him so that she could have breakfast with Ryan was not an option. She knew he liked her, but only because he wasn't getting anywhere with her. She also knew that he and Ryan were close. But what could she do? It wasn't her fault she was so attracted to Ryan. Controlling her feelings was not always possible.

"Something personal came up," she said carefully. "I'll be there tomorrow."

"Anything I can do to help out?"

"No, Don, nothing. But thanks for asking."

"You're sure?" he said, wishing she'd let him in just a little bit. She was so fucking elusive and it bugged him.

"Positive," she said firmly.

"Maybe I can buy you dinner," he suggested, feeling like the school nerd asking the prom queen for a date.

"I can buy my own dinner," she said, knowing that she probably sounded like a bitch, but she couldn't help it; her mind was firmly on Ryan.

"What's up with you?" he burst out. "You're so fucking independent."

"Something wrong with being independent?" she said, distracted as the phone guy attempted to get her attention.

"No, but—"

"I have to go," she said abruptly.

"If that's the way you want it, sweetheart," he said, experiencing a sudden flash of anger that she found it so damn easy to blow him off. Maybe Jill was right, maybe she *was* gay. "Gotta go too," he said quickly, before he made even more of a fool of himself.

"I'll be there tomorrow," she said, cool as can be. "Bright and early."

Bright and early my ass, he thought bitterly as he clicked off his phone. Enough of this chasing after her. It was ridiculous. He could have any woman he wanted, and the woman he wanted was probably gay, so fuck it, no more driving himself crazy.

He buzzed his assistant. "Get me Mary Ellen Evans," he snapped.

One thing was for sure. Tonight he was getting laid.

ANYA

*F*or several blissful days Anya discovered the joys of being in a real city where there were places to walk and things to see. It was summertime, and Amsterdam was quite beautiful with its twisting canals, fascinating old buildings and many museums. Anya felt that she had entered another world – a world where people strode along the sidewalks, rode bicycles, strolled in the parks, and were not obsessed with sex. A world where for the first time since the loss of her parents, she felt like a human being and not a mere object.

It was such a relief to be free, if only temporarily.

Velma had informed her that she was busy securing their future. "We will make plenty of money in this city," she'd told Anya. "It is important I set us up right."

Every morning for three days Velma left the small hotel they were staying in, and didn't return until late at night.

Anya wasn't lonely, she was ecstatic – exploring the city by herself was exciting. Velma – who was in charge of their hard-earned money – gave her a small amount of cash each day to buy lunch, and told her to enjoy herself. "Soon you'll be working so hard there'll be no time to see anything."

Anya didn't think to ask Velma exactly what she was doing all day, she trusted her completely.

On their third night in Amsterdam Velma brought a man back with her to their small hotel room. He was Turkish, tall and thin with long greasy hair pulled back into a tight ponytail, a scraggly beard, pock-marked skin and shifty eyes. "This is Joe," Velma announced. "He'll be our protector."

"Protector?" Anya stammered. "I don't understand."

But soon she did. Velma had decided they needed someone smart who knew the city and was familiar with the notorious red-light district, to launch them on what she was sure would be a lucrative career. Joe was that someone.

In her travels Velma had asked around and Joe's name kept on coming up. She'd finally tracked him down and informed him he was in for a treat. Joe had looked Velma over and nodded his approval. "I can handle you," he'd said. "I get you room, protection, everything you need. In exchange you hand over sixty per cent of everything you earn."

"I don't intend to be some hooker sitting in a window," Velma had informed him. "I'm after more than that."

"Then what?" he'd asked.

"Me and another girl," she'd said. "A very young beautiful girl. We put on live sex show. Then after show, the highest bidder gets to fuck her. You interested in promoting us? Fifty per cent partners?"

Joe was interested. But first he had to see this girl that Velma had promised was so young and beautiful.

That day Anya had walked all over the city. She'd visited the Van Gogh museum – staring in wonderment at the paintings; she'd fed the pigeons in Dam Square; marveled at the Royal Palace building; watched the Magere Bridge open and close several times; and finally she'd ended up in a coffee shop where all kinds of legal marijuana was on the menu.

When she'd returned to their hotel she was full of dreams of what her future with Velma might hold. Velma had talked about girl-on-girl shows being their future, but now she wasn't so sure; there were many other things they could do.

"Take off your clothes," Velma ordered. "We show Joe some of our special sex tricks."

"No," Joe interrupted, licking his thin lips. "You take off her clothes, make sure you do it slowly."

Anya tried to hide the tears that filled her eyes. She'd been so hopeful that her days as a sexual object were over. Now this evil-looking man was staring at her with his narrow bloodshot eyes expecting her to do things she dreaded. She should have known that getting out of the sex trade was impossible. How foolish of her to have imagined otherwise.

"Come, little bird," Velma coaxed, pawing at her clothes. "Pretend it's you and me alone together doing the things you love so much. Let us show the man how we make sex."

Anya nodded blankly, her eyes overflowing with helpless tears. Sex with Velma was something special for them alone. Sharing it would spoil everything.

With a heavy heart she realized there was no escape. There never was.

Chapter Twenty

Wherever Mary Ellen Evans went, paparazzi followed. She was their perfect victim. A famous TV star, currently single, recently and very publicly dumped by her movie-star husband who'd immediately hooked up with his gorgeous co-star. The press loved to portray Mary Ellen as the poor little victim. Her photo, walking on the beach looking forlorn, with just her small dog for company, sold hundreds and thousands of magazines.

It pissed her off big time, which is why she'd so determinedly set her sights on Don Verona. He was one of the few Hollywood bachelors (he'd been married twice, but that didn't count) who would raise her profile from pathetic loser in love to what a lucky girl!

She needed him, and she saw no reason at all why she couldn't have him. After all, she was eligible too, a total catch.

When Don called her at the last minute for a date that same night she was inclined to say no. But then she thought – why not? Best to catch him while she could; he was elusive and slippery, she'd already figured *that* out.

This would be their third date, which meant that sex was definitely on the agenda. And she was up for it, because once Don Verona got a taste of her action in bed – he would soon see she was not the perfect girl-next-door she portrayed on her TV sitcom. She had her moves and then some. Don would not be disappointed.

As soon as he picked her up in yet another of his impressive collection of cars – this time a gleaming metallic blue Aston Martin, she was on full flirt alert.

"We're going to *The Ivy*," he informed her.

She couldn't have been more delighted. *The Ivy* meant paparazzi frenzy. Hordes of photographers lurked across the street from the restaurant in SUVs with darkened windows waiting to pounce. Tonight they were in for a treat.

Don had chosen *The Ivy* for just that reason. Much as he hated being stalked by the photogs, he wanted Cameron to see that she had competition and she'd better do something about him before it was too late. He realized he was being perverse. Knowing Cameron, she wouldn't give a monkey's if he was linked to Angelina Jolie and Megan Fox at the same time. Cameron walked her own path, and that's what he liked about her. A beautiful independent woman who didn't give a rat's ass about fame and glory. He hadn't felt this way about a woman since high school, when he'd developed a real thing for his Latin teacher – a woman fifteen years his senior who'd taught him a lot more than Latin. Mrs Ramirez. Hmm . . . hot spicy memories.

Sometimes he wondered if she watched him on TV and remembered the boy she'd educated in more ways than one.

He kind of hoped she did.

* * *

Mandy was playing gracious daughter-in-law to the hilt. And when Mandy wanted to, she could be more adept at role-playing than any actress.

Ryan watched with astonishment. From the moment he'd gotten home she'd been in sweet Mandy overdrive, and he couldn't figure it out.

Had one of her girlfriends spotted him having breakfast with Cameron? Was that what all this was about? Or was his dear wife heading for a nervous breakdown? What the hell, it was scary stuff. Especially watching her charm the shit out of his family – particularly his mom – whom she'd never had a good word to say about.

Noreen Richards took it in her stride. She'd tried to be friends with Mandy over the years, but it had never happened. Now Mandy was acting as if they were the closest of confidantes. Ryan was shocked enough about that, but when Evie walked in with Marty he was totally taken aback. Evie had covered her black eye with cleverly applied makeup, but he knew it was there, and he had to control a strong urge to beat the crap out of his dumb-ass brother-in-law who immediately started in on the Grey Goose vodka.

Everyone came armed with presents, which on a normal occasion might've been nice. But this was not a normal occasion. This was Mandy entertaining, assisted by three attentive waiters, a barman and a chef.

Ryan was embarrassed; this was no way to entertain his family. They preferred home cooking and casual, not all this fancy crap which Mandy knew he hated. Formality was not his thing, it never had been.

He thought about Cameron for a moment. Formality would not be her thing either, somehow he was sure of it.

Evie was huddled on the couch with their two older sisters, Una and Inga. He went over and managed to extract her. "What happened?" he demanded.

"Please do *not* let Marty know I told you," she begged, her eyes filled with alarm. "He's so so sorry. Couldn't be more so. Now everything's fine, I promise. He's sworn he'll never behave like that again."

"Jesus Christ, Evie," Ryan said, frowning. "This is bullshit."

"No, no, it's not," Evie assured him, fluttering her hands. "It was all a horrible misunderstanding."

"A fucking *misunderstanding*?" Ryan said, his frown deepening.

"Don't swear. If Mom hears you she'll wash your mouth out with soap."

"Very funny," Ryan said grimly. "Why don't you get off the subject and pretend nothing happened? Isn't that the mature way of dealing with it?"

"How was your . . . work-out?" Evie said pointedly. "Does Mandy know you . . . work out?"

He couldn't believe Evie was throwing – *Leave it alone or I'll tell Mandy about Cameron* – at him. He knew she was probably aware he had feelings for Cameron; as the two youngest in the family they'd always shared a close bond.

"You're crazy," he said, shaking his head. "Taking Marty back and forgiving him is a big mistake."

"No," Evie said stubbornly. "Calling *you* was my big mistake."

At that moment Lucy and Phil arrived.

Another surprise, since Mandy had failed to tell him she'd invited them.

He threw his wife a look. Mandy smiled sweetly.

This was going to be one long night.

*　　*　　*

"Enough about me," Mary Ellen said, leaning across the table in the dimly lit *Ivy*, giving Don a long lingering look. "Tell me more about *you*."

Don shrugged. "What's to tell?"

"All your hidden secrets," she said coyly.

"Ain't got none," he quipped, wondering why he'd decided to put himself through this excruciating evening. It wasn't that he didn't like Mary Ellen, it was just that making conversation with someone he had no interest in was totally boring.

"Everyone has secrets," Mary Ellen said mysteriously.

He made a quick switch. "In that case, tell me yours."

"Are you really interested?" she asked, tilting her head coquettishly on one side.

"Go ahead," he said, encouraging her.

And so she did, enabling him to sit back and allow his mind to wander while she droned on about her cheating ex-husband, her lonely childhood, how the press wrote such nonsense about her and that her true ambition was to be accepted as a talented actress, not merely a TV star.

Nobody's satisfied with what they have, he thought, *even me*.

By this time their waiter was hovering beside their table trying to tempt them with dessert. The young waiter was obviously an out-of-work actor, and he was intent on charming Mary Ellen. "The key-lime pie is outstanding," he said, giving her an – *I think I'd be a great addition to your TV show* – look.

"No, thank you," she said politely.

"How about the Tarte Tatin?" he pressed.

"I don't think so."

Slight desperation was setting in. "Tea? Coffee?"

Mary Ellen shook her head.

"Just the check," Don said.

Defeated, the waiter went off to get the check.

"We'll have coffee at my place," Don said.

Mary Ellen nodded, trying not to look too excited.

After Don paid the check – leaving a hefty tip for the out-of-work actor for whom he had empathy – they left.

And so the paparazzi pounced. A pack of them, pushing and shoving for the best shot; tripping over each other; calling out, "Don! Don! Over here! Mary Ellen! Smile! Give us that lovely smile!"

They made it into the car.

"Whew!" Mary Ellen sighed as Don rapidly drove off. "That was an ordeal."

"But you're used to it," he remarked. "It's part of the package, right?"

"For you too."

"Not so much."

"Surely you're not blaming me for all the attention?" she asked coyly.

"You *do* get a lot of it."

"Yes," she said, her tone sharpening. "For all the wrong reasons."

He took one hand off the steering wheel and patted her knee. She responded by moving closer.

He drove fast all the way home, Mary Ellen anticipating the sexual encounter to come, and Don wondering why he'd invited her.

Too bad she wasn't Cameron. Too damn bad.

*   *   *

"Why are we here?" Phil growled to Lucy in a low voice. "This is family night at the Richards'. What the hell are we doing here?"

"Maybe Mandy considers us family," Lucy said, just as confused as her husband. She'd expected a small group of their peers, not Ryan's entire family. They were nice enough people, but they existed in a different universe. His sisters were stay-at-home moms. Their husbands – apart from Marty – were businessmen, and Ryan's mom was the definitive homemaker – a woman who'd raised a family and seemed to have no personal requirements whatsoever.

Where had Ryan and his blazing talent come from, Lucy wondered, for it sure didn't run in his family. Marty, the stuntman, immediately started coming on to her.

"Loved you in *Blue Sapphire*," he said, moving too close for comfort. "Where'd you learn to take it off like that?"

Blue Sapphire. The one movie she regretted making. She'd played a stripper, the rite of passage for every female movie star in Hollywood. If not a stripper then a hooker, and at some point in their career, preferably both.

She'd taken it all off in *Blue Sapphire* because the director had insisted that it was integral to the plot to see her naked. Tits on show. Ass for the world to see. Everything out there.

She shuddered whenever she recalled making that particular film. Especially as *Playboy* had gotten shots of her in all her glory and spread them throughout the magazine.

Blue Sapphire was an embarrassment she strove to forget, and now this drunk asshole was bringing it up.

"Can I ask you somethin'?" he slurred, following her as she attempted to move across the room toward Ryan.

"What?" she snapped, none too pleased.

"Don't think I'm bein' rude," he said, taking another swig of expensive vodka, "but your boobies in that movie – man – they were fuckin' sensational! Were they real?"

This jerk had balls as big as footballs. What a nerve!

"Excuse me?" she said, giving him the cold fish-eye.

"Well, y'know, when Demi Moore made that movie where she stripped off, she had her boobs enlarged – like for the role. So I thought—"

"Well *don't*," Lucy said, cutting him off, and giving him another icy glare.

"Nothin' wrong with gettin' implants," he mumbled, scratching his nose. "Demi had hers taken out after her movie. An'—"

Before he could finish, Lucy made her escape and approached Ryan who was concluding a heated discussion with his sister.

"Can I speak with you a moment?" she asked.

"Sure," Ryan said, glad for the diversion. He was so mad at Evie; she was an idiot if she believed that Marty was sorry and would never hit her again.

Lucy took his arm and steered him over to the patio door.

"I hope we're not intruding," she said. "Mandy never mentioned this was a family evening."

"She wouldn't, would she? That's our Mandy," Ryan said, wondering exactly when Mandy had decided to invite the Standards.

"I've been in touch with a very talented young writer," Lucy said, lowering her voice. "Don't mention it to Phil, but the writer is putting my story idea into a screenplay."

"Way to go, Lucy. But I think you might be better off telling Phil."

"Why?" she said petulantly. "He's not interested. Every time I bring the subject up he ignores me, so I've taken matters into my own hands. Can you blame me?"

Ryan shrugged. Right now Lucy's problems about her story ideas and resuming her career were not his primary concern. He had other things to think about, such as what was Mandy up to? Why had she put together this gathering of his family? A few minutes ago he'd found out it was not a pre-planned event as Mandy had said. His mother had revealed that she'd only heard from Mandy that very morning, which meant that while he was having breakfast with Cameron, Mandy had been busy putting it all together. She was a crafty one, informing him she'd planned it way ahead, since this was not the case at all. It was a last-minute move – and who the hell did she think she was fooling? Certainly not him.

"When I get the finished script I want you to promise me you'll read it," Lucy said.

"Sure," he replied, his mind still elsewhere.

Lucy leaned forward and planted a kiss on his cheek.

"Thanks, Ryan, I knew I could depend on you. And you won't be disappointed."

He moved off toward the bar. Spending time with Cameron had been a revelation, it had made him realize that there was more to life than staying with a woman he did not love. He was through punishing himself for events in the past that he'd had no control over. Neither he nor Mandy could do anything about the miscarriages and their stillborn baby. It was tragic, but it was in their past. Now it was time to move on. Divorce was the best move for both of them.

Finally he was sure of it.

Chapter Twenty-One

Cole had set up a series of interviews for new trainers to come in and show off their stuff.

"Shouldn't we wait until we open?" Cameron had asked.

"There's no way we can make it with only three of us," Cole had argued. "You, me and Dorian ain't gonna cut it. We need at least two more bodies. We gotta start off strong."

They were auditioning at their unfinished premises and Cole was being particularly picky.

"Too old," he insisted, checking out each individual applicant. "Too young." "Too sexy," followed by – "Not sexy enough."

Cameron was losing patience, so when Cole dismissed a perfectly lovely girl as – "too straight" – she snapped. "What exactly *are* you looking for?" she yelled.

Cameron didn't usually yell. Cole was surprised. He thought for a minute, then a grin spread across his face – and he said – "Someone as good as us."

Cameron shook her head. She couldn't fault him when all he wanted was the best. "The next one in, unless she/he has two left feet, they're hired," she said sternly. "We have no more time to waste."

"Got it," he agreed.

The next applicant, Cherry, was a pretty girl with a strong athletic body, a cheerful personality and excellent credentials.

"You're hired," Cameron said. "Next!"

By the end of the day they'd taken on Cherry, and Reno, a young Italian kid with rock-hard abs and an enthusiastic attitude.

Later Cameron hooked up with Cole and Dorian, and the three of them went to the *California Pizza Kitchen* on Beverly Drive where they devoured spicy chicken pizzas and large Caesar salads.

"I've got news," Cole said, munching on a slice of pizza. "Forgot to tell you earlier."

"You didn't forget," Cameron pointed out. "You were mad at me."

"True," Cole said. "Which brings up the subject of where exactly *were* you this morning? I spoke to Katie, an' you sure as shit weren't there."

"You mean Miz Paradise was on the missing list?" Dorian interjected, tossing back his golden locks.

"I was not missing, I . . . uh . . . simply forgot the time," she said, thinking about Ryan for a moment, and wondering if he was thinking about her.

No! No! No! The man is married, for God's sake.

Get over him.

What if I can't?

You have to.

"You told me you had to help out a friend," Cole said accusingly.

Yes. A friend. A new friend.

"She's being mysterious," Dorian joked. "She's hiding something from us. Look at her face! Guilty as charged, madame."

Was she coming across as guilty? About *what?* All she'd done was have breakfast with a married man. Hardly a crime.

"Will you two quit it," she said crossly. "Truth is I overslept."

"With anyone we know?" Dorian asked archly. "Seems to me you've got that 'I just got laid' flush."

"I *so* do not," she said, blushing.

"Oh yes you do," Dorian sing-songed.

"Oh yes she does!" Cole said, joining in.

"What did you forget to tell me earlier?" she asked, swiftly changing the subject.

"Natalie called. We got ourselves a new investor."

"Excuse me?"

"Someone looking for an investment opportunity. They came along at exactly the right time."

"Who?"

"Dunno. Does it matter? They're willing to put up mucho bucks."

"In exchange for *what*?"

"They're taking over a piece of Natalie's action."

Perhaps Cole was not as business-savvy as she'd thought. "We can't just allow anyone to waltz in and be part of our business without knowing who it is," she said, frowning.

"Calm down," Cole said. "If Natalie vouches for this person, they're cool. Besides, you know we're running outta money fast. This way we're set to finish everythin' an' open with a major blow-out. Natalie's got a list of celebs lined up, an' her TV show's promised to cover the openin'. Great, huh?"

Cameron nodded unsurely. The closer it got to the opening of *Paradise*, the more tense she became. *Paradise* was her future, everything she'd worked toward. It had to be a success.

But what if it wasn't?

What if it was one big devastating flop?

What if nobody came?

And she wasn't just thinking about the opening – of course people would come to that, free food and free drink – the opening party was a no-brainer.

But after that – what if it didn't take off?

Snap out of it, no negative thoughts, she told herself. *Paradise is gonna fly. No doubt about it.*

"Did you call Carlos's contact?" she asked Cole.

"Yeah," he said. "Now that the money's flowin', an' Natalie's not so uptight, I gotta feelin' he could be our man. We're meetin' at the premises at ten tomorrow. Sounds like he can get the job finished fast."

"In time for our party?"

"He talks a good game."

"He needs to do more than that."

"Natalie thinks we should hire a P.R. for the opening," Cole said. "Get us some major coverage."

"You think?"

"This is Hollywood, babe, everyone's into fitness. With the right P.R. we could be the new Pinkberry."

"Huh?" she said, wrinkling her nose.

"Remember how Pinkberry took over the yoghurt business? We're gonna do the same for bodies."

"Right on," Dorian agreed.

"*Paradise* will be *the* place to go for anyone who wants the best body in town," Cole said, full of confidence.

His enthusiasm was somewhat disturbing. What if he was expecting too much?

In spite of the smile on her face Cameron was tense and uptight. It suddenly occurred to her that she needed sex, and since Ryan wasn't available . . .

Marlon. His name popped into her head. Marlon was always available.

"Okay, guys, I think I'm gonna take off," she said, feigning a yawn.

"It's early," Dorian objected. "Surely you want to come to the Abbey with us an' watch the boys drool over me an' Cole? I promise you – it's quite a sight."

"Thanks for the offer, but I'm taking a pass."

"She's got a boyfriend," Dorian sing-songed. "It's written all over that beautiful face of hers."

"You're wrong," she said.

"I'm never wrong when it comes to sex," Dorian said. "You're gettin' it, young lady."

Oh yes, I am, in about twenty minutes after I drive myself to the beach.

"I hope she *is* seeing someone," Cole remarked. "It's about time she got some action."

"It would be so nice if you two would stay out of my sex life and concentrate on your own," she said tartly. "And I might add that I do not appreciate being spoken about as if I'm not here. You're always doing that."

"Now, now," Dorian tut-tutted. "Don't go all diva on us."

She stood up, leaned across the table and kissed both of them. "Bye, boys," she said crisply. "I'll see you tomorrow."

Once outside she called Marlon. He informed her he was working on a script, but that he'd definitely make time to see her.

Hmm . . . this was a new one, Marlon working on a script. She'd thought he was a student, now it turned out he was a wanna-be screenwriter. Why was she surprised? Wasn't that the ambition of every young guy in Hollywood?

She made the drive to Venice in record time.

As soon as she got there she wished she hadn't bothered. Marlon was so not what she was in the mood for, and while she'd thought she wanted sex, doing it with him simply didn't appeal to her anymore.

Too late. He greeted her warmly, pulled her down on his futon, and went at it until she faked orgasm and told him it was great. Then, as she started getting dressed, he decided he wanted to talk!

Bad idea. No talking, just sex.

After listening to him for five minutes, she told him she had to meet someone and raced out of there.

Sex with Marlon had lost its luster. He was just a kid, and she wanted a real man.

She wanted Ryan Richards.

* * *

"What do you think is goin' on with our girl?" Dorian asked, once Cameron had taken off.

Cole was busy making major eye-contact with a rugged-looking hunk at the bar. "Dunno," he said. "She seems normal to me."

Noticing what Cole was up to, Dorian let out a groan – "*Puleeze!* Not *him*. I had the poor slob last week, an' the only thing he can suck is a lemon!"

"What makes you think I'm not into lemons?" Cole quipped.

"Oh Cole," Dorian sighed, fanning himself with the menu. "If only I was your type, you an' I would make one hot team."

"We *are* a team," Cole said, flashing his whiter than white teeth. "Only you stay on your side an' I'll stay on mine."

"Such a bitch!" Dorian huffed.

"And don't you love it," Cole retaliated, still grinning.

* * *

Cameron drove home fast, listening to an old Sade CD. She was in the mood for some nostalgic sounds and Sade always got it right.

After collecting Yoko and Lennon, and running them around the block, she took a shower, put on some old sweats, sat down in front of her computer and began Googling Ryan Richards.

There were plenty of entries. His bio, his movies, his awards, his family.

She read all about him, absorbing every detail. When she was finished, she slipped out to her car, drove to Barnes & Noble and purchased all seven of his movies. Once home, she had an urge to start watching them immediately, but it was almost midnight, and she had Don to deal with at seven a.m. Not to mention another long day ahead.

She thought about Ryan for a moment. They'd set a time for his work-out, but they hadn't arranged a location. He'd said he'd call her, she hoped he wouldn't change his mind.

After checking her messages – none from Ryan – she went to bed and fell asleep, dreaming about opening-night disasters and falling from a cliff into a deep lagoon where she languished, floating on her back while dolphins jostled around her.

Yoko and Lennon woke her at three a.m., both of them barking frantically.

She sat up, startled, straining to hear any unusual sounds.

Apart from her noisy dogs, all was quiet.

"Shut up, guys," she yawned, thinking it might be prudent to learn to shoot a gun. Mr Wasabi had informed her there'd been a couple of break-ins on the street, and although she wasn't nervous by nature, a gun might be a smart idea.

The dogs stopped barking, and after a while she fell back to sleep. This time she dreamed about Ryan, and when she awoke it was with a smile on her face.

Chapter Twenty-Two

"Whew!" Mary Ellen exclaimed, taking in her surroundings. "This is some house!"

"I built it," Don said, as Butch – exhibiting his usual bad behavior – bounded forward and headed straight for her crotch.

She jumped back, startled.

Grabbing Butch's collar, Don pulled his dog off her. "Do you want me to put him outside?" he asked.

"That would be great. It's just that I'm not used to big dogs. I have a Chihuahua."

Of course you do, he thought as he opened up the patio doors and steered Butch out by the pool. Chihuahuas were show-off dogs, always good for a photo op. He should've guessed that was the kind of dog Mary Ellen would have.

He pressed a button and the sexy sounds of R. Kelly flooded the room. "How about a drink?" he suggested. "What can I get you?"

"I'd love a Bailey's," she said, wondering when he'd make a move. The setting was perfect. Amazing house with an amazing view of the city. The twinkling lights of Los Angeles spread out before them like a dazzling blanket.

She sat down on the leather couch and waited for him to join her.

He was in two minds about what to do.

To fuck her or not to fuck her.

That was the question.

He wasn't feeling particularly horny, yet he knew she expected sex. And if they did it, was she the kind of girl who'd consider them a couple?

Had to tread carefully with this one.

He poured her a Bailey's, himself a Jack Daniel's, and sat down beside her still unsure of what he might do.

She made up his mind for him. Downing the Bailey's in two quick gulps, she suddenly unbuttoned her blouse and unhooked her front-clasp bra, revealing two perfect perky all-natural breasts with hard extended nipples.

Done deal.

His response was instant. Nipples like that could not go to waste.

Bending his head he went to work, licking, sucking, fingering, until she was in full moan, begging him to fuck her.

And who was he to say no? His head might be full of Cameron, but his body was ready for action.

Feverishly she began unzipping his pants and wriggling out of her skirt, until the two of them were rolling about on the white rug in front of the couch, and her moans were becoming louder and louder.

His mind flashed – *Grab a condom – Grab a condom.*

His cock said – *Fuck it.*

So he did. He fucked her all the way to kingdom come and back.

And then it was over and he thought – *Damn. That was not the direction I should've gone in. No frigging way.*

* * *

Marty was getting drunker by the minute, and his pursuit of Lucy did not go unnoticed by Phil – who was hitting a few back himself.

Ryan kept a steady eye on both of them, for he smelled trouble ahead, and that was all he needed to make the night perfect.

He approached Mandy who was chatting to his mother as if they were the best of buddies.

"When is dinner being served?" he asked.

"Soon," Mandy replied, reaching out to clutch Noreen's hand.

"You'd better make it soon," Ryan said tersely. "Marty's drunk and chasing after Lucy."

"Don't you *love* it when our Ryan gets all flustered?" Mandy giggled to her mother-in-law. "He's just like a little boy."

"You should've seen him when he was ten," Noreen replied, joining in to what she thought was fun banter. "Smart as a whip and *so* grown up."

"Nothing's changed," Mandy said. "Has it, sweetheart?"

This was hardly the Mandy he knew. Had she gone through a lobotomy and he hadn't noticed?

The doorbell rang. Nobody seemed to hear it except for him, so he marched to the front door and flung it open.

Standing there was Hamilton J. Heckerling and his beautiful young bride, Pola. She was wearing a green satin Yves Saint Laurent suit and an array of tasteful diamond jewelry.

Hamilton stood tall, the proud new husband, his arm flung possessively across her shoulders.

"Ah, it's my son-in-law," Hamilton boomed, stepping inside the house. "Meet my new bride, Pola."

Pola was smiling.

The blood drained from Ryan's face.

"Well?" Hamilton said in a loud voice. "Aren't you gonna congratulate us?"

Amsterdam

Seven years earlier

The private plane, commandeered by Don Verona, arrived in Amsterdam at noon – carrying a group of hung-over men – including Don's best friend, the bridegroom-to-be, Ryan Richards. Also aboard were Ryan's other best friends – Phil Standard, Eddie Serrano, an actor who'd starred in Ryan's first movie, and Jenna, a lesbian friend from college who'd co-produced one of his films.

Four American men and one American woman with "Bachelor Party" screaming in their heads. Although Ryan's head wasn't exactly screaming, he would've been happier staying home. But Don and Phil were having none of it. Their friend, Ryan, was finally getting married and they'd all decided he deserved a worthy send-off.

Don had one divorce behind him, and Phil had been married for three years to the luscious movie star, Lucy Lyons, who'd already presented him with a son and was currently pregnant with their second child.

Phil was hot to party, as was Don – coming out of a divorce was always stressful.

Not only had Don arranged the plane, he'd also organized the hotel and a special tour guide to show them the sights of Amsterdam.

"None of that tourist crap," Don had instructed. "We're interested in seeing the real thing."

Their tour guide met them at the hotel. She was not what any of them had expected. First off they'd expected a male. Hanna might've been one once, but she certainly wasn't anymore. She was six feet tall with cascades of blonde curls, large breasts, wide shoulders and strong features. She smelled of ode to – you're going to have an excellent time. And if you don't, I am quite capable of beating the shit out of you.

Jenna fell instantly in love. So did Eddie, while Phil decided he might give it a try.

Hanna spoke perfect English in a deep masculine voice. Ryan was convinced he/she was a sex change.

"All the better," Don said. "She'll know the ins and outs of every hot place to go."

In a way Ryan felt he'd been totally railroaded so his friends could have themselves a fine old time at his expense. They'd lured him onto the plane, promising Vegas as their destination. And now here they were in Amsterdam, one of the sex capitals of Europe.

He didn't want sex, he wasn't interested in getting laid. He was thirty-three years old and up until this point – as far as women were concerned – his entire life had been one long crazy bachelor party. Now he was ready to settle down with one woman, and she was all he needed. Mandy Heckerling. She was perfect for him. Pretty, smart and quite content to be his wife. A woman with no career ambitions in Hollywood was a big plus.

"Here's the plan," Don announced after they'd checked into their hotel overlooking one of the many canals in the heart of Amsterdam. "A coupla hours to recover, then we hit the streets big time. Everybody ready?"

Everybody signaled they were indeed ready, except for Ryan, who wondered how he could get out of it. Mandy had no idea they'd dragged him across the Atlantic for fun and games in Amsterdam. She wouldn't be exactly thrilled.

"*Remember – this is your final fling,*" *Don informed him.* "*You'd better make the most of it.*"

Ryan remembered Don's final fling eighteen months ago before he married Sacha, his French movie star. It had been some blow-out. Two booze-filled nights in Tijuana with strippers and hookers galore, farm animals, and hang-overs that had lasted a week. Now Don was divorced, so it hadn't exactly been his final fling.

Ryan took a shower, readying himself for the ordeal that lay ahead. One thing he was determined about, and that was to stay sober and in control.

Yeah, sure. With his group of friends. It was his bachelor party, he'd better be prepared for anything.

It was many hours later when they finally hit the red-light district. Hours filled with the usual requisites of a bachelor party. Strippers, who did it with snakes; a live sex show between two women and a Sumo wrestler; clubs that featured women with cucumbers, bananas, little people, chickens, sheep – you name it, they could produce it. And along the way they'd stopped in cafés where grass was legal and getting high was an everyday occurrence.

The infamous street was where women sat in lighted windows waiting for someone – anyone – to choose them, fuck them, pay them and go home. Pimps lurked in the shadows, touting for customers.

"*Take your pick,*" *Don said, as they walked along the street inspecting the women for sale. There were all types. Young, old, fat, thin, big-breasted, flat-chested. Asian, European, black, Scandinavian. Something for everyone.*

"*You gotta do it,*" *Don urged.* "*If you don't, it means bad luck forever.*"

Ryan forced himself to inspect the poor pathetic creatures sitting in their windows. He felt sorry for all of them. The skinny black hooker in pink lingerie; the fat blonde in a see-though baby-doll nightdress; the hyper redhead licking her fingers and suggestively beckoning passersby to come join her.

Then he spotted her, the young girl from one of the earlier sex

187

shows they'd attended. He was sure she couldn't be more than fifteen or sixteen. She was exquisitely beautiful, but her face was sad, and her eyes were full of pain.

He'd tried not to watch earlier when she'd appeared in a show with three different men and a woman. He'd put his mind elsewhere when, after the men had screwed her, she'd been pissed on and abused for the audience's entertainment. He'd had to walk outside and wait for the others.

He'd felt ashamed of himself for witnessing things he didn't care to see, but it was his bachelor party, so what could he do? The rest of his friends were enjoying themselves, he didn't want to ruin it for them.

Now here he was on the street, and there she was again, a forlorn, lost and very beautiful little creature.

He stopped abruptly. "I'll take her," he said.

Phil roared his approval. "An' I'll take the one next door," he said, gesturing toward a comely dark-haired woman in a short red dress who sat at a table looking bored while playing Solitaire.

Hanna produced a smile, exhibiting big horse teeth. "Anyone else see anything they like?" she inquired.

Don shook his head and punched Ryan on the arm. "Make it a good one," he laughed. "'Cause after tonight, all you'll have are the memories."

"I go broker the deal," Hanna announced, approaching a tall, skinny pimp who hovered nearby.

Hanna and the pimp seemed to know each other, they exchanged pleasantries and money, then Hanna told Ryan and Phil to go into the respective rooms.

"We'll see you back at the hotel," Don said, patting Ryan on the back. "Unless you'd like us to stay and watch!"

"Not necessary," Ryan replied, forcing himself to crack a smile. "I might take longer than you think."

"That's my best friend," Don crowed. "See you back at the hotel."

"*You may tip the girl if she performs well,*" *Hanna said, all business.* "*She'll do anything you want. Everything is paid for.*"

"*Yeah, compliments of me,*" *Don said, grinning broadly.* "*An' wear a jacket if you get what I mean.*"

Seconds later Ryan found himself alone in the room with the girl.

Without looking at him she walked over and closed the flimsy curtains, cutting off the light from the street, leaving on a tall floor lamp with a red lightbulb. Then she began taking off her skimpy top.

"*No!*" *Ryan said abruptly.* "*Don't do that.*"

She turned and stared at him.

"*Can you understand me?*" *he said.* "*Do you speak English?*"

"*A little,*" *she replied.*

Yes, over the two years she'd been in Amsterdam she'd learned English. She'd learned many other things too. She'd learned that she couldn't trust anyone, even Velma, because one night – after a vicious verbal battle with Joe – Velma had vanished, never to return. And after that she'd been at Joe's mercy, and he was a hard taskmaster, forcing her to do terrible things.

"*What can I do to please you?*" *Anya asked, her face devoid of any expression.*

"*Nothing,*" *Ryan said.*

"*Nothing,*" *she repeated blankly.* "*But you have paid for me, and if I do not please you –*"

"*What'll happen if you don't please me?*" *he asked.*

She hung her head and muttered, "*Nothing.*"

Of course she was lying.

"*How old are you?*" *he said, figuring she couldn't be more than sixteen.*

"*How old would you like me to be?*" *she replied boldly.* "*I can be any age you want. I can do anything you want. You like me to suck—*"

"*Stop!*"

"*I can do anything you want, mister,*" *she said again, her tone sulky.*

He sensed that all she wanted was to get it over with. Another john. Another night. And the same tomorrow, and the day after that and so on and so forth.

"Where are you from?" he asked, noticing that her arms were covered in large purple bruises.

"Nowhere," she answered flatly.

He sat on the edge of the saggy bed with the faded blue coverlet. "Do you have parents?"

"You police?" she asked, her eyes narrowing.

"No, I'm not police. I'm just a guy who's getting married next week, and this was my friend's idea of a celebration. Believe me – it's not mine."

"You don't want to fuck me?" she said incredulously.

"No, I don't. What I'd like to do is help you."

"Help me?" she said suspiciously. "How could you do that?"

"It would be my way of making my bachelor night memorable. Helping someone who's obviously caught in a trap."

"You can't help me," she said bitterly. "You don't know anything about me."

"I'm a film-maker. That's what I do, listen to people's stories, so why don't you tell me yours?"

"You make porno?"

"No. I make legitimate movies."

"You want to buy porno?" she said, just as Joe had trained her to do. "My boyfriend – he sell filthy movies most American men want. Girls together, boys—"

"Your boyfriend, huh?" Ryan interrupted. "Don't you mean your pimp?"

Her gaze swiveled fearfully toward the door as if she expected Joe to appear at any time.

"I'm guessing," Ryan said. "But here goes. You're from a poor family – Slovakia or maybe Poland. A man came to your house one day and promised your parents he could get you a good job in Holland, so they sent you off with him in return for a small payment.

When you got here, the job turned out to be prostitution, and now you're trapped."

She shrugged. His version of her life was a fairy story compared to the real deal.

"Am I right?" Ryan asked.

She stared at him for a long silent moment, wondering if this was a trap Joe had set, a test to see if she would betray him to the authorities.

Yes.

No.

This American man seemed genuine enough, only he didn't require sex, which made him suspect, because all men wanted sex.

"Sit down and let's you and I talk," Ryan said gently. "Please don't be afraid, I'm not going to hurt you. I have three sisters and if any one of them was in trouble, I would hope someone would step forward to help them."

Anya felt dizzy. Was it possible he meant what he said?

Maybe.

Maybe not.

Anya was not sure of anything anymore.

Chapter Twenty-Three

Anya's eyes were a steely pale blue as she stared Ryan down as if she'd never seen him before, as if he wasn't the man who'd rescued her from a life of degradation and despair.

"So nice to meet you," she said, in a flat, strongly-accented voice.

"Uh . . . likewise," he managed, as Mandy appeared in the front hallway, extremely startled to see her father whom she'd thought was still on his so-called honeymoon.

"Daddy!" Mandy exclaimed with a petulant pout. "Why didn't you let me know you were back?"

"Thought I'd surprise you, Princess," Hamilton said, smoothing back his head of thick silvery hair. "Wanted you to meet Pola in person. Isn't she a little doll?"

Only Hamilton would have the nerve to call a woman a doll.

Mandy's head swiveled to take in her father's latest wife. The girl was exactly as she'd expected, another money-grubbing piece of trash. Why couldn't he just sleep with them? Why did he have to marry them?

Mandy kept her feelings to herself, but inside she was seething. What was wrong with her father? Did he really believe that people admired his taste in women when anyone with half a brain could see they were just after him for his money? And to make matters worse – this one wasn't even a woman; this one was a girl all dressed up in designer clothes and too many diamonds that were way too sophisticated for one so young.

"Hi," Mandy said, summoning a lackluster smile.

"So nice to meet you," Anya said, the same flat greeting she'd given Ryan.

Standing by, Ryan was still in a state of shock. Pola/Anya. How the hell had she gotten here? Married to his father-in-law, standing in the hallway of his house. It was quite unbelievable.

Did she even realize it was him? Ryan Richards, her rescuer, the man who'd paid plenty of money to gain her freedom, the man who'd called in so many favors to get her a Visa and entry into America. Thank God he hadn't fucked her. That would've really been bad.

No flicker of recognition crossed her exquisite face. Did she suffer from amnesia? It was only seven years ago, and he hadn't changed that much, in fact hardly at all. His hair was longer, that was about it.

She, however, had changed a great deal. No longer a frightened, abused young girl, she was sleek and groomed, with auburn hair, expert make-up, and expensive clothes on her slim body. The diamonds she was adorned with were staggering. Hamilton must really like her.

"Well," Mandy said, rallying to the occasion because she had no choice, "this is quite a surprise. Will you be staying for dinner?"

"Didn't realize you were in the middle of a party," Hamilton said, brushing imaginary lint off the lapel of his Brioni suit. "Don't wish to intrude."

"You're not intruding," Mandy replied with a dismissive wave of her hand. "It's only Ryan's family. Hardly a party."

Ryan shot her a look. Only his family indeed, as if they were so unimportant. Did words pop out of her mouth without thinking?

Yes. Mandy had a habit of always saying the wrong thing, she had no thought for other people's feelings.

"We'll stay," Hamilton decided. "You and Pola are about to become close."

"We are?" Mandy said, swallowing her indignation that he would expect her to be friends with his latest wife.

"Pola doesn't know anyone in L.A.," Hamilton continued. "And I'm not exposing her to the dragon lady wives of my friends. Besides, she'll have nothing in common with them, they're all too old. You're it, Princess. You'll show her all that girly crap such as where to get her hair and nails done, the best masseuse, what stores to frequent."

"Of course," Mandy gushed, thinking no way was she cozying up to Daddy's latest piece of ass. "Come," she said, ushering her father toward the living room. "You must need a drink. Phil and Lucy Standard are here. Wasn't Lucy in one of your movies?"

"*Blue Sapphire*," he said, eyes gleaming. "We made a fortune with that one. Overseas sales alone set all kinds of records. I was anxious to make a sequel, but Lucy balked, she wasn't prepared to show her tits again. Actresses! They have no idea how to build a career."

By this time Ryan had returned to the living room, in two minds about whether to alert Phil or not. Would Phil even remember the girl from the live sex show one drunken night in Amsterdam?

Probably not. Phil had been totally out of it, busy concentrating on his own pleasure.

None of Ryan's friends knew what had taken place that night. He'd decided he wouldn't share – not even with Don. He'd done something good, and it hadn't been exactly easy. After hearing Anya's story, he'd decided that somehow or other it was his calling to help her obtain a fresh start. He didn't know why he had to do this, he just knew that it was important to him. After all, he'd had all the breaks in life – a loving family – a college education – a burgeoning career – and on the horizon, marriage to a wonderful woman.

It seemed in his mind that it was time to give back, and helping a young girl who'd experienced nothing but misery was definitely the right thing to do.

It had cost him plenty, but he'd happily paid for her freedom. Once he'd ascertained that she was safely in America, he'd never heard from her again, which was the plan, and also fortunate, because if Mandy ever found out what he'd done, she would've been convinced he'd had sex with the girl, and then the proverbial shit would've hit the fan.

"You'd better tell your punk brother-in-law to stop bothering my wife," Phil said, sidling over and growling in his ear. "The putz is following her around as if she's a bitch in heat. I do not appreciate assholes ogling my wife."

"Hamilton's here," Ryan said, reaching for a drink.

"Are we pleased or pissed off?" Phil inquired, well aware that Ryan and his uber-successful father-in-law were not exactly close.

"Neither," Ryan replied. "I try not to let him bother me either way."

"That's the right attitude," Phil said, tugging on his beard.

"He's with the new wife."

"*Another* one?" Phil bellowed.

"Keep it down. Here they come now," Ryan said, watching Phil closely as Hamilton and Anya entered the living room.

Phil whistled through his teeth, making a sucking noise. "The old bastard sure knows how to pick 'em," he said admiringly.

"Yeah," Ryan agreed, relieved that Phil seemed to have no recollection of the girl.

Suddenly there was a shriek of anger from Lucy on the other side of the room – a shout out of "Take your disgusting hands off me, you drunken moron!" Then she tossed her drink in Marty's face.

Marty stepped forward and lifted his arm as if he was about to slap her, but before he could do so, Ryan was there, preventing Marty from taking any action, and telling them both to calm down.

Evie hurried over, ready to defend her husband. Ryan glared at his sister, who should know better than defending her piece-of-shit husband. "Be cool," he warned.

"We're out of here," she responded, grabbing Marty by the arm and marching him to the door.

Ryan shook his head. There was nothing he could do to help her, she had to find out for herself that her husband was nothing but a hopeless lecherous drunk. She'd better wise up soon and divorce the loser before it was too late and Marty totally lost it, although his mom would probably be upset.

His other two sisters wanted to know what had happened. He planned on telling them what he'd witnessed at Evie's house that morning, but he wasn't about to get into it tonight.

"Everything's fine," he assured them. "Marty just had a few drinks too many."

Gritting his teeth, he got through the rest of the evening.

Not once did Anya glance in his direction. So much for playing the Good Samaritan, although it occurred to him that perhaps she was being discreet.

He'd not acknowledged her either, which meant that she must realize it wouldn't be a wise move to bring up their history. He could just imagine Hamilton's face if he found out the truth. As it was, Hamilton had spent the evening telling everyone that his bride was a former Russian ballerina who'd come to America to study economics. They'd met at a party and fallen instantly in love.

Sure, Ryan thought. *The sixty-five-year-old billionaire and the twenty-something ex-child prostitute. A true love connection, anyone can see that.*

So much for romance.

Later, Ryan stood at the door next to Mandy bidding everyone good night.

Mandy turned to him when the last guest had left. "I simply adore your mom," she gushed, spewing insincerity. "Why couldn't Hamilton have found a woman like *her*? They're about the same age, aren't they?"

Ryan shrugged. He felt drained and exhausted. This was not the time to get involved in a heated discussion.

Tomorrow, when things were calmer, when he could get his head straight.

Tomorrow he would tell Mandy he wanted a divorce.

Chapter Twenty-Four

Mary Ellen stayed the night. Don had not planned on her spending the night in his bed, but how could he throw her out right after they'd made love? He'd never been adept at getting rid of women after he'd slept with them. As soon as they were off the premises it was easy – don't take their calls, don't answer their e-mails, and never reply to their texts. But once they were snugly settled in his bed it was a different situation.

Quite frankly he preferred sleeping alone, but what could he do? Hiring professionals had worked for a short time, although the shine of paying a woman to do things that most women would give their left tit to do for free, had soon worn off.

Now it seemed he was back on the dating trail, a place he wasn't so sure he wanted to be.

What he *wanted* was Cameron Paradise.

What she apparently wanted was not him.

But he could change her mind, couldn't he?

With Mary Ellen snuggled up beside him, he slept fitfully, not falling off until three a.m., then oversleeping, so that when Cameron rang his doorbell at seven a.m. he was still totally out of it.

The bell rang several times before the sound got through to him. Usually Butch woke him up with a few solid licks to the face, but Butch was outside by the pool where Mary Ellen had requested he stay.

"Isn't that your doorbell?" Mary Ellen murmured, twining one leg over his, her warm body closing in.

"Uh, yes," he mumbled, disentangling himself and jumping out of bed. "Stay here. I'll be right back."

He almost made it to the door before realizing he was stark bollock naked. He hurried back into his bathroom, grabbed a white terrycloth robe and headed for the door again. This time he flung it open.

"I see we overslept again," Cameron remarked.

She was standing there looking so fucking gorgeous he could barely take it. "You got me," he said ruefully.

"Y'know," she observed, walking past him into the house, "you really should stop with those late nights of yours, 'cause if I'm getting here at seven, I expect you to be ready for action."

"I'm ready for action all right," he joked, tightening the belt on his bathrobe.

She smiled slightly. "Not *that* kind of action."

"What kind did you have in mind?" he asked, moving closer.

"Are you always such a flirt?" she said, backing away.

"Only when I'm around you."

"Sorry that I bring that out in you."

"Never apologize, it doesn't suit you."

"Hmm . . . I suppose you'd like me to put on the coffee before we get started."

"How'dja guess?" he said, attempting to suppress a yawn.

"It's becoming our routine, isn't it?" she said crisply. "I make the coffee, you get into your work-out clothes, that cuts our time by about half an hour."

"You wouldn't be accusing me of slacking off, would you?"

"Never!" she said, laughing. "By the way, when *is* this event you're hosting? The one where you expect to be in optimum shape?"

"Too damn soon," he groaned. "I hate doing that shit."

"Maybe I should call you when I leave my house in future, make sure you're out of bed," she said. "What do you think?"

"I think you'd be the best-looking wake-up service in town."

"Only for you," she said with a smile.

"Why?" he said, somewhat encouraged. "Are you saying I'm your favorite client?"

"No, but you are coming to our opening party and bringing a few celebrity friends. So . . . I guess I'm obliged to give you *some* extra perks."

"I'll take 'em," he said quickly.

"Where's Butch?" she asked, glancing around.

"Out by the pool."

"How come?"

"'Cause that's where he slept last night."

"You shouldn't leave a dog outside at night in L.A.," she scolded. "Even a big dog. There's coyotes everywhere. A friend of mine had her little puppy eaten by one, and that happened during the day."

At that moment Mary Ellen emerged from the bedroom. She had put on one of his shirts and nothing else. Her hair was pinned on top of her head, and her pretty face was makeup-less.

"Oh!" she said, taken aback when she spotted Cameron. "Sorry, am I interrupting?"

Cameron glanced at Mary Ellen, then back at Don. "*Now* I understand," she said knowingly.

Jesus Christ, he thought. *Why couldn't Mary Ellen have stayed in the bedroom where I left her? Why does she have to appear, parading around in one of my shirts? Fuck!*

He'd wanted to make Cameron jealous, but he hadn't wanted her to actually run into the girl he'd spent the night with.

"Uh, Cameron, this is Mary Ellen Evans," he said, keeping it smooth. "Mary Ellen, meet Cameron, my personal trainer."

"Oh," Mary Ellen said, relieved that this tall blonde goddess wasn't competition. "Are you planning on working out? Can I join you?"

"Of course you can," Cameron said, shooting Don an amused look. She knew he was furious that Mary Ellen had emerged from his bedroom, but so what? It was fun to watch Don almost lose his cool. "It'll be a blast. I'll put on the coffee while you two get into your clothes. We'll have a joint session." A long beat. "And you know what, Don?"

"What?" he said, frowning.

"I won't even charge you double."

*   *   *

Later, after an uncomfortable work-out with both women, Don met up with Ryan at The Four Seasons dining room.

"So then," Don said, gulping down his second cup of strong black coffee, "Mary Ellen comes waltzing out of my bedroom in one of *my* shirts and nothing else, like she's taken up residence. I was pissed, I can tell you that."

"What did Cameron do?" Ryan asked, thinking that only yesterday he'd had breakfast with Cameron in the same place. He hadn't called her. Couldn't call her, especially now with Don carrying on about her as if she was the only woman in the world.

"She kind of got off on the situation," Don admitted. "Jesus, Ryan, I think I'm really falling."

"Yeah, you're falling so hard that you slept with Mary Ellen."

"It meant nothing. Cameron's the woman for me."

"That's probably because you can't have her," Ryan responded dryly, feeling a frisson of satisfaction that Cameron hadn't fallen into Don's bed like most women.

"Bullshit," Don objected. "She's just . . . well, I don't have to tell you. You met her at the party. Isn't she something?"

Ryan nodded silently. She was something all right. She was

beautiful, and smart and caring and kind. And much as he loved Don – his best friend, his buddy, she was too good for him.

Or was he thinking that because he couldn't have her for himself?

Man, he was confused. And he hadn't brought up the subject of divorce with Mandy because by the time he'd got up that morning, she was busy hosting some kind of spiritual yoga class in their living room with three girlfriends.

Chanting was not his thing, so he'd made a quick exit. Now here he was with Don, and all Don wanted to talk about was Cameron.

Ryan realized that he couldn't call her. No. Not while Don was so enamored. In all the years they'd been friends they'd never allowed a woman to come between them, and he wasn't letting it happen now.

"Sorry," Don said, realizing he'd been hogging the conversation like a teenage boy with a crush. "Tell me about *your* evening?"

"It was okay until Hamilton showed up with his latest."

"Oh, shit!" Don exclaimed. "How did Mandy take *that*?"

"She was okay, really. On her best behavior."

"How come?"

"'Cause Hamilton scares the crap out of her. She's always edgy around him."

A waiter approached their table, the same waiter who'd served him and Cameron yesterday. Handing them menus, the waiter greeted Ryan with a cheery, "Nice to see you again so soon, Mr Richards."

"Thanks," Ryan said.

"Will you be ordering the same as yesterday?"

"Uh, sure."

"I hope you don't mind me asking, but was that lady you were with a model?"

Don put down his menu and threw Ryan a quizzical look. "A

model?" he questioned. "Have you been getting a little on the side?"

"Excuse me, Mr Richards," the waiter said, flustered. "I shouldn't have asked. It was most indiscreet of me."

Somehow Ryan managed to maintain his cool.

"That's okay," he said easily. And to Don – "I was interviewing an actress."

"Over breakfast?" Don said, grinning. "You old dog, I do believe you're holding out on me!"

Chapter Twenty-Five

"Good morning, Mrs Heckerling," said Madge, Hamilton's Scottish housekeeper who'd been with him for over twenty years.

"Good morning," Anya replied stiffly, as she entered the spacious kitchen in Hamilton's Bel Air mansion.

She still could not get used to being called Mrs Heckerling, nor could she get used to the way people treated her with deference and respect, as if she was someone important.

She was well aware that they only regarded her as important because she'd married a very rich man – a billionaire, in fact. However, being married to Hamilton J. Heckerling was not all easy. She lived in fear that one day he would find out about her past, and abandon her like everyone else had – one way or the other. First her parents; then her surrogate family; next Serge; followed by Igor; and finally Velma – who'd vanished and left her in the hands of Joe – a man who'd made the rest of them seem like kindly amateurs.

The two years she'd spent in Amsterdam were worse than anything that had gone before. The things Joe had forced her to do were unspeakable.

Many nights she awoke in a cold sweat – imagining that she'd been exposed as a fraud and was forced to return to her old life, a life she'd sooner die than go back to. The sad truth was that she lived with a cloud looming over her, imagining that one day someone would discover who she really was, or perhaps recognize her.

That someone had finally appeared a week ago. That someone was the American man who'd helped her escape from Amsterdam seven years ago.

It was a cruel twist of fate that the man who'd rescued her turned out to be married to Hamilton's daughter.

Did his wife know about her?

Had he told her everything?

And if he hadn't – would he do so now?

Anya had no idea how she was supposed to handle the situation. Should she run? Take off in the middle of the night and hope that Hamilton would not come after her?

No. That would be foolish, for surely if she vanished, Ryan would talk, and then everyone would know her dirty little secret.

It was imperative that she speak to him alone, find out if he'd told anyone. Because if he had . . .

I will kill myself, she thought. *Swallow a bottle of Hamilton's potent sleeping pills and end it all.*

She'd tried to kill herself one night in Amsterdam after Joe had forced her to perform at an orgy with two lesbians, and seven drunken German men. She'd found a razor in the hotel bathroom where the orgy was taking place, and attempted to slit her wrists. But Joe had come across her slumped on the floor covered in blood. He'd kicked her as if she were a dog, and shouted that she was the most useless whore he'd ever had to deal with. Then he'd dragged her to the Emergency Room where they'd stitched her slashed wrists and sent her home.

The next night it was back to work as usual.

"Can I get you anything, Mrs Heckerling?" Madge asked, standing with her arms crossed in front of her formidable bosom.

"No, thank you," Anya replied politely.

Madge had already decided that she did not approve of her boss's latest wife; however, she always remained polite. This one was tricky though – not as transparent as the others. Madge was certain that this one had something to hide.

"Perhaps I'll make my own tea," Anya said, edging toward the fridge.

"Not necessary, Mrs Heckerling," Madge said, blocking her way. "I'll bring it out to you on the terrace."

"Fine," Anya said, realizing she was not welcome in the kitchen – it was Madge's domain and the woman wanted her to stay out.

She wandered outside. Hamilton was sitting at the breakfast table reading the *Wall Street Journal*.

"Hi, honey," he said, barely looking up.

She sat down and gazed out at the vast expanse of green lawns surrounded by well-tended flower beds and blossoming jacaranda bushes. In the distance she could see the blue sparkle of an Olympic-size swimming pool, and an all-grass tennis court.

She was married to the man who owned all this. She was married to a billionaire.

And did she love him?

No.

And was she planning on staying with him?

Yes.

Hamilton glanced up from his newspaper. "Has Mandy called you yet?" he inquired, peering over his horn-rimmed glasses.

Anya shook her head.

"That girl!" he muttered, irritated. "I told her to show you around, introduce you to people. She gets plenty of perks from me, and yet she can't do one damn thing I ask."

"Maybe she is busy," Anya said. *Or maybe she knows who I really am and wants nothing to do with me.*

206

"Busy my ass," Hamilton snapped. "Busy doing fuck all. Takes after her mother, you know."

Anya didn't know. She'd never asked about his previous wives. She didn't care.

I am Mrs Hamilton J. Heckerling now, she thought. *And that's all that matters.*

ANYA

*A*nya had wished and wished so many times for someone to rescue her from the life she was forced to live. Her world was hardly worth existing in and she'd never thought she would be lucky enough to escape. Then one fateful night, God (in Whom she did not believe – but at last He came through for her) brought someone to her who changed everything.

An American man who was about to get married. An American man who saw into her damaged soul, and decided it was his job to help her. He'd paid for her freedom, she knew that much. Not as much as Joe would've liked, but her savior had threatened him with the police, and since he had connections at the American Embassy, Joe had backed down.

Anya didn't know the details. All she knew was that the American man had arranged to get her to a safe house where a kindly couple looked after her, and then months later she was given the right papers and sent to New York where she was set up with an organization who helped girls in trouble. They put her up in a girls' hostel, and got her a job with a family, where she went to work as a day-time au pair. Her duties were light house cleaning, and taking care of a six-month-old baby. She could barely take care of herself, let alone a baby.

The young couple she worked for were nice. The father didn't *seem to expect sex, and the mother was pleasant. They were both at work all day.*

Anya was dizzy with everything that had happened. One moment she was a sex slave in one of the most decadent cities in the world. Then within months she was looking after a baby in New York – a dazzling fast-paced city that terrified her.

The girls' hostel she was staying at was clean and comfortable. The other girls in residence were a mixed group. Anya kept to herself, she went to work every morning at eight, returning to the hostel at five. After dinner every night she sat in the Recreation Room staring at the TV until it was time for bed. American TV was quite a revelation, so many pretty faces, so many nice clean houses filled with happy families. And even if they weren't happy, even if they were fighting and screaming at each other, they always ended up happy. Life on TV was very satisfying.

One of the other residents – Ella, a black girl with a mass of frizzed hair, large breasts and plenty of attitude – kept on attempting to start a conversation. Ella reminded Anya of the girls at Madam Olga's, she had so many questions.

"Where you comin' from?"

"Talk to me, girl."

"Your family kick you out?"

"Ever done drugs?"

"We need t' get our asses outta this fuckin' prison."

Ella never shut up.

"You're so fuckin' quiet," she said to Anya one day. "I can't get nothin' outta you."

Anya continued staring at the TV. It was her drug. She was addicted.

"How much they payin' you at your job?" Ella asked, sitting down beside her. "'Cause where I work the cheap bastards are payin' me shit to babysit two screaming brats. An' ya gotta know – this place is a racket. They take us girls in who got themselves in trouble, then they send us out t' work as cheap fuckin' labor. An' didja know that

when we hit eighteen they're gonna throw us out on our asses? Didja know that?"

Anya shook her head. She didn't know that.

"Mind you," Ella ruminated, "I was livin' on the fuckin' street before some fuckin' do-gooder dropped me off here. So mebbe I ain't got too much to complain 'bout. Least I got a damn bed t' sleep in."

Anya continued to stare at the TV. A homely-looking man with a wide plastic smile was giving away cars and fridges and all kinds of luxury goods. Girls in gold evening gowns fluttered around him like exotic birds, while plainer-dressed plump women jumped up and down, screaming with delight as they won things. Anya was fascinated.

"How'd you get here?" Ella wanted to know. "Didja run away from home same as me? I had a step-dad come bargin' inta my room every night t' get him some juicy pussy. That happen t' you?"

Anya thought of the family who'd taken her in when she was eleven; the father of the house who'd sexually molested her night after night while his wife tried to pretend it wasn't happening. Then she recalled the night the soldiers had invaded the house and killed every one of them – except her. Somehow she'd been spared. For what? More horrors to come.

"Well?" Ella demanded. "What's your fuckin' story?"

Anya shrugged. She'd learned not to say too much, it was safer that way.

"You're a quiet one," Ella muttered. "Ain't ya got nothin' t' say?"

"Yes," Anya said at last, pointing at the TV. "How can I get on a show like that? I would like to win things too."

Ella shrieked with laughter. "Wouldn't we all like t' get ourselves soma that shit. But we ain't gonna get nothin' stayin' here."

"Then what should we do?" Anya asked, her face quite serious.

Ella shrugged. "I dunno. You got any skills?"

"Skills?"

"Somethin' you're way good at."

"Yes," Anya said, nodding wisely for one so young. "Sex. I am very good at sex."

Chapter Twenty-Six

Cherry and Reno – the two new trainers – were major assets. Not only did each of them come with their own client lists, they were gung-ho to help out before the big opening, and there was plenty to do. Cole had fired their contractor and hired Carlos's contact, Freddy Cruise, a fast-talking tough guy originally from the Bronx. Freddy – who was quite a character with his shock of dyed black hair and a cheap cigar stuck permanently in his mouth – employed a team of workers who never quit. They were there to get the work done and there was no slacking off. It was cash all round, heavy metal blasting from a CD player all day, but things were suddenly moving at a rapid pace.

Cameron was delighted. Everyone was working toward the big opening night and excitement was building. They'd hired a P.R. woman to handle the opening, Dee Dee Goldenberg – another transported New Yorker. Dee Dee was almost like a female version of Freddy – fast-talking, acerbic, and hot to get things done as soon as possible.

Dee Dee was into lists and pinning celebrities down – which as anyone who worked in P.R. in Hollywood knew – was virtually impossible. Celebrities did not care to commit. Sometimes they'd accept an invitation and not show; sometimes they wouldn't accept and just turn up; mostly they expected to get paid.

Celebrities were mercurial creatures who danced to their own tune, which, Dee Dee informed anyone who'd listen, was a big fat pain in the butt. "It's the freakin' chicken without an egg deal," she complained. "To get the TV shows to turn out you gotta have firm acceptances."

"Don Verona is definitely coming," Cameron informed her.

"Is he bringin' Mary Ellen Evans?" Dee Dee wanted to know. "'Cause they're all over the tabloids, which means that'll get us major coverage."

"I'll make certain he does," Cameron promised, although she wasn't too sure how she was going to do that since Don was constantly telling her that he and Mary Ellen were not an item.

Busy as she was, she couldn't help wondering why Ryan hadn't called. It was disappointing, especially as she'd canceled a regular client to make room for him, and then he'd failed to follow up.

That'll teach you to get the hots for a married man.

Shut up! I don't care!

Oh yes you do.

Oh no I don't.

Trying to put Ryan out of her mind was not as simple as she'd hoped. Their time together – brief as it was – lingered in her head. Truth was, she couldn't stop thinking about him. And she wanted to stop, she was desperate to stop. Nothing was going to happen between them, so therefore she *had* to stop.

Obsessing over a man – especially a married man – was distracting and foolish and led nowhere.

Obsessing over *Paradise* was what she should be doing.

Cole sensed that something was up. "You met someone, didn't you?" he probed. "Dorian's got it right, you're finally doin' the bump an' grind with some lucky dude."

"If I was – which I'm not – you and Dorian would be the last to know."

"How come that when it's about sex, you get all uptight an'

paranoid?" Cole said, throwing her a penetrating look. "You *sure* you're playin' on the right team? 'Cause no problem if you're not . . ."

"Thanks, Cole. I'm sure. And since you're so interested in my sex life, I think I should put you out of your misery and tell you that for the last year I've been seeing a twenty-year-old guy who makes Justin Timberlake look like a girl!"

There. It was out. And so what? Now the speculation about which team she was playing on could finally stop.

"Shit!" Cole exclaimed. "A secret lover. That's hot."

"Thank you, Paris," Cameron said, tongue-in-cheek.

"When do we get to meet this hunk?"

"You don't. But trust me – he exists. Are you satisfied?"

"I am. How about you?"

"Extremely, thank you very much."

After a week or so had passed, she'd casually brought Ryan's name up to Don. "What's going on with your friend?" she'd asked.

"I thought I told you," he'd said impatiently. "Mary Ellen was a one-nighter. She's not my type."

"You have a type?"

"Yes," he said, giving her a very direct look. "You."

Ignoring his come-on she'd tried again. "I meant your friend, Ryan. The one with the shaky marriage."

"Did I say his marriage was shaky?"

"You intimated as much."

"Yeah, Ryan," Don had said, all casual. "He needs a new set of balls if he's ever gonna leave Mandy."

And that was that. She couldn't seem too interested or Don would catch on, he wasn't exactly dumb.

Cole was busy calling in favors from his phone list of big-shot, powerful ex-lovers. The gay Mafia of Hollywood responded favorably. Cole was not an easy one to forget.

Dorian consulted his BlackBerry full of mid-level TV

actors, half of them in the closet. He invited every one of them.

Cherry, it turned out, was personal trainer to pop tart Birdy Marvel. If Birdy came to the opening it would be a huge coup, for everywhere Birdy went, cameras followed.

If both Birdy Marvel and Mary Ellen Evans showed, they were set for amazing coverage.

Reno had his own group of young Hollywood which included Max Santangelo – the very pretty, very wild daughter of Vegas titan Lucky Santangelo – and Max's two best friends, Cookie – the teenage daughter of soul icon, Gerald M. – and Harry, the gay son of a TV network president.

Cameron was still nervous about the opening. She couldn't make up her mind whether to wear work-out clothes, or get all dressed up. Not that she had anything to get dressed up in – but Cherry informed her she had a stylist friend who, in exchange for an invite to the party, would set her up.

It was tempting. Both Cole and Dorian encouraged her. "You're better-looking than any of 'em," Dorian said. "You gotta work it!"

"Yes," Cole said, joining in. "Wear something that shows off that body, 'cause that's what we're sellin'."

Cherry's stylist friend picked out an amazing Dolce & Gabanna creation. A white column of a dress with a front slit from here to Cuba.

She tried it on and fell in love.

"You look fantastic!" Dorian exclaimed. "A pair of sky-high Manolos an' you're all set."

"Won't it seem as if I'm trying too hard?" she worried.

"Not at all," Cole assured her. "You're the face of *Paradise*. *And* the body. We want everyone to notice you."

Hmm . . . she wasn't sure that she was comfortable being the center of attention.

But she'd go for it. She had nothing to lose and everything to gain.

Chapter Twenty-Seven

Ryan was waiting for the right opportunity before broaching the subject of divorce. Since Mandy was on her best behavior he found it difficult to start the conversation. It didn't help that she was also upset about her father's new bride – so was he for that matter, but for different reasons. Then another family drama erupted. His sister, Evie, called in the middle of the night sobbing and crying out for help.

"You've got to come get us," Evie implored, sounding desperate. "Please hurry. Marty went crazy again. I know he's going to hurt us."

Us? Were his nephews in danger? Christ! He read about it all the time. Some husband goes berserk and blows his entire family away.

After assuring Evie he'd get there as soon as possible, Ryan jumped out of bed and hurriedly dressed. Then, since this was an emergency and he might need help, he decided to wake Mandy, who had not stirred. He stared at his sleeping wife. Her eyes were hidden beneath a black velvet sleep mask, her ears were filled with foam noise blockers because she claimed he snored – which he could swear he didn't – and she did not look as if she was going to wake up any time soon. He nudged her all the same, and she surfaced in a sleeping-pill stupor. "What?" she mumbled bad-temperedly, throwing her arms in the air. "Is there an earthquake? Wass goin' on?"

"Nothing," he said shortly. "Go back to sleep."

What was he thinking? She'd be a burden not an asset.

Cameron Paradise. Where are you when I need you?

He made it to his car and took off like a rocket.

As soon as he hit Sunset his mind began racing. Should he have taken his gun out of the lock box in the safe? Maybe called the cops? He had plenty of friends who worked in law enforcement, perhaps they could help.

Jesus! What the *fuck* was he supposed to do?

Cutting through numerous red lights, he made it to Evie's house as quickly as possible.

Evie met him at the front door, red-eyed and weepy.

"What happened?" he demanded. "Where the hell is the sonofabitch?"

"He got drunk again," she said in a low whisper. "Then he started screaming about you and your rich friends, and why didn't you give us money. Coming to your house the other night must have set him off."

"Great!" Ryan said, walking into the house with Evie close behind him.

"I told him you're always offering me money and that I won't take it. That's when he got out of control and started wrecking things."

"Did he hit you or the kids?"

"No. He stormed out, but he'll be back."

"I'm sure he will," Ryan said grimly.

"I don't feel safe here anymore," Evie said, still tearful. "We can't be here when he gets back."

"Right," Ryan said, thinking fast. "Where are the boys?"

"In their room. They're frightened, they don't know what's going on."

"Okay, okay," he said. "I want you to run upstairs and pack

an overnight bag for all of you – you're coming with me. We'll sort out what to do in the morning."

"Thank you, Ryan," Evie said softly. "I knew I could depend on you."

"Go get packed," he said gruffly.

He walked into the living room, observing that once more Marty had done an excellent job of destroying whatever he could. The couch was overturned, the TV smashed, photos strewn across the floor, broken glass from the frames they were in scattered everywhere.

Ryan made a decision and he was sticking with it. He was bringing them home with him. Mandy would throw one of her childish fits, but it was his house too, and if he wanted to have members of his family stay there for a few days until he got everything sorted – then so be it.

The one big drawback was that he'd have to put the divorce conversation on hold yet again. But he'd been married to Mandy for seven years, another few weeks wouldn't make that much difference. The important thing was to have Evie and the kids settled somewhere safe.

The three boys came downstairs rubbing their eyes and looking confused. Benji, the youngest, was crying.

Ryan gave them each a big hug and told them everything was going to be okay. He loved his nephews, and if Marty so much as touched them . . .

"Let's go, boys," he said, leading them outside and bundling them into the back seat of his car. "We're taking off on an adventure."

*   *   *

Lucy Lyons Standard was sitting on a bean bag in Marlon's room at the beach, feeling like she was back in college. She was reading the latest pages of Marlon's screenplay based on her brilliant idea, and she had to admit that to her delight they were pretty good. Just as she was about to tell Marlon this, he hovered in front of her, shot her a sly look, and said, "I rented one of your movies."

"You did?" she said, glancing up.

"*Blue Sapphire*," he said, a satisfied smirk crossing his boyish face. "Some trip!"

Lucy frowned. Why were men so obsessed with *Blue Sapphire*? Yes, she'd stripped off in the film and twirled around a slippery pole a few times, but why this fascination? She'd made a dozen other movies where she'd shown what an accomplished actress she was, yet all men ever wanted to talk about was *Blue Sapphire*. Personally she would prefer to forget the entire experience, especially when she recalled the producer of the movie, Hamilton J. Heckerling, leching after her as if she were a bitch in heat. *That* was a story she'd never shared with Mandy. Hamilton had appeared on the set every single day, his beady eyes taking in every inch of her exposed body. "We gotta make a sequel," he'd said to her one memorable afternoon. "You'll do a Sharon – flash your snatch."

"I'll do no such thing," she'd replied, quite insulted.

"Jesus Christ!" he'd responded, used to everyone agreeing with him. "What's wrong with you girls today? Don't you wanna see your career sky-rocket?"

Fortunately it was around that time that she'd started getting together with Phil, so Hamilton – who had Phil working on two other projects – backed off, wise enough not to upset his Oscar-winning screenwriter. They had history and a future.

"*Blue Sapphire* is not my best work," she said, slightly irritated that Marlon would even bring it up.

"It's like – wow!" Marlon said enthusiastically. "Hadda keep on pausing the DVD t' make sure I didn't miss anything!"

"Spoken like a true teenager," she murmured, hardly impressed.

"I'm not a teenager," he said, scowling like a little kid. "I'm gonna be twenty any moment."

219

Then act like it, she wanted to say. But she didn't. Since he was doing such an excellent job on the script it wouldn't be smart to put him down.

Placing the script on the floor, she stood up and stretched. Sitting on a bean bag was killing her back, it wasn't as if she was sixteen. Why couldn't he get a couch like normal people?

Without warning Marlon came at her like a raging bull, slamming his lips down on hers while going for a quick feel of her breasts.

"Hey!" she objected, pushing him away. "What *do* you think you're doing?"

He stood there, nonplussed in his tight jeans with a visible hard-on.

"Uh . . . sorry," he mumbled, running a hand through his bleached-by-the-sun hair. "I thought—"

"Exactly *what* did you think?" she asked, putting on a cross face, but secretly quite flattered. After all, she was old enough to be his . . . hmm . . . older sister. "Surely you have a girlfriend?" she said, recovering her composure.

"I got a few," he muttered. "Thing is – they're not like you. You're . . ."

"Yes?"

"You're like the real deal."

She liked that. The real deal. This boy obviously appreciated a mature woman, unlike Phil, who took her totally for granted.

But Phil was her husband, and didn't all husbands take their wives for granted? Which was one of the reasons she was trying to resurrect her career. Perhaps if she reclaimed her movie-star status, *that* would get the great Phil Standard's attention.

"Marlon," she said, the smooth voice of adult reason, "I'm a married woman. I have kids who could be your . . . uh . . . siblings. And in case you haven't noticed, I'm a tad older than you."

"Yeah, but you're way hot," he said lustfully. "I don't give a crap if you're married and old."

Old!! Had he actually called her old?

Briskly she strode toward the door. "I'm leaving," she said coldly. "I'll be back tomorrow at the same time. And perhaps you should think about being more professional." A long beat. "Oh yes, and Marlon, the first twenty pages need a lot of work."

And with those words she made a dignified exit.

Old indeed! She was a movie star. She'd always be a movie star. And no would-be screenwriter teenage boy was getting away with calling her old.

*   *   *

Sometimes Mandy slept late, other times her sleeping pills wore off too early and she was up with the dawn. The thing she hated more than anything was being physically jolted awake, and that's exactly what Ryan did to her on Tuesday morning. She vaguely remembered that he'd made an attempt to wake her earlier, that hadn't worked, now he was at it again, roughly shaking her shoulder until she pulled off her sleep mask and reluctantly opened her eyes. "What?" she mumbled, leaving behind a delightful dream where Patrick Dempsey – or was it Don Verona – had been pursuing her across the sandy beaches of Mystique.

"I need to tell you something," he said, sitting on the edge of the bed.

"Can't it wait?" she said, sensing danger.

"No, it can't."

"Then what?" she said, struggling to sit up.

"Evie and the boys are here."

"Where?"

"Here, Mandy, in our house."

She tried to recall whether – in a moment of weakness, while trying to be especially nice to Ryan – she'd invited them over. But no such recollection came to mind.

"Why, Ryan?" she asked petulantly. "Why are they here?"

"Because they're staying with us for a few days," he said calmly.

This information made her sit up in a hurry. "Excuse me?" she said, not quite sure she'd heard correctly.

"It's an emergency," Ryan explained. "Marty's finally lost it, so I had to go get Evie and the kids in the middle of the night."

"And you brought them here?" she said incredulously. "Here, to my house."

"*Our* house," he corrected.

That's what *he* thought. When Hamilton had supposedly wedding-gifted them the house, he'd left the title in the name of one of his companies – just in case. *It's* my *house*, Mandy thought. *Hamilton is no fool.*

Her mind was running in different directions. Lately she'd been trying hard with Ryan, ever since she'd sensed him pulling away. She'd organized the dinner with his family; she hadn't sulked when he'd gotten drunk and stayed out all night; she'd offered him sex; in fact, she'd been behaving like the perfect wife.

Was this how he repaid her? By dumping Evie and the kids on their doorstep? Damn! This was not acceptable.

"I'm a little confused," she said, reaching for her robe.

"Don't be," he said sharply. "It's a done deal, and I'd appreciate it if you'd try to be nice to them."

She could tell that her husband was still edgy; better tread carefully and keep up the perfect wife act.

"I'm always nice," she said, deciding to make the most of a sticky situation. "Where is everybody?"

This was not the reaction he'd expected. Who was this

amiable woman who'd taken over Mandy's body? It certainly wasn't the Mandy he knew and didn't love.

"They're downstairs," he said slowly. "Consuela is making them breakfast."

"Then let's go join them," Mandy said cheerfully, slipping her feet into cozy cashmere slippers. "I haven't seen the boys in ages."

Chapter Twenty-Eight

Twenty-four hours before kick-off and Freddy – the eccentric contractor and his team – had done a phenomenal job of finishing everything. It had been costly, but their new mystery investor didn't seem to care; the money was flowing.

In her mind Cameron had pinned the investor down to Natalie's current boyfriend – a successful real-estate developer with money to burn. This was all fine as long as the affair lasted, but what if they broke up? Cameron had high hopes that *Paradise* would be making plenty of money by that time, and they could pay off their investors and be done with outside interference.

She was feeling quite optimistic and full of excess energy when she turned up for her regular seven a.m. work-out with Don.

"Hey, beautiful," he said, greeting her at the door of his house.

"You're all dressed," she observed, thinking that she usually saw him only in his work-out clothes. "I certainly hope this doesn't mean we're not working out today."

"Right on, Miz Paradise," he said, stepping outside and closing the door behind him. "It means I am taking you for breakfast to celebrate the opening of your establishment tomorrow night."

"You make it sound like a brothel," she joked, wondering what he was up to.

"Now *that's* a quaint old-fashioned word," he said, mildly teasing her. "I didn't think brothels still existed, what with the Internet and all."

"Don't look at me," she said with a casual shrug. "I know nothing about such things."

"And so she plays innocent," he said, starting to smile.

Was Don Verona charming himself into her good graces? Perhaps.

Recently she'd made time to watch his evening show. He came across as slightly cynical, witty and original. His interviewing skills were playful but right on point. She'd enjoyed seeing the professional side of him; now she could understand why his show was so popular.

So . . . Don Verona was smart, great-looking, and he always made her laugh. And since she'd decided to give up Marlon, and it was quite obvious that Ryan – damn him – was never going to call, what would be so wrong about going out with Don?

Why?

Why not?

Idly she wondered what it would be like to date a man like Don. He was into the chase, she knew that. Twice divorced – everyone knew that.

But . . . he was a player, and that was not such a good thing.

Ha! Better than being with a married man.

Like I have a choice. Ryan hasn't called. Remember?

"Okay, so where are you taking me for breakfast?" she asked, figuring she wouldn't mind a break.

"You mean you're not putting up a fight?" he said, raising a quizzical eyebrow.

"Now why would I do that?" she answered lightly.

"'Cause you always do."

"You'd better tell me where we're going before I change my mind."

"Malibu."

"I don't have time for Malibu."

"Yes, you do – that's if you want me to appear at *Paradise* tomorrow night."

"I smell blackmail," she said accusingly. "You're always doing that to me."

"True," he said, unabashed. "Seems to be the only way I can get through to you."

"You're bringing Mary Ellen to the opening, right?"

"Do I have to?" he groaned.

"You most certainly do."

"Then I definitely need you to come to Malibu. If I give a little, you've gotta learn to do the same."

"Well . . . if you insist," she said, giving in far too easily. "But I have to be back by ten."

"Deal, Cinderella," he said, sensing victory.

"Promise?"

"Have I ever let you down?"

"You mean apart from never being ready in the morning when I get here, and forcing me to make the coffee?"

He laughed.

She had to admit he had a great laugh.

"What are you thinking?" he said, as he led her over to his Ferrari parked in the driveway.

"That's for me to know and you to guess," she answered succinctly.

"Jesus, Cameron," he said, his expression perplexed. "Do you ever come out with a straight answer?"

"Isn't – *what are you thinking* – a very seventh-grade question?"

"My bad," he agreed. "I'm a talk-show host, guess I need my writers around me telling me what to say."

She got into the passenger seat of his Ferrari. *This is crazy*, she thought. *I shouldn't be doing this.*

Why not? I'm my own boss, I'm allowed to take time off. Natalie and Cole have taken over arrangements for the party, so what's wrong with stealing a break?

'Cause you're starting to weaken.

No. I am not.

Don was a speed demon, darting his Ferrari in and out of traffic as if it were a toy and they were zooming around on one of those fun-fair car tracks. He roared down Sunset like he was competing in the Indie 500, hit the Pacific Coast Highway and never once slowed down.

"You're crazy!" she gasped, kind of getting off on the speed since she wasn't exactly a slow driver herself.

"Never said I wasn't."

"Do you always drive like a maniac?"

"Only when my date's in a hurry."

"I'm not your date," she corrected. "I'm your trainer."

"Point taken," he said, finally making another sharp turn before racing down Old Malibu Road.

"There's a restaurant here?" she asked, surprised.

"Yup. My restaurant."

"*Your* restaurant?"

"S'right," he said smoothly. "I make the best pancakes this side of Mississippi, an' bacon that'll bring tears to your eyes."

"Really?" she said suspiciously.

"You got it," he said, pulling up outside a rustic beach house. He jumped out the car, opened the passenger door and helped her out. "This is my escape hatch," he explained. "Nobody knows about it except me and my business manager."

"Then why tell me?"

"'Cause you're kinda special. And I want you to know you can use it any time. All you have to do is call, tell me when, and it's yours."

"I might take you up on that."

"I wish you would."

"Can I bring my dogs? They love the beach."

"Dogs are welcome."

The house was so unlike his ultra-modern masterpiece in town. No TVs, no computers. It was a comfortable one-bedroom beach house with shabby chic decor and a real cozy feel. A well-worn dog bed took front position in the living room, next to an all-wood kitchen that appeared to be very cook-friendly.

Don led her through the house to a small deck overlooking the ocean.

"You're sitting out here staring at the waves while I make breakfast," he informed her, settling her on a comfy lounge chair. "Drift off, you've been working too hard."

He was right, she had been working hard. Ever since she'd left Hawaii she hadn't actually stopped. She'd worked her butt off, saved money, and now *Paradise* was about to open and it was all because of her vision.

She closed her eyes for a moment, savoring the smell of the sea and the light breeze ruffling her hair. The sound of the waves was mesmerizing. How nice it was to relax for once, forget about work, forget about everything.

She must've fallen asleep, for the next thing she knew, Don was serving her his famous pancakes and bacon, along with a glass of freshly squeezed orange juice. He'd set everything on a wicker table, then he pulled up a chair and sat opposite her.

"Please tell me you didn't slip me the date rape drug?" she sighed, pushing a hand through her hair.

"I would've," he dead-panned. "Only we're not on a date. Remember?"

"Oh, that's *right*."

"However . . ."

"It's too late now," she said, picking up a strip of bacon with her fingers and nibbling on it.

"Don't you think it's about time you went out with me?" he said, serious for once.

"No," she answered on automatic pilot.

"Why no?"

"Why yes?"

"Here she goes again with the slippery answers," he said, rolling his eyes.

"My answers are not slippery. I told you upfront I do not believe in mixing business and pleasure."

"In that case I'll hire myself another trainer. Will that solve your problem?"

"Fine with me," she said casually, knowing he didn't mean it.

"You wouldn't miss me?"

"God!" she gasped. "You're so persistent."

"I like you. Is that a crime?"

"You *do* need writers," she joked. "That's a *really* old line."

"Screw you," he said, a grin spreading across his face as he contemplated how refreshing it was to spend time with a woman who knew how to banter.

"What about Mary Ellen?"

"So I say screw you – and you immediately bring up Mary Ellen?"

"C'mon, Don. You must admit that she's very sweet, and she obviously adores you."

"I made a mistake, I shouldn't have gone there."

"Well you did, so now you've got to treat her nicely. The poor girl's been through tabloid hell, she doesn't need you dumping her on top of everything else."

"You sound like my mom."

"You have a mother?"

"Man! You're something else," he said, shaking his head.

"I'll take that as a compliment."

"Listen to me," he said seriously. "Here's the deal. I am not responsible for Mary Ellen. She's a big girl who makes her own choices. I slept with her once. Nobody forced her."

"Ah yes, but she thinks you like her," Cameron said, feeling genuinely sorry for the girl.

"What *are* you – a mindreader?" he said, perplexed. "You don't even know her."

"As a matter of fact, I do."

"Oh really?"

"Yes. After the three of us worked out that day, she called me for a private session. I went to her house, and all she could talk about was you."

He frowned. Mary Ellen had no right contacting Cameron without his knowledge. The thought of them exchanging information about him was not a welcome one.

"What did she say about me?" he couldn't resist asking.

"How much she likes you. That you're witty, smart, oh yes, and that you're a lousy lover."

"Hey –" he said, starting to grin. "If there's one thing I've never been accused of –"

"Just f-ing with you, Don," she teased.

"I should hope so," he said, getting up.

"Hmm . . ." she said, pausing for a moment. "Did I get too close to your ego?"

"You can get close to any part of me you want," he said, moving around the table.

"According to Mary Ellen—"

Before she could finish he bent down and kissed her, taking both of them by surprise.

"What was *that* about?" she asked breathlessly.

"Do not act all shook up and innocent. You know how I feel about you, and it's time we did something about it."

"Yes?"

"Most *definitely* yes."

"Okay," she murmured, surprising herself. "You bring Mary Ellen to the *Paradise* opening, and I'll go out with you."

"Finally!"

"It wouldn't be fun if I'd said yes immediately, would it?" she said, smiling at him.

He had to admit she was right. And now he had something to look forward to.

ANYA

*E*lla was a resourceful girl. Once she discovered what Anya claimed to be good at – and that was quite a shock – she made it her business to try and make a connection. Ella was street smart; she might be only seventeen – the same age as Anya – but she'd been around. And it did not escape her notice that Anya was better-looking than most. "I know this dude who says if we do sex stuff together," she informed Anya, "he can get guys t' pay us."

"I am not interested," Anya said, her voice flat and devoid of any emotion.

"Why not?" Ella demanded. "We can make us some money an' get our butts outta this creephole."

It was the same old story – sex, sex, sex – but Anya was not listening. She was in America now, and things were different. Circumstances had turned her into a whore, but she'd decided that if it was her destiny to stay a whore, then she'd become a whore who made a lot of money like the girls on Sex and the City. Television had taught her plenty. She'd watched Sex and the City many times and noted that the girls on the show slept with different men all the time. And not only did they sleep with them, they were treated with respect and handsomely rewarded. None of them appeared to have serious jobs, yet the money seemed to flow. They all lived in luxury apartments, they all wore beautiful

232

clothes. And the shoes . . . oh, how Anya yearned to own a pair of shoes like that.

She was deeply impressed. "I want to be like those girls on TV," she informed Ella.

Ella laughed in her face and said, "Doncha get it? Those bitches are actresses. Everythin' on TV's a big fat dumb-ass shitty fairy story."

"I don't care," Anya said, her expression stubborn. "It is possible. I am in America now. Anything is possible."

"No it ain't," Ella argued. "You gotta put out or you don't get nothin' in this crappy world."

Anya did not believe her. She had plans and Ella did not factor into them.

Chapter Twenty-Nine

Between Natalie de Barge and Dee Dee Goldenberg, the two of them had made sure that *Paradise* was *the* place to be seen on opening night. Dee Dee had received instructions to pull out all the stops, so that's exactly what she'd done. Outside the building a neon sign flashed *Paradise*, while a red carpet snaked its way from the valet service to the entrance, and silver ropes held back a healthy gathering of photographers and TV crews. Two of Dee Dee's assistants manned the entrance, each armed with a guest list. Inside, *Spago* was catering. Champagne and special drinks christened *The Paradise* abounded. The drinks were carried aloft on trays held by waiters clad in tight black pants and nothing else. Dorian had personally conducted the ab inspection to make certain that every one of their waiters for the night were up to par.

Cameron felt like a princess as she made her entrance escorted by Cole on one side and Dorian on the other.

Dee Dee immediately instructed the photographers to get busy, even though they didn't know who Cameron was. Dee Dee soon told them, embellishing somewhat. "She's Cameron Paradise, the owner of *Paradise*," Dee Dee announced. "Remember the name, she's soon getting her own reality show on Bravo, and in September she'll be guesting on *Two and a Half Men*, playing herself as Charlie Sheen's love interest."

Cameron opened her mouth to object, but Dee Dee shot her a look that screamed – "*Don't you dare!*"

The photographers went to town. She might not be famous – yet, but she was certainly beautiful enough. Posing for the cameras she felt quite ridiculous. It was a relief when Natalie turned up with Nicollette Sheridan and Michael Bolton, because the cameras immediately swiveled away from her. Grasping the opportunity, she rushed inside. The spotlight was not for her.

"Two and a half men?" Dorian inquired, raising an arch eyebrow.

"Speak to Dee Dee," she said, giggling. "It's her vivid imagination, not mine."

"I *looove* people with out-of-control imaginations," Dorian sighed, his mane of blond hair freshly highlighted for the occasion. "Do you think she could make up a story about me and Josh Duhamel getting it on in Vegas?"

"Come on you two, stay focused," Cole said, getting agitated. "This is our big night, we gotta be on top of our game."

"You're right," Cameron agreed. "And Cole – perhaps you can tell me exactly how we're paying for all this? It's way over what we budgeted for."

"Natalie's silent investor requested the best," Cole said, resplendent in a black Armani suit – purchased for him by one of his many admirers. "The dude's payin', so who gives a fast one?"

"I don't understand," Cameron said, perplexed.

"What's to understand?" Cole responded. "It's his money."

"Yes, but it's *our* business," she pointed out. "How can we work with someone who thinks they can come in at the last moment and call the shots?"

"This is a party to get us on the circuit," Cole explained. "Tonight is gonna pay off big time, you'll see. Let's go with it, babe. Natalie's cool, we should be too."

"I hope you're right," she said, worried about all the extra money being spent.

"I'm always right," Cole boasted, taking off to greet a major Hollywood mogul who was waving at him across the room.

Lynda darted over, all excited. "Oh, mama! You look hot!" she exclaimed. "Lookit *you* in a dress all slit up an' sexy. It suits you so fine."

"Make the most of it," Cameron said dryly. "It'll be a long time before I wear another one."

"Why's that, sister? *Mucho* sexy suits you."

"I'm not going for sexy," Cameron said, perplexed. "I'm going for fit and healthy."

"Yeah, yeah," Lynda said, her abundant curves bursting out of a short scarlet wrap dress and very high strappy gold sandals. "Didja see Carlos around?"

"Is he here?"

"Of *course* he's here," Lynda said, plucking a smoked salmon canapé from a passing waiter. "I gotta keep a sharp eye on that bad boy, 'cause women – they chase after him like crazy. You got no damn clue what I gotta go through shooing off the crazy bitches who get too close. He's got that Antonio Banderas vibe goin' on."

"Sure," Cameron said, thinking that Carlos resembled Antonio Banderas like Pamela Anderson resembled Nicole Kidman!

She wondered when Don was going to show. She'd told him a dozen times he had to come with Mary Ellen, now she was kind of regretting that she'd insisted. Ever since their kiss at the beach she was definitely regarding him with new eyes. Should she go out with him? Would it be a mistake? Was he too much of a player?

What the hell – why not?

Natalie was standing at the temporary bar set up in front of a row of gleaming new treadmills. She was holding court with a group of friends. Mr Moneybags, her real-estate boyfriend, was by her side.

Cameron contemplated going over and saying something to him, then she remembered he wished to stay anonymous.

So be it.

Where are you, Don? she thought. *Don't let me down. I need you to show your face here tonight.*

A few minutes later, Katie arrived. She'd flown in from San Francisco especially for the opening.

"Wow!" Katie said excitedly as they exchanged hugs. "I'm so glad I made it in time. My plane was late, I grabbed a cab and came straight here."

"Where's Jinx?" Cameron asked, delighted to see her best friend.

"He finally scored a record deal," Katie said, beaming. "He's in the studio, sends big kisses."

"That's such great news! Give him my love and congrats."

"Ah, but I have even *more* exciting news," Katie burbled. "We finally got engaged last night!"

"You did?"

"We certainly did," Katie said, flashing a modest diamond ring.

"Fantastic!" Cameron said, throwing her arms around Katie. "I'm so happy for both of you, I know it's what you wanted."

"We're getting married on the day Jinx gets his first gold record," Katie said confidently.

You might have a long wait, Cameron thought, before slapping herself metaphorically on the wrist for being mean-spirited. Jinx was talented, but he wasn't John Mayer or even Adam Levine of Maroon 5.

She felt her cell vibrating in her purse and quickly pulled it out.

"Running late," announced Don. "The show ran over, technical problems. Don't worry, I'll be there."

"With—"

"Yeah, yeah," he said resignedly. "I'm picking her up as soon as I leave the studio. Reluctantly, I might add."

Cameron laughed softly.

"You having fun without me?" he asked.

"I'm managing."

"Don't forget our bargain. Tomorrow night is date night."

"You make me feel like I'm back in high school."

"Wait until I move in for second base," he said with a knowing laugh. "That's when you'll *really* feel it!"

"Is that a promise?"

"You want it to be?"

"Concentrate on your date tonight," she reminded him. "Remember to smile nice for the photographers."

"Jeez, you're a tough one," he grumbled.

"Hurry up. Your name's on the list and the press are getting impatient."

"Soon," he promised.

She snapped her phone shut, slid it back in her purse and looked around. The place was buzzing. Was *Paradise* about to become L.A.'s hot new fitness center? If only people signed up to join, they'd have it made. Cole was already talking about expanding – putting in a tanning booth and a beauty spa. "Let's get the gym off the ground first," she'd said cautiously. "Then we can think about adding other elements."

Lynda approached balancing a drink, a canapé and her spangly purse. "Are we open for business tomorrow?" she wanted to know.

"The day after," Cameron said, wondering if anyone ever listened to her. She'd told them all ten times that the day after the party was clean-up day, but that they should all come in anyway to field calls and get organized.

"Carlos has a cousin who makes T-shirts," Lynda said, popping the canapé between her glossy lips. "He wants to know if you'll place an order."

"Carlos has more cousins than the Queen of England," Cameron remarked.

"He'll print *Paradise* on the front," Lynda promised. "They'll be so cute, an' we can sell 'em at the front desk."

"*No*, Lynda, maybe later."

"Okay, okay," Lynda said, all put out. "No need to snap at me."

"Who's snapping? I'm trying to concentrate on one thing at a time. Our focus right now is signing members, not selling T-shirts. Membership is what guarantees a steady income."

"Oh . . . my . . . *God*!" Lynda exclaimed. "Take a peek at who's walkin' through the door. It's Mister Potty-mouth himself."

"And that would be?"

"Mr Lordy el creepo."

"Who put *him* on the list?"

"Certainly not me," Lynda said, indignant that Cameron would even think such a thing.

"I don't even train him anymore," Cameron said. "So what the hell is he doing here?"

"Maybe Cole sent him an invite."

"I hardly think so."

"Shall I get Carlos to throw him out?"

"No, leave it. Hopefully he'll blend in."

"That'll be the day," Lynda said, rolling her expressive brown eyes. "Watch out, he's comin' this way."

And so he was. Everyone's un-favorite client.

Cameron searched for an exit strategy, couldn't spot an escape route, and faced him head on.

"Cameron, Cameron, Cameron," Mr Lord said in an accusing voice, his black wig slightly askew, with caterpillar eyebrows almost forming a unibrow. "You left me high and dry."

Mr Lord always managed to include a cliché or two in his conversations.

"Actually," she said, determined not to get agitated, "I wasn't allowed to take any of my clients from *Bounce*. House rules."

"Screw house rules. You were my trainer, and one day you were there – all sexy and creamy in your little shorts – the ones where I could get a load of your juicy crack, and the next day your wet little pussy was history."

Realization dawned. She didn't need to get agitated, she had her own place, she wasn't desperately trying to save money, she could tell him to piss off.

It was an empowering sensation.

"Mr Lord," she said calmly, "your *saggy* old dried-up ass is history. So you can take your dirty mouth and sexist diatribes and get the hell out of here. *Paradise* does not welcome perverts."

And with those satisfying words, she turned and walked away.

Chapter Thirty

Two hours into the party, Don finally showed, making a grand entrance with Mary Ellen. Following right behind him were Mandy and Ryan Richards.

Noting his arrival from across the room, Cameron felt her heart-rate accelerate. Why hadn't Don told her he was bringing Mandy and Ryan? At least if she'd been forewarned she could have prepared herself.

Grabbing Cole away from his major mogul, she dragged him over to Don and the Richards, and made introductions all round.

"Hey – you've got yourself quite a turn-out," Don said, glancing around. "And I must say the place looks fantastic, better than I expected."

"Thanks," Cameron murmured, determined not to look at Ryan.

"You remember Mandy and Ryan, don't you?" Don said.

Oh yes, I remember them all right.

"Sure," she answered casually, still trying not to look. But then she couldn't resist, and she was shocked to realize that Ryan's eyes were as blue as ever, his long hair was tousled and slightly mussed, and the small indentation in the middle of his chin sent shivers up her spine.

She felt a stab of hopeless longing for this man she barely knew.

"Hi," Mary Ellen said, all bright and chirpy because this was her fourth date with Don, and the press were writing about them as if they were a couple. She hoped that her former husband was reading about them and choking over his coffee and his man-stealing movie-star girlfriend.

"Hey –" Cameron said, dragging her eyes away from the object of her desire.

"You'd better be nice to Mandy," Don said. "If she gets behind this place, you're all set."

"I think we're kind of set already," Cameron said, green eyes narrowing. "My schedule is fully booked, how about you, Cole?"

"All booked," he said, playing along.

"But you'll fit *me* in, won't you?" Mary Ellen bubbled. "I start back on my series soon, so I was thinking early morning."

"I can take care of you," Cole promised, putting his hand on her arm. "It'll be my pleasure."

"That would be so great," Mary Ellen said, hoping that attention from this extremely handsome African-American man would make Don jealous.

"Here's my card," Cole said, fishing in his pocket. "Call me, an' we'll set something up."

"Oh, I will," Mary Ellen said, shooting Don a quick look to make sure he noticed.

"Yoga's *my* thing," Mandy observed, clinging onto Ryan's arm. "I'm trying to get my husband into it, but he's so stubborn, aren't you, sweetie?"

Christ! Ryan hated it when she called him sweetie. And he hated it when she clung onto him. It wasn't like Mandy to play the little woman, and that's exactly what she was doing. Had she sensed that he was hopelessly attracted to Cameron?

"Yoga's very satisfying for some people," Cameron said

evenly, attempting to stay cool and businesslike. "I prefer a more vigorous work-out."

"Tell me about it," Don joked. "She works me so hard I can barely stagger to the studio."

"But it's worth it," Mary Ellen said, gazing at him all starry-eyed. "Your body's ripped."

"You can thank Cameron for that," Don said. "She's the best."

"If you're the best, then perhaps I should try you," Mandy said, completely ignoring the fact that Cameron had informed her she was fully booked.

"I'm sure we can set you up with one of our trainers, Mrs Richards," Cameron said.

"*Touché!*" Don laughed.

Mandy pulled on Ryan's arm, she didn't quite get what was going on. Don had insisted they come with him to the opening of this new sports club, and he'd brought Mary Ellen as his date. Now it turned out that the girl he'd been with at Ryan's birthday dinner was one of the partners at this place.

Hmm, Mandy thought. *Perhaps he's looking for a threesome, that would be about Don's style.*

"I need a drink," she announced. "Our house is full of screaming kids. I cannot tell you what a *relief* it is to get away from the annoying little brats."

What kids? Cameron thought. Ryan had told her that since Mandy couldn't have children of her own she didn't allow anyone else's in the house.

"My sister and her boys are staying with us," Ryan explained, as if reading her mind. "Three little guys under eight, I have to admit they're quite a handful, but they're certainly entertaining."

"I'm sure nobody's interested in our domestic situation," Mandy said, spotting the well-heralded arrival of Birdy Marvel. "Come on, Ryan, we should go over and say hello to Birdy."

"You go," he said. "I need to talk to Don about something."

Mandy was torn. Should she stay with her husband or should she go speak to the very famous pop tart whom she was after to appear at her next big charity event?

Pop tart won, and she was off, which left Mary Ellen, Don, Cole, Ryan and Cameron.

"How about I give everyone a tour?" Cole suggested. "We got a state-of-the-art steam room, and vibrating massage chairs in what we call our relaxing room. You're gonna love it."

"Yes, please," Mary Ellen said. "Coming, Don?"

"Later," he said, waving her off. "Ryan and I have to talk."

And then there were three.

"Satisfied?" Don said, looking straight at Cameron. "I had to drag myself through paparazzi hell getting in here tonight. You'll have all the coverage you want, and I'll be Mister Mary Ellen Evans for the next six weeks. Exactly what I don't need."

"I do appreciate it," she managed. Her throat was dry and she couldn't bring herself to look at Ryan again. This was ridiculous!

"Cameron forced me to bring Mary Ellen tonight for the P.R. explosion," Don explained to Ryan. "Can you imagine? This is what I have to go through to get a date with this woman! She's a hard taskmaster, but an amazing one." He grinned at Cameron and took her hand. "Did I tell you how spectacular you look tonight?"

"Thanks," she murmured, feeling the heat – and it wasn't coming from Don's hand.

"Isn't she something?" he said – once again to Ryan, who nodded silently.

Natalie de Barge drifted over, looking somewhat spectacular herself in a lime-green Versace creation with plenty of daring cleavage. "Don," she said, greeting him with a kiss on both cheeks, "may I steal you for a moment? Don't worry, kids, I'll bring him right back."

"You'd better!" Don joked. "Otherwise my best friend is likely to run off with my girl!"

"I thought Mary Ellen Evans was your girl?" Natalie said.

Don winked at her. "Long story."

Linking her arm through his, Natalie led him away.

And then there were two. Cameron and Ryan.

Cameron experienced an insane urge to bolt, but she didn't; instead she said – genuinely concerned, "Is your sister okay?"

"Right now she is," Ryan replied. "We had to get a Restraining Order against Marty."

"You did?"

"He went on another rampage, so I brought Evie and the boys over to my house. I'm not comfortable sending them home yet. Marty's too unpredictable."

"How is Mandy handling everyone being at your house?"

"I guess you could say she's trying."

"Uh huh."

An awkward silence.

Ryan broke it. "Uh . . . Cameron, I didn't call," he said hesitantly, stating the obvious.

"I noticed," she said, swallowing hard.

"I wanted to, but I figured my timing was off, what with you and Don, and then of course my home situation."

"You don't have to explain," she said, searching for a waiter so she could grab another drink, which she desperately needed.

"Yes I do," he said earnestly. "I said I'd call and I didn't. That's not like me; when I say I'll do something it usually happens."

"No worries," she said, spotting a waiter and frantically waving. "I get it. You're a married man, and I'm seeing your best friend. Besides, nothing happened between us, so no big deal, right?"

Wrong! screamed in her head. *Something did happen between us, a connection I've never experienced before.*

"Then it's true, you are seeing Don?" he said, willing her to say – *No, he's not for me. He just thinks he is.*

"Uh . . . yes."

"Well, that's nice," he said stiffly.

"It is," she said, lifting a glass of whatever from the waiter's tray. She didn't care what it was, she simply needed a drink.

"You know," Ryan ventured, unable to help himself, "Don's a great guy, but he's been divorced twice, and he does have a love 'em an' leave 'em reputation."

"Is that a warning?" she asked coolly. "Because if it is, I'm sure Don wouldn't be thrilled to hear it, especially as you say he's your best friend."

"You're pissed at me, aren't you?" Ryan said, suddenly getting it.

"Why would I be?" she said, gulping down her drink – which was one of the *Paradise* specials and quite potent. "I mean, I agreed to be your trainer at a time you chose, and I moved a regular client to accommodate you, but that's okay. Although it would've been nice if you'd called to let me know that you wouldn't be keeping your appointments."

"I'm sorry. You're right. I should've—"

"Hey –" she interrupted. "No problem."

"The thing is—"

"You'll have to excuse me, Ryan," she said, realizing that she couldn't stand another moment of this torture. "There's a thousand things I have to take care of."

Forcing herself to move, she took off before she changed her mind or said something she would regret, such as – *I was desperately waiting for your call. I've been thinking about you every day. Surely you know there's something going on between us? Surely you feel it too?*

Ryan watched her walk away, out of his life again and into

Don's. And there was nothing he could do about it, except leave Mandy – which right now was too complicated, with Evie and the kids ensconced in their house.

A feeling of deep frustration gnawed at the pit of his stomach. Was she sleeping with Don yet?

Oh Jesus, he didn't want to know.

Chapter Thirty-One

"I love that it's so star-studded here," Katie confided, cornering Cameron by the bar where she was downing yet another *Paradise*. "And gimme the inside, what's the deal with you and the incredibly hot Don Verona?"

"Huh?" Cameron said, feeling somewhat light-headed because one drink was usually her limit and now she was on her fourth.

"He's gorgeous!" Katie exclaimed. "And he hasn't stopped watching you all night."

"Don't be crazy, he's with Mary Ellen Evans."

"You could've fooled me," Katie said knowingly. "There's something going on between you two – I can smell it!"

"Actually," Cameron said, keeping it vague, "I guess Don *is* kind of chasing me."

"I told you!" Katie crowed. "How cool is *that*."

"But it's no big deal, he's my client. We work out every morning."

"And?" Katie questioned, eyes gleaming with the anticipation of juicy gossip to come.

Cameron shrugged. "Nothing. He's just another guy."

"Don't give me that," Katie scoffed. "You're the girl who used to tell me everything."

"Ah yes, when we were young and restless."

"*Young and Restless* is a TV soap."

"I know."

"So?"

"So . . ." Cameron said, desperately feeling the need to share. "If I tell you something you have to swear to keep it to yourself."

"Like who am I gonna tell?"

"Jinx."

"Ha!" Katie snorted. "As if."

"Well . . . you see that guy over there, the one standing next to Don."

"Yes," Katie said, peering across the room. "Got him in my sights."

"He's the one," Cameron sighed.

"The one what?" Katie asked, perplexed.

Downing her drink, Cameron signaled the barman for another. "He's married," she said glumly.

"Who's married?"

"God, Katie!" she said, suppressing an unexpected hiccup. "Why are you being so dense? The guy standing next to Don."

"Oh!" Katie said. "I get it. You're into the married one. And from what I can see – he's pretty cute himself. Man, they grow 'em tall and handsome in Hollywood."

"He's married," Cameron repeated glumly. "Married, married, married."

"So are you," Katie pointed out.

"What?" Cameron frowned, hiccupped again. "I'm *married*?"

"Oh man," Katie said, laughing. "I think you've had enough."

"Enough what?"

"Enough *booze*," Katie said. "And here we go. Mr Verona is on his way over – bee-lining straight for you."

Cameron leaned against the bar to steady herself.

"Hi," Katie said to Don as soon as he came over. "I'm Katie, Cameron's best friend, and—"

"I feel dizzy," Cameron interjected. "Think I'd better lie down."

"She's had a few too many," Katie explained.

"I can see that," Don said. "Can you help me get her into the office?"

"Love to," Katie said. "And may I say that you're much more handsome than on TV. And taller. Do you get that a lot?"

"Why don't we concentrate on Cameron before she falls down," he said, putting his arm around Cameron's shoulder.

"Hey, Don, wassup?" Cameron mumbled, dissolving into a full giggling fit.

"Hey, Cam," he answered, raising an amused eyebrow. "Anyone mentioned that you're bombed?"

"Bombed?" she questioned. "Who bombed?"

He attempted to remove the drink from her hand, but she held on so tightly that the liquid shot out of the glass, splashing down the front of her dress.

"Ooops!" she giggled again. "Nipple alert!"

"Take her other arm and we'll move her nice and slowly," Don instructed.

"Got it," Katie said, impressed with his take-control attitude.

Together they maneuvered Cameron into the office.

"Now what?" Katie inquired, shutting the door.

"You'll go summon up a cup of strong black coffee while I stay here with her."

Katie nodded. Tall, dark, famous, rich, caring and handsome. Was Cameron nuts? If what she said was true, she was turning down this one and going for Mister Married. The woman was insane!

"I'll be right back," Katie said.

"She'll be right back," Cameron giggled, suddenly flinging her arms around his neck and pressing her lips against his.

Summoning major willpower, he gently extracted himself.

"Wassamatter?" she questioned. "Thought you *liked* kissing me."

"You know," he said, guiding her to a chair, "if I wasn't a gentleman, I could take big advantage of you tonight."

She smiled at him, a somewhat boozy smile. "Go ahead, big boy, take advantage."

"Oh man," he said, shaking his head. "You're so going to regret this in the morning."

"Rugrat who?" she asked, widening her eyes.

"Cameron, Cameron," he said, laughing softly. "I can't wait for our date tomorrow night so I can tell you all about this, 'cause if I know you, you'll be mortified!"

"Yeah, yeah, yeah," she said, leaning back in the chair, her breasts falling out of her dress. "Mort E. Fied. What a name!"

He quickly adjusted the top of her dress so that she was covered.

"Thank you, Mister Policeman," she said, as a wave of dizziness enveloped her. "A flash in time saves nine."

"Huh?"

She closed her eyes, then quickly opened them. "Are we on a boat?" she asked, perfectly serious.

"No, we're not on a boat," he said patiently. "Why would you think we are?"

"'Cause everything's *really* spinning."

He stared at her thinking how beautiful she was – even in her drunken state she was a knock-out. And no – he would not touch her while she was incapacitated, it wouldn't be right. Although it was sure as hell tempting.

Katie returned with the coffee. "Your girlfriend's searching for you," she remarked. "Asking everyone where you are. I didn't say anything."

"I don't have a girlfriend."

"I read the tabloids, y'know. Mary Ellen Evans."

"Oh, *her*."

"Yes, *her*."

Pulling out his cell phone, he made a quick call to Ryan.

"Where are you?" Ryan asked. "Mandy wants to leave."

"Don't repeat what I'm saying," Don said, lowering his voice. "I'm with Cameron, she's having some kind of crisis, so do me a big one – make my excuses and drop Mary Ellen home for me."

"Jesus, Don!"

"Yeah, I know, but Cam needs me, so I'm here for her."

"What am I supposed to tell Mary Ellen and Mandy?"

"Tell 'em I got called back to the studio, had to re-tape a segment. Big emergency."

Ryan couldn't help himself, he had to ask. "Is Cameron all right?"

"She's better than all right."

Ryan clicked off his phone in a foul mood. This thing with Don and Cameron was not going to be easy for him to deal with. But he knew that he'd have to face up to it. There was no other way.

ANYA

*T*he young couple Anya worked for, Diana and Seth Carpenter, were both lawyers and dedicated to their work. Every morning Anya arrived at their apartment promptly at eight thirty. Shortly after that, Diana and Seth left together. Once in a while Seth returned home at lunch-time, locked himself in the cubby-hole he called his home office, and worked on his computer.

Anya began studying him carefully. In her young life she'd observed many men, and Seth did not seem like the men who'd visited the brothels she'd worked in. He was quite serious, not at all sexual, and extremely work-oriented.

On some days she asked him if he would like her to fix him lunch. Occasionally he said yes, and while she was busy making him a sandwich he would play with the baby for a few minutes and make some phone calls. Then he would eat his sandwich and leave again.

Anya continued to study him. Seth Carpenter was a very tense man, he did not seem at all happy.

Sometimes when Anya arrived early in the morning, she heard Seth and his wife fighting. It happened more than once a week. The two of them argued about money, and his mother whom Diana didn't like. They argued about the phone bill and how much time he spent on his computer. They argued about the clothes she wore and how long it took her to get ready. In fact, they argued about everything.

As the days, weeks and months drifted by, Anya formed a master plan. Her plan included never allowing herself to be used by men again. She would use them to make something of herself. They deserved to be used, they were all pigs, even if they presented a decent front – like Seth. She knew that she could use Seth whenever she felt like it. He was a man, wasn't he? And all men had an undeniable weakness, a weakness she'd learned to exploit to her advantage.

One afternoon Seth returned home in a particularly black mood. She could see at once that he was angry.

"Should I make you lunch?" she asked.

"Not today, Anya," he answered gruffly. "I have calls to make, then I'm off again. Are you taking Ali to the park?"

"I take baby to the park today, yes."

"It's good for her to get out."

"You look tired, Mr Carpenter," she said, softening her voice.

"I am tired," he admitted. "I never stop."

"In Russia I sometimes work as massage therapist," she said. "You take jacket off, I give you shoulder rub. Very invigorating."

"I don't think so," he said, although she could tell he was tempted.

"It would be relaxing for you," she encouraged.

"I certainly need some of that."

"You will work better this afternoon, you will see."

"Well, if you're sure . . ."

She nodded, indicating a hard-backed chair by the kitchen table. Shrugging off his jacket he sat down.

Anya moved behind him, and began pressing her thumbs deeply into the soft tissue behind his neck.

"That feels good," he said.

"I told you," she said. "In Russia we are trained to do this. A man who works hard must learn to relax."

"You do it very well."

"Thank you, Mr Carpenter," she said, moving closer to him so that her small breasts brushed against his back.

An involuntary gasp passed his lips.

Married Lovers

Men, they were so easy. Very soon he would be growing hard, and after that there would be no problem getting him to do anything she wanted. And she wanted plenty. She wanted retribution for all the years she'd been treated as if she were nothing but a piece of unfeeling flesh to be passed around from man to man.

She wanted revenge.

Chapter Thirty-Two

"You're having lunch with my daughter today," Hamilton said, his tone brooking no argument. "My driver will drop you off at *Spago*."

"I hardly know your daughter," Anya said, hoping somehow or other to get out of meeting with Mandy. She could tell that Hamilton's daughter did not like her.

"What's that got to do with anything?" Hamilton said curtly. "Mandy will show you around, advise you where to shop, what beauty salon to frequent, things like that."

"If you insist, I'll do it," Anya said reluctantly.

"Yes, you will," Hamilton said. "I spend a lot of time in L.A. so you'd better get used to being here."

"You could leave me in New York," she suggested. "I wouldn't mind."

"Ah yes," he said, his voice ripe with sarcasm. "*Now* I know why I married you, so I could leave you by yourself in New York with every old billionaire friend of mine trying to fuck you."

"You know I would never be unfaithful to you, Hamilton."

"Yes, *I* know it. But do they?"

Hamilton was extraordinarily possessive and jealous. He didn't approve of her looking at other men, let alone talking to them, so she'd learned to practically ignore all his peers when they were out at a dinner party or a formal charity event. Wherever they went, Hamilton always had one of his many assistants call ahead to make sure they were seated together.

Anya wasn't quite sure whom he didn't trust – was it her or was it his horny old friends? And they *were* horny, this army of very rich very married billionaires with mistresses on the side and multiple women at their beck and call.

In America, Anya had soon discovered, money can buy you anything you want. Hamilton knew this, and he had no desire to see his exquisite young wife offered the temptations of more than he could give her. And since he could give her plenty, Anya didn't care about his possessiveness. In fact, she didn't much care about anything except her shoe collection. Oh, how she loved her shoes.

Over the last five years – two years after first arriving in America – she'd accumulated five hundred pairs of shoes – most of them Jimmy Choos. They were her most prized possessions. Nobody would ever come between Anya and her shoes.

* * *

"Where did you and my father meet?" Mandy asked, vexed that she'd been forced to take Hamilton's new wife to lunch. Her dear father had insisted – and there was no point in refusing Hamilton when he wanted her to do something.

She'd elicited the help of Lucy and Mary Ellen, she'd even invited Birdy Marvel, who so far had not put in an appearance, which was probably just as well since the baby Diva was usually so stoned out of her pretty trashy little head that she couldn't even follow a conversation.

They were sitting on the patio at *Spago*. It was a glorious spring day and usually Mandy would be enjoying herself, but not today, not with three screaming brats running around her house to come home to – and some young Russian gold-digger whom she was being forced to entertain. Things were far from perfect.

Anya's expression was blank. "A dinner party," she said at last. "In New York."

"Whose dinner?" Mandy asked, pushing for information.

"I do not remember," Anya said, fervently wishing she were somewhere else. She was just as uncomfortable as Hamilton's daughter, for she had still not had an opportunity to speak to Ryan and discover if he'd told anyone about her shameful past.

Was it possible that Mandy knew?

Yes, it was possible.

"You don't remember?" Mandy said, imbibing her voice with just the right amount of disbelief. "How peculiar that you wouldn't remember where you were the night you met your future husband."

"God!" Lucy exclaimed, sipping a Mimosa. "I'll never forget the first time I set eyes on Phil. He was at Brett Ratner's house sitting by the pool in *the* most ridiculous Speedo you've ever seen! His rolls of fat were on fire, and the man was so hairy, like a gorilla!"

"Sounds enchanting," Mandy murmured. "I bet you couldn't wait to lure him into bed."

"After a while we started to talk," Lucy said, smiling fondly at the memory. "And before long he ambushed me with his amazing and outrageous stories. Phil is *such* a brilliant raconteur. I fell in love with his words."

"I met my husband – well, I suppose I should say *ex*-husband – on a blind date," Mary Ellen piped up. "We shared a mutual business manager who thought we'd make a great couple."

"Hardly a *blind* date," Mandy interjected. "You were both famous so you probably knew all about each other."

"I suppose," Mary Ellen agreed. She was not sure why Mandy had invited her to lunch. She'd decided to accept the invitation because it would probably please Don if she began mixing with his friends, and more than anything she wanted to please him. Don Verona was such a catch, so handsome and eligible and witty.

The press loved him, and they'd already labeled them a couple. It was an exciting time.

She fervently hoped her ex was finally regretting dumping her in front of the entire world. Bastard!

"Well, yes, of course she knew what he looked like," Lucy pointed out. "But even so – he could've turned out to be a big bore."

"What – instead of a cheater?" Mandy said.

Mary Ellen gulped down her glass of sparkling water. Ignoring Mandy's barbed comment she said, "And you, Mandy, where did you meet Ryan?"

Mandy flashed back seven years. She was twenty-five and desperate to settle down with someone her father *hadn't* chosen for her. Hamilton was always pushing men he could control in her direction, and she was always shying away. Instinctively she knew – in fact her shrink had warned her – that she had to meet a man who was not under her father's influence – a strong-minded man who could stand up for himself. So who better than independent film-maker, Ryan Richards?

She'd been following his career and liked what she saw. He was young, hot and happening. The perfect candidate. The perfect antidote to Daddy.

After finding out everything she could about him, she'd set her stalking skills to work. Within three months he'd asked her to marry him and she'd said yes.

Hamilton was not pleased with her choice. Too damn bad. She was.

"Ryan saw my photo in the *Hollywood Reporter* and relentlessly pursued me," she said, weaving fantasy. "How could I resist?"

"How romantic," Lucy said, not revealing that Phil had told her that Mandy had introduced herself to Ryan at the première of his second movie and from that moment on she'd never let go. According to Phil, the poor guy hadn't stood a chance. Like her father, Mandy was relentless.

"Did you hear from Don this morning?" Mandy asked, turning back to Mary Ellen.

"Actually, no," Mary Ellen replied, somewhat crestfallen because Don hadn't taken her home the night before. At least he should have called and apologized, but not one word. "I guess he's very busy," she added lamely.

"We were all at the opening of some new fitness place last night," Mandy explained to Lucy. "Bit of a rat fuck, but the place might be worth investigating."

"I need a new trainer," Lucy said, waving at Wolfgang Puck who was diligently making his usual rounds of every table.

"I met a hunky trainer with an amazing body," Mary Ellen offered. "He gave me his card. It's a membership gym, I think I'll join."

"Give me his number," Lucy said, fiddling in her purse for her BlackBerry while wondering how soon she could take off. Marlon had texted her that he had more pages for her to look at, and she couldn't wait to read what he'd come up with.

Anya gazed off into the distance. She had nothing to say to any of these women. In a way they reminded her of the actresses from *Sex and the City* – all three of them immaculately groomed with their glossy hair and perfect complexions; dressed stylishly with ridiculously expensive accessories; indulging in light conversation that went nowhere.

Sex and the City was still her favorite TV show. She'd purchased the boxed set of DVDs and watched them often.

"Whereabouts in Russia are you from?" Lucy inquired, trying to include her in their conversation because she felt sorry for the girl – she was so young, Hamilton had to be at least forty years older than her. Naturally Mandy was ignoring her. Mandy could be such a bitch without even trying. She should at least give the girl a chance.

"Moscow," Anya replied, adding – "It is a magnificent city. Very cold in the winter."

"She sounds like a tourist guide," Mandy muttered under her breath.

"Excuse me?" Anya said.

"Nothing, dear," Mandy said airily. "Oh goody, here comes Birdy. Now we can have some fun."

*   *   *

"I'm renting you a house," Ryan informed Evie. "And I am not listening to *any* arguments."

"That's so foolish," Evie said, immediately getting into it. "Why should we move? We'll go back to Silverlake. Marty can't come near us with the Restraining Order and all."

"That's what you think," Ryan said ominously. "I spoke to a detective friend of mine, and he warned me that you shouldn't get too comfortable simply because you've got a piece of paper. According to him those things don't mean shit; people ignore Restraining Orders all the time, and that's exactly when something really bad goes down."

Evie stared out of the window watching her three boys splashing about in the large swimming pool. Was it right that she was about to deprive them of a father? Should she give Marty another opportunity to make amends?

"I don't know, Ryan," she said hesitantly. "Maybe I should give him one more chance."

"For crissake!" he said, frustrated and angry. "Get it through your head, you've *got* to move on. Marty is *never* going to change, and deep down you know it."

"I suppose so," she said, reluctant to admit that maybe he was right.

"Then it's settled," Ryan said firmly. "I'm renting a house for you, and enrolling the boys into a local school. Don't worry about money, I'll take care of everything."

Unbeknownst to Evie, he'd already called a realtor and viewed several rental properties. He hadn't taken her with him because he knew she'd try to back out of moving.

It was all well and good having Evie and the boys around, but he was anxious to return to work. His latest movie was in the can and would be coming out in a couple of months, so therefore it was time for him to start prepping his next project, a gritty drama set on the streets of downtown L.A. The script was almost finished, and very soon he'd have to start concentrating on putting his crew together, scouting locations and casting. Getting back into production was his favorite thing to do.

Upon waking that morning he'd made a decision that he had to stop thinking about Cameron Paradise. He was only going to drive himself nuts by going over what might have been, and that was destructive and stupid. She was Don's new girlfriend – end of story.

Cameron had to play out whatever was going to happen between her and Don, and he had to do the same with Mandy.

It was the only sane decision he could make.

Chapter Thirty-Three

The clean-up crew at *Paradise* were in full action when
Cameron walked in. Cole, Dorian, Lynda, Cherry and Reno
were all sitting around the office eating take-out pizza from the
California Pizza Kitchen – everyone's favorite – while helpers ran
around with large black trash bags clearing up the debris of what
had turned out to be an extremely successful opening party.

"She's here! Madame Paradise herself!" Dorian called out,
jumping up and affecting a mock bow.

"Not so loud," Cameron groaned, holding her head. "Have
a little consideration."

"Oh, is madame feeling a touch delicate?" Dorian inquired,
trying to sound solicitous, but not quite pulling it off.

"Delicate!" Lynda exclaimed, bountiful breasts straining to
escape a skimpy orange tank top. "That girl was reelin'!! An' so
would this girl be if I'd had Don Verona chasin' me around all
night."

"Go ahead," Cameron sighed, wishing everyone would lower
their voices. "Once again talk about me as if I'm not here."

"We made the *L.A. Times*," Cole remarked, waving the newspaper at her. "Big picture of Mary Ellen with your friend Don,
and a stoned Birdy Marvel with her latest tattooed stud."

"And," Cherry said, joining in – "Jillian mentioned us on

Good Day L.A. this morning. She recommended us as the hot new place to get movie-star abs. Dorothy said she can't wait to get here, and Steve said he'll be right behind her. How great is *that*?"

"Natalie's running a four-minute segment on her show tonight," Cole said. "The phones haven't stopped. We are off to a fantastic start."

"I'm sorry I missed all the excitement," Cameron said, sinking into a chair. "Can someone please remind me to never drink again. Never *ever*!"

"Consider yourself reminded," Dorian said with a cheeky grin. "Although I have to say you're quite something when you've had a few. *Very* free and easy."

"Please! I don't want to hear about it," she said, her head still throbbing sledge-hammer style. God! She'd really done it. Drunk too much and probably behaved like an idiot. She had grainy memories of Don driving her home, and she vaguely remembered slobbering all over him. How humiliating!

Thank God Katie was with them, otherwise she probably would've done something she'd regret in the cold light of day. As it was, Katie had watched out for her. And she had to give Don points for behaving decently, because once he'd helped Katie get her into her house and onto her bed, he'd taken off.

When she'd finally awoken in the morning, feeling like the dregs in the bottom of a stale bottle of red wine, Katie was preparing to leave for the airport.

"I've called a cab," Katie had informed her. "You look like crap, and if you don't choose Don Verona you're out of your freaking mind."

"Oh," she'd moaned, head throbbing. "Do you *have* to go? I need to hear what I did last night. Was I appalling? Does everyone hate me?"

"Everyone loves you," Katie said matter-of-factly. "I walked the dogs, brought in the papers, your couch has springs from hell.

Oh yes – and Don's sent you an unbelievable arrangement of roses. Gotta go, my cab's waiting."

"Call me later."

"I will."

Katie had rushed off, back to the arms of her would-be rock star fiancé, and Cameron had finally made it to *Paradise*.

She looked around at everyone's smiling faces, and realized that Cole was right, they were off to a fantastic start.

It was a little surreal that all her dreams were finally coming true; she should be enjoying the moment, not suffering from the worst hangover she'd ever experienced.

Damn Ryan Richards. It was all his fault.

Don started calling around noon. "I'm planning our evening," he informed her, sounding very self-satisfied.

"Please don't," she croaked. The thought of going anywhere except back to bed was not a welcome one.

"You'd sooner unplanned?"

"I'd sooner crawl into my bed and go to sleep so that I can wake up tomorrow feeling like a human," she explained, hoping that he understood.

"Oh no," he said warningly.

"Oh no what?"

"Oh no," he repeated in a firm voice. "You are *not* wriggling out of our deal."

"What deal?" she asked innocently, although she knew perfectly well what he meant. A date. Their first date. Although technically it was their second because she *had* gone to Ryan's birthday party with him.

"Miz Paradise," he added sternly, "do not even *think* about fucking with me."

"Can I tell you something, Don?" she said softly.

"Go ahead."

"You do not want to see me tonight."

"That's where you're wrong."

"I look like crap, and I feel even worse." She paused for a moment, hoping he wouldn't force her to keep her part of the deal. "Believe me, I'll be horrible company."

"You?" he said gallantly. "Never."

"Please," she begged. "Can we do it tomorrow night instead?"

"Do it?" he said, amused.

"You know what I mean."

"No, Cameron."

"Please, Don, please," she urged.

"Ah jeez," he said, weakening. "I suppose, if you insist."

"Thank you!" she said gratefully.

"I'll see you in the morning though, right?"

"Seven a.m. sharp. Can you try to be dressed and ready to get to work?"

"Yes, ma'am!"

She clicked off her phone and couldn't help smiling. There was something very appealing about Don. Maybe *he* was the one, and Ryan was simply a silly crush.

Somehow or other she got through the day. At four o'clock they all gathered around the TV in the office to watch Natalie's show on the New York feed.

Natalie – seductively gorgeous in her low-cut green Versace – roamed around interviewing celebrities, asking them about their fitness regimes and health tips.

Don was funny. "As long as I can haul my butt out of bed in the morning I consider myself fit," he joked. "But seriously, Miz Cameron Paradise is responsible for some of the best bodies in town."

Natalie – who'd produced the segment herself – cut to a shot of Cameron arriving.

Everyone in the office cheered.

"So here's my recommendation," Natalie said, once more taking center stage on the TV screen. "If getting into shape *fast* is your goal, then *Paradise* is *the* place to go."

"That was unfuckingbelievable!" Cole enthused. "Sis really came through."

"And you, madame," Dorian said, turning to Cameron, his voice filled with admiration, "looked better than anyone. You're *such* a star! Our star!"

She did not want to be anybody's star, all she wanted to do was to go home and crawl under the covers.

And right after Natalie's show, that's exactly what she did. Two extra-strength Tylenols, two big bottles of Evian, a burrow into the depths of her comfortable duvet, and she was out.

* * *

Meanwhile, Cole got together with Natalie at *Argo* to celebrate. He'd wanted Cameron to come with him, but she'd flatly refused – opting for bed.

"The piece you ran was so fuckin' great!" he said. "Thanks, sis. You're a keeper!"

"Gotta help baby bro' make it big," Natalie said with a warm smile. "Where's Cameron? I have to tell you – our website is buzzing, everyone's dying to find out more about her. I might even interview her on our show."

"She's suffering from a major hangover," Cole explained. "Too many shots of somethin' or other."

"Are you saying that with a body and a face like that, she drinks?" Natalie asked with a note of surprise in her voice.

"I guess last night she was feelin' it," Cole said, drinking beer from the bottle.

"I guess so," Natalie murmured.

"Here's my question," Cole said, getting serious. "Who's our mystery investor droppin' the big bucks?"

"Can't tell you," Natalie said, sipping a Cosmopolitan.

"Waddya mean you can't tell me? I'm your brother. An' not only that – we're in business together."

"We certainly are," Natalie said, completely unfazed.

"So give," he insisted, taking another swig of beer.

"Can't. It's a privacy issue."

"Shit, Natalie! Cameron wants to know."

"Sorry, baby bro', no can tell. But as long as he's putting up big bucks and not asking for anything in return – why is anyone bothered?"

"'Cause who doesn't want anything in return?" Cole said, perplexed.

"My silent investor doesn't. He's rich, and he's doing this as a favor to me, so don't worry about it. None of the extra money he's putting up affects our original deal."

"The dude has to be crazy."

"Maybe."

"Just tell me this – was he at the party?"

"Of course. He paid for it."

"Uh-huh," Cole said. Now he was convinced it was Natalie's real-estate boyfriend, it had to be.

"My entire crew wants to join the gym – have someone send over membership forms," Natalie said, getting off the subject because she had faithfully sworn to Don that she would not reveal his name under any circumstances.

"Sure," Cole said. "Did you happen to mention that it's gonna cost them a thousand bucks a year?"

"They'll make their own decisions when they get the forms," she said, waving at superstar Venus and her husband – the over-a-decade-younger Billy Melina – a star in his own right. The two of them were making their way to a table on the outdoor patio.

"Shit!" Cole exclaimed, sitting up straight. "You *know* them?"

"Yes, Cole, I know everyone, and they know me – that's as long as they can put me in context."

"An' *that* means?"

"It means I'm a celebrity journalist on TV," Natalie said matter-of-factly. "So when I interview them it's best friends all round. And when they see me somewhere else, they're not so sure how to place me. It's all a game."

"Billy Melina is some sexy-lookin' stud," Cole remarked, throwing a lustful stare after the actor. "I wouldn't mind workin' *his* cute butt."

"Stop droolin' after the straight ones," Natalie scolded. "That's always been your problem."

"Could be he's in the closet," Cole mused.

"He's married to Venus," Natalie observed dryly. "I hardly think so."

"You never know," Cole replied, refusing to be shot down. "How many times I gotta tell you it's always the ones you never suspect."

"God help us!" Natalie sighed. "When are you *ever* going to find the right man?"

"When are you?" he countered. "You go through 'em as fast as I do."

"Maybe tomorrow, maybe never," she answered vaguely. "I'm in no hurry."

"So it runs in the family," he said. "We're just gonna havta keep lookin'."

"Well quit looking in Billy Melina's direction," she said tartly. "I'm telling you, Billy is straighter than a ruler."

"Yeah, sure," Cole mocked.

"Freako!" Natalie exclaimed.

"Takes one—"

"To know one!" she said, finishing the sentence for him.

They both burst out laughing.

* * *

Cameron awoke feeling great after ten hours' sleep. Wow! Hangover completely gone.

She lay in bed for a moment going over the events of the last

269

couple of days. It was all so exciting, the total realization of her dreams. *Paradise* actually existed! How cool was that?

Yoko and Lennon sprawled on the bed beside her, farting and snoring in their usual fashion.

"Up!" she commanded. "Jump to it!"

Both dogs leaped off the bed and immediately began barking.

"Calm down, guys," she ordered. "We've got a lot to do today."

Singing to herself she took a shower, threw on her work-out clothes, fixed a healthy breakfast, ran the dogs around the block, dropped them off at Mr Wasabi's, and set off for Don's.

True to his promise he was up, dressed and ready. "I even made the coffee," he said, adding a sly – "Thought you might need it."

"Nope. I do not need it," she said cheerfully, heading for the stairs and the gym. "Today I feel great."

"Glad to hear it."

"And thanks for your very nice comment on Natalie's show. Much appreciated."

"It worked," he said, following her up the stairs. "Everyone's bugging me for the number so they can check the place out."

"That's amazing."

"You're an instant success, kiddo."

"Thanks to your support, and Natalie of course. That woman is such a dynamo."

"Yes, she is. Did I tell you I'm doing an interview with her?"

"Is she guesting on your show?"

"No," he said, keeping it casual. "I'm giving her an exclusive."

"I thought you told me you never did interviews."

"I don't, but Natalie asked me, and since she's been trying to get me for years, I finally caved."

"I didn't realize you were so close."

"We're not, but I've always thought that out of the crowd of entertainment interviewers, she's one of the best. Besides, she cornered me at the party, I couldn't say no."

"Of course you'll mention *Paradise*?"

"Man!" he said, laughing. "What am I – your P.R. whore?"

"If you like," she said, giggling.

"What I *like* is seeing you in such a happy mood."

"Okay," she said briskly. "You – on the treadmill, no more time to waste."

"And then – just when the sun is shining – out comes her bossy side," he said, breaking a smile.

"I'm not bossy," she objected, "simply organized."

"Yeah, yeah, *sure*," he teased.

"By the way, I'm giving up house calls and asking everyone to switch to the gym."

"Except me," he said confidently, stepping onto the treadmill.

"Well . . ."

"I'm your exception, right?" he said, flashing another one of his devastating smiles. "After all, I'm the guy who rescued you the other night. Without me taking care of you, you'd be sprawled on the floor singing 'The Star Spangled Banner' with your dress around your waist."

"I would so not," she said, her cheeks flushing.

"You don't remember, do you?"

"I remember enough, thank you."

"Bet you don't," he said, provoking her.

"Can we drop it?" she begged, cringing at some of the memories.

"Fine. As long as you don't forget our deal."

"Deal?"

"C'mon, Miz Paradise, don't give me that," he scolded. "Tonight. Our date. I'm picking you up at eight."

"You are?"

"I am."

"In that case I promise to stay sober."

"Hey –" he said, with an irresistible grin. "And I was hoping for a repeat performance!"

"Shut *up*," she said, leaning over and switching the speed on the treadmill to the highest.

"Jeez, Cam," he said, as the treadmill took off and he attempted to keep up, almost falling off. "What are you trying to do – kill me?"

Now it was her turn to smile. "Maybe."

Chapter Thirty-Four

"We should throw a dinner party," Lucy suggested, entering their large comfortable kitchen where Phil was sitting at the table finishing his breakfast. "We never entertain at the house, I think it would be a nice thing to do."

"What's the occasion?" Phil inquired, putting down *Variety*, his daily read.

"No particular occasion," she said, casually shrugging. "I just thought we might enjoy a few laughs."

Phil regarded his beautiful former movie-star wife with a jaundiced eye. Since when was Lucy into entertaining at the house? Perfect little dinner parties were not her thing, she left those kind of events to her friend, Mandy. "How many people?" he asked. "And even more important – what'll it cost me?"

"You're so bloody loaded, darling, does it really matter?"

"I'm loaded 'cause I know how to keep an eye on my fuckin' money," he growled.

Fuck you! squawked the parrot, picking up on the F word. *Fuck you!*

Phil chuckled. "God! I love that bird."

"I know you do," Lucy said calmly. "And so do the kids. Their playmates' mothers – not so much."

Phil was pleased that he and his wife appeared to be having a

273

civilized conversation. For the last few months she'd done nothing but bug him about resurrecting her stupid career. Thank God she seemed to be over such nonsense.

"Okay," he said, downing the rest of his coffee. "We're having a party. Go ahead and arrange it."

"I will," she said, secretly delighted, for she had a big surprise in store.

Phil took off for his study – located in his special tree house overlooking their pool. He would stay locked away for the rest of the day, refusing to be disturbed under any circumstances. Nothing came between Phil and his scripts.

Lucy was used to his ways; at least when he was writing he wasn't out screwing around.

After throwing a cover over the parrot's cage, and shooing the dogs out of the kitchen, she phoned Marlon.

His machine picked up, so she left him a message. "Marlon. It's Lucy. Loved the pages I read today. Do you think you can finish very soon? I've decided to throw a launch party for our script, so keep working."

*   *   *

"Great news," Ryan announced, catching Mandy in her enormous dressing room where she was busy trying to choose a pair of sneakers from her extensive collection. "I've found a house for Evie and the boys."

"Thank God!" she gasped, sitting cross-legged on the floor surrounded by unopened shoe boxes. "I don't think I could take one more day of them running riot around here."

"They haven't been exactly running riot, Mandy," Ryan pointed out, irritated that she would say such a thing. "They've been pretty well behaved considering they were uprooted from their home."

"Whatever," she answered vaguely.

"Are you going somewhere?"

"Yes," she said, settling on a pair of brand new Chanel sneakers. "Mary Ellen's picking me up, we're taking a proper look at that new place."

"What new place?"

"*Paradise.*"

Paradise! Was she kidding him? Why was she going back there?

"Kind of a dumb name, don't you think?" Mandy continued. "And that girl who runs it doesn't seem too bright. Do you think Don's banging her?"

"No," he said shortly, overcome with all kinds of mixed emotions. How dare Mandy call Cameron dumb, that's the last thing she was.

"Poor Mary Ellen," Mandy sighed. "She's under the impression Don is the one. Should I tell her he's nothing but a bad boy womanizer who can't keep it in his pants?"

"And what would you have to gain by telling her that?" Ryan asked, waiting to hear his wife's agenda, because she always had one. "Besides, Phil's the one who can't keep it zipped, not Don."

"You never know," Mandy mused. "Mary Ellen could come in useful at one of my events – after all, she *is* a star. I know it's only on TV, but according to all the magazine coverage she gets, she's very popular. Maybe you should put her in one of your movies."

I want a divorce. The words screamed in his head. *I want out. I can't do this anymore.*

But now he had to wait until Evie and the boys were settled in their new home. God! There was always something.

After that, he promised himself he'd go for it – there was only so much more of Mandy he could take.

* * *

Miss Dunn, Hamilton's most trusted L.A. assistant, approached Anya who was laying out beside the pool. Like most of Hamilton's employees, Miss Dunn had worked for him for almost twenty years. Thin, with scraggly brown hair pulled back in a tight bun and slightly crossed eyes, she harbored an unrequited crush on her overbearing boss. Originally he'd imported her from New York. Hamilton did not want any L.A. glamour babes working for him. Business was business, and he liked the women who worked for him to be plain and dedicated. Miss Dunn fit the bill.

"Yes?" Anya said, languidly raising herself up on one elbow.

"Mr Hamilton asked me to give you these," Miss Dunn said, trying to avoid staring at the young woman's slender body – the body that was giving her boss so much pleasure.

"What are they?" Anya asked, shading her pale blue eyes from the sun.

"Charge cards," Miss Dunn said. "Neiman Marcus, Saks, Barney's. Mr Heckerling thought you should have them. And your new black American Express card."

"Okay," Anya said, sinking back down. "Put them on the table."

How ungrateful, Miss Dunn thought to herself. *At least she could have said thank you.*

"Mr Heckerling asked me to tell you that he took the helicopter to Santa Barbara," Miss Dunn continued. "He'll be back at six p.m. in time for dinner."

Anya sat up all the way. If Hamilton was out of town for the day it might be the perfect opportunity for her to contact Ryan Richards.

"Can you get me Mr Richards's business phone number," she said.

"Perhaps you mean Mr Heckerling's *daughter's* number?"

"No," Anya said abruptly. "Ryan Richards's."

"As you wish," Miss Dunn said, tight-lipped, wondering why

Mrs Heckerling would want to contact Mr Heckerling's son-in-law.

Reaching for a flimsy top to put over her barely there bikini, Anya said – "I'll walk up to the house with you."

"Very well," Miss Dunn said. She could never understand why her boss had to marry these women. Why couldn't he simply sleep with them and be done with it? Marriage was such a big commitment, and he always managed to choose the wrong woman. This one was no exception; she was also young enough to be his grand-daughter, which Miss Dunn found somewhat disgusting. That very morning she and Madge, his loyal Scottish housekeeper, had discussed the situation over tea in the kitchen.

"He marries them to make his friends jealous," Madge had confided, as if she had inside information. "He wants them to envy him."

"Perhaps they won't sleep with him unless he puts a ring on their finger," Miss Dunn had suggested.

Madge had let forth a hearty guffaw. "In this day and age? Nonsense!"

Anya followed Miss Dunn into Hamilton's all-leather book-lined study, then through to the ante-room where she worked within calling distance of her boss. Going straight to her computer, Miss Dunn printed out Ryan's details, then handed the sheet of paper to Anya, who took it and went upstairs.

As soon as her boss's new wife left, Miss Dunn made a notation in the detailed list of the day's happenings she always handed to Mr Heckerling before she went home. He was a man who liked to know everything, especially when it came to the activities of his wives.

* * *

"Don't faint," Lucy said over the phone. "But we're throwing a dinner party at our house."

"Ex*cuse* me?" Mandy said, quite surprised. "You're actually inviting people to your home? This is a first."

"I know, I know," Lucy agreed. "We're kind of lax on the entertaining at home front. But what with the kids and the dogs and Phil's crazy parrot who won't stop screaming *Fuck you!* it's not exactly easy."

"But you're definitely doing it?"

"We are. And I thought you could tell me what caterer I'm supposed to use."

"Oh Lucy, Lucy, you're such a babe in Hollywood," Mandy sighed. "So ignorant about how things are done."

"Is that an insult?"

"Of course," Mandy said gaily. "Can't you tell? But only in a very loving way."

"How about lunch tomorrow?" Lucy suggested. "Come armed with a list of things I have to do to make it all work."

"I suppose . . ."

"*Chow's?* One o'clock?"

"I'll be there."

*　*　*

Anya stared at the piece of paper with Ryan's phone numbers. Home. Office. Cell. Which should she choose?

Certainly not home. Mandy was an alarming and pushy woman she wanted nothing to do with.

Office? Maybe.

Or cell? Probably her best bet.

Tentatively she reached for the phone.

ANYA

*T*aking it slowly was the best way to reel Seth Carpenter in. Anya knew it was the only way.

The mid-afternoon back rubs soon became a regular occurrence. Seth began coming home almost every day, and Anya was there, looking after his baby, fixing him a sandwich, ministering to his every need – well, almost – because he was riddled with guilt that every time she gave him the shoulder massage with her breasts pressed firmly against his back, he got hard.

She pretended not to notice, and when she was finished massaging his shoulders, he rushed into the bathroom as if he had to go.

One day he said, "It's best if you don't mention to Mrs Carpenter that I come home so much." A nervous laugh. "She'll think I'm slacking off."

Or jacking off, Anya thought. TV was teaching her so many quaint American expressions.

Back at the hostel, Ella was still pestering her about getting together and putting on a sex show for money. "I got this dude lined up," Ella insisted. "He'll pay us fifty bucks each. Whaddya think?"

"No," Anya replied primly.

Fifty bucks indeed! She was in America now. The stakes were much higher.

After six weeks of playing with Seth, acting naive and innocent and caring, he finally cracked.

She'd known it was coming because the morning fights with his wife had escalated; their arguments were continuous.

"Anya," he said, after a particularly vigorous neck rub. "We've got to stop doing this."

"Doing what, Mr Carpenter?" she asked, all wide-eyed and innocent.

He stood up, faced her and began speaking. "I'm . . . I'm developing feelings for you, and that's not right."

"Feelings, Mr Carpenter?"

"Oh God," he groaned. "You're so young."

"I'm seventeen."

"Yes, but you've led a sheltered life, I can see it in your face. You're innocent, sweet . . ." He trailed off.

"I've had a boyfriend," she murmured, hoping that the baby wouldn't awaken, because this was the moment she'd been working toward.

"A boyfriend?" he said, startled. "You never mentioned you had a boyfriend."

"He left me," she said sadly, her eyes dropping to the very evident bulge in his pants.

"Why's that?" he asked, his voice thick with lust.

"There were certain things he wanted me to do," she said timidly. "Things that didn't seem right."

"What things?" Seth asked, licking his lips.

Anya summoned up a blush. "Things that only married people should do . . ."

"Such as what?" he insisted.

Her voice dropped to a whisper. "Oral sex."

"I see," Seth said, feeling beads of sweat form on his brow.

"What do you think, Mr Carpenter? Is it wrong if two people love each other?"

"Did you love him?"

"No."

"Did you . . . uh . . . do anything else with him?"

"He touched my breasts. That's all."

"Show me how," Seth mumbled, unable to control himself any longer.

This girl was an angel with her delicate innocent face, long fair hair, and extraordinary pale blue eyes.

She'd been sent his way to save him from a wife who constantly berated and criticized him.

Fixing him with a direct gaze, Anya slowly began peeling off her T-shirt and started fingering her nipples. "Like this," she said. "He touched me like this."

Mr Seth Carpenter was about to be her first American victim.

Chapter Thirty-Five

"I thought you'd prefer coming here rather than going to a restaurant," Don said, escorting Cameron onto the outdoor patio around his infinity pool where a dining table for two was set up with all the requisites for a romantic evening. Candles in tall silver holders; purple roses arranged in a series of delicate small glass bowls; a scarlet tablecloth with matching napkins; black thin-stemmed wine glasses; and the pièce de résistance – an all-male trio playing soft Brazilian music.

She stifled an urge to break out in a fit of giggles. This was so predictable. The Seduction Dinner. And his bed was probably covered in rose petals.

She hadn't expected this of Don, she'd thought he would come up with something more original.

"Uh . . . lovely," she managed.

"Private," he said, quite pleased with himself.

Yes, very private, she thought. *Two waiters, a chef, a couple of maids and the three-man group. What was up with entertaining in Hollywood?*

One of the waiters approached her with a flute of champagne.

"No thanks," she said, shaking her head. "I'll have water."

"Water?" Don questioned.

"After the other night—"

"Understood." He nodded at the waiter. "Get Miz Paradise some Evian. Room temperature. No ice."

She was impressed that he remembered.

"Let's sit over here," he said, taking her hand and leading her to a couple of lounge chairs strategically set up to take advantage of the spectacular L.A. view.

"Don—" she began.

"Yes?"

"This is all so unnecessary."

"What is?"

"Everything," she said, indicating the table and the waiters and the musicians. "It's excessive."

"I thought you'd enjoy it."

"Why would you think I'd enjoy something like this? It's *way* too formal."

"Hey – it's better than a restaurant where people keep on coming over requesting me to sign bits of stupid paper," he said, frowning slightly because he'd gone to a lot of trouble – or rather his assistant had.

"For you – maybe," Cameron said. "For me – no. I'm not a formal kind of girl."

"You're not, huh?" he said, arching an eyebrow.

"Can't you tell?"

"I wasn't sure."

She laughed softly. "You know, Don, you didn't need to go to all this trouble just to lure me into bed. I've already decided tonight's the night."

"Aren't *you* little Miss Romantic," he said, throwing her a perplexed look.

"What can I tell you," she answered with a casual shrug. "Playing games is not my thing."

"Apparently not," he said, totally flummoxed by her offhand attitude.

"So," she continued, "this entire set-up is somewhat redundant."

"It is, huh?"

"Yes, I'm afraid it is."

"Okay," he said, getting up. "Never say I don't listen to reason. Stay here. Do *not* move."

"I'm not moving."

"Promise?"

"Yes, Mr Verona."

He hurried inside the house, returning a few minutes later with a big wide grin on his face.

"What did you do?" she asked.

"Told everyone to get the hell out," he said, still grinning. "Believe me – I'm no slouch when it comes to following orders."

"You really did that?"

"Everyone will be gone in five minutes," he assured her, taking her hands and pulling her up. "Satisfied?"

"I didn't think you would—"

"Yes, you did," he said, swooping in for a long hot kiss.

"This doesn't mean you can rush me," she warned him, breathlessly extracting herself.

"Who's rushing?" he questioned, moving in again for a leisurely second kiss.

This time she found herself unable to resist. Twining her arms around the back of his neck and pulling him close, she realized how satisfying it would be to make a real connection. And now, with *Paradise* opening, she felt so much more secure and quite ready to move forward.

After a few minutes he began kissing her in earnest, his tongue exploring her mouth. They could both feel the heat building between them, and neither of them cared to stop.

By the time they surfaced for air, everyone had left the house.

"You did it," she gasped, drawing away from him. "We're alone."

"Would I lie to you?"

"I hope not."

"So," he said, throwing her a meaningful look. "No music, no food. What *are* we gonna do?"

"I wonder," she breathed, quite light-headed and full of expectations.

They began kissing again, standing beside the pool, the lights of L.A. spread out before them.

It was a long time since she'd enjoyed kissing a man and it was quite a heady experience. She savored every moment – the roughness of his mouth, the feel of his tongue, the sensation of breathing in his aura.

Gently she reached up and touched his face, stroking the slight stubble on his chin, then moving her hands once again to the nape of his neck.

He was tall, so was she, their bodies seemed to meld together. Soon she could feel him hard against her thigh and it was turning her on.

How many times has he done this?

How many women has he slept with?

Am I one of hundreds? Thousands?

Who cared? He was a great kisser, so much better than over-enthusiastic Marlon – the only man she'd been with since fleeing Hawaii.

She knew she was taking a risk, embarking on an adventure with Don Verona.

Was she making a mistake?

Ryan's warning drifted into her head – *Don's a great guy, but he's been divorced twice, and he does have a love 'em and leave 'em reputation.*

Right now she didn't give a damn. She had a strong urge to be with someone who cared about her, really cared, and hopefully Don was that someone.

And if he wasn't? The thing was, she had to take a chance sometime, may as well go for it.

Slowly he began peeling down the straps of her white silk camisole, exposing her breasts. "God, you're beautiful," he marveled, caressing her nipples with a great deal of expertise.

The sensation of Don touching her was taking her breath away. She'd only slept with two men, Gregg and Marlon – and neither of them had been into foreplay. She had not expected it to feel this heady and exciting.

Waves of desire overwhelmed her as she feverishly began unbuttoning his shirt, suddenly desperate to feel his skin against hers.

"Slow down," he commanded, gripping her wrists. "I'm the guy here, remember?"

She was so used to calling the shots with Marlon that she wasn't prepared to be with a man who knew exactly what he was doing. And Don knew all right – his touch sent shivers of ecstasy throughout her entire body.

His practiced hands started moving down to her waist, then they began undoing the zipper on her white silk pants.

"This isn't fair," she murmured. "I'm not standing here naked while you're still fully dressed."

"You standing out here naked has been my dream ever since you turned up at my house that memorable morning," he said, husky-voiced. "I saw you at my door that day and I was a goner. That was it for me."

And I saw Ryan pacing up and down outside Chow's *and that was it for me.*

Don't go there, Cameron. You're making a move with this guy.

The twice-divorced, love 'em and leave 'em guy?

Shut up, Ryan. You're married. It's none of your business.

Okay, okay.

"Get your clothes off," she ordered, kicking off her shoes and stepping out of her pants.

"And she's *still* bossy," he said, obligingly starting to strip.

"Aren't you glad I made you send everyone home?" she said breathlessly.

"I gotta admit," he said, dropping his pants. "You're an excellent decision maker."

"You'll need a condom," she managed, admiring his strong physique and impressive hard-on.

"It's okay, I just got tested," he said, his eyes soaking up every inch of her beauty. "You have nothing to worry about." She was beyond the point of no return. Condom. No condom. Whatever.

And then it was on, neither of them able to hold off another second. They sank back on one of the loungers and he was on top of her and inside her, and somehow she reversed positions and maneuvered herself astride him. It felt so damn *good*!

The sex was hot and frenzied and carnal. They were both so into it. And it went on for quite a while before they reached the pinnacle together.

"Jesus Christ!" Don exclaimed, rolling off her. "You do not disappoint."

"And you," she murmured, every fiber of her body tingling, "must've been working out. I'm very impressed with your stamina."

"Hey – gimme ten minutes," he said, with a lazy grin. "I gotta thank my trainer – she keeps me in tip-top shape."

"I can tell. She must be quite something."

"Oh yeah, she certainly is."

They both started to laugh.

After a few moments he stood up, pulling her up with him.

She felt totally invigorated, her skin still tingling with waves of deep-seated pleasure.

"You're so goddamn beautiful," he sighed. "Why'd you make me wait this long?"

"'Cause I could," she said, teasing him, all thoughts of Ryan temporarily banished.

"Jesus, Cam—"

"What?"

"I . . . uh . . . I think I could be falling in like."

"Now let's not get carried away," she said lightly, remembering that this guy was a player and that she should tread carefully. Didn't want to fall. Didn't want to get hurt.

"Gonna try," he said. "Can't promise anything."

Was he full of smooth lines? Or was he genuine?

She hadn't quite figured him out.

With a sudden burst of energy she jumped up and made a running dive into the pool. "Last one in the pool's a chicken," she called out, challenging him.

By the time she surfaced from her dive he was in the water next to her. And once again it was on.

Making out in the pool was a challenge, but they were both into it, nearly drowning in the process as they came together in a tangle of arms and legs, choking and spluttering for air.

They finally emerged from the pool, wet and giggling.

"Wow!" she gasped. "I gotta say – you're pretty active for an old man."

"Old my ass," he said, picking up a couple of large cabana towels and tossing one at her.

"How old *are* you?" she asked, wrapping the towel around her, sarong-style.

"Thirty-nine. And you?"

"Twenty-five."

"Seems to me that's about right," he said, toweling his hair dry.

"For what?"

"For you and I to be together."

"Yeah, yeah . . ." she drawled, not quite sure what he meant. It wasn't as if she was about to move in.

He threw her a quizzical look. Somehow he knew the chase was only just beginning. Cameron was elusive, he'd have to tread carefully to get her to make any kind of commitment, and wasn't *that* a joke, considering *he* was supposed to be the commitment-phobic one, the one who usually ran in the other direction once the deal was sealed.

It was getting chilly out, so they made their way into the house.

"Where's Butch?" she asked.

"Had to shut him in the gym."

"Why would you do that?"

"'Cause he jumps up on the kitchen counter and eats the chef's food. The guy's French, hates dogs."

"Great!" Cameron said, frowning. "Can you please go let him out, it's not fair to shut him away like that."

"Yes, ma'am!"

"Will you stop saying that."

"You've got to admit – you *are* bossy."

"I told you before – I'm *not* bossy."

"Whatever you say."

"Go get your dog."

"Yes, m—"

"Don't you dare!"

Laughing, he ran upstairs to release Butch.

"I'm taking a shower," she called out after him. "Is that okay?"

"Go ahead," he yelled over his shoulder. "I'll join you in a minute."

Hmm . . . was he insatiable or simply gifted?

She couldn't help smiling. The sex was sensational and he was so easy to be around, not at all what she'd expected.

Do not take it too seriously. The guy's a big player. Divorced twice. A love 'em and leave 'em kind.

I'm not looking for an involvement.

Oh yes you are.

His shower was state of the art, with jets shooting water from eight different angles, and a glass-enclosed TV.

A TV in the shower! How wild was that!

By the time he joined her he was ready to rock 'n' roll again.

"What are you – a Viagra freak?" she questioned breathlessly as he soaped her body with the most amazing fragrant soap he informed her he had imported from the South of France.

"Just lucky, I guess," he said, smoothing soap onto her nipples, a move which started driving her into a frenzy. "Tried Viagra once, and ended up with a hard-on that lasted three days."

"Lucky you," she murmured.

"Not so lucky," he said ruefully. "Had to go to the hospital where a nurse slapped it down."

"Sounds painful."

"It was," he said, gently pushing her up against the glass block walls of the shower and maneuvering himself inside her.

After a few minutes she couldn't take it anymore.

"Oh God!" she gasped, climaxing for the third time that night. "You're—"

"What?"

"Pretty . . . damn . . . good."

Later, swaddled in white toweling bathrobes, they raided the kitchen to see what the chef had left behind. They discovered plenty of hors d'oeuvres – including a selection of tiny baked potatoes filled with caviar, miniature duck pancakes with plum dipping sauce, and baby pizzas.

Don grabbed a bottle of red wine, and they put everything on a tray and took it into the living room, where they settled in front of a fire, with Butch comfortably stretched out at their feet.

"Y'know, this is maybe the best night I've spent in a long time," Don mused, putting his arm around her. "You gotta admit we're very compatible, Cam. Are you feeling it too?"

"And that would be because –?"

"'Cause I don't get the vibe that you want anything from me. Most people do."

"What do they want?" she asked curiously.

"Oh, y'know, my money, my fame . . . oh yeah," he added with a hollow laugh, "and my body. But *you* got that now."

"I do?" she said, snuggling close.

"If you want it."

"I'll take it on a rental," she said, nibbling on a duck pancake.

"A rental?"

"That way it's nothing permanent."

"Oh, so I guess that means you're not into anything permanent?"

"Are you?" she responded, tossing it right back at him.

"You're an odd one, you know that?" he said, giving her a long, penetrating look.

"Odd, how?"

"Mysterious. Not like other women. Do you realize that I don't know anything about you. Your likes, your dislikes, your dating history. Most women can't wait to spill all that crap."

"That's because I live in the present, not the past," she said carefully.

"Which suits me just fine," he said, fixing her with another long look, and deciding that yes – she was indeed the perfect woman.

Chapter Thirty-Six

"How was your visit to that new gym?" Ryan asked, unable to stop himself from going there.

He'd worked late at his office the previous evening, and when he'd arrived home Mandy was out at one of her charity event meetings. Now it was morning, and he was in his bathroom, shaving, and Mandy had wandered in looking as if she was ready to ask him something. What a relief if the words that came out of her mouth were – *I want a divorce.*

He could fantasize, couldn't he?

"We didn't go," Mandy said. "Mary Ellen got called to the studio."

"It's probably just as well," Ryan said, keeping his voice even.

"Why's that?"

"Gym's aren't your thing. You're more into yoga, aren't you?"

"I'm into whatever keeps me looking good," she said, leaning over his shoulder and peering at her reflection in the mirror.

He knew it was his cue to say – *You always look good, honey.* But he couldn't bring himself to do so.

He hated that he was filled with such animosity toward his wife; it wasn't her fault she'd never been able to have his baby.

Jesus! It suddenly occurred to him – was *that* the real reason his marriage was breaking up? He wanted children and she couldn't deliver. Although she'd tried, hadn't she? Two miscarriages and a stillborn baby were tragic enough for anyone.

"I've been thinking," Mandy said, moving away from the mirror.

"What about?" he asked cautiously.

"I was thinking that maybe we should go away for a long weekend, somewhere relaxing before you get all bogged down with your next production."

"Mandy –" he said, feeling his stomach tighten. "I've been thinking too, and—"

Before he could finish the sentence his youngest nephew, Benji, burst into the room.

"Uncle Ryan, Uncle Ryan," Benji yelled, his words tumbling over each other. "Mom says we're gonna have a basketball hoop at our new house. That's so cool, Uncle Ryan. You gotta play. Can you? Can you?"

Mandy threw the little boy a disgusted look. "Have you ever heard of knocking before you enter a room?" she said coldly.

Benji ignored her, or maybe he just didn't hear her. "When we goin', Uncle Ryan? When we goin'?" the young boy asked, his longish hair falling in his eyes. "I packed all my stuff."

"Soon, Benji," Ryan assured him. "Where's your mom?"

"Dunno," Benji mumbled.

"Go find her, I'll see you in a minute."

Benji raced off, yelling – "Mom! Mom!"

"Those kids are so rude," Mandy huffed.

"Benji is five," Ryan pointed out.

"It's never too soon to develop manners," she sniffed.

Then her phone rang, and Benji came racing back with one of his brothers, and before long it was time for Ryan to pile everyone in his car and transport them to the house he'd rented for them, which was only a couple of blocks away on Alpine.

Evie and the boys were thrilled as they toured their new

house, the boys racing from room to room at top speed screaming with excitement. It was a family home with four bedrooms, a
swimming pool and a miniature basketball court.

"This has to be costing a fortune!" Evie exclaimed. "How will
I ever be able to pay you back?"

"That's okay, don't worry about it," Ryan said, delighted that
he could finally do something for his sister.

"As soon as the boys are settled in school I can start working
on your next movie, that's if you'd like me to."

"You know I'd like you to," he said, and he meant it.

Evie was a talented set designer, one of the best. She'd met
Marty when they were thrown together on a location shoot in
Arizona. At least she had three great boys out of the marriage, but
that was about it.

Fortunately, since getting served with a Restraining Order,
Marty appeared to have vanished. He wasn't at the Silverlake
house, and no one had heard from him. Ryan had plans to put
Evie together with a good divorce lawyer as soon as possible.

After Evie and the boys were organized, he took off for his
office, where Kara handed him his usual phone sheet.

He scanned it quickly, his eyes lingering on one name in particular. Mrs Heckerling.

What did *she* want?

Well yes, he knew what she wanted, but he wasn't in the
mood to deal with it. Besides, she had left a rather terse message
saying not to call her – she would call again.

Great! Exactly what he didn't need. Anya surfacing seven
years later married to his father-in-law. It didn't seem possible.
And yet it was.

No good deed goes unpunished.

Famous slogan. Undeniably true.

He couldn't help wondering how much Hamilton knew
about her past. Had she told her husband about Amsterdam and
her activities there? He sincerely doubted it.

Kara buzzed him. "Don't forget your lunch today with Don Verona and Phil Standard," she reminded him.

"Sure," he said, hoping that Don would not have something to tell him that he sure as hell didn't care to hear.

* * *

Cameron was just about to sit down with Cole in their office at *Paradise* to go over things, when Katie caught her on the phone.

"Have you seen the freaking tabloids?" Katie shouted, sounding excited.

"No," Cameron answered, balancing a mug of green tea and a slice of wheat toast. "What's up?"

"Get your ass out and buy 'em, 'cause you're all over the place."

"What *are* you talking about?" Cameron said, taking a bite of toast.

"You. Mary Ellen Evans and Don Verona. There's a big freaking story."

"I . . . I don't understand," Cameron stammered, almost choking on her toast.

"They've got pictures of Don arriving at *Paradise* with Mary Ellen. Then they've got a pic of *you* draped all over him on the way out. He's helping you into his car and the two of you look very cozy." Katie paused for breath. "*I* never saw photographers when we left, did you?"

"Oh God!" Cameron groaned. "This sounds really bad."

"The headline reads *LADIES' MAN – DON VERONA – STILL DOUBLE DIPPING.*"

"Huh?"

"I don't know what it means either," Katie said, "but if I was Mary Ellen I'd be way pissed. The whole story is about how she's always getting dumped on by guys. You gotta feel sorry for her."

"Damn!" Cameron exclaimed. "Why would they do this?"

"Anything for a juicy bit of scandal," Katie said. "And you gotta know that Mary Ellen's kinda one of the tabloids' faves. So is Don Verona."

"Yes, but how can they drag *me* into it?" Cameron said, quite agitated. "I'm not a public person."

"'Cause you were there," Katie said, adding a pissed off – "So was I, but they managed to crop me out."

"I'll call you later," Cameron said.

"You'd better."

"What's the deal?" Cole inquired as soon as she clicked off her phone. "Sounds dramatic."

"Apparently I'm in the tabloids," she explained, shaking her head.

"You?"

"Yes, me."

"Doing what?" Cole asked as if he didn't quite believe her.

"According to Katie, being carried out of here by Don."

"Oh shit! That ain't fly for business."

"Tell me about it," she said, trying to remember her exit from the party. Was it only three days ago? So much seemed to have happened since then. *Paradise* was taking off like a rocket, and last night she'd had sex with Don. Amazing sex, hot sex, different from sex-with-Marlon sex. And no – she was determinedly not thinking about Ryan – he was off her radar.

Last night had been pretty damn great, so great that she'd almost stayed the night at Don's house. But since she didn't want it to be too much too soon, she'd finally asked him to drive her home – which he'd done, reluctantly. On the way they'd collected Yoko and Lennon, then sat around talking until three a.m. Somehow or other he'd ended up spending the night in *her* bed, sharing *her* toothbrush in the morning and not leaving until eight. "No work-out today," he'd said triumphantly, like he was getting away with something.

In her mind she'd already decided that if she was sleeping with him, she would be sending somebody else to work him out. Maybe Reno or Dorian. She hadn't told him because she was sure he'd object. But since her motto was never mix business with pleasure, and since Don was now purely pleasure, she had no choice.

"I'll get Penni to go to the newsstand an' pick 'em up," Cole said, bringing her back to the present.

Penni, a skinny sixteen-year-old with enormous eyes and an enthusiastic attitude, was Carlos's very young niece whom they'd hired as an assistant to take care of all the things nobody else had time to do.

As soon as Cole asked, Penni raced out to pick up the offending tabloids.

Cameron wondered if she should call Don and warn him, then she figured he was probably at the studio, so somebody must have mentioned it to him by now.

Then why hadn't *he* called *her*?

Hmm . . . maybe Don Verona was into the chase, and now that they'd done the deed . . .

No! she told herself firmly. *Don isn't like that.*

Really? Exactly how well do you know him?

Penni returned with three of the weekly tabloids. Don and Mary Ellen had made the front page of all three – with an assortment of lurid headlines, and a smaller picture of Don with Cameron. She was indeed – to her chagrin – draped all over him.

"How did this happen?" she asked blankly, staring at the pictures.

"You tell me," Cole replied, being absolutely no help at all.

* * *

"You're supposed to control this kind of crap," Don steamed to Fanny, his show's publicist, a weary woman who'd been in the business too long to take anyone's shit – even Don Verona's.

Fanny made a hopeless gesture. "*People, Esquire, US* – those kind of publications I can control to a degree, but the tabloids – forget about it."

She wanted to add – *Stop sleeping with two women at a time and this might not happen* – but she didn't, because it would only infuriate him further. Besides, Don's producer, Jerry Mann, was shooting her a warning look.

"I hate the goddamn tabloids," Don grumbled, continuing his rant. "They slime their way into people's lives printing a shit-load of half-truths, doing their best to fuck everyone up."

"It's yesterday's trash," Jerry pointed out. "Nobody reads 'em."

"You mean nobody *admits* to reading them," Don corrected. "It's like *Playboy* when guys say they only buy it for the articles and the interviews – when meanwhile they're jerking off all over Miss Fucking January three times a night."

"Three times?" Jerry said with a hearty laugh. "That's impressive!"

"Not me – you putz!" Don said, finally cracking a smile as he recalled that last night with Cameron it had indeed been three times, and every one of them memorable.

"You're smiling," Jerry said. "That's a good sign. Now maybe we can go over tonight's guests?"

"Sure," Don said. "But first can someone tell my assistant to send Mary Ellen Evans two dozen roses with a note that says something like *Sorry about the rags, will call soon – Don*."

"Not roses," Fanny interjected.

"Why?" Don said, frowning.

"Not roses if you don't intend to see her again."

"Excellent point. What then?"

"An orchid plant," Fanny suggested. "Expensive and appropriate."

"Okay. Can you arrange it, sweetheart?"

"*Sweetheart?*" Fanny said, her penciled eyebrows shooting up.

"You know I love you," Don said, turning on full-wattage charm. "So please do this one little thing for me."

"While I'm taking care of your dirty work – how about the other one?" Fanny asked, unable to resist.

"The other what?"

"The other woman you're photographed with."

"Uh . . . don't worry about her. I'll take care of her personally."

Fanny and Jerry exchanged knowing looks. "Roses!" they both said in unison.

"Get fucked," Don said, but suddenly he was smiling again.

"See you later," Fanny said, heading for the door.

"Do me a big one," Jerry said as soon as Fanny left. "Try not to screw the guests then dump 'em. It makes re-booking them a big problem, and that problem always seems to end up in *my* lap."

"Who've we got tonight?" Don asked, ignoring Jerry's request. "And if you tell me another of those dumb would-be celebutants, I'll fucking kill you."

"You'll be happy," Jerry said. "Don Rickles."

"Thank Christ! Finally someone I can talk to!"

"Yeah," Jerry agreed. "Someone you don't get to fuck, and that alone makes a refreshing change."

Chapter Thirty-Seven

A rmed with a list of suggestions for Lucy's forthcoming dinner, Mandy turned up at *Mr Chow* ten minutes early. She was in an excellent mood, looking forward to Evie and her kids being gone by the time she got home. What a nightmare it had been having three wild boys running throughout her house screaming and breaking things. Ryan hadn't seemed to mind, but then he'd always loved kids.

Sometimes she felt guilty about her failure to provide him with an heir – because everyone knew that's what all men wanted – a little mirror image of themselves. But it wasn't meant to be. She'd tried, hadn't she? It wasn't her fault things hadn't worked out. Although . . . if she really thought about it, which she didn't like to do, maybe it *was* her fault.

From the beginning of their marriage Ryan had always wanted children. Unbeknownst to him, having babies was the last thing on her mind, but of course she didn't tell *him* that. Instead, after they'd been married a year, she informed him she was pregnant – a lie – and then eight weeks later she informed him that sadly, she'd experienced a miscarriage – another lie.

He was so considerate and caring that it had made their marriage even better. Men were so naive and pliable – it was ridiculous.

Eighteen months later when she was planning on pulling the same stunt again, she discovered to her horror that she was actually pregnant. Panic ensued; she did not want kids under any circumstances. No! No! No! She'd seen what having children had done to some of the women she knew. None of them ever properly recovered their pre-baby shape, and – in spite of legions of nannies who came and went on a regular basis – they were always exhausted and sleep-deprived. Quite frankly, having babies made them incredibly boring.

Mandy hatched yet another of her devious plans. After telling Ryan the good news, she lived with it for a few weeks – quite enjoying the attention and love he lavished upon her, all the while waiting for him to go off on a four-day location shoot. As soon as he left, she high-tailed it to a doctor in Mexico who came highly recommended, and went through a quick abortion.

When Ryan returned from his trip he found her in bed with more sad miscarriage news. The disappointment on his face was palpable, but once again he rallied and was totally there for her.

Then three years ago, Hamilton had summoned her to his house and told her quite bluntly that he required a grandson, and if she didn't drop a baby within the next year, he'd marry a woman young enough to give him as many children as he wanted, and those kids would be the ones to share her inheritance.

Get pregnant or share her inheritance! No! That was impossible. So after much thought she'd decided that she'd better have a baby, and fast. Filled with a steely determination, she'd immediately set about conceiving.

Within three months she was pregnant. Triumphant, she suffered through eight and a half uncomfortable and infuriating months before giving birth to their baby. And shockingly their baby – a son – was stillborn.

It was devastating. To think that she'd gone through so much and the result was a baby who apparently had died in her womb.

Over the next few months she couldn't help wondering if it had anything to do with the abortion she'd never told anyone about, especially when her doctor informed her that because of certain complications she would not be able to conceive again.

Was this God's way of punishing her?

She refused to entertain the thought.

Once again Ryan was there for her, but this time it wasn't enough. Slowly they began drifting apart, cumulating with their discussion in the car when Ryan had mentioned that they should consider going to couples counseling. Anyone with half a brain knew that couples counseling was the beginning of the end, so Mandy had determined to make things right, but it wasn't proving to be easy. Ryan was becoming more and more distant, and the nicer she was to him, the more he drew away.

It wasn't the perfect situation, and for once she was not quite sure what she could do to correct it.

Somehow there had to be a solution, there always was.

*   *   *

For the second day *Paradise* was packed. Looking around the crowded gym, Cameron experienced a shiver of pure joy. She'd done it! She'd actually done it. She'd opened her own place and it was a big success. What a sensational feeling.

Who would've thought that everything would move onto the fast track from day one. They'd only been open for two days and each trainer was fully booked for the rest of the week. It was amazing what a little publicity achieved, although she could've done without the damn tabloids.

Cole was working with an actress client; Dorian was watching Roger – his favorite closeted actor – lift weights; Cherry was bouncing around with a couple of her younger clientele; and Reno was conducting a spinning class out on the terrace.

Over at the front desk Lynda was valiantly trying to man the phones – which never stopped. She was also attempting to organize the membership paperwork.

Cameron could see that Lynda desperately needed someone to help her out, and Penni was not exactly that someone. The young teenager was fine for running errands, fetching coffee and picking up the tabloids, which Cameron was trying to forget about. It was obvious that they had to hire more help.

Glancing at her watch, Cameron realized it was now noon and Don had not called. Was she expecting him to?

Yes. They'd had sex, hadn't they? They'd spent the night together in *her* bed – that was a first.

She tried to recall how they'd left it.

They were sitting in her kitchen drinking coffee, when he'd suddenly glanced out the kitchen window which overlooked the street, and yelled – "I'm getting a goddamn ticket. I don't believe it!" And with that, he'd thrown her a quick kiss and made a run for his precious Ferrari.

Goodbye, Don Verona.

Now she knew how Mary Ellen felt. Or did she? Unlucky Mary Ellen splashed across the tabloids again, portrayed as loser girlfriend of the month. It wasn't very nice. And Cameron was partly to blame.

But hey – it wasn't as if she'd stolen him. Don had told her quite clearly that he and Mary Ellen were not an item, except she'd witnessed the actress emerging from his bedroom early one morning.

Sighing, she wondered if she'd made a mistake. And as she was wondering this, three dozen purple roses arrived with a note that read – *You're not bossy, you're organized. And I'm definitely in like. See you later? D.*

What was the question mark all about? Did it mean that *she* was supposed to call *him*?

I told you not to get involved. I warned you it would be a distraction. Weren't you better off with Marlon where it was just sex for sex's sake?

No. I have no regrets. I knew exactly what I was doing.

Before she could think about it further, Charlene Lewis walked in, followed by a sallow-faced man who Cameron presumed was Charlene's bodyguard – someone had to watch the diamonds.

"Too busy to come to me," Charlene scolded, resplendent in a lime-green cat suit and full makeup. Clouds of *Angel* enveloped anyone who ventured within two feet of her. "I'll try it here once," Charlene continued, wagging a finger at Cameron who was standing by the front desk contemplating her flowers and Don's note, "but I'm sure you're aware how much I cherish my privacy."

Her huge diamond ring caught the light, blinding Lynda, who scowled at Charlene – one of her least favorite clients.

"Are you Cameron Paradise?" the bodyguard asked, shoving his way in front of Charlene.

"Yes," Cameron said, thinking how rude the man was. "And if you'd like to wait—"

Before she could finish her sentence, he thrust an official-looking document at her. "Consider yourself served," he said, and swiftly departed.

*   *   *

It was a busy day at *The Grill*. Ryan found himself stopping at almost every table before he made it to Phil and Don, who were already seated.

"You're late," Don said, tapping his watch. "I can only spare an hour. Got to get back to the studio. Don Rickles is on tonight – for him I have to prepare."

"Rickles is something else," Phil said admiringly. "A true original. I presume you're ready to have the shit insulted out of you?"

"Ready and happy about it," Don said, waving a greeting at fellow talk-show host, Craig Ferguson, who was sitting at a nearby table. Craig and Jon Stewart were the only late-night shows he made an attempt to watch – their monologues were always insightful and sometimes quite brilliant.

"What's new?" Ryan asked, noting that Don seemed particularly relaxed – a sure sign that he'd recently gotten laid.

"What's new is that my insane wife is insisting we throw one of those dumb-ass dinner parties that you all seem to like so much," Phil complained. "People wandering all over our house, crapping in our toilets, disturbing the animals. On top of which I have to feed a bunch of ungrateful assholes. I'm not happy about it, I'm not in favor of it—"

"But you said yes," Don interrupted with a knowing grin. "She had your balls in the palm of her hand, and before she squeezed—"

"I said yes," Phil admitted, stroking his beard which looked like it was in dire need of a trim. "'Cause what's a fellow supposed to do if he's after a little peace in his everyday world?"

"I thought you had yourself a little piece every morning," Don quipped. "That's the word on the street."

"Had to fire her," Phil grumbled. "Lucy didn't like me doing it so close to home."

"How *do* you get away with it?" Ryan asked, ordering a Jack Daniel's because he felt like it.

"Drinking – in the middle of the day?" Don said, raising a caustic eyebrow. "What's going on with you?"

"You sound like a fuckin' A.A. sponsor," Ryan snapped. "And since I'm not an alcoholic – keep your shit to yourself."

"Somebody needs to get laid," Phil said, guffawing.

"Aw, leave him alone," Don said good-naturedly. "He's trying to work something out. Right, buddy?"

Damn! Ryan thought. *He slept with her. I know it. It's written all over his too-handsome-for-his-own-good goddamn face.*

Fucking asshole.

Fucking prick.

Why did he have to include Cameron in his long list of conquests?

Why the *fuck*?

* * *

"How many people are you thinking of inviting?" Mandy asked, casually dipping a shrimp in plum sauce and popping it in her mouth.

Lucy shrugged. "I haven't really thought about it."

"Well, think," Mandy said, in full bossy mode. "I can't advise anything unless I know how many guests are on your list."

"Hmm . . ." Lucy frowned. She knew she wanted to launch her script – but the group shouldn't be too large. "Maybe twelve including Phil and me," she said at last. "Our big table just about accommodates twelve."

"Then two chefs, three waiters, a barman, valet parking, and two helpers," Mandy said briskly, ticking off the amount of help on her fingers. "I'll e-mail you the number of my party organizer, she'll do everything for you."

"God!" Lucy exclaimed, imagining Phil's face when she handed him the bills. "It sounds expensive, Phil will be pissed, he hates spending money."

"What man loves it?" Mandy observed. "Men are all tightwads unless they happen to be a big spender – and there's not very many of those around – not in this town."

"True," Lucy agreed.

"Have you ever known an actor to pick up a check?" Mandy continued. "Believe me, that's a rarity – unless you're out with Michael Caine."

"I worked with Michael once," Lucy said, remembering the English movie star and his exotically beautiful wife, Shakira. "He was a sweetheart – he taught me so much about acting."

"And as I said – generous," Mandy added.

Lucy gave a vague nod, she was busy thinking about who she should invite to her dinner. The Richards, of course, and Don with a date, Hamilton and his new wife – although she wouldn't mention she was asking them to Mandy – one never knew with Mandy, it might not be a popular move. She'd also invite a couple of key producers who might be interested in her script. Maybe Anne and Arnold Kopelson – producers of such successful movies as *Seven* and *The Fugitive*. Or the Bruckheimers, although Jerry was knee-deep in übersuccessful TV shows such as the *CSI* series – so he might not be available.

Marlon – she decided – would be her surprise guest. She'd bring him out over dessert, introduce him to everyone, and then they'd hand out copies of the finished script.

She might even do a reading. Yes, that was a brilliant idea, although she'd need an actor to read with her. Hmm . . . someone who wouldn't send Phil into a jealous rage.

It never occurred to her that Marlon might set her possessive husband off.

"You're so quiet," Mandy remarked. "Don't tell me you're worried about Phil spending money, the man is *loaded*. What's he saving it for? Dinner parties are fun, and if you listen to me and hire the right people, yours will be great."

Lucy nodded her agreement. Yes, it would be. She'd make sure of it.

ANYA

At first Anya wasn't sure what she wanted from Seth. Was it his money?

No, because he was certainly not rich.

Was it his power?

He didn't have any power. He was a hardworking lawyer at a big law firm.

Was it his life?

Ah . . . to be an American housewife with a baby and a husband to look after. Was that her dream?

She didn't have dreams anymore, they'd all been shattered the day she'd watched the soldiers slit Svlenta's throat, and shoot the girl's parents in the head, then set their house on fire while she cowered in a corner, whimpering with fear. No more dreams after that as she was passed around from man to man, all of them relentlessly using her. No more dreams . . .

Seth Carpenter would be her stepping stone to better things. She had to start somewhere, and he was it.

Before Velma had so cruelly deserted her – leaving her to the mercies of Joe – Velma had drummed into her head the three things to say to a man that would ensnare him for however long a girl wished to keep him around.

Anya had not forgotten Velma's wise words.

Your cock is so big.

You're the best lover I've ever had.

You make me come so hard.

She tried the first line on Seth after they'd made love on the bed he shared with his wife while the baby was asleep in the other room. It was lunch-time, and the rain was pounding down outside. She'd opened her legs and welcomed him inside her as if he was the first man she'd ever allowed to visit such a sacred place.

They'd been building toward this moment for weeks. He'd been coming home at lunch-time almost every day, and very slowly she'd drawn him in, until he was so desperate to have her that she was quite certain he couldn't wait a moment longer.

"Your cock is so big." The admiring words made him swell up with pride.

Actually, his cock was not big at all, but Anya could see how the words worked magic.

After the first time it was easy to leave telling clues around the apartment — an earring in the bed, a pair of black lace panties in the bedroom.

Diana was not stupid – it didn't take her long to discover what was going on.

By this time Anya had Seth exactly where she wanted him. He was besotted with her, and could not imagine spending another day without her, so when Diana fired her and threw her husband out, Seth did exactly as Anya hoped he would, he suggested that he rent an apartment, and that she should move out of the hostel and come live with him.

Step one accomplished. An American man of her own.

It was a promising start.

Chapter Thirty-Eight

Somehow Ryan got through lunch, going out of his way not to ask Don any questions. It infuriated him that his best friend had the attitude of a strutting peacock, he was so pleased with himself it was sickening. And of course, Don could not resist mentioning his latest conquest. "I'll be bringing Cameron to your dinner," he informed Phil. "So be warned – keep your sweaty hands to yourself. She's not the kind of woman who appreciates getting groped."

"Who's Cameron?" Phil boomed.

"Someone I'm kind of getting involved with," Don allowed, a sly smile creeping across his face.

Ryan experienced a sour feeling in the pit of his stomach. *How* involved? Was Cameron just another one of Don's conquests? Or was this time the real thing?

"What happened to TV Girl?" Phil asked, busily attacking a formidable steak and a side order of French fries.

"TV Girl is not for me," Don said, dismissing Mary Ellen with a casual shrug.

"And this new one is?" Phil wanted to know.

"Could be," Don replied, his smile widening. "Ryan's met her. Cameron's a peach, right, Ryan?"

Ryan grunted; he was not about to encourage this

burgeoning affair. The truth was, he was hoping it would go away as quickly as possible.

"Y'see, he's in like too," Don said, laughing. "But seriously, Phil, this one's special, you'll see."

"You fucked her?" Phil asked in his usual crass way.

"For crissake," Don said, shaking his head. "If I had, you'd be the last person I'd tell."

"Never stopped you before," Phil observed.

"Jesus Christ! You are such a horny old dog."

"It takes one to know one," Phil said, happily chewing on a succulent piece of steak.

* * *

"You'll have to get rid of the children and the animals for the night," Mandy decided, all bossy and in control. "You can bundle them off to your mother's."

"My mother is living in Palm Springs with a twenty-six-year-old out-of-work landscaper," Lucy said dryly. "I doubt if she'd be interested in babysitting."

"Really?" Mandy said, surprised. "You never told me."

"You never asked," Lucy retorted. "Besides, why would I even mention the woman after she wrote that tell-all book about me filled with nothing but disgusting lies."

"Wasn't that years ago?" Mandy said, vaguely remembering a scandalous book about the very famous Lucy Lyons that had caused a mild sensation at the time. "Before you married Phil?"

"Ten years," Lucy stated, trying to control the feelings of anger and hurt that swept over her whenever she recalled her mother's betrayal. "I was at the height of my career, so the bitch couldn't help herself from cashing in."

"Mothers!" Mandy sighed. "I never had one – merely a series of step-mothers, each one more annoying than the last."

"Maybe you lucked out," Lucy said bitterly. "Mine is not exactly a day at the beach – more nightmare on Elm Street."

"Well then," Mandy said, bored with the subject of mothers, "have you got a neighbor who'll take the kids?"

"Can't I just tell Nanny to make sure they stay in their rooms?"

"Absolutely not," Mandy said, her voice firm. "Kids are disruptive, they'll come running in and start annoying everyone. Besides, the staff hate tripping over kids, it ruins their entertaining flow."

Lucy couldn't help wondering how Mandy knew all this, considering she had no children of her own. "I can ask Nanny to take them to her aunt's house," Lucy said. "That'll work."

"*And* the animals," Mandy reminded. "Oh yes, and you should get in a proper cleaning crew to spiff up your house."

"Why?"

"Because it's the thing to do since you haven't entertained in I don't know how long. I can't remember the last time you had people over."

"That would be because we haven't entertained at home since the night of our wedding," Lucy revealed. "Phil was too cheap to throw the reception elsewhere."

"Oh my *God*!" Mandy exclaimed. "Has it been that long?"

"Time goes quickly when you're having fun," Lucy said with a dry chuckle.

"I was sleeping with that sexy German chef my father loathed," Mandy recalled, eyes gleaming at the memory. "I hadn't even met Ryan – was he there?"

"Ryan was away on a location shoot, but Don was very much present with his first wife – the ballet dancer. You remember her?"

"How could I forget?" Mandy said. "All the guys were drooling over *that* one. She had exceptionally long legs and her party trick was doing the splits. What a show-off!"

"You must admit she was quite a stunner. Don was a very happy camper."

312

"Not for long," Mandy said quickly.

"You're absolutely right," Lucy said, as it all came flooding back. "Didn't he divorce her a year later after he caught her cheating with their building contractor?"

"Oh yes!" Mandy squealed. "Who could forget *that*."

"Don was beyond furious," Lucy said.

"I'm sure it didn't do much for his ego, although he soon bounced back," Mandy said. "But then our Don always does. Anyway," she added, through with reminiscing, "the kids must go, *and* the animals. Work it out."

"I'll try," Lucy said unsurely. "Although Phil will not appreciate losing his parrot for the night; he's crazy about that damn bird."

"The one you told me screams *fuck you* all the time?"

"That's the one," Lucy said grimly.

"If it was in my house I'd shoot the little bugger," Mandy said, tapping her freshly manicured nails on the table.

"If I did that, Phil would shoot *me*," Lucy replied.

"Ah, but think of all the publicity if he did," Mandy said with a sly chuckle. "You'd be right back in the headlines."

"Thanks, Mandy," Lucy said tartly. "I do believe there are better ways of getting there."

"Mary Ellen's coming for coffee," Mandy announced. "After lunch we're going to try and check out that new fitness place again – *Paradise*. Why don't you come with?"

"I might do that," Lucy said thoughtfully. Yes, if she was to resume her career she'd better be in fantastic shape.

Joining a gym was definitely top of her list of things to do.

* * *

"Hey," Don said, speaking on the phone in his car.

"Hey," Cameron responded, taking a quick peek at her watch. It was almost three and Don was finally calling.

313

It infuriated her that she was fast becoming the kind of girl who waited for a man to call her, instead of picking up the phone herself and calling him. They'd had great sex. He'd run out of her house early in the morning. He should've called before this.

"How are you today?" he asked.

"Really good," she answered caustically. "Considering I just got served with a writ from Mister Fake Tan."

"Who's Mister Fake Tan?" he asked, sounding faintly amused.

"The asshole I used to rent space from. He's suing 'cause he claims we're taking business away from him."

"Did you sign an employment agreement with this guy?"

"No. I told you," she said impatiently. "I merely rented space in his gym and paid commission."

"Then it's no problem," Don said smoothly. "I'll have my killer lawyer deal with it."

She knew she should say – *No, I'll deal with it myself.* But Don's killer lawyer sounded like a far better option.

"Okay," she said, hoping she didn't sound like too much of a weakling.

"I'll send a messenger to pick up the relevant papers."

"Are you sure?"

"For you – anything," he said gallantly, then after a quick beat – "Did you get my flowers?"

"They're beautiful," she said. "Oh yes, and I also saw the tabloids."

"Ignore 'em," he said casually, as if they didn't matter. "It's all total crap. They never get anything right."

"But what about Mary Ellen?" Cameron said. "I feel bad for her."

"Not your problem."

"I know, but shouldn't you phone her?"

"For what?"

"To explain."

"Yeah, I'll give her a call," he said, with no intention of doing so. He hadn't forced Mary Ellen into his bed, she'd come willingly. It wasn't anyone's fault that they shared no chemistry, and furthermore he'd sent her an expensive orchid plant as a consolation prize. "Are we on for dinner tonight?" he asked, abruptly getting off the subject of Mary Ellen.

"I don't know," Cameron answered tentatively. "Are we?"

"It's your call."

Why was it her call? Shouldn't he be saying – *I must see you – last night was amazing*?

Yes, he should.

"It's been pretty hectic here today," she said, keeping it casual. "I sense an early night in my future."

"You do, huh?"

"You don't mind, do you?"

"Not at all, but I was thinking that maybe this weekend we'd take your dogs and mine and veg out at my Malibu house. Does that work for you?"

Yes, it definitely worked for her.

"Sounds great," she said.

"Anyway, I'll see you in the a.m. We'll make a plan. Try to watch my show tonight, Don Rickles is on, it'll be a riot. Rickles is still the funniest guy around."

"If I'm awake."

"Haven't you ever heard of TiVo?"

"Don't have one."

She clicked off her phone feeling strangely disappointed. What had she expected? He was Don Verona, he wasn't just another guy.

Tomorrow morning she decided to send Reno to work out with him. Don probably wouldn't like it, but if she was going to continue seeing him, that's the way it had to be.

Well . . . at least she had the weekend to look forward to. Maybe he'd open up then, be a little warmer and more loving.

Loving? Is that what you want?

Absolutely not.
I warned you not to get involved.
Oh, screw off!

*   *   *

Back at the studio Don contemplated his conversation with Cameron. She'd sounded a tiny bit cool, hardly as into him as he would've expected after last night. Determined not to have her back away, he'd played it cool himself, not coming on too strong. Although after one night of exceptional sex and tantalizing company he was almost on the verge of asking her to move in with him.

How insane was *that*? He was Don Verona, for crissakes, not some love-sick jerk with a hard-on and a crush.

And yet . . . he couldn't stop thinking about her. The way she looked, the way she smelled, the way she was in bed . . . everything about her was a turn-on.

Making him wait had only heightened his attraction toward her. He was hooked in a very big way. And he liked it.

Or did he?

Jesus! She was confusing the hell out of him, messing with his concentration. And that he didn't need.

Jerry ambled into his office smelling of cigars and garlic – a bad mix.

"We're gonna have a great show tonight," Jerry offered. "Everyone around here gets excited when Rickles puts in an appearance."

"I know," Don said, nodding. "Smart move giving him all three segments. We'll both have a blast."

"No dumb starlets flashing their panties – or lack of 'em – tonight," Jerry said with a hearty chuckle. "Disappointed?"

"Are you kidding me?" Don replied. "That ditzy blonde last night sent her stylist to my dressing room with a card on which she'd written her private number and a scrawled message – *Call me – let's continue our interview all the way to my bedroom.*"

"Didja call her?" Jerry asked, eyes bugging.

"Jerry," Don said patiently, "I'm seeing someone. And even if I wasn't, desperate actresses with fake tits are not my style."

"So who're you seeing?" Jerry inquired, his interest perked.

"Nobody you know," Don replied, not ready to share.

"If you read the tabloids, you'd know," Jill Khoner announced, entering the office with the proposed questions for the Rickles interview.

"I've read the tabloids," Jerry said. "It's neither of those two."

"How do you know?" Jill asked, handing Don a sheaf of papers.

"'Cause they're both getting kiss-off flowers."

"Jesus!" Don said. "Go ahead and discuss my love life. Feel free."

Jill laughed. "And what exactly *were* you doing with our dyke friend?"

For a moment he was lost for words, and that wasn't like him. But Jill was totally out of line, so what the hell – he went for it.

"Cameron is not gay," he said forcibly. "And even if she was, I don't like you using the word 'dyke' as if it's something to be ashamed of."

"Sorry!" Jill said, exchanging a startled look with Jerry. "I didn't realize—"

"*What* didn't you realize?" Don said, fixing her with a steely look.

Jill knew exactly when to shut up.

317

Chapter Thirty-Nine

Mary Ellen arrived at *Mr Chow* trailed by a ferocious pack of paparazzi who were immediately barred entry. Bitching and complaining, they were forced to gather outside while Mary Ellen ran into the restaurant to join Mandy and Lucy.

She appeared stressed, although it was obvious she had made an effort to look her best in a short white Donna Karan dress and a light blue Richard Tyler jacket. Her eyes were hidden beneath enormous Dolce & Gabanna black-out shades, and she kept on squeezing her hands together in an agitated fashion.

"What's the matter?" Mandy asked, as Mary Ellen sat down at their table.

"Your friend, Don Verona," Mary Ellen hissed. "He's another cheating low-life sonofabitch! I hate him!"

"Oh God! What's he done now?" Mandy inquired, always anxious to get the details.

"Well," Mary Ellen said, still agitated, "I thought we had something good going on, but apparently *he* thought otherwise."

"That's Don for you," Mandy said, acting as if she knew him better than anyone.

Digging into her oversized Prada purse, Mary Ellen produced a page torn from *Truth and Fact* and proceeded to read out the headline. *"LADIES' MAN – DON VERONA – STILL*

DOUBLE DIPPING." She threw down the offending page in disgust. "Double dipping! How does that make *me* look?"

"Not great," Lucy said sympathetically.

"Damn right!" Mary Ellen snapped, completely out of the girl-next-door mode. "Don Verona is a lying creep. And so is that bitch – Cameron Shitface Lying CUNT!"

"Why don't you tell us how you really feel," Lucy murmured.

"She feels like crap," Mandy said, picking up the torn page and reading more. "And quite frankly I don't blame her, do you?"

"I thought he was the one," Mary Ellen said sadly, a lone tear emerging from her black shades and snaking its way down her cheek. "Now he does this to me."

"Did you sleep with him?" Mandy asked, mentally ready to take down even more details.

"Of course she slept with him," Lucy said scornfully. "Who wouldn't? The man is a hunk."

"Is he as expert in bed as everyone says?" Mandy asked. She'd been dying to get the real inside on Don's bedroom prowess for years, and now was the perfect opportunity.

"Yes," Mary Ellen muttered. "Although I gave him head for fifteen minutes and he didn't reciprocate."

"Not acceptable," Mandy said.

"Ha!" Lucy exclaimed, quickly joining in. "You should sleep with Phil – that's *all* he wants to do."

This was news to Mandy, who would now regard Phil with new eyes. Men who *really* enjoyed going down on a woman were not thick on the ground. Ever since her first fake pregnancy Ryan had not gone down on her once. It wasn't that she cared, sex was hardly her favorite activity, although when she put her mind to it she could be an enthusiastic participant. At fifteen she'd perfected the art of giving a great blow-job, just so boys would really like her.

It had worked – she'd landed Ryan, hadn't she?

"I think I'll become a lesbian," Mary Ellen mused. "That'll *really* give the rags something to gossip about."

"Interesting choice," Lucy mused. "Have you *seen* how beautiful the actresses are on Showtime's *The L Word*?"

"She was only joking," Mandy said, throwing Lucy a look. "Weren't you, dear?"

"If we're going to drop by that new fitness place we'd better get moving," Lucy said, glancing at her watch. "I have to meet a writer at four."

"What writer?" Mandy asked.

"A young guy I hired," Lucy answered vaguely, wondering if Marlon would try to kiss her again. She hadn't minded that much when he'd made his first attempt. It was quite refreshing to be desired by someone other than her husband, and Marlon *did* desire her – oh yes, big time.

"I can't go to that gym," Mary Ellen said, spitting her anger. "It's where *that woman* works."

"What woman?" Lucy asked, not making the connection.

"The one who's throwing herself all over Don," Mary Ellen said, her voice rising. "The *bitch* who pretended to me that she was just his trainer."

"Maybe that's all she is," Lucy offered.

"Sure," Mary Ellen responded, a spiteful twist to her mouth. "She's training his cock to head straight for her lying cunt!"

*   *   *

"Mrs Heckerling is on the line," Kara said, buzzing Ryan in his office where he was in the middle of a meeting with his line producer.

"Give me a minute, Keith," he said. "I've got to take this."

Keith ducked out of the room and Ryan picked up the phone.

He really didn't have to take the call at all, but he was anxious to hear what Anya had to say seven years later.

"We should meet," Anya said, her voice low and secretive.

"Why's that?" he responded.

320

"I need to talk to you," she said. "Hamilton is flying to Japan next Saturday. I can see you then. Is there a place we can meet that is discreet?"

Discreet? Ryan thought. In L.A.? A mogul's young wife and the mogul's son-in-law. Nothing discreet about that. TMZ and Perez Hilton would lap it up.

He considered their options.

A hotel room?

No! No! No!

A motel somewhere like Culver City?

Even worse!

A bar?

Forget about it.

Then it came to him. A friend's house. Somewhere completely private.

Don's house.

In a perverse way, Ryan felt that Don owed him.

* * *

When Cameron left *Paradise* with Cole, she was not expecting an onslaught of photographers. They rushed her, merrily flashing away while shouting out a laundry list of questions.

Are you and Don Verona an item?

Have you known him long?

When are you seeing him again?

How do you feel about Mary Ellen?

Are you two rivals?

She held onto Cole's arm. "This is ridiculous," she whispered. "I'm nobody. Why are they doing this?"

"I guess you're somebody now," he said, not as put out as she would have expected.

"I'm making a run for my car," she informed him.

"Good luck," he said. "Try not to freak. I'll check in with you later." Then he gave her a quick kiss on the cheek and headed for his motorcycle.

She made it to her Mustang, still trailed by photographers. The attention was horrendous. She wasn't used to it and she didn't like it – in fact, she hated it. If going out with Don Verona led to this, she wanted no part of it.

When she reached her house there were two men and a small truck blocking the entrance to her garage. She honked her horn, and one of the men meandered over to her open window.

"You're blocking my way," she pointed out.

"Are you Miz Paradise?" he asked.

Oh Christ! Not another writ.

"Who wants to know?" she said, staring at him suspiciously.

"We have a delivery for Miz Cameron Paradise."

"What delivery?" she asked, frowning.

"A TiVo and TV," the man said. "Compliments of Mr Verona. If you let us into your house, we'll set everything up."

An hour later she was staring at a brand new flat screen high def TV and a complicated TiVo that she had no idea how to work.

Was this a reward for sleeping with Don Verona? Great! Did he send every one of his conquests a new TV?

The whole thing was surreal. She didn't want his gifts, she would have preferred a more intimate phone call. But apparently that was not about to happen, so a TV and TiVo it was, whether she wanted them or not.

* * *

While Cameron was trying to figure out why Don had sent her a TV, Don himself was preparing to be interviewed by Natalie de Barge. He was not happy about it, but since he'd given Natalie his word there was no backing out.

Fanny, the P.R. for his show, was puzzled. "You can't stand being interviewed," she reminded him. "Why are you doing it?"

"I made a promise," he said off-handedly. "Besides, Natalie de Barge is controllable; she won't ask me anything I don't care to answer."

"*She's* not in control," Fanny muttered ominously. "Her producer is. You know that."

But nobody argued with Don when he'd made up his mind to do something, so Fanny went along with him to the studio where Natalie shot her hugely successful daily celebrity gossip-fest.

Natalie greeted Don with a hug and a whispered, "How about our investment taking off so fast? You must have the magic touch."

"I've been told that a time or two," he drawled.

"Hmmm . . ." Natalie said, smiling flirtatiously. "That's something I'll get to wonder about all day."

"What?"

"Your magic touch."

"Yeah?" Don said, smiling back at her.

"Do you need makeup?" she asked. "The girls in the makeup room are creaming to meet you."

"Sorry to disappoint, never wear it."

"Not even on your show?"

"Nope."

"Most guys on TV require more makeup than Marie Osmond," Natalie joked. "I should've guessed that you ride bare-backed."

"That too," Don said, grinning.

"Let's get on with this," Fanny interjected in her best bossy publicist voice. "Mr Verona has an extremely full schedule."

"I'm sure he does," Natalie murmured, thinking how much she couldn't stand publicists. They were always interfering, shoving in their two cents' opinions while attempting to control their clients. There were a few competent ones around, but Natalie did not consider Fanny to be one of them. Over the years they'd experienced several run-ins. However, Natalie decided, Fanny was not about to win this one, especially as Don had promised her this interview.

"If you're ready, Don, we can go straight through to the studio," she said, linking her arm through his, successfully shutting out Fanny, who silently fumed as she was relegated to walking behind them. "You can watch in the Green Room," Natalie threw over her shoulder.

"That's all right," Fanny answered, clenching her teeth. "I prefer to be on the set."

"Is that okay with you, Don?" Natalie asked.

"Sure," he said, anxious to get the ordeal over of answering questions as opposed to asking them.

"It's fine, Fanny," Natalie said off-handedly. "You can be on the set."

Black bitch, Fanny thought.

Dried-up white hag! Natalie thought.

The interview went smoothly enough until Natalie decided to get personal. Well, *she* didn't actually decide, her producer did, telling her through the earpiece stuck in her right ear that since the story of Don and two women was splashed all over the tabloids, it was her duty as a competent journalist to ask him about it.

He'd just finished telling an amusing antidote about Warren Beatty and Justin Timberlake who'd appeared together on his show, when Natalie launched in with questions about his love life. *How come two divorces? Who are you seeing now? Are the stories the tabloids print true? What is going on between you and Mary Ellen Evans? Are the two of you still dating? And why does she have such bad luck with men?*

Inwardly annoyed that she'd crossed the boundaries he'd set, Don deflected most of her questions with tact and charm. But when it came to Mary Ellen he was at a loss for words. She was one conquest he never should have made.

Finally it was over, and he left abruptly, listening to Fanny crow about how she'd warned him he shouldn't have appeared on such a gossip-fueled show.

Too late now, he thought wryly.

Depending on how Natalie cut the segment, he'd end up looking like an uncaring son of a bitch, or a player who was only interested in the game.

It was a no-win situation.

* * *

On his way home, Ryan stopped by Evie's to see how she and the boys were settling in.

"They're in heaven!" Evie informed him. "A swimming pool *and* a basketball court, it's too much."

"Next week you're seeing a lawyer," he said sternly. *And so am I*, he thought.

Evie gave a half-hearted nod. She'd finally come to the conclusion that Ryan was right and that she had to sever all ties with Marty and start afresh, but it wasn't easy.

The boys were delighted to see their uncle. He played hoops with them for a while before heading home, deciding that tonight could be the night he confronted Mandy.

But no, once again it was not to be. She had six girlfriends over and an Indian guru who was teaching them the meaning of life.

The meaning of life, indeed! Mandy had no clue – she simply got a high from following trends, and the current trend was spirituality.

The women were chanting. Several of them looked exactly alike with their long straight blonde hair, glowing complexions, and unlined faces. Their uniform seemed to be True Religion jeans, a James Perse white T-shirt and a Birkin pastel leather bag by their side.

Hollywood wives. The younger generation.

Ryan went straight upstairs and called Don. He was anxious to get the whole Anya meeting over and done with.

Don didn't answer.

Ryan imagined that Don was off somewhere with Cameron. Maybe in bed with Cameron . . . maybe making love to Cameron . . .

Dammit! He hardly knew the girl and he was hooked. Hopelessly, helplessly, hooked.

Chapter Forty

For a variety of reasons everyone was looking forward to the upcoming weekend. Cameron – because she was anxious to see how it was, spending more time with Don, and also simply wanting to get away and take a break. To her delight, *Paradise* was all systems go: the place had been packed all week.

Ryan was preparing to meet with Anya, see what she had to say. Don had called him back and agreed that he could use his house. Of course, Don was thinking that Ryan was getting it on with a woman other than Mandy. "Go for it!" Don had encouraged. "It's about time."

Ryan was intrigued to find out exactly how Anya had met Hamilton, and why Hamilton had married her without eliciting a thorough background check. It seemed so unlikely that Hamilton – who was usually so anal about every little detail – wouldn't do that.

Lucy was getting all set for her script launch party the following Saturday. She was excited about it. Phil wasn't.

Mandy was happy to have the house to herself without screaming children running everywhere.

While Don couldn't wait to spend a long weekend at his beach house with Cameron.

What could be better?

He hadn't felt this way in a long time, and he was filled with anticipation of good things to come.

* * *

Saturday morning, Yoko and Lennon sensed something was up. They roamed around the house freshly bathed, ready for some beach action. Cameron swore they understood every word she said, and since she'd told them where they were going, excitement was in the air. She hoped her dogs got along with Don's Labrador, Butch.

Wow! she thought, smiling to herself as she packed a weekend bag. *It's almost as if we've got kids and they're all meeting for the first time! Will they get along? Will they like each other?*

She'd had a couple of days to get over the shock of the tabloids and the trailing photographers. Dorian and Lynda were in heaven – they kept on popping out of the building to see how many cameramen lay in wait. Then they insisted on accompanying Cameron to her car, so that with any luck they'd be in the shot!

By Friday the photographers were gone. Don Verona had not put in an appearance at *Paradise*, so their interest had waned. Lynda and Dorian were disappointed. Cameron was delighted, since being the center of attention did not thrill her at all.

She hadn't seen Don since their romantic night together, although they'd spoken on the phone every day. He wasn't happy that she'd sent Reno to work him out.

"I want *you*," he'd complained.

"Told you my motto," she'd replied. "I never mix business with pleasure."

"Yeah, yeah, I know. So does that mean that right now I'm pleasure?"

"Kind of," she'd allowed.

"Kind of?" he'd said. "You should be salivating for more."

"Don't push it."

On Saturday he arrived to pick her up at noon wearing khaki chinos, a black T-shirt, and a white baseball cap. She had to admit that he looked pretty damn great.

The feeling was mutual. "Hey," he said, giving her a quick hug. "Aren't *you* looking gorgeous."

"Would you like to see my TiVo?" she inquired, tongue-in-cheek.

"That's not what I had in mind, but if you insist," he joked. "Are you loving it?"

"I have no clue how to work the damn thing!"

"I'll teach you."

"Not now. Yoko and Lennon are driving me nuts. They know they're in for a treat."

"And how about you?" he said, moving closer and nuzzling her neck. "Are *you* in for a treat?"

"Ah, Mr Verona," she said lightly. "I guess that's up to you."

He broke into a grin. She grinned back. Yes, it was definitely nice to see him.

"Let's go," he said, "before I get a ticket on this shitty street and somebody tries to dognap Butch. He's waiting in the car."

"Kindly do not call my street shitty," she objected. "This is a nice friendly neighborhood street."

"Yeah, where I got a nice friendly neighborhood ticket the other morning."

"Then maybe you shouldn't have stayed over."

"Next time, we spend the night at *my* house," he said confidently.

"What makes you think there'll be a next time?" she shot back.

They bantered all the way out to the car, where Butch was sticking his head out the window of a large black SUV. As soon as Butch spotted them approaching he began to bark, hurling his body against the car window, livid to see Don in the company of two other dogs.

Yoko and Lennon retaliated, barking back like crazy.

"This might not be the greatest idea," Cameron said unsurely. "Lennon gets protective around Yoko when there's another male dog around."

"*Now* she's telling me," Don said wryly.

"Sorry, didn't think about it."

"Butch is not a fighter," Don said. "But introducing them in the car – not a plan."

"What do you suggest?"

"Why don't you take them back into your house, run 'em around the garden, then I'll bring Butch out, and once they've done enough sniffing it'll be fine."

"Good thinking," she said, handing him her overnight bag and heading back into her house with Yoko and Lennon close behind her.

Don glanced up and down the street. No paparazzi in sight. Thank God they hadn't discovered where Cameron lived yet. She was pissed enough about them hanging around outside *Paradise*, she'd be really angry if they started camping outside her house. The last thing he wanted was to frighten her off right at the start of something that could turn into more than just another casual fling.

There was one guy hovering at the corner he'd noticed when he'd driven up, but the man was keeping his distance, and even better, he didn't appear to have any cameras.

Over the years Don had been bothered by several death threats, and once a crazed female so-called fan had taken to sending him impassioned letters that had turned into hate mail when he'd failed to respond. She'd broken into his house twice, sent him an assortment of weird gifts, and one day she'd appeared at his office and stabbed his assistant with a letter-opener, fortunately not fatally. After that little incident he was super-careful, always aware of everything around him.

The second he opened the car door, Butch bounded out like

he had a rocket up his butt. New friends were on Butch's agenda and the enthusiastic Labrador couldn't wait!

Walking toward Cameron's front door, Don decided it bothered him that she lived right on the street with no security gates and no protection. Plus nowhere to park his goddamn car as her tiny garage only had room for her prized Mustang.

Memo to self: *Buy the girl a decent car.*

Second memo to self: *Ask her permission first, she's a difficult one.*

Out of the corner of his eye he noticed the man on the corner suddenly approaching.

Shit! Was the guy a journalist? Another nutty fan? A threat?

Before he could give it any further thought, the man came right up to him and said, "Excuse me, mate, mind if I ask you a question?"

Don automatically took a step back. He was tall, six foot one, but this guy was even taller and quite heavy-set, with sandy hair and a deeply weathered suntan. His accent sounded Australian, so maybe he was a tourist.

"Sure," Don said, careful to keep a distance between himself and the stranger.

"I'm looking for Sunset Boulevard. Am I anywhere near?"

BINGO! Tourist! Don felt a slight rush of relief. He gave the man directions to Sunset and walked up the path to Cameron's house.

"'Scuse me for bein' nosey," the man called out to his back. "I heard tell the girls were pretty in L.A. but that one you were out here with earlier is a real beaut. She your girlfriend?"

Tourist? Or journalist digging for dirt?

Now Don wasn't so sure. Where was Fanny when he needed her?

"Sister," he said casually, his hand on the doorknob.

The stranger wasn't giving up. "She married?" he yelled. "'Cause if not, I sure wouldn't mind taking her out."

Ignoring the anonymous stranger, Don made it through the front door, shutting it firmly behind him. What a freak! Some people had a lot of nerve.

Butch raced straight through the small house and into the tiny garden in back, where he immediately began paying too much attention to Yoko.

Lennon growled and made a move to warn Butch off.

Don forgot all about the journalist, tourist, whatever, and stood next to Cameron as they watched their dogs get acquainted.

Half an hour later they were on the road to Malibu.

* * *

"Where are you going?" Mandy asked.

To see the teenage hooker I saved and your daddy married.

"Over to Evie's," Ryan replied calmly. "I promised the boys I'd take 'em to lunch. Want to come?"

This threw her. "No thank you," she said crisply. "I've had enough of those little monsters to last a lifetime."

He wondered what kind of mother Mandy would have made if they had been lucky enough to have children of their own.

Probably not the greatest.

"Okay, don't say I didn't offer."

"If it was the two of us on the patio at *Spago*, I'd be happy to join you," she said, trying to make him feel guilty – one of her favorite things to do.

"Nope," he said casually. "It's just me and the boys."

"Shame."

"Yeah."

And then he came up with a plan. Since he was finding it almost impossible to broach the subject of divorce, what if the two of them had a quiet *dinner* at *Spago*? That way they'd be in a public place, and it was unlikely Mandy would make a scene.

332

He couldn't understand why he was finding it so difficult to tell her they were over. Mandy was a smart woman, surely she must know?

"How about we do dinner at *Spago*?" he said quickly, before he changed his mind. "Don't invite anyone else."

Once again Mandy was caught off-guard. She could not remember the last time she and Ryan had gone out to dinner alone. Was this a romantic gesture? Or did he plan on bringing up couples counseling again?

Hmmm . . . she was immediately suspicious, but she didn't let on.

"That's a lovely idea," she said. "I'll book a table."

And already she was formulating a plan of defense. There was no way she was going to couples counseling.

No way at all.

*   *   *

It was purely by chance that Lucy walked in on Phil screwing his assistant, Suki, the very same assistant he'd assured her that he'd fired weeks ago.

Lucy never made the trek out to the tree house where Phil liked to lock himself away when he was writing. But today was Saturday, and she'd honestly thought he'd gone out.

She'd been thinking that the tree house might be the perfect place to stash the animals during their upcoming dinner party. Certainly the parrot and the dogs. The pot-bellied pig she wasn't so sure about. Anyway, she wanted to see for herself how messy the tree house was, as Phil refused to allow the housekeepers in there to clean. The tree house was his domain, he'd designed it and had it built as his own private retreat. He claimed it was the only place where his creative juices could flow uninterrupted.

They were flowing today all right. They were flowing all over

Suki's flat chest as Phil heaved and grunted, pulled out, and then came all over Suki's non-existent tits.

Lucy stood in the doorway frozen like a statue, too shocked to move. Oh yes, she knew her husband played around on her – who didn't know about Phil Standard and his sexual conquests? But she'd never expected to find him making out with another woman on their property.

"You cheating whore-mongering *bastard*!" she yelled.

She'd never used the phrase "whore-mongering bastard" before, except in one of her movies. It seemed to fit the occasion.

Startled, Phil's hairy ass shot into the air as he leaped off Miss Suki with a roar of disapproval.

"What the hell are *you* doing here?" he yelled. "You know you're not allowed in here. Nobody is."

"Fuck you and the horse you rode in on," Lucy spat, another line from one of her movies – or maybe it was a Clint Eastwood Western classic.

How dare he imagine he could get away with being mad at *her*. Reverse psychology. Phil's way of dealing.

Suki sat up from the couch, Phil's juices dripping down her chest. Lucy noticed that she might not have any tits, but she did have unappealing extended brown nipples.

"In case my *husband* forgot to tell you," Lucy said in her best icy voice, "you're fired." And with that she turned on her heel and headed straight for her car – the new Mercedes Phil had bought her only last week.

She took off before anyone could stop her. Not that anyone was trying.

She was all alone with her fury, and right now that suited her just fine.

ANYA

After living with Seth for a few months and telling him constantly he was the most wonderful man in the world, Anya made sure he got a divorce. Several weeks later he took her to Niagara Falls where they were married.

Once she had the ring on her finger, things changed. She did not care for Seth, she never had. He was a man, wasn't he, and all men were the enemy. They craved sex day and night. They were controlled by their penises and they were violent and ugly. Like the soldiers who'd raped her. Like Greedy Boris and Igor. Like all the men she had been forced to service since she was fourteen.

And most of all Joe. The pimp in Amsterdam who'd degraded her worse than anyone.

Joe was the man of her nightmares. He always came to her in them with his pointed face, evil eyes and greasy hair.

The things Joe had forced her to do were beyond shameful. The sex shows, the orgies, the animals, the perversions . . .

Joe had crushed her will to live. Almost.

Once again she'd survived, thanks to a stranger who had taken pity on her and given her a new start. A man. Yes. A man she didn't know, so therefore she had no interest in him.

Seth professed to love her. She didn't believe him. How could he love her?

What he loved was how she made him feel when he was inside her and she began moving her pelvis in a way he'd never experienced before.

He loved the way she put him in her mouth and sucked him until he came with a ferocity he had not believed possible.

He loved her because she allowed him to put his hard cock anywhere he wanted, while she sighed and cried out his name and professed to enjoy it.

That's *why he loved her. No other reason.*

As soon as his divorce was final, Anya set about alienating him from his wife and child. It was easy. Once you knew the key to a man's sexual desires, anything was possible. Velma had taught her that. The same Velma who'd run out on her and left her in the care of Joe.

Or *had* Velma *run?*

In Anya's dreams Velma sometimes came to her naked, soaking wet and distressed, her long hair matted and tangled across her muddy, broken face, smashed teeth protruding from her mouth.

"He drowned me!" Velma would scream, her eyes popping out of her head. "Joe drowned me!"

Anya dreaded those dreams because they were so real.

After a while it began to occur to her that the vivid dreams were merely reflecting the truth. Joe had murdered Velma.

It made sense because she'd never truly believed that Velma would abandon her. They'd been so close, shared so much. Besides, Velma had left her clothes and other possessions behind, which Joe had quickly disposed of.

The more Seth fawned over her, the more Anya turned to ice. She stopped telling him how wonderful he was. She stopped granting him sexual favors whenever he wanted. She took whatever money she could get out of him and began her precious shoe collection.

The colder she became, the more he wanted her, making her realize that men were interested in two things as far as women were concerned – wild unfettered sex, and the chase.

A year into their marriage Seth got a promotion at the law firm where he worked. Shortly after that he was invited to a formal event hosted by the chief partner at his firm.

He gave Anya money to go out and buy a dressy outfit suitable for such an important occasion.

She came home with a black leather bustier and an extremely short skirt, which she paired with six-inch Jimmy Choos.

Seth was horrified. His delicate exquisite wife looked like a hooker in such a get-up.

He tried to make her change. She refused.

When they arrived at the event all eyes were on Anya. She resembled a young girl masquerading in someone else's clothes. Most of the men were transfixed by her slutty child-like appearance. The women hated her.

Seth was embarrassed. How could she do this to him?

Anya soothed him with whispered promises of the sexual favors she would bestow on him when they got home.

Later she asked him to point out his boss. He did so, and without hesitation she set off in the man's direction.

His boss, Elliot Von Morton, was caught off-guard when Anya marched up to him and introduced herself as one of his junior associate's wives. But, after his initial surprise, Elliot sat up and took notice, for in spite of her flashy outfit and excess of makeup, beneath it all he could see that Anya was a true beauty.

"And what can I do for you, Mrs Carpenter?" Elliot – a tall thin man with drooping eyelids and a sparse moustache – asked.

"I was thinking," Anya replied, fingering the soft leather rim of her bustier, her pale blue eyes fixed firmly on him, "if there is anything I can do for you?"

Elliot glanced around to see where his wife was located. Mrs Von Morton was busy talking to friends across the room.

This girl was coming on to him, he was sure of it.

Where was her husband?

Fast approaching.

"Call me at the office," Elliot said to Anya, boldly slipping her his card. "I'm certain I can think of something."

A mortified Seth, red in the face, rushed up to them. "Uh, excuse me, Mr Von Morton," he said, stumbling over his words. "Anya is new to these events. I hope she isn't . . . uh . . . bothering you."

"Not at all," Elliot replied with a crocodile smile. "Your wife is charming," he added, his eyes raking over every inch of Anya's tight black leather cleavage, while he imagined this girl with the face of an angel standing over him armed with a leather whip, beating the crap out of him. "Quite charming."

Six weeks later Anya left Seth, Elliot split from his wife, and Anya moved into Elliot's Park Avenue penthouse.

Her journey was gaining ground.

Chapter Forty-One

Stretched out on a lounger in her bikini watching Don barbecue hamburgers and corn on the cob, Cameron felt totally at ease. Three exhausted dogs lay on the deck around her, lazily sunning themselves. After a ten-minute battle with Lennon for control, Butch had backed down, quite content not to be the Alpha dog.

"Y'know," Cameron remarked, "you need to get Butch a companion – see how happy he is?"

"*I'm* his companion," Don joked. "He comes to the studio with me, makes out with a couple of French poodles on the lot. Believe me, Cam, he has a great old time. And speaking of great old times – guess who's entertaining at my house today?"

"Entertaining? While you're away?" she said, reaching for the suntan lotion.

"Not exactly entertaining in the 'we're throwing a party sense.' More like getting together with someone other than his old lady."

Cameron experienced a quick jab in the pit of her stomach. It was Ryan, she knew it was Ryan.

"Who is it?" she asked calmly, smoothing suntan lotion onto her legs.

"Birthday Boy," Don said triumphantly. "He's finally giving

himself the present I've been urging him to give himself for years."

For a moment she was silent. Ryan wasn't like that. Or was he?

How well did she know him? Hardly at all. And yet she felt that she'd known him for years.

"So . . ." she said, forcing herself to sound casual, although she was desperate to know. "Who's he seeing?"

"Dunno," Don replied, expertly flipping burgers. "Ryan's a close-to-the-chest kinda guy. Although he *was* spotted out with a knockout A.M. the other day – surprised the shit out of me."

"What's an A.M.?"

"Actress/model. Sometimes an escort when the money's tight."

"Isn't escort a polite word for call girl?"

"C'mon, Cam," Don said, amused. "Ryan would never pay for it. He has women falling over themselves to get near him, although he never notices – until now, that is."

"Then I guess you're pleased he's playing around on his wife?"

"Don't sound so uptight," Don said, throwing her a quizzi- cal look. "You met Mandy. She's impossible, nags the crap out of him. I'm hoping this will be the precursor to the end of his mar- riage. Ryan deserves a life without Mandy hanging around his neck, he's a great guy."

"I suppose so," Cameron murmured, imagining Ryan in Don's house making love to a gorgeous A.M. who may or may not request payment. She hated the thought of him being just like other men. She'd hoped he was different, a man with a high moral compass. How wrong was *she*.

"Cheese or no cheese on your burger?" Don called over his shoulder.

She'd lost her appetite. "Whatever," she answered vaguely. She'd choke it down one way or another.

* * *

Running several red lights, Lucy was in a reckless frame of mind as she headed for Venice and Marlon. Phil Standard screwed around, everyone knew that. But in *her* house with some skank assistant that he assured her he'd fired weeks ago? No damn way.

Lucy Lyons was one furious ex-movie-star wife.

Running her fourth light in a row, she didn't even care when a cop car slid out of a side street and flashed her down.

She swerved her new Mercedes into the curb and pulled to a sharp stop.

The cop got out of his car and approached her window with a cocksure swagger. "License and registration," he said, barely glancing at her.

She checked him out. Approximately thirty-six or seven. Quite a few pounds overweight. White. Disinterested. Simply doing his job.

She'd soon change that.

"I'm so sorry, Officer," she purred. "I recently caught my husband with another woman, and as I'm sure you can imagine, I was extremely upset." Pause while he digested *that* little piece of information. Then straight in for the kill. "I'm Lucy Lyons," she added, raising her sunglasses. "You probably saw me in *Blue Sapphire*. Most everyone did."

The cop snapped to immediate attention. Bending his head to get a better look, he licked his lips and swallowed hard. "Uh, yeah, I sure did," he said, thinking who could ever forget *that* rack. Lucy Lyons was built and then some. And she still looked hot – not that he could see much more than her face and that sweep of long jet-black hair. Like his other favorites, Sharon Stone and Demi Moore, she was ageing well. "You *did* jump a light," he managed, clearing his throat.

"Once again I'm so very sorry," she said, lowering her voice to a sexy new level. "I can promise you that it won't happen again."

"Uh well, I guess I can let you off this time," the cop said, adding a stern – "But you'd better make *sure* it doesn't happen again."

"Of course, Officer," she purred once more. "Thank you so much."

She drove off, slightly calmer than before.

At least she hadn't lost it. Lucy Lyons could *still* weave her particular brand of magic. No ticket for *her*.

* * *

Anya didn't drive. She had Hamilton's driver drop her off at *Barney's* and instructed him to meet her at the back of *Neiman's* in three hours.

As soon as the driver left, she headed down the street to the Beverly Wilshire Hotel, walked though the lobby and got into a cab at the back entrance, giving the driver Don's address.

She was nervous. She was on her way to see a man who knew far too much about her past. And what did she know about *him*?

Not a lot. Only the information she'd gleaned from Hamilton, and a few of his credits from IMDB on Miss Dunn's computer.

After checking out his movies, it was clear he made meaningful films that mattered. Hamilton had called him a do-good loser; Anya only knew he'd been kind to her.

But now that she was married to his father-on-law, would Ryan Richards continue to keep her secrets?

It was imperative that she find out.

* * *

Before noon Ryan stopped by Evie's to make sure everything was okay. His mother was there, all set to scold him for not informing her about what was going on with Evie and her drunken husband. "Why didn't you tell me?" Noreen demanded, speaking to him as if he was six.

"Sorry, Mom, but I didn't want to worry you," he explained.

Noreen shook her head and scolded him some more.

He wondered if now was the time to tell her that he was asking Mandy for a divorce. Then he decided against it; best to wait.

After hanging around and playing a few hoops with his nephews – their favorite pastime – he headed for Don's house. Don, who was so sure he was having a secret sex tryst that he'd left champagne on ice, and a pound of caviar in the fridge.

Caviar and sex. The two didn't seem to go together. Hey – maybe in Don's glamorous bachelor existence they did.

Ryan wandered around the house biding his time until Anya arrived. Don's house wasn't very homely; it was all glass and chrome, pale beige leather furniture, modern art and too much technology. Everything was very pristine and ordered, the way Don liked things.

Ryan thought back to their USC college days when they'd shared a minuscule apartment. Even then Don was a neat freak, constantly tidying up after both of them. Who would have thought that he would become such a big star?

Ryan prowled around the bedroom searching for clues of Cameron. Had she spent the night? How did she really feel about Don? Was she about to move in?

Christ! Why torture himself?

She was Don's latest girlfriend, that's the way it was, and he'd better learn to accept it.

* * *

"This is the most relaxing day I've spent in a long time," Don announced, settling on the lounger next to Cameron.

"Me too," she murmured, raising her chin to the sun.

"There's nothing like the sound of waves breaking," he said, leaning over and trailing his fingers across her stomach. "It's almost hypnotic, sends me off into another zone."

"I know what you mean," she agreed, feeling very comfortable.

"Ryan and I used to hit the beach every weekend when we were in college," he said, laughing. "Two horny young guys, totally broke and full of big ideas."

"You must have been quite a duo."

"Yeah. Anyway, I always promised myself I'd get myself a beach house one day. And now here I am with you. Hey," he added. "I got the beach house *and* I got the girl. How about that?"

"Not quite," she said coolly.

"Still playing hard to get, huh?"

"Not used to it, Don?"

"Right."

"You mention Ryan a lot," she said, switching to a subject that interested her.

"Why not? He's my best buddy and I want to see him in a good place with a woman who really cares about him."

"Mandy doesn't?"

"Are you kidding me?" Don snorted. "Mandy has her own agenda, always has."

"Then how come Ryan stays?"

"Guilt. She lays it on thick about the miscarriages and the baby they lost at birth. She makes sure that in some insane way Ryan blames himself. Believe me – she encourages him to think like that."

Reaching over, Don began caressing her thigh. "But that's enough about Ryan and Mandy, it's time for more about you and me." His hand began moving upwards. "Is it my imagination, or do we have a very real connection going on here? I feel it – how about you?"

*　*　*

The woman who walked into Don Verona's house was light years away from the damaged teenage whore with the defeated attitude and glassy-eyed stare Ryan had rescued from a life of misery and degradation. This young woman was assured, confident, or at least that's the impression she gave.

"Whose house is this?" she asked upon entering.

"A friend of mine," Ryan replied.

"It is like something from a magazine," she said, moving over to gaze out of the glass doors at the spectacular view. "I like it."

"Glad you approve," he said, a touch sarcastically.

"Yes," she said slowly. "It is nice. Hamilton prefers more traditional."

Jesus – was *that* what this meeting was about? Home décor?

He wasn't wasting anymore time. "Anya," he said.

"My name is now Pola," she replied. "Anya ceased to exist years ago."

"Really?"

"Yes. It is all legal. I changed my name by deed poll when I married my second husband."

"Hamilton is your *second* husband?"

"Third," she stated matter-of-factly. "And I am now an American citizen."

"Congratulations," he said, his mind racing. She'd accomplished a lot in seven years, three marriages and a citizenship, no wonder she wanted to make sure it didn't all come crashing down around her because of what he knew. She might be Mrs Hamilton J. Heckerling now, but his memories of her were very clear. The young girl forced to perform in a graphic live sex show. The young girl who was pissed on and humiliated and treated like she was less than human. And then the same young girl sitting forlornly in a room with a window in the famed red-light district of Amsterdam, offering herself for sale to anyone who passed by.

He would never forget the look in her eyes. A look so filled with pain and sadness and hopelessness.

Now the look in her eyes was different. He would have to say it was watchful, weary, calculating and quite hard.

"So," he said, "I understand why you considered it important that we meet. You're scared that I might reveal where I first saw you, what you were doing back then, and how I came to your assistance."

Anya gave him a long penetrating stare. "It is human nature to reveal secrets," she said flatly. "Have you told Mandy about me? Does she know?"

"Absolutely not," he said quickly. "I haven't told anyone, and I have no intention of doing so. You've made a new life for yourself, Anya, and you're to be congratulated for that. I'm happy you've been able to forget about everything that happened to you in the past and move on. Really – you're to be commended. Not everyone could get over the things you suffered."

A half-smile flickered across her face and she moved toward him. "Thanks to you," she said, her voice softening. "And now the time has come for me to repay you."

"There's no way you can repay me," he said, automatically taking a step back.

"Yes," she said firmly. "There is a way."

And before he could stop her, she stepped out of her dress and stood in front of him in nothing but a lacy black thong and extremely high Christian Louboutin stilettos.

"Jesus Christ!" he said, taken completely by surprise. This was the last thing he'd expected. "No, Anya, no!" he said. "Put your clothes back on right now."

"Why?" she asked, seductively licking her index finger, then touching her left nipple. "You know you want me."

"No, I don't," he said, trying not to stare at her perfect little body, everything in the right proportion to her size, for without heels she couldn't be more than five foot one or two. He felt a stirring where he shouldn't be feeling a stirring, and once more he demanded that she put on her clothes.

Her eyes dropped to his crotch, and she was not surprised to notice the effect she had on him.

Men were so damn easy. Once they were hard, nothing else mattered.

"Do you like my breasts?" she murmured, still touching herself. "They're real, you know, not like many American woman with bags of silicone filling their chests so they look like stuffed turkeys."

Ryan bit down hard on his lower lip, experiencing pain, willing his hard-on to take a hike.

No way was he falling into this trap. No way at all.

Chapter Forty-Two

The man lurking on Cameron's street had watched her emerge from her house twice. The first time she was with two dogs, and carrying an overnight bag. The second time she was with the guy he'd accosted on the street – the handsome dude driving the black SUV. Don Verona, that was the dude's name. And according to the stuff he'd been reading, Don Verona was some kind of famous person on TV.

Trust Cameron to trade up without a second thought about the husband she'd left behind in Hawaii.

Trust the bitch to act as if she had no past.

Well, she had a past all right, and he was here in Los Angeles to prove it.

Gregg Kingston. Husband. The same husband she'd left lying on the floor in their condo in Maui, his head bashed in by a table lamp, blood everywhere, unconscious for six hours until the cleaning woman had discovered his almost lifeless body at eight a.m. and frantically called for an ambulance.

He'd lain in a coma for almost three months. Everyone had given up on him, until one day he'd opened his eyes and struggled back into the land of the living.

Gregg was strong. He was a survivor. He was a god-damn *angry* survivor. And he wanted his fucking wife to know that she could never escape from him, however hard she tried.

And the bitch had obviously tried very hard indeed. She'd left Hawaii and vanished. Poof! Like that she was gone, and nobody could help him discover where she was. She'd taken their address book of contacts, so he had no one to chase. She could have gone anywhere – back to America, Australia, Thailand. The bitch could've gone anywhere in the world. She was a world-class traveler.

Gregg had no choice but to wait, hoping that one day she'd turn up again. She had to, because knowing Cameron as well as he did, eventually she'd want a divorce, and the only way she could get that was to return to Hawaii and face him.

Unless she thought she'd killed him.

Christ! Was that what she thought? Just because he'd pushed her around a little she'd imagined she could get away with fuck-ing *murder*!

Not on *his* watch. No way. He would find her and punish her if it was the last thing he did.

And then, one day, purely by chance, he discovered exactly where she was.

Fate was a strange and wonderful thing. After his forced time off, he'd returned to his job at the luxury hotel in Maui, a hotel filled with vacationing families, couples and women.

Ah . . . the women. Single and horny as hell – all searching for a little vacation romance. And who better than the king of the beach, the surfing pro teacher – Gregg Kingston himself – to give it to them?

He screwed his way through three or four a month. They came to the island with great expectations, and he didn't let them down.

Since getting out of the hospital his sexual appetite seemed to have increased tenfold, and he was determined to enjoy himself.

Problem was, none of the women were Cameron . . . none of

them were as beautiful or as sexy or as smart as his murdering
bitch of a wife.

He missed her.

He hated her.

And he was determined to punish her.

One afternoon while he was enjoying oral sex from a vacationing schoolteacher with an insatiable urge to give him head
three times a day – he spied a tabloid magazine on the table by
her bed. And on the front of the magazine was a photo of a
woman who looked exactly like Cameron. In fact, it *was*
Cameron.

Jerking his erection out of the woman's mouth, he grabbed
the magazine.

"What's the matter?" the woman wailed. "Did I do something wrong?"

Ignoring her, he read the magazine, devouring every morsel
about his wife, who now called herself Cameron Paradise, and
who was in the clutches of some famous American talk-show host,
and who had opened her own fitness studio called *Paradise*.

He could hardly believe his eyes. There she was, carrying on
like she didn't have a care in the world. She'd left him for dead,
and proceeded to make a new life as if he'd never even existed.

Fury overcame him. A white-hot fury that made him itch to
find her, get her back, and force her to pay for the way she'd
treated him.

Two days later he'd taken a leave of absence from his job, and
now here he was in Hollywood, and it had only involved a small
amount of detective work to track her down.

Now that he had her in his sights he decided that he was not
in a hurry. First he had to find out exactly what she was up to –
hence stationing himself on her street to observe her movements.
She had two dogs and a rich prick famous boyfriend. The two of
them looked like they were off on a weekend get-away.

Did the Famous Prick understand that she was *his* property?

She was Mrs Gregg Kingston – that's who she was. And if he didn't understand, he soon would.

After the black SUV took off, Gregg made his move. He approached her house, made his way around the back, and easily slid a credit card to open the lock on the side door that led into what was obviously her bedroom. Cameron never had been big on security; he was surprised the door was locked at all, and naturally there was no alarm system.

The house was neat and clean and quite small. One bedroom, one bathroom, a living room connected to the kitchen that overlooked the street.

Gregg surmised that it was not a house that Famous Prick would want to hang out at.

He took his time checking everything out, going through her closet, reading her mail, opening every drawer. When he came to her underwear drawer he stuffed a couple of thongs into his jeans pocket. Maybe later he could put them to good use.

Finishing his inspection, he let himself out the same way he'd come in, and headed back to his rented car parked on the next street. Then he set off for the hills above Sunset, where he knew Famous Prick lived. Easy enough to find out where anyone lived nowadays. If you couldn't find an address on the Internet, all a person had to do was buy a *Where the Stars Live* map on the street. Gregg had done both, so he knew he had the right location.

Now that he was here, in Los Angeles, near to Cameron, he felt a real sense of satisfaction.

He knew exactly where she was and what she was doing.

And the kicker was that she didn't know shit.

Tough luck, bitch, I'm coming to get you.

Chapter Forty-Three

Never had Ryan felt so trapped. Anya stripping off her clothes and trying to seduce him was the last thing he'd expected to happen. If he'd wanted to have sex with her he would have done it in Amsterdam when she was up for sale. But no, he'd rescued her, hadn't he? And did she honestly believe that this was the best way to repay him?

Wrong. Very very wrong.

After finally realizing she was not about to get anywhere with him, Anya reluctantly slithered back into her dress and asked him if he was gay.

"You're screwing with me, right?" he said, shaking his head in wonderment that she would even think such a thing.

"All men want sex," Anya stated flatly.

"Maybe with the right woman," he replied.

"And I am not the right woman?" she asked sulkily.

"I'm married, Anya, and so are you. I don't need repayment for anything."

"You are an unusual man."

"And you are a *married* woman who should have more respect for yourself," he said, making yet another attempt to get through to her. "You don't have to do this. You're free now."

She shrugged as if his words didn't matter. "Is respect what

Hamilton has for me when he brings in other women to make love to me while he watches and pleasures himself? Is that respect?"

Ryan held up his hand. "No details of your married life, please," he said firmly. "I am not interested. This is America. If you don't want to do something – refuse. You're not sitting behind a window with a pimp controlling your every move."

She stared at him for a long thoughtful moment. "You are a decent man, Ryan Richards," she said at last. And then, to his relief, she asked him to call her a cab, and when it arrived she left the house.

Anya. Pola. She was a complicated woman. So young and so damaged, and the unfortunate thing was that like all the men before him, Hamilton was still using her.

* * *

"So here's the deal," Don said, feeling quite at ease opening up to Cameron about his career as they strolled along the shoreline. "The way I look got me on local TV in the first place – not as a regular, but as a roving reporter on a news show. Then one night the anchor called in sick, and since they couldn't get hold of anyone else – I got to take over for a few nights. That was kind of the beginning of it. My aggressive personality took me all the way to my own talk show, and I never looked back."

"Did you want to?" she asked, watching as their three Labs frolicked in the surf, having a fine old time.

"Want to what?"

"Look back."

"Well, sure," he said, kicking a clump of seaweed out of the way. "My big ambition was to be a serious war correspondent covering all kinds of shit across the globe."

"That sounds *really* interesting."

"Yeah, I know," he said ruefully. "Only problem is that it

never happened for me. Instead of being on the frontline in Iraq, I find myself sitting behind a desk making small talk with Charleze Theron and Jessica Alba."

"Hey," she said, surprised by his candor. "Don't knock it – most men would kill to be doing that."

"I'm not most men, Cam," he said, quite serious.

"No, you're not," she said, thinking that if Ryan didn't exist she and Don might have a shot.

"Y'know," he said, stopping abruptly, taking both her hands in his, "you're gonna think this is kind of sudden, and you'll probably say no – but how about moving in with me?"

Things were speeding along much too fast. She liked Don, but she was certainly not at a point in their brief relationship where she would even consider moving into his house. Besides, she had a perfectly comfortable place of her own, and now she had what looked to be a successful business to run.

"You don't have to answer me immediately," he continued. "But give it some thought." A beat. A grin. "Think of all the money you'd save in rent."

"What gives you the impression that I don't own my house?" she asked coolly.

Hmm . . . It wouldn't do to let on that he'd done a spot of investigating.

"Do you?" he asked casually. "'Cause if you do, think of the score you'd make selling it – the market is high right now."

"Actually, I rent," she admitted.

"There you go," he said, as Yoko ran up to them and began shaking out her fur, spraying them both with droplets of water. "You'd save a fortune every month."

"Maybe I don't want to," she said, shielding her eyes from the bright sun.

"Maybe you should give it a bit more thought," he said, bending down and brushing off his pants, which he'd rolled at the ankle.

"A little splash of water's not about to ruin your day – is it?" she asked lightly, glad for the diversion.

"It's not the water," he said, taking a long look around. "We're approaching Paris Hilton territory, and that means the paps will be out in full force."

"You think?"

"Yeah, they're all over the place – hiding like cockroaches. So far they've not caught on that I have a beach house, so let's do the smart thing, go back in the other direction and not tempt Fate."

"You know, Don," she mused, "that's why I could never live with you."

"And that would be because?" he said, quite perplexed that she'd turned him down.

"All the attention, the photographers, fans coming up to you. I could never be one of those women standing by their man at film premières while he gives an interview and they hover next to him with a fixed smile looking like nothing more than an appendage."

"You, my dear," he said gallantly, "could never look like an appendage. And besides, I loathe film premières. Only go when I'm doing a friend a favor." And with that he swooped in for a kiss; a slow, practiced, leisurely kiss.

She kissed him back, feeling totally free and quite content. This weekend of doing nothing much except enjoying herself was exactly what she'd needed.

"We'd better beat a quick retreat," he said, pulling away. "Come on, I'll race you back to the house. First one there gets to choose what we do tonight."

"You're on!" she said.

He had no idea how fast she could run.

*　　*　　*

Marlon was lounging outside his place on the boardwalk cleaning the spiked wheels on his bicycle when Lucy showed up.

Bronzed and hunky, he wore nothing but a pair of low-rider denim shorts, faded and torn.

Two teenage girls in barely there bikinis hovered nearby. Lucy couldn't decide whether they were with him, or merely hanging around with the hope of getting lucky.

"Lucy!" Marlon said, genuinely pleased to see her. "Wasn't expecting you today. Wassup?"

What's up is I caught Phil fucking his assistant in my house and I feel like killing him.

"Nothing much," she said with a casual shrug. "I figured I'd drop by, make sure we'll have a finished script by the end of next week."

"Sure we will," Marlon said, long dirty-blond hair flopping in his eyes. "Like I promised, didn't I? And your party's not till Saturday, so we got like plenty of time."

"One week is not plenty of time," she admonished.

"Are we gonna see you later, Marlon?" one of the bikini-clad girls called out. "We should meet up at *Villa*. I got the ID thing down, an' there's a late party up at Kim's, her parents are outta town. It'll be chronic. See you there?"

"Maybe," he said, throwing them a desultory wave.

"I hope I didn't break anything up," Lucy said, her eyes drawn toward his tanned and taut six-pack.

"Nah." He stood up and stretched. "Wanna come inside an' grab a Coke or somethin'?"

"Great," she said, finding herself unable to stop checking out his body. It was truly a work of art – all young rippling muscle, not an ounce of fat. So unlike Phil, who'd let himself wallow out of shape years ago.

She flashed onto Phil's big hairy ass leaping off Suki, and the image fueled her anger even more.

Sonofabitch! She needed to do something to get back at him, and she needed to do it today.

*   *   *

"Is Lucy with Mandy?"

Ryan had the phone to his ear as he left Don's house. It was Phil on the line, sounding agitated.

"I've no idea," Ryan replied. "Is she supposed to be?"

"Who the fuck knows," Phil mumbled. "We had an . . . uh . . . altercation. She ran out of here."

"You had a fight, big deal, she'll be back."

"Give me Mandy's cell number."

"Is it *that* important that you talk to her?"

"Yes, it is."

"What was this big fight about?"

"She caught me with my pants around my ankles."

"And?"

"And my cock happened to be inside Suki at the time."

"Oh Jesus, Phil, I thought you fired her."

"I did, I did," Phil groaned. "But I owed her a check, so she came by to collect, and one thing led to my cock somehow making its way into her—"

"Okay, okay," Ryan said, not interested in hearing details – he had enough on his mind. "I get it."

"No, you don't," Phil said miserably. "Lucy's never actually caught me in the act before. This is not a healthy situation. The woman has a temper, she could do anything."

"Well, she's not going to kill herself, we know that for sure," Ryan said dryly. "Maybe she's out buying a gun and she's going to shoot *your* dumb ass."

"Not funny, Ryan," Phil growled. "Where's Don? He's not answering his phone."

"Oh, so my advice is not good enough, now you need Don."

"No offense. You're too married. Don deals with unhinged women all the time."

"Yeah," Ryan said with a rueful laugh. "Like Mandy's not unhinged."

Phil managed a grunt.

"Take down Mandy's number, I'm getting another call," Ryan said, giving Phil her number and switching to his other call.

It was his mother on the line, frantic and verging on hysteria.

"Get here as fast as you can," Noreen gasped. "Something terrible has happened."

ANYA

*L*iving in a Park Avenue penthouse with Elliot Von Morton was a far different proposition from life with Seth in the small apartment they'd resided in on Lexington. Elliot was much older than Seth, and his tastes were far more sophisticated – but men were men, and Anya was used to catering to all different types.

Elliot was into whips and chains and punishment. He was into being collared and put on a leash, while Anya led him around his tony penthouse on all fours. He wanted her clad in tight black leather and six-inch heels. Sometimes he wanted her to wear a mask. He appreciated a thorough beating, and Anya was happy to give it to him.

Elliot was the chief partner in a powerful New York law firm. He dealt with many important clients. In a way he was the man controlling their lives, therefore it was no surprise that his main form of relaxation was surrendering all forms of power.

Anya was so much more obliging than his wife, who refused to have anything to do with his perversions, forcing him to frequent a house of ill-repute on Forty-Seventh Street. He'd never felt comfortable going there, he was always on the alert for hidden cameras and spies who'd report his activities to the press. Not that he was famous – merely powerful. However, he had enemies who would like nothing better than to bring him down.

One look at Anya on that fateful night when she'd walked into his event with Seth Carpenter – a very junior associate at his firm – and he'd immediately had a strong hunch that here was a girl who might be able to fulfill all his needs.

And he was right. Anya turned out to be a devil with a whip, and she was a devil who showed no mercy.

After their third assignation he informed his wife that he required an immediate separation. His wife was not surprised; she knew all about her husband's sexual needs, and she had no intention of fulfilling them.

Fortunately there were no children involved, only their New York penthouse, a magnificent house in the Hamptons, and a fleet of expensive cars.

Elliot kept the penthouse, while his wife claimed the Hamptons house.

Getting rid of Seth was not so civilized. When Anya informed him she was leaving he broke down and cried, sobbing like a heart-broken fool. She did not tell him she was moving in with his boss, she merely said it was time for her to go.

When Seth found out about her and Elliot, he'd stormed his boss's office, and been fired for his trouble. Later that night he'd gone to a bar, gotten hopelessly drunk, and been picked up by a woman who'd lured him outside into an alley – where her pimp had robbed him, then stabbed him to death when he'd attempted to fight back.

When Anya was informed by the police of her husband's untimely death, she had not shed a tear. Death was something she'd witnessed too many times to be upset.

While Elliot approved of her trashy outfits in the privacy of his home, he did not care to take her out in public looking so trampy. Anya was such a beauty, and yet she had no idea how to make the best of herself. He soon hired a stylist to teach her about clothes and makeup and hair.

He wanted to be proud of her when they attended big social events. He did not relish the thought of being regarded as a laughing stock. His main desire was that every one of his peers – stuck with their original wives – would envy him.

Once Anya had gone through her makeover – including a name change to Pola, which was her idea – other men did indeed envy him, for Anya/Pola was such a delicate and refined beauty in her Chanel and Valentino outfits, her exquisite evening gowns and fine jewels.

Elliot got a kick out of spoiling her, and in return she beat him on a regular basis while secretly enjoying his pain.

She did not love him.

Anya did not know what love was.

Chapter Forty-Four

Marlon was everything Lucy had expected, and yet he wasn't Phil. He was young, strong, hard-bodied and horny, but still he wasn't Phil. His kisses were amateurish. His fumblings with her clothes were juvenile. Foreplay? Apparently he'd never heard of it.

And just when he was about to do the deed, she aborted the situation. She simply couldn't go through with it. Bad as Phil was, she loved him and she couldn't bring herself to cheat on him. Besides, she missed the feel of his furry belly and rolls of comforting fat. She missed his cigar breath and the way he kissed her. She missed the special way he touched her and went down on her and made her come a hundred different ways. She missed his all-encompassing love, his genuine warmth and his loud raucous laugh.

Damn Phil Standard. He was a cheating lying sonofabitch. But he was *her* cheating lying sonofabitch.

"I can't do this," she said to Marlon, pushing his young hard body off her.

Marlon was stunned. "Huh?" he mumbled, his mouth hanging open in shock.

"It's not right," she said, quickly jumping up and starting to dress. "I'm sorry."

His eyes were fixed on her breasts, the same breasts he'd fantasized about ever since watching *Blue Sapphire* ten times on his DVD player. They were the best tits he'd seen in a while, still firm and luscious and big and round. Man, he just wanted to bury his head in them and never surface.

Now she was saying no after getting him all primed for action. Blue balls were on his horizon; this was turning out to be a real bummer.

"I . . . uh . . . I love you," he said, trying out a line that always worked, especially with all the surfer chicks who stopped by his place on a regular basis.

"Don't talk such nonsense," Lucy said crisply, fastening her bra – removing those great tits from his sight.

"But I do," he protested, still hard as the proverbial rock.

"Go jerk off and get over it," Lucy said, all business. "We've got work to do on the script."

Marlon slunk off to the bathroom, defeated.

Older women, they sure weren't as easy as the younger ones.

* * *

"I can't believe you beat me," Don grumbled, climbing up on the deck behind Cameron.

"And I can't believe you honestly imagined I wouldn't," she teased, collapsing onto a lounger. "I'm a personal trainer – emphasis on the *trainer*. Besides, I'm younger than you."

"Oh, she's playing the age card, is she?" he joked, falling down on top of her.

"I'm all sandy and sweaty," she objected, attempting to push him off. "I need to go inside and take a shower."

"No," he said firmly. "What you need is me. Now. Right now."

"Out here? What about the paparazzi?"

"Fuck 'em."

* * *

On the cab ride back to the Beverly Wilshire, Anya reflected on Ryan's behavior. What kind of man was he? He'd resisted having sex with her, and that was not normal at all.

She had learned over the years that by offering sex she could get men to do anything she wanted – including marrying her. She'd even got Hamilton Heckerling to marry her and he wasn't easy.

But of course Hamilton had no clue she was damaged goods, that from her early teenage years she'd been used and abused by men. If he ever discovered how many men had availed themselves of her body, he would *never* have even considered marrying her, he would have run like the wind.

Was that why Ryan didn't care to have sex with her? Too many men before him?

Yes, she decided, that must be it.

But if she had nothing to hold over him, how could she expect him to keep his silence?

It was a big problem.

Could she trust him?

Maybe. Maybe not.

She decided she would have to keep on trying to seduce him. Ryan Richards wasn't made of stone, eventually she'd succeed.

Directing the cab driver to the back entrance of the hotel, she paid him off, walked down the street to *Neiman Marcus*, went inside, and headed straight for the shoe department.

* * *

"Since you won the race, then *you* get to choose what we do tonight," Don announced. "Do we stay in or do we go out?"

"Hmm . . ." Cameron mused, playing him because she knew

he'd sooner stay in and so would she, but why not have a little fun at his expense? "Where would we go if we went out?"

"*Nobu*," he said. "*Taverna Tony's*. There's plenty of places around here." A beat. "Or . . ."

"Or what?"

"Or we could order in, sit out on the deck, catch the sunset, go to bed early and—"

"Sold!"

"Huh?"

"We're staying in."

He grinned. "I *knew* you were my kind of girl!"

*   *   *

"Pola?"

For a moment Anya did not respond – sometimes she forgot she'd renamed herself.

"Pola." Mandy's beringed hand clamped down on her shoulder, startling her. "What are *you* doing here? Spending Hamilton's money?"

"Excuse me?" Anya said, not appreciating Mandy's tone.

"Just joking," Mandy said with an insincere giggle. "After all, it's yours to spend as much as it is his. Nice shoes," she added, sitting down beside Anya, and picking up the other shoe to the one Anya was trying on. "Hmm . . ." she said, checking out the price. "Eight hundred dollars. You have expensive taste."

Silently Anya snatched the shoe back. She knew Mandy hated her; it gave her a frisson of satisfaction to realize that she'd hate her even more if she ever found out that she, Anya, had been standing in front of her husband, naked.

If only Ryan had responded . . .

"Tell me," Mandy said, "did Hamilton make you sign a prenup?"

"What is pre-nup?" Anya asked, although she knew perfectly well what it was.

"In America we have a little thing called a pre-nuptial agreement. Men give it to their intended to sign, so that when the divorce comes . . . oops, sorry! I mean *if* a divorce comes . . . then his money is protected."

"I sign nothing," Anya said, delighted to observe an expression of fury and frustration flit across Mandy's face.

The truth was that she *had* signed a pre-nuptial. It guaranteed her half a million dollars for every year she stayed married to Hamilton.

She planned on staying married to him for a long, long time.

A half million dollars a year was not enough for Anya.

* * *

Ryan made it down the hill to Evie's house on Alpine in record time, cursing all the way. What was wrong with his mom, sticking him with a cryptic message and then not picking up her phone when he tried to call back? Was she attempting to give him a heart attack, for crissakes? Didn't she realize he was forty, and forty was fucking *old*, goddammit!

He was depressed. Anya had depressed him with her pathetic come-on. And he was ashamed for almost falling into her trap. But sex had ceased to exist between him and Mandy, so it was hardly his fault that the sight of a naked woman had caught him off-guard.

Don was no doubt having incredible sex with Cameron and that pissed him off – although it shouldn't. He should be pleased that Don had finally found someone who made him happy.

If it lasted.

Which it probably wouldn't, since Don was the definitive player.

Ryan's worst fears were realized when he drew near to the

house. There was an ambulance in the driveway, and a couple of police cars.

Jesus! Evie . . . The boys . . .

Heart pounding, he jumped out of his car and raced toward the front door.

Chapter Forty-Five

Gregg Kingston drove his rented Chevy up to Don Verona's house to check it out. Had to find out what he was up against, since the gossip rags seemed to be linking Cameron to Famous Prick, and he'd observed with his own eyes her taking off with him for what looked like a weekend jaunt.

Don's house was gated. No problem.

Making sure no one was watching, Gregg scaled the gate with ease. There was a car parked in the driveway, so in case someone was home, he stealthily made his way round the side of the house, credit-carding his way through a locked side-gate.

He moved slowly – wouldn't do to get caught. He could hear the slight movement of a pool, and as he rounded the corner, there it was – a blue infinity pool overlooking Hollywood.

This was some lush set-up – quite different from Cameron's modest little shack down in the cheap streets. No wonder she was chasing this dude.

Noticing big glass doors, he edged toward them, flattening himself against the side of the house.

Then he saw them. Two people. A man and a woman standing close together inside the house.

The woman was naked except for her shoes. The man was fully dressed.

Gregg took a sharp breath, and at that moment his eye caught the glint of something in the surrounding bushes – was it a telescope, a camera? Yeah, someone had a camera and they were taking pictures, pretty pictures of the couple in the room.

Moving fast, Gregg backed up out of sight and retreated the same way he'd come in, making it back to his car which he'd parked half a block down the street.

He sat there for a while, listening to Linkin Park and Chris Brown on the radio. He didn't know why he was sitting there, just had a hunch there might be something to see.

Sure enough, ten minutes later a cab came barreling round the corner, stopping outside Famous Prick's house. And then the naked woman emerged from the house, all dressed now. She got in the cab, but before she did, Gregg spied a shadowy figure with a camera snapping her picture.

The woman had no clue that she was being photographed, and Gregg had no clue what was going on, but it was sure as hell interesting – especially when a black Lincoln town car fell in behind the cab as the driver took off.

Naked woman in Famous Prick's house having clandestine photos taken and then being tailed.

Something was up.

Twenty minutes passed before the man who'd been standing with the naked woman came out. He got in the car that was parked in the driveway, activated the gates and left. House now empty, Gregg surmised.

Once more he scaled the gate, making his way round the back where he'd observed the sliding glass doors. His luck was in because they were not locked.

Entering the house, he stood there for a moment, listening intently for any sound of movement.

Nothing.

House definitely empty.

Gregg was enjoying himself. How powerful it was having free run of someone else's house. Snooping in every nook and cranny and they didn't know!

Famous Prick, Cameron's new boyfriend, had a lot of clothes. There were rows of expensive suits, jackets, shirts, all neatly lined up on matching hangers – the shirts were color coordinated. And there were dozens of shoes, mostly shiny and new. And many ties of all hues.

"Faggot!" Gregg muttered, suppressing a sudden urge to piss all over everything.

He checked out the bathroom. The usual shit. Dozens of packs of vitamins, and in the bathroom cabinet, prescription bottles of Vicodin and Ambien.

Gregg was way familiar with both drugs. He emptied out half the contents of both containers and shoved them in the pocket of his jeans. Nice haul. Worth the visit.

The bedroom was next. Huge oversize bed, black-out blinds, TV hanging from the ceiling on chrome chains. Too modern for Gregg's taste. He opened the drawer in the cabinet next to the bed, and BINGO! Good stuff. Packets of condoms – magnum size. Yeah! Who was this dude kidding? Breath mints – strong ones. Hand cream. Several remotes. A digital camera. And best of all – a nine-millimeter hand gun.

Gregg picked up the gun and slowly caressed it. He had a thing about guns, always had, and this one was a beaut.

He checked the clip, fully loaded. In back of the drawer he discovered an extra box of bullets. Very convenient.

Shoving the gun down the waist of his jeans and pocketing the bullets, he ran through the images on the digital camera. A few pretty girls who looked vaguely familiar sitting or lying in various stages of undress on Famous Prick's bed, nothing too raunchy, no images of Cameron. Too bad. He was almost in the mood to jerk off.

He thought about taking the camera, decided against it. The

370

gun was the real prize. He couldn't wait to wave it in Cameron's face and take her the fuck back to where she belonged.

Hawaii.

With him.

Suddenly the doorbell rang, startling him. His eyes swiveled to the security cameras and he observed a pretty girl in pink shorts and matching tank top standing by the outside gates. Gregg took a second look and recognized her as the other girl from the photos of Famous Prick in the rags. Mary Ellen Something. He'd seen her on TV in some stupid sit-com.

What did *she* want?

Maybe he should invite her in and show her a *real* good time.

But no, he wasn't in L.A. to have a good time. He was here to collect his fucking out-of-control cheating murderous wife.

After a couple of minutes the girl put an envelope in the mail-box, turned around, plumped her pretty ass in a white convertible Mercedes, and drove off.

Gregg waited a beat, then decided it was time to go before Famous Prick had any more visitors.

On the way to his car he flipped open the mailbox and scooped up Mary Ellen's note.

Why not? It was a free country.

Chapter Forty-Six

Marty was dead. Stone cold utterly dead.

Ryan stood near the pool in Evie's rented house, and stared in stunned silence as the police photographer finished his job. Marty's body was sprawled beside the pool, his head blown to pieces, blood and fragments of human flesh scattered everywhere.

A broad-faced detective approached Ryan. "I'll never understand why they havta do it in front of the kids," the detective said, digging at his teeth with a wooden toothpick. "Makes me sick. This is the second one this week."

"Second what?" Ryan asked, his stomach churning.

"Second bastard who blew himself away with his kids watching."

"My sister had a Restraining Order," Ryan muttered.

"Yeah," the detective drawled. "An' I got a note from Bank of America saying they're gonna give me a million big ones."

Ryan understood what the detective was saying. He'd been warned that Restraining Orders were a waste of time. Why hadn't he had the sense to hire a security guard to watch over Evie and the kids?

Thank God for small mercies. Marty had taken his own life and not Evie's or the boys. It could so easily have gone the other way.

He walked inside the house where Evie was being questioned

by a female detective, his mother also. The three boys had been whisked away by his older sister, Inga.

Making his way out to the front yard he pulled out his phone and called Mandy. She didn't pick up. Same thing with Don.

He ached to call Cameron, she would understand better than anyone, but he couldn't do that, could he? No. She was with Don. They were enjoying their weekend together. He wasn't about to ruin it for either of them.

Back inside the house the female detective had finished taking Evie's statement.

Evie spotted him, got up and ran into his arms.

Ryan hugged her tightly. "You can cry if you want," he encouraged. "Go ahead, let it all out."

Between choked sobs she began explaining what had happened. She told him that the boys were out in the pool, all three of them excellent swimmers, while she and her mother watched them from the kitchen window as they prepared lunch. Then out of nowhere Marty suddenly appeared, screaming at the boys to get out and come home to Silverlake with him where they belonged.

Confused, the boys started climbing out of the pool. Evie ran outside, followed by Noreen.

Marty was drunk and a mess. He looked like he hadn't slept in a week.

"You're not supposed to be here," Evie shouted.

"Too fuckin' bad," he responded. "You're all comin' home with me."

"No, they're not," Noreen said, bravely stepping forward to protect her brood.

That's when Marty produced the gun, waving it randomly in the air. "Gonna give you a choice," he said, turning to Evie. "You're all comin' home with me or I'm blowin' my fuckin' brains out. Whaddya think of *that*?"

"Go ahead," she said, never imagining he'd do such a thing.

But he did.

As she finished telling him, Ryan held her even closer. "It's not your fault," he assured her. "Marty was unbalanced, he wasn't thinking straight. You didn't cause him to do this, he did it all on his own."

"Yes, but I told him to go ahead," she sobbed, tears trickling down her face. "And the worst thing is that the boys saw everything."

"He would've done it anyway. It had nothing to do with you telling him to go ahead."

"I don't know," she said unsurely. "What if I'd stayed in Silverlake? What if I hadn't taken the boys?"

"Stop second guessing yourself. You did the right thing, that's all there is to it."

"Are you sure, Ryan?"

"About as sure as I can be about anything," he said, once more enclosing his sister in the safety of his arms.

* * *

After going over the script with a somewhat subdued Marlon, Lucy got in her Mercedes and drove home, her fury at Phil's indiscretion somewhat abated. She'd gotten her revenge – of sorts. She'd been half-naked in front of another man, and that was enough to boost her confidence and infuriate Phil if he ever found out.

Of course, she could never tell him it was Marlon, that would ruin any future relationship the two of them might have regarding her script. Actually she was quite excited about them meeting one day. Phil was often into mentoring young talent, and when he read Marlon's work, who knew what would happen?

Humming softly to herself she parked her car in the driveway and entered her house.

"Mommy! Mommy!" both her children chorused, greeting her in the hallway. "Look what Daddy got you. Look! Look!"

She looked, she couldn't *not* look. The hallway was filled from one end to the other with an amazing array of Lalique vases filled with all different colored roses and tulips.

"It's not your birthday, Mommy, is it?" asked Abigaile, who was seven and a petite version of her mother.

"No, it's not her birthday, stupid," countered Andrew, aged nine and quite stocky with Harry Potter-style glasses and sticking-up hair.

"Daddy says you're special, so you should have special things," Abigaile sighed. "I wish *I* was special, Mommy."

"You are, sweetheart," Lucy said, patting her little daughter on the head.

"No, she's not," Andrew snorted. "She's stupid!"

Nanny put her head around the door. "Homework, children," she called out. "Come along. Snap to it."

Thank God for Nanny, Lucy thought. She could never manage without her.

Abigaile and Andrew rushed off.

Phil appeared, balancing several small packages. "I'm an idiot," he boomed, his voice louder than ever. "An oversexed, dumb-ass goddamn idiot."

"That's true," she said, playing it cool as he thrust bags from *Cartier*, *Tiffany* and *Prada* at her. "What's all this?" she asked.

"Gifts for my beautiful amazing forgiving understanding wife."

"What makes you think I'm forgiving?" she said, narrowing her eyes.

"Because I adore you," he proclaimed. "I worship you. You mean everything to me."

"In that case . . ." she said, sensing a great and unexpected opportunity.

"Yes?" Phil said anxiously. "Anything you want. Just name it."

"Help me get my career back on track," she said quickly. "I have a plan."

* * *

375

Returning home from her shopping spree, Mandy was surprised to find Evie and Noreen sitting in her living room. She did not recall Ryan telling her they were coming over, and she wasn't exactly thrilled. Dropping several *Neiman's* and *Saks* bags, she threw Ryan a questioning look.

"Hi, everyone," she said. "Did I forget you were coming over?"

Ryan took her arm. "There's been a terrible tragedy," he said in a low voice. "Marty shot himself."

For a moment she thought he was joking, then observing their serious faces, she realized he wasn't.

As Ryan relayed the story to her, she thought how bizarre it was. Why did Marty shoot himself at Evie's, when he could've done it at their Silverlake house and saved everyone a lot of trouble? A selfish bastard right up until the end.

Mandy had a sinking feeling that Evie and the boys were coming home to roost, for they certainly wouldn't want to stay in the rented house, not after this.

She wasn't quite sure what to say. Somehow – *I'm sorry for your loss* – did not seem appropriate.

She looked at Ryan who was pouring brandy into several glasses. "I suppose I should cancel our reservation at *Spago*," she said lamely.

He fixed her with a grim stare. "Yes, Mandy, I suppose you should."

* * *

They'd made love outside. Now, less than two hours later, they'd made love again – this time inside the house.

Could this weekend get any better? As far as Don was concerned – no. And Cameron had no complaints.

"You never tell me anything about you, your family, your ex-boyfriends, how you got into the personal fitness business. I don't even know where you're from," Don said, lazily reaching over and stroking her hair as they lay on his bed in the bedroom, sun streaming down on them from an open skylight.

Don was getting curious. She wasn't sure she liked that.

"Chicago," she said at last. "When my mom died, I left home and traveled around the world with a friend from school."

"How old were you?"

"I guess I was about eighteen."

"That's a very adventurous thing to do for one so young," he remarked.

"I was always an old soul, always capable of looking after myself."

Now that was a lie. If she was so capable, why had she let Gregg get away with abusing her? Why hadn't she run at the first sign of violence?

"How about ex-boyfriends?" he asked, his curiosity aroused. "Anyone I should be jealous of?"

"What is this?" she said, starting to get edgy. "An inquisition?"

"I'm interested," he said, still stroking her hair.

"Here's the thing, Don," she said, willing him to stop with the questions. "It's just not that interesting."

"How'd you end up in L.A.?" he asked, determined to keep going.

Enough was enough, it was time to turn the questioning around. "How did *you*?" she countered, sitting up.

"I'm that strange breed – a tried and true L.A. native."

"That's unusual, isn't it?"

"It sure is," he said, thinking how naturally beautiful she was. "Most people *come* to L.A., they're not born here."

"And your parents – are they still alive?"

"My mom's around."

"Do you see her often?"

"Once in a while." He paused for a moment before continuing. "She lives in the valley with a house full of cats and a live-in girlfriend."

"Girlfriend? You mean partner girlfriend?"

"Yeah," he said casually. "My dad ran out on us when I was six, so it kinda put her off men, then a few months after he beat it she changed tracks."

Silently Cameron thought that his dad deserting the family, and his mother becoming a lesbian explained a lot. Don Verona. Player. Of course.

"Hey," he said, perplexed. "How did this get turned around and now *I'm* the one answering all the questions?"

"'Cause you love talking about yourself," she said, smiling. "It feeds your ego."

"No, it doesn't," he protested.

"Yes, it does."

"Says who?"

"Says me, and I'm hungry. Isn't it about time we sent out for something to eat?"

"And so she changes the subject," he drawled, reaching for his phone and checking the messages. "You're such a slippery one, you never reveal anything."

There were three messages from Phil, which made him think that something must be up.

"One quick call to Phil and I'll order food," he promised.

Cameron jumped off the bed. "I think it's about time I took a shower."

"What?" he said, throwing her a meaningful look. "You can't wait two minutes?"

"Join me," she said, her voice full of promise. "I'll keep the water cold for you."

"Don't you mean hot?"

"For you – cold. You're insatiable."

"And you're complaining?" he said, raising an eyebrow.

"Not really," she said, heading for the bathroom with a smile on her face.

Nothing like great afternoon sex. Cole and Dorian would be proud of her.

* * *

"I'm going over to Ryan's," Phil informed Lucy after hearing the news about Marty's suicide. "There's no reason for you to come."

"Perhaps I should."

"No. You weren't that fond of Marty, there's no need for you to tag along."

"You weren't that fond of him either."

"That's beside the point. I feel bad for Evie, she's such a sweetheart. I'll run by, give her a hug from both of us."

"That's nice of you."

"It's what friends are for, isn't it?"

Lucy nodded. Loyalty to his friends was one of Phil's most endearing qualities.

"I love my gifts," she said, because it was obvious he was trying hard.

"Excellent," he said, sounding more confident now that she didn't appear to be about to dump him – a thought that frightened the crap out of him. "Because I love you, my dear. You are always number one in my heart, and you always will be."

Lucy had forgiven him, but not all the way. He had to keep his promise and do something major about getting her script off the ground before she totally forgave him.

And then . . . once she was Lucy Lyons again, he wouldn't dare risk cheating on her.

* * *

Having been married five times, Hamilton J. Heckerling knew women very well; he also knew how devious they could be. Over the years he'd caught two of his wives having affairs, another one

379

squirreling money into an offshore account, and one wife had been supporting her entire extended family by forging his signature on checks.

Yes, Hamilton knew a thing or two about women. He understood that if a man was smart he would keep a very strong eye on them, especially if the wife in question was forty years his junior.

Pola was a true beauty. She catered to his every whim. But he did not trust her. Not one little bit.

Since their marriage he'd never left her alone, so when he decided to make a business trip to Japan without her, he put in place the appropriate arrangements to make sure he knew exactly where she was and what she was doing every minute of every day.

The report that came through on his e-mail, accompanied by photographs, was the last thing he'd expected.

It was shocking. Quite shocking.

The proof was in the pictures.

ANYA

*E*lliot Von Morton was well aware that his affair with Anya wouldn't last. He was a high-powered divorce attorney, he'd seen the worst of what went on between men and women, he was wise enough to know that it couldn't last.

One thing he did know for sure – Anya had turned into a drug – his drug. When he was with her, all sense of reason deserted him. She was a prize he'd never imagined he'd find. A young beautiful creature who understood his sexual needs and catered to them like a dedicated maestro.

There was nothing she wouldn't do. Nothing that shocked her.

She had a past, this girl with the face of an angel. A dark past Elliot had no desire to investigate. He was quite certain there were things he would not care to know about. She was his now, and that's all that mattered.

The day his divorce became final, things changed. Anya changed. She became sulky and not so obliging.

Elliot did not understand why, but it didn't take long before Anya enlightened him, "I want you to marry me," she said. "I want to be Mrs Elliot Von Morton."

At first he refused to entertain the idea. He was fifty-six years old, and to marry a girl young enough to be his daughter would be beyond foolish. But Anya was adamant, and the more he said *no, the more she stopped catering to his very specific sexual needs.*

He soon began noticing how flirtatious her attitude was becoming toward his male friends and acquaintances, and it worried him that she might leave him and move on to bigger and better, exactly as she had done to Seth.

Dammit! Why not marry the girl? He'd spent enough time and money on her. He'd pulled strings and arranged for her to become an American citizen. He'd facilitated her need to change her name. He'd buried her past – whatever that might be. The truth was that he'd re-invented her. She'd come to him as a slutty-looking waif, and he'd turned her into an impeccably groomed and stylish young woman.

Yes, Elliot decided, he would marry her. He had nothing to lose and everything to gain.

It wasn't a big wedding – quite low-key, in fact. They honeymooned in the Bahamas and returned to New York after a week. Elliot did not wish to stay any longer – he missed his chains and whips and handcuffs. Elliot was addicted to the pain Anya inflicted.

Anya was not sure what she was addicted to. Shoes. They were the only thing that gave her any pleasure. Other than her shoe collection, nothing mattered. She was empty inside, unable to feel anything except a cold indifference. She had thought that marrying an important man like Elliot might fill the void, but no, nothing helped.

And then one day Elliot took her to the première of a movie one of his clients had produced, and she met Hamilton J. Heckerling. He was older than Elliot. And richer.

In Hamilton's eyes Anya recognized a ruthlessness that matched her own. Hamilton J. Heckerling was a far more glamorous figure than Elliot Von Morton. Elliot worked in a New York office. Hamilton J. Heckerling roamed the world making huge blockbuster epic movies.

Anya decided it was a way of living that might appeal to her, so she set about seducing Hamilton, and when she discovered that his fetish was watching women together, she knew he was all hers.

There was only one problem. Elliot Von Morton.

He did not remain a problem for very long. Sadly, he expired in the middle of one of their sexual games – suffering a massive heart attack.

Anya had not heard him utter the "safe" word – a word that signaled he'd had enough.

Six months later Hamilton announced their engagement at a New York dinner party.

Shortly after that, Anya became Mrs Hamilton J. Heckerling.

Chapter Forty-Seven

"We're on the biggest friggin' roll *ever*!" Cole announced. "We've signed almost fifteen hundred memberships in ten days – it's unbelievable what's happenin'."

Cameron agreed. It *was* unbelievable, a success neither of them had imagined. Don's killer lawyer had dealt with the Mister Fake Tan situation – the whole thing had gone away, so now they had nothing to worry about except keeping up the pace.

"We're gonna havta expand," Cole declared. "This is just the beginning, babe. We're on fire!"

They'd already hired two more trainers and a massage therapist, and what with so many new clients, space was at a premium.

"I'll speak to Iris," Cameron said. "I know there's an empty floor downstairs, it might be perfect."

"Yeah, call her first thing Monday."

"I will."

Cole threw Cameron a long penetrating look. "What's up with you lately?" he inquired, leaning across the desk. "You should be doin' handstands, yet you're sittin' here all quiet an' moody. You're not your usual self."

"I'm tired," she confessed.

"New boyfriend runnin' you ragged?" Cole said with a sly smile.

"Don's great," she said half-heartedly. "He gives me my space."

"Then what?"

"Nothing, Cole," she said, wishing he'd leave her alone. "Really – I'm fine."

Although she wasn't fine, she was utterly confused. The previous weekend she'd spent with Don at the beach, it had been idyllic – comfortable and fun and the usual amazing sex because Don was a master in the bedroom – and anywhere else they cared to get it on. But on Tuesday he'd informed her he had a big aversion to funerals (like who didn't?) and that he simply couldn't go to Marty's without her by his side. And of course he had to attend, out of respect for his best friend's sister. And who was his best friend? Ryan Richards.

So she went with him, albeit reluctantly.

Walking into the church, the first person she saw was Ryan. Their eyes met, and that was it. She'd felt the same way she had that night outside *Chow's*. It was a seminal moment.

Later, when everyone went back to the Richards's house, she and Ryan had experienced a short time alone together. She'd walked outside to the back patio while Don was busy talking to other people, and two seconds later Ryan was there.

"Hey –" he'd said.

"Hey –" she'd responded.

They'd stared at each other for a long silent beat, sparks flying.

"Uh, I hope Evie's okay," she said at last, feeling quite dizzy.

"I hate to say it, but I know she's better off."

"And you?" she said, noting that he looked stressed. "Is everything okay?"

"I've been better," he replied, suppressing an insane urge to grab her hand and get the hell out of there. "How about you?"

They were both being so polite, and yet who cared? She wasn't listening to the words coming out of his mouth – she was too caught up in his bluer than blue eyes. So intense, so sexy, so tempting.

Leaning toward her, Ryan said in a low voice – "I've been thinking about you."

"You have?" she replied, feeling ridiculously light-headed.

"You're with my best friend," he said, clearing his throat. "So I guess you're on my mind."

"In a good way, I hope?"

"Cameron," he said sincerely, "all I want is for you to be happy, and if Don makes you happy—"

"He does," she said, a tad too quickly.

"Are you sure?"

"Yes," she said, unconvincingly.

"You don't sound it."

"Well, I am."

"Don can be difficult, you know. He has a reputation. Loves women, but has a habit of moving on when it suits him."

"Why do you keep on warning me about your so-called best friend?"

"Maybe I don't want to see you get hurt."

"Does it really matter to you?"

"You know it does."

"Hey – hey – hey – what's going on with you two?" Don said, appearing beside them. "Trying to sneak off for an illicit affair behind my back?" He grinned, enjoying what he knew to be a foolish assumption. "Making a run to steal my girl, Ryan?"

"Right," Ryan responded, summoning a forced smile. "We're busy planning our escape."

"That's okay," Don said, still joking as he threw his arm around Cameron and deposited a kiss on her cheek. "I think I got a lock on the situation. Right, beautiful?"

She smiled weakly. It was the kind of humor she didn't need.

Later, driving her back to *Paradise*, Don had said, "You know, I think Ryan really likes you. Good thing I got you first."

"What makes you think that?" she'd murmured.

"I dunno – he's kind of different around you. Like he's got a thing for you."

"It's your imagination," she'd said, her heart pounding.

And ever since then she'd been thinking about how to break it off with Don.

Tonight they were going to a dinner at Phil and Lucy Standards'. Maybe tonight she'd tell him it was over.

She'd miss him, but she knew for sure that he simply wasn't the one.

* * *

Lucy raced around her house making sure everything was set for her very important dinner. Phil was completely on board. Ever since she'd discovered him screwing his now very ex-assistant, he couldn't do enough for her. Plus he was still bombarding her with gifts. So far she'd received the very latest Cartier watch, an antique diamond bracelet from Neil Lane, exquisite gold and diamond necklaces from XIV Karats, and the offer of yet another new car.

"Enough," she'd admonished. "You're spending a fortune."

"And you, my dear," Phil had replied, "are worth every red cent."

Talk about guilt ridden!

She didn't care about the gifts, she only cared about her script, and the dinner party – which was to be her launching pad for a big career comeback.

Once she included him in her plan, Phil changed the dynamics of the dinner. "We do not want a house full of people," he warned her. "Two producers are more than enough. Keep it down to Ryan and Hamilton."

"Are you certain they're the right two?"

"Definitely. Nobody's going to read your script while they're here. But with Hamilton and Ryan you've got that competitive thing going on between them. They'll both take it home. Ryan will read it himself, and Hamilton will give it to one of his development people to look at. Who knows? You might even create a bidding war."

Phil wanted – or at least he pretended that he wanted – to read the script before the big night. She'd said no, because she would prefer for him to be surprised along with everyone else. Besides, she was nervous for him to read it at this late stage; he'd have criticisms and comments, and now was not the time to deal with his professional opinion.

She wondered how Phil would react when he got a look at Marlon. Hmm . . . a touch of payback was not such a bad thing.

Once they'd cut the number of guests down, she'd decided to hire only one chef and a helper who would double as a barman. None of Mandy's suggested army of people, and they certainly didn't need valet parking. Their enormous driveway – way off the main road – could accommodate dozens of cars.

The children had gone off with Nanny, most of the animals were ensconced in the tree house, the table was set, there was nothing left for Lucy to do except get ready.

She had a hunch it would be a very special evening.

*　*　*

"I'm engaged!" Lynda shouted out the good news as she sashayed into *Paradise* later than usual, flashing a small diamond ring on her engagement finger. "Carlos asked me last night and I said yes – yes – YES!"

Everyone gathered around her, Dorian already planning what style of dress she should wear, and how the flower arrangements at the reception should look.

"I am so happy for you," Cameron said, giving her a big hug. "You've wanted this for a long time."

"You bet your fine ass!" Lynda exclaimed. "Carlos has been dragging his feet forever, but last night he finally came through."

"Everyone – this calls for a celebration," Cole announced. "*Obar*, tonight – eight o'clock. Are we on it?"

"You bet!" Lynda grinned, her brown eyes sparkling. "I'll tell Carlos."

"Yeah," Dorian said dryly. "Carlos in a gay bar. Can't *wait* to see *that*!"

"He'll be fine," Lynda giggled. "He's been around you guys long enough. I am so HAPPY!"

"Let me see the ring," Cameron said.

Lynda proudly displayed her hand.

"It's lovely."

"Tell that to Carlos later," Lynda said, beaming. "He spent *mucho* bucks."

"Oh, God!" Cameron suddenly remembered the dinner party at the Standards'. "I can't come tonight, I promised Don—"

"Cancel!" Dorian said sharply. "Our Lynda getting engaged is more important than whatever you have to do with your big star boyfriend."

"I can't cancel, but I'll try to come by later."

"Ha!" Dorian sniffed. "I think I liked it better when you *weren't* getting laid."

"For your information," Cameron retorted, "I was always getting laid, you just didn't know it!"

"Uh *ha*! Now I understand why you would never let me fix you up with Carlos's friends!" Lynda exclaimed.

"She's a secretive one," Cole said.

They should only know just *how* secretive. Which reminded her, wasn't it time she did something about getting a divorce?

Yes. Perhaps Don's killer lawyer could help her. The only problem with that was that she hadn't told Don she was married. And now, with breaking things off with him on her mind, it was not the right time.

She had two things other than work on her agenda – the first was to break up with Don, and the second – to find her own lawyer.

She'd do both things. Soon.

*   *   *

"I wish we didn't have to go tonight," Ryan grumbled.

"We have to," Mandy responded. "Lucy would never forgive me if we canceled two hours beforehand. She's gone to a lot of trouble – they haven't had people over in years."

Ryan was thinking what a difficult week it had been, dealing with Evie and the kids after Marty's unexpected suicide. He'd found himself taking care of everything – starting with the funeral, getting out of the six-month lease on the rented house, Marty's Will – in which he'd left jack-shit – and dozens of other small matters. He was tired, and he still hadn't faced Mandy about the divorce situation. Every time he came close, something happened to stop him. The last thing he felt like doing was going to a dinner party.

Seeing Cameron at the funeral with Don had done nothing to help his frame of mind. It had only reminded him of how stuck he was in a loveless sexless marriage.

And to make matters worse – Don had not been able to wipe the smile off his face. Now his best friend really did have everything.

But what about Cameron? Was she just as happy? Was Don the man she wanted to be with?

Obviously yes. She was with Don Verona, and that was that.

*   *   *

"If you moved into my house," Don said, as Cameron opened her front door, "I wouldn't have to dodge photographers and take a different route every time I pick you up."

"Yes," she said, smiling. "But you love giving them the slip. It's a game you enjoy winning, and so far you're doing an excellent job. Apart from that night at *Paradise*, we're totally flying under the radar."

"That we are," he agreed. "The gossip rags are *still* linking me with Mary Ellen. How about that?"

"She must be thrilled."

"Poor kid. I *do* feel sorry for her."

"No, you don't."

"Do you really think I'm that heartless?"

"No, just a big player."

"By the way, Miz Paradise, I think I should tell you that you look amazing tonight."

"Thank you."

"No need to thank me, it's a fact," he said, escorting her outside to yet another of his many cars. "This is my new baby," he said proudly. "A Bugatti Veyron." He didn't bother to add that it was the fastest sports car around *and* the most expensive – his latest toy had set him back almost a million bucks. Things were pretty hot in the talk-show business.

"Wow!" Cameron murmured. "It's a fantastic-looking car, but I still prefer my Mustang."

Laughing, he held the car door open for her. "You're a funny lady," he said. "Nothing impresses you, does it?"

"Hey Don," she said, suddenly remembering Lynda and her engagement, "if the dinner finishes early, can we go by *Obar*? Cole and Dorian are throwing a little celebration for Lynda – she and Carlos finally got engaged."

"Who is Lynda? And where's *Obar*?"

It irritated her that he did not remember the people she worked with, even though he'd come by *Paradise* and met them all.

Maybe they weren't famous enough for him.

No. Don wasn't like that, he was merely forgetful.

"Oh c'mon, you can't forget Lynda, she's our receptionist. Latina. Gorgeous. And *Obar* is a fun restaurant on Santa Monica."

"Sure, we'll stop by if we get through in time. But only if you spend tonight at *my* house."

"You're always trying to blackmail me."

"Deal?"

"Do I *have* to say yes?"

"Actually, you do."

One more night wasn't about to make any difference. It wasn't as if Ryan was single and waiting for her, he was still very much married.

And what could she do about that?

Absolutely nothing.

*　*　*

Anya was puzzled. Hamilton had been home for twenty-four hours and so far he had not touched her or ordered in an expensive call girl so he could watch the two of them make love for his enjoyment. This was unlike Hamilton, who, with the help of Viagra, had quite a robust sexual appetite, especially as he'd been away for almost a week.

Anya did not mind enacting scenes for Hamilton with other women. In her mind she turned every other woman into Velma – the only person she'd truly felt anything for.

She wondered what Hamilton had done in Japan. She didn't ask. Silence was a far more powerful tool.

He'd brought her back a dress, a slinky satin dress – bright scarlet and extremely form-fitting with deep side slits.

"You'll wear it tonight," he informed her.

"Are we going out?" she inquired.

"Yes. We're attending a dinner party at Phil and Lucy Standard's house. You met them at Mandy's."

She remembered a tall, striking woman with long jet-black hair – and a heavy-set rumpled bear of a man with a beard. The man with the beard had been sitting next to Ryan at the live sex show in Amsterdam. She recalled him roaring with laughter and applauding. When he'd met her in L.A. he hadn't remembered her. Why would he? In his eyes she was nothing but a disposable whore. She'd loathed him then, why should tonight be any different?

Now Hamilton was forcing her to go to his house, eat his food, and be in the presence of his hateful face.

Would Mandy and Ryan be there, since they were all friends? Yes, and she dreaded seeing them.

Later in the afternoon she approached Hamilton in his study. "I'm feeling unwell," she said. "Would it bother you if I stayed home tonight?"

There was a malevolent spark in his eyes. "Yes, Pola," he said, tapping the tips of his fingers together, "it would bother me a great deal. We leave here at seven thirty. Be ready."

Chapter Forty-Eight

Unbeknownst to Cameron, Gregg visited her house whenever he felt like it. He knew where she was at all times. He knew where she deposited her two dogs every day with her Japanese neighbor. He knew exactly when and what time the cleaning woman arrived – twice a week – Tuesdays and Fridays between nine and one.

When Cameron wasn't there he treated her house as if it was his home – which in a way it was. They were married, weren't they? He was her husband, wasn't he? He had rights.

He watched sports on her TV. Drank her booze. Ate her snacks. Jerked off in her bedroom. In fact, he did whatever the fuck he wanted to do. Best of all he kept a sharp eye on an appointment book she left lying on the kitchen table. He didn't have to follow her anymore, he knew every one of her movements, her book really helped him out.

After she'd spent the weekend at the beach with Famous Prick, Gregg observed that she'd seen him only twice. One time she'd gone with him to a funeral – Gregg had followed her to *that* one – very depressing. And on Thursday night she and Famous Prick had shared a quiet dinner for two at *Il Sole*, a cozy restaurant on Sunset.

Cameron had turned into a workaholic. She spent most of her

time at *Paradise*, occasionally taking off to work with private clients at their homes.

One day, certain that she was out, Gregg sashayed into *Paradise* and introduced himself to the busty little piece of Mexican ass sitting behind the reception desk. He told her he was a journalist for a big sports magazine in Sydney, Australia, and that he needed information about *Paradise* so he could write the place up in his magazine.

"Fantastic!" Lynda cooed, batting her eyelashes at him. "But you should really speak with one of the owners."

"Who are the owners?" he asked, giving her some major eye-contact.

"There's Cole, but he's busy with a client. And Cameron, she's out right now."

"That's a drag. I'm on a time deadline and I gotta speak to someone today. Who is this Cameron anyway?"

"Cameron Paradise – the place is named after her 'cause it's her baby. 'Scuse me," she said, reaching for the phone.

"What's *your* name?" he asked when she got off the phone.

"Lynda," she answered coyly, enjoying the attention.

He played it smart with Lynda. Invited her for a sandwich on her lunch-break, promised that he'd write something very positive about *Paradise* in his magazine, and that he'd send it to her and she could surprise her bosses with it and take full credit. "We'll even run your photo," he said, sealing the deal.

Over a quick tuna fish sandwich Lynda spilled everything, thinking it was all for this great piece he was preparing to write.

Yeah. Sure. In your dreams, you Salma Hayek wanna-be.

So ... Cameron had told no one that she was a married woman. Interesting.

And now she was carrying on a full-blown affair with Famous Prick as if she didn't have a care in the world.

The time had come to burst her fucking bubble.

The time had come to take his wife back.

Chapter Forty-Nine

The first guests to arrive were Hamilton and his new bride. Lucy greeted them at the door herself. She'd opted to wear a low-cut bronze Hervé Léger dress – her new gold and diamond casual necklaces strung around her neck, her Cartier watch on her wrist. With her long black hair and porcelain skin she cut a dramatic and sexy figure.

"*So* glad you could make it," she said warmly, kissing Hamilton on both cheeks, while offering Anya/Pola a casual wave.

"I was worried you'd be stuck in Tokyo, and have to cancel."

"I never get stuck anywhere," Hamilton opined. "One thing about me – if I have a schedule, I stick to it."

"I'm sure you do," Lucy said, flirting a little bit. "I remember when we worked together, you were always so organized." A beat. A flutter of her long eyelashes. "It was one of the things I enjoyed most about working with you – your unswerving dedication."

It immediately struck Hamilton that the actress wanted something from him. No doubt during the course of the evening he'd find out what that something was.

Don and Cameron arrived next. Don, so handsome and charming, displaying his usual self-deprecating humor. And Cameron, quite lovely in silky pants and a loose top.

Phil was busy playing genial host to the hilt, dismissing the barman – telling the man to go help the chef in the kitchen – while he poured the drinks himself. He was intrigued to find out what Lucy had in store. Her script presentation could turn out to be a major embarrassment, but he was on for the ride, he owed her that.

The first thing Mandy realized when she and Ryan walked in, was that she was overdressed in her Narciso Rodriguez backless purple dress and Elsa Peretti diamonds. Where were the parking valets? The other help she had distinctly told Lucy to hire? And why was Phil behind the bar?

Even more infuriating – what was Hamilton doing there? And Don Verona with that pushy blonde who'd stolen him from Mary Ellen?

"Where is everybody?" she asked Lucy in a hoarse stage whisper.

"Change of plan," Lucy said, all wide-eyed innocence. "Didn't I tell you?"

"No, you didn't," Mandy hissed. "Who else is coming?"

"This is it," Lucy said. "Phil thought it best to keep it small."

"Thanks for letting me know," Mandy said, unable to keep a lid on her aggravation.

"Sorry," Lucy said, too excited about her upcoming surprise to worry about Mandy being upset.

"And may I ask why Hamilton is here?" Mandy demanded.

"Phil wanted him," Lucy replied, making a quick escape to the kitchen to check on the chef.

Mandy was furious. She'd been expecting an elegant evening with interesting and important guests. Instead she was stuck with her father and his wife, and Don plus his current fling. Why had she bothered to dress up and get her hair done? It wasn't worth it.

"Let's make this an early night," she muttered to Ryan as Phil poured their drinks.

Ryan didn't really hear her, he was too busy making eye-contact across the room with Cameron.

"Lucy should've told me it was a small dinner," Mandy complained.

"I thought you two spoke every day," Ryan said.

"We do, that's why I can't understand why she didn't tell me."

"Here comes your old man," Ryan said. "I'm going over to say hi to Don." And picking up his glass of vodka, he headed for the couch.

Hamilton descended on his daughter. "How are you, my dear?" he asked. "Doing well, I hope?"

It was so unlike Hamilton to give a damn about how she was. Maybe he was mellowing in his old age. Anya stood behind him in an unflattering and quite tarty scarlet dress, looking sulky. Somehow, the mere sight of her father's latest wife put Mandy in a bad mood.

"Everything's good," she said. "I'm sure you heard about Ryan's sister's husband blowing his brains out."

"No," Hamilton said, completely disinterested. "I've been in Japan scouting locations."

"Another big blockbuster in the works?" Mandy asked, wondering when he'd give it up. Hadn't he had enough of the limelight? She wished he'd hand his company over to Ryan, and she wished that Ryan would accept it. But that wasn't going to happen any time soon.

"As always," Hamilton replied, proffering his glass to Phil for a refill, then once more engaging his daughter in conversation. "How is Ryan?"

First he asked how she was, now he wanted to know about Ryan. What *was* going on with him?

"Why don't you ask him yourself?" she suggested, gesturing toward her husband. "He's right over there."

"Are you two having problems?" Hamilton asked, giving her a long intent look.

She felt a blush rise and color her cheeks. Oh yes, Hamilton would love it if she and Ryan were experiencing difficulties.

"Why would you even *ask* something like that?" she said, determined to remain calm.

Hamilton favored her with one of his annoying chuckles, and turned away to talk to Phil.

Anya stared at her.

Ha! Mandy thought. *If she's expecting me to stand here and talk to her, she can think again.*

Grabbing her glass of wine, Mandy hurried over to join Ryan, Don and his girlfriend – whose name she couldn't remember.

It didn't matter; her loyalty was with Mary Ellen, and if she knew Don, this one was nothing but a temporary replacement.

*　*　*

Lucy had a quick word with the chef before dashing to the back of the house where she'd stashed Marlon in a cubbyhole of a maid's room after smuggling him onto their property earlier.

Marlon was edgy and nervous. He wasn't in favor of Lucy's plan to surprise everyone with him and their script. What if the great Phil Standard didn't like it? What if her plan backfired and *nobody* liked it?

"Stay in control. Be nice," Lucy said, hoping to calm him. "None of them will read it here. They'll take it home. Between you and me we'll tell them the thrust of the script, and we'll make it sound so enticing that they'll probably want to make an offer on the spot! Anyway, that's what Phil thinks."

"When can I come out?" he whined. "I'm gettin' claustro-phobic stuck back here."

"Be patient. We have to eat first."

"Yeah, well, how about me?" he complained, cracking his knuckles – an annoying habit he'd developed recently. "I'm hungry too."

"I'll get you some food," she said, watching him turn into a sulky nine-year-old before her very eyes.

He was not good under pressure, she'd have to remember that.

* * *

Dinner was an avocado and Cajun shrimp salad, followed by thinly sliced steak, whipped potatoes, and a mélange of vegetables. Dinner-table conversation encompassed everything from politics to sex. Phil enjoyed bringing the conversation around to sex, it always ensured a lively discussion. One of his favorite table games was – "Who is the most famous person you've ever fucked?"

Usually he won, but not with Hamilton and Don at the table, so tonight he didn't bring it up. Instead he concentrated on politicians' predilections toward hookers. "They love getting their dicks dirty," he crowed. "Don't they know that if they pay for it they'll always end up getting caught."

"Everyone gets caught," Hamilton said sagely. "Nobody gets away with anything." He stared directly at his son-in-law sitting across the table. "Right, Ryan?"

"Why are you asking *me*?" Ryan said, irritated.

"Yes, why are you asking him?" Mandy said, joining in. "If there's one person in this room who has nothing to hide, it's Ryan."

Anya's eyes darted from Ryan to her husband. Something was definitely going on with Hamilton. Did it have anything to do with Ryan?

No. That was impossible. She believed Ryan when he said he had told no one about her. Ryan Richards was a man of integrity.

"Pola," Hamilton said, speaking to his wife for the first time since they'd arrived, "what do *you* think of Ryan? Do *you* think he might have something to hide?"

Anya shrugged, endeavoring to keep her face expressionless, although small shivers of apprehension attacked her body.

"I barely know Ryan," she said at last. "I am not the right person to answer that question."

"Jesus, Hamilton," Phil boomed. "What's your sudden interest in poor old Ryan tonight? He done something to you we don't know about?"

Hamilton's eyes turned into lethal slits. "Maybe," he said ominously. "Why don't *you* all be the judge."

And with those words he reached into his breast pocket and produced an envelope of photos. Taking them out one at a time, he proceeded to pass them around the table.

"What do you think, everybody?" he asked, his expression deadly. "Does Ryan have something to hide – or not?"

Chapter Fifty

Saturday morning Gregg awoke with a crusty hangover and a cheesy blonde Cameron look-alike lying in bed beside him. In the cruel light of day the girl no more resembled Cameron than his mother – a woman he loathed.

He woke the slag up, got rid of her, sat on his bed and brooded about what the fuck he was doing. He was following and tracking a woman who was already his, the fucking devious cunt who'd thought she'd killed him. Oh yes, she'd left him for dead and gone on her merry way.

Well, not so fast, bitch, because now the time had come to do something about re-claiming his bride. Miz Cameron Paradise was riding high and mighty, and now it was her turn to experience a sharp jolt of reality. And what better way to do that than in front of her friends and Famous Prick boyfriend? The boyfriend who didn't even know she was married.

Earlier in the week he'd noted that she'd written in her appointment book *Saturday, dinner at the Standards' with Don, 8 p.m.*

Was it a big dinner? Small gathering? He didn't care, he was following her anyway. Tonight was the night for retribution.

He spent most of the afternoon drinking with a rowdy bunch of Australians who hung out at a pub near the Venice boardwalk.

They were a wild group of guys – although he could drink most of them under the table and still have room for more.

Later in the day, he staked out his usual spot near Cameron's house, biding his time until Famous Prick came to get her.

Famous Prick turned up on time, driving a ridiculously flashy car. *What an asshole!* Gregg thought. Trust Cameron to choose an asshole.

She got into the car, and they set off.

Gregg followed at a discreet distance, tailing them all the way past Brentwood and up into the hills.

The Standards – whoever they were – sure lived off the beaten track in a huge rambling ranch house set way back from the road. The large property was gated, but the gates weren't closed. Rich people in big houses. Hollywood was full of them.

Gregg stopped his car outside the open gates, reached down to the floor of the passenger seat and picked up a bottle of Scotch he'd started on earlier. Nothing like getting back in action to cure a hangover.

After taking a few hearty swigs he left the car and made his way by foot up the long winding driveway. He was feeling better already. Yeah, better and ready for action.

The big problem was, he had no clear plan of what he was about to do, but whatever he decided, he knew for sure that he was not leaving without his bitch wife.

Cameron was his, and if he couldn't have her – then sure as shit – nobody else could.

Chapter Fifty-One

Reactions to Hamilton's photos as they were passed around the Standards' dinner table differed.

Mandy cried out in shock.

Anya simply stared blankly at the incriminating photos.

Cameron shook her head in disbelief.

Don let out a long low whistle.

Phil suppressed a crazed guffaw.

Lucy was livid. Her script surprise was supposed to be the big deal of the night. This had ruined everything.

And Ryan – well, Ryan was speechless as he realized that somehow he'd been set up.

The photos – six of them – were a series of shots of him and Anya in Don's house. Anya, standing in front of him naked but for the lacy black thong, while he – thank God – remained fully dressed.

He knew *exactly* what the photos represented, but to an uninvolved observer they told a completely different story.

"Anything to hide now?" Hamilton crowed, quite enjoying himself.

"You *bastard*!" Mandy hissed at her husband. "How could you do this to Daddy and me?"

"It's not what it looks like," Ryan managed, unable to face Cameron across the table. God! What must she think of him?

"I'm under the distinct impression it's exactly what it looks like," Hamilton said coldly. "It *looks* as if you are about to fuck my wife while I'm conveniently out of town. I knew you were a no-good sonofabitch the moment Mandy dragged you home, and now you've finally proved it."

Ryan glanced at Anya. Now was the time for her to speak up, rescue him like he'd rescued her seven years earlier. But she remained silent, her face devoid of expression.

"We were talking, nothing else," Ryan said, making an attempt to explain, and realizing how lame he must sound.

"Talking?" Hamilton sneered. "Is that right, Pola, dear? The two of you were just talking?"

She kept her silence, eyes downcast.

"You two must have so much to talk about," Hamilton said with a sarcastic smirk. "My wife and the man who's married to my daughter."

Surprising everyone, Mandy leaped to her feet and unexpectedly slapped Ryan hard across the face. "Bastard!" she yelled for the second time. "How dare you humiliate me!"

Don jumped up. "You know something, Hamilton," he said angrily. "You're totally out of line bringing this up here tonight. It's your business, not ours, and none of us appreciate being dragged into it. You should have more consideration for your daughter's feelings. What kind of a father are you?"

"A very generous father," Hamilton said, his tone icy. "A father who cares about the scum his daughter associates with."

"Oh," Don said scornfully. "And I suppose it's not your wife in the photos bare-assed naked."

"Please, everybody," Lucy said, desperate to get the evening back on track, although deep down she realized it was impossible. All her scheming, all her plans, and now *this*. Damn Hamilton, she'd never liked him. "Can we all calm down."

"I'm sorry, Lucy," Don said. "Cameron and I are out of here. This isn't our business, and we don't care to be involved." He put his hand on Cameron's shoulder, and she started to push her chair back from the table. As she did so, a loud crash came from the direction of the kitchen.

"Oh my God!" Lucy exclaimed, simmering with frustration. "What now?"

Phil got up. "Please all stay put," he said, taking charge. "I'll be right back."

As he hurried toward the kitchen he thought about the girl in the photos. Hamilton's wife. There was something about her without her clothes on that struck a chord. Phil never forgot a naked woman, and he'd seen this one before. But where? He couldn't quite place her.

Pushing open the swing doors to the kitchen he came face to face with a man holding a gun.

Christ! If he'd written a script for this evening he could never have come up with this. He spotted the chef and the barman both tied up on the floor. This was a fucking home invasion on top of everything else.

Shit! Where was the panic button? He couldn't remember.

"Evenin', mate," said the man with the gun, a big fellow, around thirty, with a weathered and deeply tanned complexion. "Nothin' t' get alarmed about, this is a social visit."

Double *shit*! An Australian burglar who thought he could be cute and get away with it.

"Take it easy," Phil said, speaking slower than usual. "I'll lead you to the safe. You can take whatever you want and go. Nobody's going to get in your way."

"It's not money I'm after," the burglar said, breathing heavy whisky fumes in Phil's direction. "Although I can always use a few thou' cash."

"What is it then? Jewelry? Computers?"

"You're damn generous, mate, but what I really came for is my wife."

"Your wife?" Phil said, his mind racing. Could this be one of Lucy's deranged fans from the past? Yes, it was possible. She still received a stack of crazy fan mail and sometimes a few obscene scribbled notes.

"That's right," the gunman said. "My fuckin' evil wife."

Phil took a deep breath, this evening was getting weirder by the minute. Then it suddenly occurred to him that maybe this had something to do with Lucy's script presentation. He wouldn't put it past her to conjure up some insane goings-on, her way of making sure he was punished properly for his major indiscretion.

The maybe or maybe not burglar jerked his gun at Phil. "Let's take a trip back inside an' join your friends," he ordered.

Phil blinked rapidly and tugged on his beard. "Certainly," he said, playing along. "Phil Standard at your service."

* * *

"We're going," Don said to Cameron in a low voice. "I can't take anymore of this. You don't mind, do you?"

"Of course not," she replied, watching as Mandy began berating Ryan, screaming in his face. "I feel so bad for Ryan."

"Yeah, so do I, but this isn't the time or the place to handle anything. He's a big boy, he'll deal."

Cameron wondered what exactly was going on. Ryan was not the kind of man who would cheat with his father-in-law's wife. Besides, he was fully dressed in the photos, so something wasn't right.

"Lucy," Don said, turning to his distressed hostess, "we really gotta go. I know you understand."

Lucy couldn't think of anything she could say to keep them there.

As Cameron and Don walked toward the door of the dining room there was a sudden commotion. Phil was roughly shoved through the door, almost knocking Cameron down. Right behind him was a man with a gun.

Cameron recovered her balance and then she froze.

The man with the gun was Gregg. The husband she'd thought she'd escaped from years ago.

Chapter Fifty-Two

Marlon was getting more than antsy – he was also getting stoned. Lucy had smuggled him into her house like a criminal and stashed him in a windowless box of a maid's room. Wasn't there some kind of law about bedrooms without windows? Yeah, he was sure about it.

His dealings with Lucy were not exactly the way he'd imagined writing a script would go. No proper script meetings, only an occasional visit from her with her comments scribbled on the back of the page. No fancy lunches out with an agent, he'd negotiated the deal himself. Ten grand cash and he'd write her a script. No contract. Nothing.

His dad, the lawyer, would freak if he got wind of what he'd agreed to. But – shit – it was Lucy Lyons he was working with – she of the great tits. Man, he'd jacked off thinking about those tits many a long lonely night. And now he'd seen 'em – up close and personal – and that had to be better than some half-assed contract.

She'd stopped by earlier with a plate of hors d'oeuvres – like that was going to solve his hunger problem. He'd scoffed the lot, but he was still starving.

Lighting up a third joint, he tried to alleviate the boredom by thinking about his sex life. It wasn't bad – he had three girlfriends on the go – three hot foxy girls all under nineteen. And there lay the problem. They were girls, not women, and it seemed he'd developed a taste for women. Ever since Cameron Paradise he'd had a yen to get together with another woman like her. It wasn't as if they'd indulged in long philosophical conversations or anything like that – but the bed action – sweet. And then one day Cameron vanished, changed her cell number and never came back.

If only Lucy hadn't chickened out it could've been even sweeter. Yeah . . . much much sweeter.

He checked the time, it was getting later by the minute.

Hmm . . . later by the minute – did that even make sense?

Hell, no.

Jeez, how long did she expect him to sit here? He wasn't doing it for much longer, that was for sure. If she didn't come and get him soon – script presentation or not – he was out of there.

Chapter Fifty-Three

G regg had them all lined up in a row, sitting on the floor against the dining-room wall. The gun in his hands made him feel all-powerful – especially as none of them knew who he was yet, and Cameron hadn't opened her mouth.

His intention had not been to hold up a room full of people. His intention had been to crash the party, humiliate Cameron, and take her off with him back to where she belonged. But circumstances had a way of evolving, and when the bartender had come across him trying to prise open the kitchen door, they'd gotten into an altercation which had ended with Gregg beating the crap out of the man, then bursting into the kitchen, overcoming the chef and tying them both up.

Gregg was strong. Muscles of steel. Back in Hawaii he'd worked out twice a day. Don't even think about messing with Gregg Kingston.

Then he'd remembered he had a gun with him – and why not use it? So he'd taken it from the waistband of his pants, and that sure made everyone jump to attention. Yeah, including Cameron. He was getting off watching the expressions on her face. At first she'd registered total shock, followed by bewilderment and finally resignation.

The bitch knew exactly why he was here. But her boyfriend

didn't. Famous Prick was in for one helluva big surprise. Gregg couldn't wait to see *his* face when the truth came out.

Before he had a chance to say anything, Cameron spoke up, infuriating him. "I have to apologize to everyone," she said in a strained voice. "This man is my . . ." she could barely get the words out – "husband."

Don gripped her arm tightly. "Tell me you didn't just say that," he muttered. "Tell me you're lying."

"*What*?" yelled Mandy, outraged. "Your *husband*! Oh my *God*! Is this a robbery? Did you two set it up?"

"Gregg," Cameron said, keeping her voice low and even, "you don't want to do this. Put the gun down, let everyone go, and you and I will talk."

"Fuck!" Gregg yelled, continuing to brandish the gun around. "The bitch wants to *talk*. Can you believe it? The bitch left me for dead in Hawaii three years ago. Yeah, you heard me – " he shouted, focusing his attention on Don. "Left me for dead an' ran off in the middle of the night." Picking up a bottle of red wine from the table he took a few solid gulps. "Yeah, I was in a fucking coma for months, but she didn't give a shit; she thought I was a goner."

"Daddy!" Mandy moaned, quite appalled. "*Do* something."

Hamilton started to stand up, a look of controlled fury on his face.

"Forget about it, old man," Gregg growled, turning on him. "You ain't goin' nowhere."

Hamilton sat down again.

"What do you want?" Ryan asked, remaining calm, even though the shock of finding out that the man with the gun was Cameron's husband was quite a revelation. "Tell me what it is and I'll try to arrange it."

Gregg's bloodshot eyes swiveled to encompass Ryan. "Who died an' made *you* king of the group?" he snarled.

"You must want something," Ryan said, persisting.

"Yeah, *her*," Gregg said, gesturing toward Cameron with his gun. "I want the lying bitch to come with me now."

Cameron rose to her feet. She could not believe this was happening, she only knew there was no way she could allow it to continue. She had to do something.

"Okay, okay, I'm coming," she said.

"You're coming all right," Gregg sneered. "Every night with your new boyfriend. But didja know that while you're comin', he's been fuckin' the shit outta Mary Ellen whatever, an' she's knocked up by him? Didja know *that*, my lovely wife?" Reaching into his shirt pocket he produced Mary Ellen's note. "Ya don't believe me, read this," he said, throwing it at her.

The note fell to the floor and Don picked it up.

"Where's the panic button in here?" Phil whispered to Lucy.

"Under the table," she whispered back. "Right where you sit."

"See if you can get to it."

"I'll try."

Gregg was busy swigging more red wine and enjoying Don's expression as he quickly scanned Mary Ellen's note.

"I'll write you a check for fifty thousand dollars right now if you let us go," Hamilton said, speaking up.

"Fifty thou –" Gregg said, squinting at the famous producer. "Is that all your friends are worth t' you?"

"A hundred thousand."

"Do I look stupid?" Gregg demanded, his voice rising. "Do I look like a Sheila with no frigging brains?"

"How much?" Hamilton said.

"How much, the man asks me," Gregg said, quite in his element. "How friggin' much. Well, I dunno – a million or two might do it."

"Fine," Hamilton said.

Gregg roared with laughter and gulped wine from the bottle. "You rich fuckin' assholes think you can buy anythin', doncha?

Well, you can't buy Gregg Kingston, no siree, no can do. Gregg Kingston's not for sale."

Cameron recognized the frame of mind Gregg was in only too well. Drunk and belligerent, violent and out of control. She'd seen him like this so many times, but never with a gun in his hands. This was a nightmare, there was no predicting what he was capable of.

"I need water," Lucy said, standing up and leaning against the wall. "If I don't have water I think I'm going to faint."

Gregg looked at her for the first time, his eyes dipping to her breasts – on display in her Hervé Léger dress. "Aren't you that movie-star piece of ass?" he said, checking her out. "Saw you in—"

"*Blue Sapphire*," she said, moving over to the table and reaching for a glass of water, surreptitiously sliding her other hand under the table and pressing the panic button.

"Yeah, that's it," Gregg said, pleased with himself for recognizing her.

Lucy put down the glass and returned to sit with the others. "Did it," she whispered to Phil. He squeezed her hand.

Cameron could not take her eyes off Gregg. She'd kept her marriage a dirty little secret, and now Gregg was here because of her – threatening everyone. It wasn't right. She'd left this man three years ago, this man who'd beaten and abused her. She'd left with a broken arm and a battered face and she'd been scared out of her mind.

But things were different now, she wasn't scared anymore. Oh no, she'd grown up, discovered new strengths within herself, and now she possessed an inner confidence she'd never known she had. If only she could persuade him to leave with her, then maybe no one would get hurt.

"Gregg," she said, her voice sharp and clear. "Let's go. Leave these people alone, they've done nothing to you."

"Fuck it, little Cammy," Gregg said, rocking back and forth on the heels of his cowboy boots. "I'm kinda enjoyin' myself. I'm getting' offered all kinds of money, meetin' movie stars, an' I like it. I can see why you get off on livin' here, it's a cushy set-up for a gal from the sticks." Once again he swiveled his head to stare at Don. "How's she doin' in the sack now? I taught her everything she knows. Cammy was a virgin when I got her. Not a bad learner, had to teach her to suck a cock. You likin' it?"

"You sonofabitch—" Don said, starting to get up.

Moving swiftly, Gregg whacked him across the side of his face with the butt of his gun, cutting Don's cheek and drawing blood.

Mandy screamed. Ryan tried to get up and do something – anything. But Gregg was quicker. Twirling the gun like a movie gunfighter, he fired off a shot.

The bullet hit the wall and ricocheted across the room.

"That's like a warnin' I mean business," Gregg snarled. "An' just so you rich motherfuckers know, the next one hits flesh. So fuckin' settle your asses down, an' stop pissin' me off."

Chapter Fifty-Four

Marlon had fallen into an extremely pleasant stoned sleep. He was dreaming he was in a harem surrounded by curvy naked babes catering to his every need, while Amy Winehouse crooned 'Rehab' and Kate Moss – clad in a leopard print nun's habit – massaged his feet.

It was a wild dream, until Kid Rock appeared and shot Kate Moss straight between the eyes.

Marlon sat bolt upright. Man, he might be stoned, but he could swear the gunshot was for real.

He took a peek at his Swatch watch. Jeez, it was almost eleven, and he was still stuck in the maid's room like some kind of dumb prisoner. This was not the way he'd expected the evening to go.

Hauling himself up, he began pacing around the room. Enough of this bullshit, he'd been cooped up for three hours.

Had he heard a gunshot or not?

No way. It was in his dream.

Taking out his phone he checked his messages. Three from various girls and a text from his friend, Randy, informing him there was a happenin' party going on at the House of Blues, and he should try to make it.

He inspected the pile of scripts, neatly stacked on a side table.

Six pristine copies of his work ready to be distributed. Tonight was supposed to be the beginning of the career he really wanted, not the lawyer route his dad expected him to follow.

Time to get this thing going, he thought, refusing to skulk around any longer.

Gingerly he opened the door, making his way down the long corridor that led to the kitchen.

Yeah, food, and then he'd poke his head around the dining-room door and attract Lucy's attention.

He sauntered into the kitchen – and what did he see? Holy shit! Two dudes on the ground trussed up like a couple of freakin' chickens!

Either he'd smoked too much pot and was experiencing hallucinations, or this was the real deal.

Whatever.

Better investigate and figure out what was up.

Chapter Fifty-Five

Now that Gregg had a room full of people captive, he had no plan what to do with them. He'd come here for Cameron. He hadn't intended to take out the gun, but he'd done so, and that meant he could be in big trouble when this was over.

Problem was, they all knew his name – because – like a fool, he'd told them. And he'd smashed Famous Prick in the face with a gun – which would probably be regarded as an assault.

Fuck! This was all Cameron's fault. The bitch was responsible for everything. Best to tie everyone up and get the fuck out. Yeah, that was it. Grab her and go.

While Gregg was trying to decide on his next move, Cameron was attempting to staunch the flow of blood from Don's cheek-bone.

Don managed to give her a wan smile. "You couldn't tell me you were married, huh?" he said, shaking his head. "Had to keep it to yourself."

"Yes," she answered ruefully. "Just like you told me, I'm a slippery one."

"Who *is* this guy?"

"Someone from far away and long ago. And for your information, I never tried to kill him."

"That was your first mistake."

Meanwhile, Ryan was trying to reassure Mandy that everything was going to be all right.

"Don't touch me!" she spat at him. "You make me sick! I
hate you!"

"It's all a big misunderstanding," he said, determined to
explain, although how was he supposed to do that without giving
Anya away?

"Daddy was right about you all along," Mandy said, filled
with a mixture of fury at Ryan, and fear at the situation they were
caught in. "I thank God we never had children together."

"That's not fair. We tried."

"Did we?" she said spitefully. "My first miscarriage I was never
even pregnant. The second one I aborted. And you know what,
Ryan? I'm not even sorry."

Her words cut him like a knife. She'd aborted their child.
She'd lied to him all this time, and he'd believed her, felt sorry for
her, stayed with her because of everything he imagined she'd
gone through.

Waves of sadness and regret rushed over him. Suddenly it all
became so easy. "When we get out of here we're over," he said.

"Yes, Ryan," she hissed back at him. "We're over, all right."

Gregg was now balancing on the edge of the table rocking
back and forth, still trying to decide on his next move.

Cameron knew him well enough to understand that for now
it was best for everyone if she stayed silent. Gregg had put himself in a corner, and that wasn't good for any of them.

She glanced over at Ryan. He and Mandy were involved in
some heated whispered conversation.

Hamilton was sitting ramrod straight, an expression of cold
fury on his distinguished face.

His young wife stared off into space, her pale blue eyes blank.
Cameron saw that the girl was not afraid, and that was strange. A
man had a gun pointed at them, their lives were in danger, the girl
should be petrified. But she wasn't.

Phil had his arm around Lucy, protecting her.

Damn Gregg. How could he do this? How could he march back into her life and ruin everything?

And then the phone rang and everyone jumped.

"Ignore it," Gregg instructed.

But it kept ringing.

He waved the gun at Lucy. "Shit! Answer it, get rid of them fast."

Lucy stood up and walked over to the phone, her heart pounding. Thank God the children weren't home, that's all she could think of. "Hello," she said, picking up the phone.

"Mrs Standard?" a male voice said.

"Yes."

"This is Detective Saunders. Are you all right?"

"No."

"Is there a gunman in your house?"

"Yes."

"Hang up," Gregg commanded.

"Put him on the line," the detective said.

She stretched out her arm and handed Gregg the phone. "It's for you," she said, and then everything turned to black as she fainted.

Chapter Fifty-Six

Marlon untied the chef and the barman, and the three of them made it outside the house where Marlon immediately got on his cell phone and called the police.

Man, he thought to himself, when two minutes later a couple of squad cars arrived at the end of the long driveway, *these mother-fuckers are swift*.

It turned out that they'd received some kind of silent alarm signal from the house, which is why they'd arrived so quickly.

Both the chef and the barman needed medical attention for cuts and bruises. While they were getting attended to, a detective took down their statements. Marlon also gave a statement, only he didn't have much to say.

"I never saw the dude," he informed the detective, "but I sure as shit heard the gunshot. Woke me up outta a deep sleep. Scared the crap outta me."

"What were you doing at the house?" the detective wanted to know, as if he, Marlon, might be involved.

Marlon explained about Lucy and their script, but the detective still instructed him to stay put. Like he was about to leave – *not*. He had a front-row seat to a real-life drama, there was no way he was going anywhere.

Within the hour TV camera crews turned up, which pissed the

detectives off. But hell, there was a siege situation going on, so there was nothing they could do about it.

Marlon latched onto a young blonde reporter in a short skirt and knee-high leather boots. "I was in there," he told her. "You know whose house it is, don't you?"

"Actually no," she responded, all soft crimpy curls and gleaming lip-gloss. "Why don't you tell me."

"Lucy Lyons."

"The old movie star?"

"She's not so old."

"Wow! My dad took me to see that movie – *Blue* something or other, when I was twelve years old. He thought it was about dolphins. We got quite a surprise!"

"I bet," Marlon responded, figuring Miss Glossy Lips was around twenty-three. Exactly the right age for his next older-woman fling.

"So," she said, interest perking, "tell me everything you know."

"Oh, I will," Marlon said, giving her a lopsided grin.

Chapter Fifty-Seven

Sweating and filled with rage, Gregg was confused and angry. This whole fucking thing had turned into a siege, and that's not what he'd wanted at all. Without a doubt it was all Cameron's fault, she was the one responsible for everything that was happening to him. He'd come to Los Angeles to find her and punish the bitch for trying to kill him, and now he was caught up in this no-win situation.

Some shit-ass detective had spoken to him on the phone like he was a fucking moron. "Put the gun down, come outside with your hands up and everything will be all right," the detective had said.

Oh, thank you, Detective, you'll just give me a smack on the wrist and send me back to Hawaii, is that it?

Yeah. Right.

Who'd called the cops, that's what he'd like to know. Had one of the assholes in the kitchen gotten loose and summoned them?

"You!" he said, jerking his gun at the girl in the scarlet dress sitting against the wall by herself. She hadn't said one word all night.

"Yes?" she answered, staring at him with lifeless pale blue eyes, exhibiting no fear.

What was up with her? The rest of the group were shit-scared he might suddenly go berserk and shoot them, but not this one – nothing.

"What's your name?" he said, swiping a hand across his sweaty brow.

"Anya," she said flatly.

Ryan shot an alarmed look in her direction. Why was she reverting to Anya when everyone knew her as Pola?

Cameron leaned close to Don. She'd managed to staunch the blood from his cut cheek, and now he held a table napkin against it.

"Are you okay?" she whispered.

"Nothing a plastic surgeon can't fix," he answered with a wry shrug.

"Go check out the kitchen, Anya," Gregg commanded. "See if there's anyone in there, then get your ass back here or I'll pop a bullet in your daddy's face."

Hamilton bristled. He'd personally see that this criminal received the maximum sentence when he was caught.

Slowly Anya stood up, taking her time, sensuously smoothing down the skirt of her clinging scarlet satin dress. She knew why Hamilton had bought it for her, it was the kind of dress a prostitute would wear. That's how Hamilton saw her – as a prostitute. He was right, that's exactly what she was. A prostitute, a whore, a hooker, a tart. As long as they paid, men could use her whenever they liked. They could spit on her, degrade her, beat her, fuck her. She was a piece of flesh for sale. Sex mattered. In the world Anya lived in – it was all that mattered.

"Move it," Gregg muttered, sweating profusely. "And while you're up, see if you can score me a bottle of Scotch. This wine shit ain't doin' the job."

Anya stared directly at him, licking her lips in a suggestive fashion. "Do you want to fuck me?" she said in a low husky voice. "You will not be disappointed. I am very accomplished in bed. I can do anything you want me to. Anything at all."

"Jesus Christ!" Hamilton exclaimed.

"Oh my God!" Mandy gasped.

Gregg was speechless. This girl coming onto him was the last thing he'd expected. Had Cameron put her up to it? Was his bitch wife playing games?

Ryan jumped to his feet. He got it. Anya was in shock. She didn't know what she was saying – or doing – because now she was starting to peel her dress off.

Gregg suddenly realized this *was* a trick – some kind of scheme to catch him off-guard. But he wasn't falling for it, oh no – he wasn't *that* dumb.

Did these people honestly think they could trick him? He was Gregg fucking Kingston! Nobody could trick him. He was invincible.

"Sit down!" he roared at Ryan, his hands starting to shake. "An' you," he yelled at Anya. "Sit the fuck down too."

But Anya wasn't stopping, she was allowing her dress to drop to the floor and then, quite naked, she was walking straight toward him.

Cameron had a horrible feeling that something bad was about to happen. Gregg was panicked, she could see it in his face. She attempted to rise, but Don prevented her from doing so. "Stay still," he muttered, gripping her arm.

"Sit back down or I'll shoot," Gregg yelled at Anya as she continued on her path. "I'M NOT FUCKING WITH YOU, BITCH!"

Ryan couldn't take it anymore – he leaped forward, making a last vain attempt to stop Anya. But he was too late.

Once more the gun went off, and this time there was a river of blood and a deathly silence.

Epilogue

Eighteen months later

The première of *Blue Sapphire 2* was an all-out Hollywood affair. Klieg lights, the red carpet, a live Internet feed, TV crews from around the world, old-fashioned bleachers to accommodate the legions of fans, and a lavish party due to take place when the movie finished.

Natalie de Barge manned her post, interviewing a stream of celebrities, asking the usual inane questions about designers and hairstyles – but managing to throw in a zinger or two – because Natalie had no intention of remaining an entertainment reporter forever. Her ambition was to host her own TV show with three other smart women – kind of an L.A. version of *The View*.

Don Verona had promised that his production company would help her set it up, and why not – they were partners with Cole and Cameron in *Paradise* – the most successful sports club in L.A. Everyone was making money.

Natalie flattered the women, flirted with the men, smiled broadly and asked all the right questions. Like her brother, Natalie possessed the likeability factor, making the stars feel completely at ease in her presence.

She greeted Birdy Marvel with kisses all round. The sweet-faced baby diva – who suffered from a wicked sex addiction –

babbled on about how tough her last stint in Rehab was, but now she'd found God, and was helping to feed starving children across the world, while working on her new CD, preparing a cross-country tour, and launching her own fragrance and clothing line.

"That's so great," Natalie said, moving Birdy on because she spied Lucy Lyons being shepherded toward her.

Lucy was the big star of the evening, for not only did she star in *Blue Sapphire 2* – her comeback movie – but she'd also been credited as an executive producer.

The movie, produced and written by Lucy's husband, Oscar winner Phil Standard, was supposed to be hot, hot, hot. Co-produced by Hamilton J. Heckerling and co-written by a talented young newcomer – Marlon Robert – the word on the street was that *Blue Sapphire 2* went places that even *Basic Instinct* hadn't dared to go.

The two women greeted each other with the Hollywood kiss, a ritual involving lips never actually touching flesh.

"You look beautiful," Natalie gushed. It was her job to go over the top, although she had to admit that at forty-two, with a couple of kids and a famously eccentric and randy husband, Lucy Lyons did indeed look great. Glowing, in fact, with her sweep of long black hair, generous lips and well-toned body.

"Tell me all about the movie," Natalie urged. "I hear it's quite something."

"That it is," Lucy said, with a big 'I'm a movie star again' smile. "*Sooo* sexy, and I only take my clothes off once. The real star of the movie," she added generously, "is Mary Ellen Evans who plays my niece. Just wait until America gets a look at Mary Ellen taking it all off! She's no longer the girl next door, she's the girl that every man would like to – oops!" She stopped, placing a coy finger to her lips. "I almost said the F word on live TV!"

"Not to worry, we've heard worse," Natalie said with an all-encompassing smile. "But back to the movie, Lucy. I hear that the two of you are wonderful. According to *Variety* you both give stellar performances."

"Thanks, Natalie," Lucy said modestly. "We tried our best."

"I'm sure you did. Now – let's talk about the important stuff – who are you wearing?"

* * *

Sitting in a rented limo on their way to the première was Lynda – eight and a half months' pregnant – Carlos – the proud papa-to-be – although they still hadn't gotten married – Dorian with a twenty-year-old male model, and Cole – alone and loving it. They were discussing the new premises *Paradise* had just acquired. Only Cole and Cameron had seen the space, and according to Cole it was spectacular, featuring lavish outdoor gardens, a full spa, and a lap pool.

"Pool aerobics, *very* now," Dorian said, pursing his lips. "Can't wait!"

"And I can't wait to see this movie tonight," Lynda sighed. "I'm *so* in the mood to watch me some steamy sex."

"That's about all you can do," Carlos grumbled. "Watch."

"Are you complaining?" Lynda said, brown eyes flashing as she patted her enormous stomach. "'Cause this big bundle I'm carryin' is *your son,* so snap it shut."

"Okay, chicken," Carlos said with a cocky smirk. "But the second you've laid this egg, this stud is expecting *mucho* action."

"Oh *God!*" Dorian groaned. "Do we have to listen to baby talk all night? Where's Cameron when I need her?"

"She had somethin' more important to do," Cole said.

"More important than a night out with us?" Dorian sniffed. "I don't *think* so."

Cole grinned. Sometimes he was the only one privy to Cameron's secrets. And this could turn out to be a good one.

* * *

"Doesn't she look gorgeous!" Natalie exclaimed, helping Mary Ellen Evans onto her platform in front of the TV camera. "I can't believe that you had a baby seven months ago, then went on to star in this movie, and look at you now. You're stunning!"

"Thank you, Natalie," Mary Ellen said, basking in the spotlight.

"Your jewelry is sensational, and your gown. Who are you wearing?"

"Armani, of course."

"Of course." A beat, and then – "How's the baby's daddy? Is he still in the picture?"

Mary Ellen didn't hesitate, she had her answer down pat. "Don Verona is a caring and hands-on father, but we're not together anymore, although I have the utmost respect and love for him."

"So tell me about your role in this movie," Natalie said, moving on. "Lots of nudity, I hear. How did you *really* feel about taking it all off?"

* * *

"Don't fidget," Mandy scolded.

"I'm not fidgeting," Marlon retorted.

"He's not fidgeting," Hamilton said.

The three of them sat in the back of Hamilton's Bentley, while a chauffeur took care of the driving.

Mandy was excited. She knew *Blue Sapphire 2* was going to be huge, and she stood to gain on two counts. Hamilton had promised her a piece of his profits as a reward for finally coming to her senses and divorcing Ryan.

And Marlon . . . well, Marlon was her prodigy – she'd discovered him.

Hmm . . . *almost* discovered him, for Lucy had gotten to him first – fortunately not in a sexual way. Mandy would never have accepted sloppy seconds.

Blue Sapphire 2 was all her idea. After their nightmare

experience at the Standards', Lucy had been on a downward spiral, and who could blame her? A girl getting shot and killed in their dining room was enough to put anyone in a slump.

Since it was Hamilton's fifth wife who took a bullet from the deranged husband of Don's girlfriend, Mandy had not been filled with total grief. Although it sure was one hell of a traumatic evening – what with finding out about Ryan's affair and all.

Anyway, when Lucy told her about Marlon, the script, and the lost opportunity, Mandy had offered to show the script to her father as a gesture of friendship toward Lucy.

Reading Lucy's script first, Mandy found it to be unoriginal, but the dialogue was brilliant, and that's when she'd come up with the idea for *Blue Sapphire 2* – because *Blue Sapphire* had been one of Hamilton's biggest movies.

Once Mandy suggested the project to her father, everything had fallen into place. Hamilton was not in mourning for his deceased wife. He had found out more than he ever wanted to know, and that was enough to make him erase Anya from his memory forever. He was determined to make *Blue Sapphire 2* a mega-success. Lucy was thrilled, and since Phil was desperate to please his wife, he agreed to have Marlon write the script and he would do a polish. It was all systems go, and Mandy had suggested Mary Ellen for the role of the young nympho. Inspired casting.

The result was a movie that was destined to be another huge box-office hit, perhaps even bigger than the original.

It didn't take long before Mandy embarked on a steamy affair with Marlon – even though he was almost thirteen years her junior.

Their age discrepancy didn't bother her. In fact, it made her feel very fashionable and of the moment. After all, it seemed to work for Demi Moore and Ashton; Madonna and Guy; Susan Sarandon and Tim; and now Mandy Heckerling and Marlon.

As Marlon would say – *sweet!*

* * *

Don and Phil sneaked away from the red carpet and grabbed a drink in the manager's office.

"I have to admit," Phil said, exhibiting all the signs of an extremely proud husband, "Lucy is a marvelous talent. Wait until you see her in this. Y'know, Don, she was absolutely right about making a comeback."

"And Mary Ellen?" Don asked. "How's she in the movie?"

"Surprisingly good." Phil took a long beat. "I presume you two are over?"

"We were never really on," Don said, quite casual. "She's nice enough, but she's not for me."

"You see the baby though?"

"All the time. She's the most adorable little girl in the world. I'm in love!"

"Finally!"

"Hey – " Don said with a wry grin. "I've been in love before, but it never seems to work out. You and Lucy – what can I say? You're one lucky sonofabitch."

"And don't I know it!"

*　　*　　*

And while the extravagant *Blue Sapphire 2* première was taking place on Hollywood Boulevard, Ryan was having a screening of his latest film, the heart-wrenching story of a young Russian prostitute. Shot documentary-style, he considered it the best movie he'd ever made. Over the last eighteen months he'd immersed himself in the film, put his heart and soul into it – traveling across Europe and filming in many different locations.

His film was called *Anya* – in memory of a girl he'd never known very well. A girl who'd been hurt in more ways than anyone could imagine. A girl who'd finally met her fate in the dining room of a Hollywood mansion.

While filming, he'd forgotten about everything else. He'd

instructed his lawyers to take care of his divorce and to give Mandy anything she wanted. He didn't care about material possessions, he only cared about his work.

The actress he cast in his movie, Tamara Yakovlev, was a luminous brunette with unfathomable eyes and a lithe body. Born in St Petersburg, she'd come to America when she was ten with her affluent parents. Her story was the complete opposite of Anya's, but somehow Tamara inhabited her spirit, and her acting was flawless. She became Anya.

They had a brief affair while filming in Poland. It didn't last, she wasn't the woman for him.

He often thought about Cameron. After that tragic evening at the Standards', they had not been in touch. He'd cut himself off from everyone to concentrate on his movie. Along the way he'd heard that she was no longer with Don.

Now that he was back in L.A. he'd thought about calling her, but he hadn't done so.

Perhaps he was romanticizing something that wasn't real. Best to leave it alone.

*   *   *

Dropping Yoko and Lennon off at Mr Wasabi's was kind of a ritual for Cameron. They liked him. He liked them. So even though she could afford a dogsitter, she preferred the familiar routine.

"Is it okay if they stay the night?" she asked Mr Wasabi.

The old man winked knowingly. He might be too old to indulge in adventures himself, but he certainly envied the man his incredibly beautiful and charming neighbor was spending the night with.

After depositing the dogs, she stopped back at her house, took a shower, applied a small amount of makeup, changed clothes about six times – eventually settling on jeans, combat boots, a simple tank – and her most expensive piece of clothing – a Dolce & Gabanna butter soft beige leather jacket. Finally satisfied, she left the house, got in her Mustang, and headed for the screening room in Santa Monica where she'd found out – purely by chance – that Ryan Richards was showing his movie.

Ryan Richards. A name from a while ago.

Ryan Richards. A man who to this day she had not stopped thinking about.

They had not been in contact since the fateful night Gregg had shot and killed Hamilton's young wife. It was such a tragedy and sometimes Cameron was overcome with guilt about what had taken place, for basically she blamed herself.

If Gregg hadn't come looking for her . . .

If she'd had the guts to fly to Hawaii and divorce him . . . If, if, if. Everyone told her it was inevitable, that Gregg was a psycho, but she knew she could have prevented it.

After the shooting the cops had stormed the house, and then it had all turned into pure chaos.

Don had wanted her to come home with him. She'd refused. She'd told him she needed space. Then several nights later she'd sat down with him and been as honest as she could. It was the break-up talk and he wasn't happy.

"*You* lie to *me*, and *I'm* the one getting the shaft," he'd steamed. "I don't fucking believe this."

"I'm sorry," she'd said, genuinely regretful, because she did have feelings for him, but it wasn't enough. "I don't fit into your lifestyle, Don. It's simply not for me."

He was so angry that he'd blurted out that *he* was the silent investor in *Paradise*. *He* was the one who'd put up all the extra money to get it off the ground.

So be it. She wasn't even mad, Gregg had left her shell-shocked.

"That's okay," she'd said. "I want us both to benefit from your investment."

It had taken him a while, but eventually he'd accepted the fact that all she wanted from him was his friendship. His ego was bruised, but the great thing about Don was his self-deprecating sense of humor. They still saw each other occasionally, and he still kept on telling her she was making a mistake, but to Cameron's delight, they were able to remain friends.

Gregg's trial came months later. After two days of deliberation, the jury's verdict was manslaughter. He received an eight-year jail sentence.

As soon as the trial was over, Cameron consulted a lawyer and started divorce proceedings. Six months later, she was free.

The gang at *Paradise* rallied around her, and once more work became her life. Until yesterday, when a young actress lifting weights with Cole had happened to mention that there was a screening of Ryan Richards's movie tonight.

Cameron had blown off going to the première of *Blue Sapphire 2* with Cole and the others. Instead she'd decided to take a chance. A big chance. A crazy insane chance.

Maybe this thing between her and Ryan was all in her imagination. Maybe he wouldn't even remember her.

Slipping into the screening room after the movie started, she sat transfixed. *Anya* was a magnificent piece of work – understated, yet extraordinarily powerful.

The audience applauded at the end, and she noted a few people dabbing their eyes.

She looked around for Ryan, and finally spotted him. The beautiful star of his film had her arms around him, she was kissing and hugging him.

Cameron experienced an ache in the pit of her stomach. Of course he'd moved on, why wouldn't he?

And just as she was contemplating a stealthy exit, a young man extracted the actress from Ryan, and the two of them walked off with their arms around each other.

Taking a long deep breath Cameron headed in Ryan's

direction. More people were surrounding him, shaking his hand, patting him on the back. Congratulations and accolades were thick on the ground.

She stood behind a large woman waiting her turn to tell him how meaningful his movie was.

And then he saw her.

For a tantalizing moment their eyes met, and she knew in her heart that nothing had changed. They both felt the same way.

"Hi," she murmured softly.

"Hey – you," he responded.

"Loved your movie."

"You did?"

"I did," she said, noting that his eyes were still that intense blue that took her breath away.

"So," he said, filled with optimism and delight, "how come it took you so long to find me?"

She smiled. A dreamy smile, a happy smile. "Just lazy, I guess."

And he pulled her toward him, close, very close.

Somehow she knew this was the beginning of something very special.

CORINTHIA
PALACE HOTEL & SPA
MALTA

**WIN A LUXURY TWO-WEEK SPA
BREAK FOR TWO AT THE EXQUISITE
CORINTHIA PALACE HOTEL AND SPA, MALTA.**

Perfectly situated at the centre of the island, close to the Presidential Palace, Malta's
premier five-star hotel and spa is set within its own landscaped gardens
and is the ideal retreat for pampering and relaxation.

The hotel offers the best in accommodation, luxury and facilities, the perfect
base to discover Malta's major historical and cultural sites. A unique feature of
the Corinthia Palace Hotel is the Athenaeum SPA, a centre for
Vitality, Beauty and well being.

To enter answer the following question:

The lead character of *Married Lovers* is called Cameron Paradise.
What is her occupation?

a) Fitness Instructor

b) Driving Instructor

c) Bus Conductor

To enter this competition visit **www.simonsays.co.uk**

Terms and Conditions

Open to all UK & Ireland residents age 18 and over. No cash alternative.
Prize valid until end 2009 and subject to hotel availability. Prize includes flights,
transfers between airport-hotel-airport and half board accommodation.
Two signature spa treatments per person to be booked and chosen by hotel and spa.
A full list of terms and conditions is available at www.simonsays.co.uk

For more information on other Corinthia hotels visit **www.corinthia.com**